The Far Side
of the World

The sails of a square-rigged ship, hung out to dry in a calm.

1	Flying jib	12	Mainsail, or course
2	Jib	13	Maintopsail
3	Fore topmast staysail	14	Main topgallant
4	Fore staysail	15	Mizzen staysail
5	Foresail, or course	16	Mizzen topmast staysail
6	Fore topsail	17	Mizzen topgallant staysail
7	Fore topgallant	18	Mizzen sail
8	Mainstaysail	19	Spanker
9	Maintopmast staysail	20	Mizzen topsail
10	Middle staysail	21	Mizzen topgallant
11	Main topgallant staysail		

Illustration source: Serres, Liber Nauticus.
Courtesy of The Science and Technology Research Center,
The New York Public Library, Astor, Lenox, and Tilden Foundations

The Works of Patrick O'Brian

Biography

PICASSO
JOSEPH BANKS

*Aubrey/Maturin Novels
in order of publication*

MASTER AND COMMANDER
POST CAPTAIN
H.M.S. SURPRISE
THE MAURITIUS COMMAND
DESOLATION ISLAND
THE FORTUNE OF WAR
THE SURGEON'S MATE
THE IONIAN MISSION
TREASON'S HARBOUR
THE FAR SIDE OF THE WORLD
THE REVERSE OF THE MEDAL
THE LETTER OF MARQUE
THE THIRTEEN-GUN SALUTE
THE NUTMEG OF CONSOLATION
THE TRUELOVE
THE WINE-DARK SEA
THE COMMODORE
THE YELLOW ADMIRAL
THE HUNDRED DAYS
BLUE AT THE MIZZEN

Novels

TESTIMONIES
THE GOLDEN OCEAN
THE UNKNOWN SHORE

Collections

THE RENDEZVOUS AND OTHER STORIES

PATRICK O'BRIAN

The Far Side
of the World

W. W. Norton & Company
New York • London

FOR WOLCOTT GIBBS, JR.
WHO FIRST ENCOURAGED THESE TALES

ISBN 0-393-03710-X

W. W. Norton & Company, Inc.
500 Fifth Avenue, New York, N.Y. 10110
W. W. Norton & Company Ltd.
10 Coptic Street, London WC1A 1PU

7 8 9 0

AUTHOR'S NOTE

Perhaps few authors are wholly original as far as their plots are concerned; indeed Shakespeare seems to have invented almost nothing, while Chaucer borrowed from both the living and the dead. And to come down to a somewhat different plane, the present writer is even more derivative, since for these books he has in general kept most doggedly to recorded actions, nourishing his fancy with log-books, dispatches, letters, memoirs, and contemporary reports. But general appropriation is not quite the same thing as downright plagiary, and in passing it must be confessed that the description of a storm's first aspect on p. 308 is taken straight from William Hickey, whose words did not seem capable of improvement.

If these tales are to continue, however, it is clear that the writer will soon have originality thrust upon him, for he is running short of history. Some ten or eleven years ago a respectable American publisher suggested that he should write a book about the Royal Navy of Nelson's time; he was happy to agree, since both the period and the subject were congenial, and he quickly produced the first of this series, a novel based upon Lord Cochrane's early days in command of the *Speedy*, which provided him with one of the most spectacular single-ship actions of the war as well as a mass of authentic detail. But had the writer known how much pleasure he was to take in this kind of writing, and how many books were to follow the first, he would certainly have started the sequence much earlier. For the 14-gun *Speedy* did not capture the 32-gun *Gamo* until 1801 and this was followed by the ill-judged

Peace of Amiens, which left enterprising sailors less time to distinguish themselves than they could have wished and deprived later writers of a great deal of raw material. Historical time has not yet run out for these tales, and in the present book the naval historian will detect an echo of HMS *Phoebe*'s pursuit of the USN *Essex*; but even in the early nineteenth century the year contained only twelve months, and it is possible that in the near future the author (if his readers will bear with him) may be led to make use of hypothetical years, rather like those hypothetical moons used in the calculation of Easter: an 1812a as it were or even an 1812b.

Yet if he should do so it will be strict chronology alone that is affected; he will continue to respect historical accuracy and speak of the Royal Navy as it was, making use of contemporary documents: the reader will meet no basilisks that destroy with their eyes, no Hottentots without religion, polity, or articulate language, no Chinese perfectly polite, and completely skilled in all sciences, no wholly virtuous, ever-victorious or necessarily immortal heroes; and should any crocodiles appear, he undertakes that they shall devour their prey without tears.

The Far Side
of the World

CHAPTER ONE

'Pass the word for Captain Aubrey, pass the word for Captain Aubrey,' cried a sequence of voices, at first dim and muffled far aft on the flagship's maindeck, then growing louder and more distinct as the call wafted up to the quarterdeck and so along the gangway to the forecastle, where Captain Aubrey stood by the starboard thirty-two-pounder carronade contemplating the Emperor of Morocco's purple galley as it lay off Jumper's Bastion with the vast grey and tawny Rock of Gibraltar soaring behind it, while Mr Blake, once a puny member of his midshipman's berth but now a tall, stout lieutenant almost as massive as his former captain, explained the new carriage he had invented, a carriage that should enable carronades to fire twice as fast, with no fear of oversetting, twice as far, and with perfect accuracy, thus virtually putting an end to war.

Only a flag-officer could 'pass the word' for a post-captain, and Jack Aubrey had been dreading the summons ever since the *Caledonia* came in, a little after dawn: within minutes of receiving it he would have to tell the Commander-in-Chief how it came about that his orders had not been obeyed. Seeing that Aubrey's small, elderly, but sweet-sailing frigate *Surprise* was to return from Malta to England, there to be laid up or sold out of the service or even sent to the breaker's yard, Admiral Sir Francis Ives, the Commander-in-Chief, Mediterranean, had directed him to go by way of Zambra on the Barbary Coast, there to reason with the Dey of Mascara, the ruler of those parts, who showed a tendency to side with the French and who had uttered threats of hostile action if he were not given an enormous sum of money: if the Dey proved stubborn, Aubrey was to embark the British consul and to tell his Highness that the instant any of these threats were carried into action, all ships bearing the Mascarene flag should be seized, burnt, sunk, or otherwise destroyed, and the Dey's ports blocked up. Aubrey was to sail in company with the *Pollux*, an even older sixty-gun ship that was carrying Rear-Admiral Harte back to England as a passenger, but the mission to the Dey was his alone; and having accomplished it he was to report to the Commander-in-Chief at Gibraltar. It seemed to him a fairly straightforward assignment, particularly as he had an unusually well qualified political adviser in his surgeon, Dr Maturin, and off the mouth of Zambra Bay he left the *Pollux* with an easy mind, or at least with a mind as easy as was right in one who had spent most of his life on the sea, that dangerous, utterly unreliable element, with nothing but a plank between him and eternity.

But they had been betrayed. At some point the Commander-in-Chief's plan had become known to the enemy and a French ship of the line together with two frigates appeared from the windward, in evident collusion with the Mascarenes; the Dey's forts had fired on the *Surprise*; and in the subsequent activity Aubrey had neither had an interview with the ruler nor embarked Mr Consul Eliot. The *Pollux*, closely engaged by the French eighty-gun ship, had blown up with the loss of all hands, and although by her brilliant sailing qualities the *Surprise* had run clear, Jack Aubrey had in fact accomplished nothing of what he had been sent to do. To be sure, he could represent that in the course of the manoeuvres he had wrecked a heavy French frigate by luring her over a reef, and that the *Pollux* had so mauled her adversary in the fight and had so shattered her in blowing up that there was little likelihood of her ever regaining Toulon; but he had nothing tangible to show, and although he was satisfied in his own mind that materially the Royal Navy had gained rather than lost by the encounter he was by no means sure that the Commander-in-Chief would see it in the same light. And he was all the more uneasy since adverse winds had delayed his run from Zambra Bay to Gibraltar, where he had expected to find the Commander-in-Chief, and since he could not tell whether the boats he had sent off to Malta and Port Mahon had reached the Admiral in time for him to deal with the crippled Frenchman. Sir Francis had an alarming reputation, not only as a rigid disciplinarian and a right Tartar, but also as one who would break an erring subordinate without compunction. It was also known that Sir Francis longed for victory even more than most commanders-in-chief: for evident, positive victory that would please public opinion and even more the present ministry, the effective source of honours. How the Zambra action would appear in this respect Jack could not decide. 'Another couple of minutes will tell me, however,' he said to himself as he hurried aft in the wake of a nervous, inaudible youngster, keeping his best white tights and silk stockings well clear of the buckets of pitch that were carrying forward.

But he was mistaken: the call had originated in the other flag-officer aboard, the Captain of the Fleet, who was confined to his cabin by the present bout of influenza but who wished Jack to know that his wife had taken a house no great way from Ashgrove Cottage, and that she should be very happy in Mrs Aubrey's acquaintance. Their children were much of the same age, he said; and then, they being fond parents and long, long from home, each gave the other a pretty detailed account of his brood, while the Captain of the Fleet showed his daughters' birthday letters, received some two months ago, and a little scrubby rat-gnawn pen-wiper, the work of his eldest's unaided hand.

During this time the Commander-in-Chief himself carried on with what was left of his paper-work, a task that he had begun just after sunrise. 'This to Captain Lewis, and his damn-fool words about an enquiry,' he said. ' "Sir, Your letter has not contributed in the smallest degree to alter the opinion I had formed of your having determined to avail yourself of this influenza to get the *Gloucester* again into port. The most serious charge made against you is the savage rudeness offered to Dr Harrington on the quarterdeck of the *Gloucester*, wholly unbecoming the character of her commander and particularly reprehensible in the desponding state in which your improper conduct has placed the crew of His Majesty's ship under your command. If you continue to court enquiry in the style of the letter I am replying to, it will come sooner than you are aware of. I am, Sir, your most obedient servant." Damned rogue, to try to bully me.' The two clerks made no reply to this, but kept their pens plying fast, the one on a fair copy of the previous letter, the other on a rough of this, though the other inhabitants of the great cabin, Mr Yarrow, the Admiral's secretary, and Mr Pocock, his political adviser, responded with a 'Tut, tut, tut'.

'To Captain Bates,' said Sir Francis, as soon as one pen had stopped squeaking. ' "Sir, The very disorderly state of His Majesty's ship under your command, obliges me to require that neither yourself nor any of your officers are to go on shore on what is called pleasure. I am, Sir, etc." And now a memorandum. "There being reason to apprehend that a number of women have been clandestinely brought from England in several ships, more particularly so in those which have arrived in the Mediterranean in this last and the present year, the respective captains are required by the Admiral to admonish those ladies upon the waste of water, and other disorders committed by them, and to make known to all, that on the first proof of water being obtained for washing from the scuttle-butt or otherwise, under false pretences, every woman in the fleet who had not been admitted under the authority of the Admiralty or the Commander-in-Chief, will be shipped for England by the first convoy, and the officers are strictly enjoined to watch vigilantly their behaviour, and to see that no waste or improper consumption of water happen in the future." ' He turned to the second clerk, now ready to write. 'To the respective captains: "The Admiral having observed a flippancy in the behaviour of officers when coming upon the *Caledonia's* quarterdeck, and sometimes in receiving orders from a superior officer, and that they do not pull off their hats, and some not even touch them: it is his positive direction, that any officer who shall in future so forget this essential duty of respect and subordination, be admonished publicly; and he expects the officers of the *Caledonia* will set the example by taking off their hats, and not touch them with an air of negligence." ' To Mr Pocock he observed, 'The young people now coming up are for the most part frippery and gimcrack. I wish we could revive the old school,' and then continued, ' "To the respective captains: the Commander-in-Chief having seen several officers of the fleet on shore dressed like shop-keepers, in coloured clothes, and others wearing round hats, with their uniforms, in violation of the late order from the Right Honourable the Lords Commissioners of the Admiralty, does positively direct, that any officer offending against this wholesome and necessary regulation in future, is put under arrest, and reported to the Admiral, and, let the sentence of a court-martial upon such offenders be what it may, that he is never permitted to go ashore while under the command of Sir Francis Ives." '

While the pens flew on he picked up a letter and said to Mr Pocock, 'Here is J.S. begging me to intercede with the Royal Bird again. I wonder at it: and I cannot but think that this form of application must end ill. I wonder at it, I say; for surely, with such a high mind and unrivalled pretensions, a peerage is an object beneath him.'

Mr Pocock was a little embarrassed to reply, particularly as he knew that the clerks, in spite of their busy pens, were listening intently; for it was common knowledge throughout the fleet that Sir Francis longed to be a lord, thus rivalling his brothers, and that he had fought with unparalleled fury for the Mediterranean command, as the most likely means to that end. 'Perhaps . . .' he began, but he was interrupted by a scream of barbarous trumpets close at hand, and stepping over to the stern-gallery he said, 'Bless me, the Emperor's envoy has put off already.'

'God damn and blast the man,' cried the Admiral, looking angrily at the clock. 'Let him go and . . . no: we must not offend the Moors. I shall not have time for Aubrey. Pray tell him so, Mr Yarrow – make my excuses – force majeure – do the civil thing – bid him to dinner and let him bring Dr Maturin; or let them come tomorrow morning, if that don't suit.'

It did not suit. Aubrey was infinitely concerned, but it was not in his power to dine with the Commander-in-Chief today; he was already engaged, engaged to a lady. At Jack's first words to Mr Yarrow the Captain of the Fleet's eyebrows shot up under his nightcap; at his last, the only excuse that in a naval context could acquit him of being a wicked contumelious discontented froward mutinous dog, the eyebrows reappeared in their usual place and the Captain of the Fleet said, 'I wish I were engaged to dine with a lady. I may draw a rear-admiral's pay, but I have not seen one, apart from the bosun's wife, since Malta; and what with this damned influenza and having to give an example I do not suppose I shall see another until we drop anchor in the Grand Harbour again, alas. There is something wonderfully comfortable about having a lady's legs under one's table, Aubrey.'

In principle Aubrey was all agreement: by land he was quite devoted to women – indeed, his devotion had very nearly been his undoing before this – and he dearly loved to have their legs under his table. But in the case of these particular legs (an uncommonly elegant pair) and of this particular dinner, his mind was far from easy: in fact uneasiness of one sort or another fairly crammed his mind today, leaving little room for its usual cheerfulness.

14

He had given Laura Fielding, the lady in question, a lift from Valletta to Gibraltar, and in ordinary circumstances it was a perfectly usual thing to carry a fellow-officer's wife from one port to another. These circumstances however were very far from ordinary: Mrs Fielding, an Italian lady with dark red hair, had appeared in the middle of a midnight downpour with no baggage, under the protection of Stephen Maturin, who offered no explanation of her presence, only observing that in Captain Aubrey's name he had promised her a passage to Gibraltar. Jack knew very well that his intimate friend Maturin was deeply concerned with naval and political intelligence and he asked no questions, accepting the situation as a necessary evil. But as a very considerable evil, since rumour had connected Jack's name with Laura's at a time when her husband was a prisoner of war in the hands of the French: yet in this instance rumour was mistaken, for although Jack was at one point very willing to give it consistency Laura was not. Nevertheless the rumour had reached the Adriatic, and there the escaping husband, Lieutenant Charles Fielding of the Navy, had met it aboard HMS *Nymphe*; and being of an intensely jealous nature had believed it at once. He had followed the *Surprise* to Gibraltar, landing from the *Hecla* bomb the night before. On hearing the news Jack had at once sent the pair an invitation to dinner the next day; but in spite of Laura's kind note of acceptance he was by no means convinced that he might not have an exceedingly awkward situation on his hands at half past two o'clock, when he was to receive his guests at Reid's hotel.

Landing at the Ragged Staff a little before noon he sent his barge back to the *Surprise*, with very unnecessarily repeated instructions to his coxswain about the rig, the cleanliness and the promptitude of those hands who were to assist at the dinner; for the Navy, though often reduced to salt horse and hard tack, ate it in style, every officer and guest having a servant behind

15

his chair, a style that few hotels could equal. Then, observing that the Parade was almost empty, he walked along towards the Alameda gardens, meaning to sit on the bench under the dragon-tree; he did not choose to return to his ship at present, for not only was it painful to him to see her, knowing that she was condemned, but in spite of his efforts the news of her fate had spread and sadness with it, so that the *Joyful Surprise*, as she was known in the service, was now but a dismal place. The tight, well-knit community of some two hundred men was about to fall apart, and he reflected upon the pity of it, the waste – a hand-picked crew of able seamen, many of whom had sailed with him for years and some, like his coxswain, his steward, and four of his bargemen, ever since his first command – they were used to one another, used to their officers – a ship's company in which punishment was extremely rare and where discipline did not have to be imposed since it came naturally – while for gunnery and seamanship he did not know their equal – and this invaluable body of men was to be dispersed among a score of ships or even, in the case of the officers, thrown on shore, unemployed, simply because the five-hundred-ton, twenty-eight-gun *Surprise* was too small a frigate for modern requirements. Instead of being reinforced and moved as a whole to a larger ship, such as the thousand-ton, thirty-eight-gun *Blackwater* that Jack had been promised, the crew was to be scattered; while the promise had gone the way of so many promises. The influential Captain Irby had been given the *Blackwater*, and Jack, whose affairs were in a state of horrible confusion, had no certainty whatsoever of another ship, no certainty of anything at all but half-pay of half a guinea a day and a mountain of debt. Just how high a mountain he could not tell, for all his skill in navigation and astronomy, since several lawyers were concerned, each with a different notion of the case or rather cases. These thoughts were interrupted by a cough and a diffident 'Captain Aubrey, sir. Good day to you.' Looking up

16

he saw a tall thin man of between thirty and forty with his hat raised from his head. He was wearing naval uniform, the threadbare uniform of a midshipman, its white patches yellow in the sun. 'You do not remember me, sir: my name is Hollom, and I had the honour of serving under you in *Lively*.'

Of course. Jack had been acting-captain of the *Lively* for a few months at the beginning of the war, and in the early days of his command he had seen something of a not very efficient, not very enterprising midshipman of that name, a passed midshipman with the rating of master's mate: not a great deal, since Hollom, falling sick, had soon removed to the hospital ship, not particularly regretted by anyone except perhaps the schoolmaster, another elderly passed midshipman, and the grey-haired captain's clerk, who formed a little mess of their own, well away from the more usual and more turbulent midshipmen in their teens. As far as Jack could remember there was no vice in Hollom, but there was no obvious merit either; he was the kind of midshipman who had not improved in his profession, who had no evident zeal for seamanship or gunnery or navigation and no gift for dealing with men, the kind of midshipman that captains were happy to pass on. Long before Jack first met him, a good-humoured board had passed Hollom as fit for a lieutenant's commission; but the commission itself had never appeared. This happened often enough to young men with no particular abilities, or no patron or family to speak for them, but whereas most of these unfortunates bore up after a few years and either applied for a master's warrant if their mathematics and navigation were good enough, or left the service altogether, Hollom and a good many others like him went on hoping until it was too late to make any change, so that they remained perpetual mids, perpetual young gentlemen, with an income of about thirty pounds a year when they could find a captain to admit them to his quarterdeck and nothing at all if they could not, midshipmen having no half-pay. Theirs was perhaps the most unenviable position in the whole service and Jack pitied them extremely: nevertheless he hardened his heart against the request that was sure to come – a forty-year-old could not possibly fit into his midshipman's berth. Besides, it was evident that Hollom was an unlucky man, one that would bring bad luck to the ship; the crew, an intensely superstitious set of men, would dislike him and perhaps treat him with disrespect, which would mean starting the hateful round of punishment and resentment all over again.

It was clear from Hollom's account of himself that he was finding more and more captains of this opinion: his last ship, *Leviathan*, had paid off seven months ago, and he had come out to Gibraltar in the hope either of a death-vacancy or a meeting with one of his many former commanders who might be in need of an experienced master's mate. Neither had occurred and now Hollom was at his last extremity.

'I am very sorry to say so, but I am afraid it is quite impossible for me to find room for you on my quarterdeck,' said Jack. 'In any case, there would be no point in it, since the ship will be paying off in the next few weeks.'

'Even a few weeks would be infinitely welcome, sir,' cried Hollom with a ghastly sprightliness: then, clutching at a straw he added, 'I should be happy to sling my hammock before the mast, sir, if you would enter me as able.'

'No, no, Hollom, it would not do,' said Jack, shaking his head. 'But here is a fi'pun note, to be repaid out of your next prize-money, if it would prove useful to you.'

'You are very good, sir,' said Hollom, clasping his hands behind his back, 'but I am not . . .' What he was not never appeared; his face, still retaining something of its artificial sprightly expression, twitched oddly, and Jack dreaded a burst of tears. 'However, I am obliged for your kind intention. Good day to you, sir.'

'God damn it, God damn it,' said Jack to himself

as Hollom walked away, looking unnaturally stiff. 'This is infernal goddam blackmail.' And then aloud, 'Mr Hollom, Mr Hollom, there.' He wrote in his pocketbook, tore out the page, and said, 'Report aboard the *Surprise* for duty before noon and show this to the officer of the watch.'

A hundred yards farther on he met Captain Sutton of the *Namur*, Billy Sutton, a very old friend, since they had been youngsters together in HMS *Resolution*. 'Lord, Billy,' cried Jack, 'I never thought to see you here – I never saw *Namur* come in. Where is she?'

'She is blockading Toulon, poor old soul, and Ponsonby is looking after her for me. I was returned for Rye in the by-election. Stopford is running me home in his yacht.'

Jack congratulated him, and after some words about Parliament, yachts, and acting-captains Sutton said, 'You look most uncommon hipped, Jack; like a cat that has lost its kittens.'

'I dare say I do. *Surprise* is ordered home, you know, to be laid up or broke, and I have spent some truly miserable weeks, making preparations, fobbing off whole boatloads of people who want a lift for themselves or their families or friends. And not five minutes ago I did a very foolish thing, clean against my principles: I took a middle-aged master's mate off the shore because he looked so goddam thin, poor devil. It was mere sentimentality, mere silly indulgence. It will do him no good in the end; he will be neither grateful nor useful, and he will corrupt my youngsters and upset the hands. He has Jonah written all over his face. Thank Heaven the *Caledonia* is in at last. I can make my report and be away as soon as my launch returns from Mahon, before anyone else comes aboard. The port-admiral has tried to foist a number of horrible creatures on to me, and to take away all my best men by one dirty trick or another. I have resisted pretty well so far; after all, the ship may come into action between this and the Channel, and I should like her to do herself credit; but even so . . .'

'That was a sad business in Zambra Bay, Jack,' said Sutton, who had not been attending.

'It was, indeed,' said Jack, shaking his head; then after a moment, 'You know about it, then?'

'Of course I do. Your launch found the vice-admiral at Port Mahon, and he sent *Alacrity* away for the C-in-C off Toulon directly.'

'How I hope she reached him in time. With any luck he should be able to snap up the big Frenchman. There was something very dirty about that affair, you know, Billy. We sailed straight into a trap.'

'So everyone says. And a returning victualler spoke of a great turmoil in Valletta – some high civilian cutting his throat and half a dozen people shot. But it was all at second or third hand.'

'There was no news of my cutter, I suppose? I sent it off for Malta with my second lieutenant as soon as the wind came right round into her teeth, so there was no hope of fetching Gibraltar for a great while.'

'Not that I have heard. But I do know your launch was put aboard the *Berwick*, since she was to rendezvous with the C-in-C here. We sailed in company until yesterday evening, when she carried away her foretopmast in a squall, and as Bennet dared not face the Admiral until everything was perfectly shipshape, he signalled to us to go ahead. But with the wind veering like this,' said Sutton, glancing at the high ridge of Gibraltar, 'he will be backstrapped, if he don't mend his pace.'

'Billy,' said Jack, 'you know the Admiral far better than I do. Is he indeed still so very savage?'

'Pretty savage,' said Sutton. 'Have you heard what he did to the midshipman that looted the privateer?'

'Not I.'

'Well, some boats from the squadron boarded a Gibraltar privateer, found her papers all in order, and left her in peace. Some time later a midshipman belonging to the *Cambridge*, a big hairy sixteen-year-old who loved to be popular with the hands, went back and made them give him and his boat's crew porter, and then, having lost his wits entirely I suppose, he put on the master's blue jacket with a silver watch in its pocket and walked off laughing. The master complained and it was found in his hammock. I sat on the court-martial.'

'Dismissed the service, I suppose?'

'No, no: not so lucky. The sentence was "to be degraded from the rank of midshipman in the most ignominious manner, by having his uniform stripped from his back on the quarterdeck of the *Cambridge*, and to be mulcted of the pay now due to him,' and it was to be read out aboard every ship in the command – you would have come in for it if you had not been in Zambra. But that was not enough. Sir Francis wrote to Scott of the *Cambridge*, and I saw the letter: "Sir, You are hereby required and directed to carry out the sentence of the court-martial on Albert Tompkins. And you are to cause his head to be shaved, and a label affixed to his back, expressive of the disgraceful crime he has committed. And he is to be employed as the constant scavenger for cleaning the head, until my further orders." '

'Good God,' cried Jack, reflecting upon the head of an eighty-gun ship of the line, a common jakes or privy for more than five hundred men. 'Was the wretched boy of any family, any education?'

'The son of a lawyer in Malta, Tompkins of the Admiralty court.'

They took some steps in silence, and then Sutton said, 'I should have told you that the *Berwick* has your former premier aboard, too, the one who was promoted for your action with the Turk, going home to try to find himself a ship, poor fellow.'

'Pullings,' said Jack. 'How happy I shall be to see him – never was such a first lieutenant. But as for a ship . . .' They both shook their heads, knowing that the Navy had more than six hundred commanders and not half that number of sloops, the only vessels they could command. 'I hope she has her chaplain aboard as well,' said Jack. 'A one-eyed parson by the name of Martin, a very fine fellow and a great friend of my surgeon.' He hesitated for a moment and then said, 'Billy, would you do me the kindness of dining with me? I have rather a difficult party this afternoon and a witty cove like you rattling away would be a great advantage. I am no great fist at conversation, as you know, and Maturin has an awkward way of turning as mum as an oyster if the subject don't interest him.'

'What kind of party is it?' asked Sutton.

'Did you ever meet Mrs Fielding in Valletta?'

'The beautiful Mrs Fielding that gives Italian lessons?' asked Sutton, cocking an eye at Jack. 'Yes, of course.'

'Well, I gave her a lift to Gibraltar: but because of some silly rumours – false, Billy, false upon my honour, completely false – it seems that her husband conceived some suspicion of me. It is the Fieldings that are coming to dinner, and although her note assured me they should be delighted to come, yet I still feel that a source of sparkling repartee would not come amiss. Lord, Billy, I have heard you address the electors of Hampshire in the most fearless way – jokes, badinage, anecdotes, topics – why, it was almost eloquence.'

Captain Aubrey's fears were unfounded. Between her husband's arrival yesterday evening and the hour of dinner, Laura Fielding had found means of convincing him of her perfect fidelity and unvarying attachment, and he came forward with an open smiling expression on his face to shake Jack's hand and to thank him again for his kindness to Laura. Yet even so Captain Sutton's presence was by no means unwelcome. Both Jack and Stephen, who were very fond of Mrs Fielding, felt uneasy in her husband's presence; neither could understand what she saw in him – a heavy, dark man with a thick forehead and small deep-set eyes – and they both resented her obvious fondness. It somewhat diminished her in their opinion, and neither felt so strong an inclination for social effort as they had before; while for his part Fielding, once he had given a bald account of his escape from a French prison, had no more to say, but sat there smiling and fondling his wife under the table-cloth.

It was now that Sutton proved his worth. His chief qualification as a Member of Parliament was an ability to speak at great length in a smiling, cheerful way upon almost any subject, urging universally admitted truths with the utmost candour and good nature; he was also capable of reciting bills and other Members' speeches by heart with perfect accuracy; and he was of course a defender of the Navy in the House and out of it, whenever the service was adversely criticized in any way.

At the first remove Laura Fielding, who was perfectly aware of her husband's limits and of her admirers' feelings, tried to revive the conversation (now grown monstrously insipid) by crying out against the Commander-in-Chief for his treatment of the wretched Albert Tompkins, who was the son of an acquaintance of hers in Valletta, a lady whose heart would be broken when she heard of her boy's hair, 'which fell in such lovely curls, scarcely needing the tongs at all.' Sir Francis was worse than Attila; he was a bear, a worthless.

'Oh come, ma'am,' said Sutton. 'He may be a little strict at times, but where should we be if all midshipmen wore their hair like Absalom and spent all their leisure stealing silver watches? In the first place they could scarcely go aloft without danger, and in the second the service would fall into sad disrepute. And in any event, Sir Francis is capable of great kindness, astonishing magnanimity, Jovian lenience. You remember my cousin Cumby, Jack?'

'Cumby of the *Bellerophon*, that was posted after Trafalgar?'

'The very man. Now, ma'am, some years ago, when Sir Francis was C-in-C before Cadiz and when there was a great deal of murmuring and discontent in the fleet, with undisciplined and even half-mutinous ships coming out from the Channel, Sir Francis ordered the Marines to parade at ten every morning aboard every line of battle ship – anthem played – arms presented – everyone present – all hats off – and he always attended himself in full-dress uniform, blue and gold: all this to promote discipline and a sense of order, which it did effectually. Once, I remember, the captain of the main-top forgot himself and kept his hat on after the anthem had begun: Sir Francis had him flogged out of hand, and after that all heads were as bare as the palm of my hand. But young men are sometimes thoughtless ma'am; for as Friar Bacon said, you cannot expect *old* heads on *young* shoulders; and my cousin wrote an irreverent skit on the C-in-C and the ceremony.'

'So he did, the dog,' said Jack, laughing with pleasurable anticipation.

'And somebody took a copy of the skit and conveyed it to the Admiral, who invited my cousin to dinner. Cumby had not the least notion of what was afoot until the end of the meal, when a tall chair was brought in and the Admiral bade him sit in it and read *that* to the assembled company, all of 'em flag-officers or post-captains. Poor Cumby was dumb-founded, as you may imagine; but however there was no help for it, and when the Admiral said "Sing out" again in a stern voice, he began. Shall I repeat it, Jack?'

'Aye, do. That is to say, if it would not be disagreeable to Mrs Fielding.'

'Not at all, sir,' said Laura. 'I should very much like to hear it.'

Sutton took a draught of wine, straightened himself in his chair, and adopting a pulpit voice he began, 'The First Lesson for the morning's service is part of the third chapter of Discipline.

1. Sir Francis Ives, the Commander-in-Chief, made an image of blue and gold, whose height was about

24

five feet seven inches, and the breadth thereof was about twenty inches. He set it up every ten o'clock, on the quarterdeck of the *Queen Charlotte*, before Cadiz.

2. Then Sir Francis Ives, the Commander-in-Chief, sent to call together the Captain, the officers, the parson, the seamen, and the Marines, to come to the dedication of the image which Sir Francis Ives, the Commander-in-Chief, had set up.

3. Then the Captain, the officers, the parson, the seamen, and the Marines, were gathered together, unto the dedication of the image which Sir Francis Ives had set up; and they stood before the image which Sir Francis Ives had set up.

4. Then the Captain cried aloud, To you it is commanded, O officers, parson, seamen, and Marines, that at what time ye hear the sound of the trumpet, the flute, the horn, the clarionet, the drum, the fife, and all kinds of music, ye take off your hats, and worship the blue and golden image that Sir Francis Ives, the Commander-in-Chief, hath set up; and whoso taketh not off his hat and worshippeth, shall be surely visited with the Commander-in-Chief's displeasure.

5. Therefore, at that time, when all the people heard the sound of the trumpet, the flute, the horn, the clarionet, the drum, the fife, and all kinds of music, they took their hats off and worshipped the blue and golden image which Sir Francis Ives, the Commander-in-Chief, had set up.

6. Wherefore, one morning after that time, a certain officer drew near, and accused a thoughtless thoroughbred seaman.

7. He spake, and said to Sir Francis Ives, O, Commander-in-Chief, live for ever!

8. Thou, O Commander-in-Chief, hast made a decree that every man that shall hear the sound of the trumpet, the flute, the horn, the clarionet, the drum, the fife, and all kinds of music, shall take his hat off and worship the blue and golden image; and whoso taketh not off his

hat and worshippeth, shall be surely visited with thy displeasure.

9. There is a certain seaman whom thou hast made a petty officer, and hast set over the affairs of the maintop: this man, O Commander-in-Chief, regarded not thee this morning: he took not off his hat and worshipped the image thou settest up.

10. Sir Francis Ives, in his rage, commanded to bring the captain of the maintop. Then they brought this man before the Commander-in-Chief.

11. Then was Sir Francis Ives full of fury, and the form of his visage was changed, against the poor captain of the maintop.

12. Therefore he spake, and commanded that they should rig the grating, read the Articles of War, and call the boatswain's mates; and commanded the boatswain's mates to take their thief's cat-o'-nine-tails.

13. And he commanded the most mighty men that were in his ship to seize up and bind the captain of the maintop, and that he should be punished with one dozen lashes.

14. Then the captain of the maintop, in his trousers, his hosen, and his shoes, but without his jacket and his shirt, was bound up to the grating, and was flogged with one dozen lashes.

15. Then was the captain of the maintop sore at the displeasure of Sir Francis Ives, the Commander-in-Chief.

Here endeth the First Lesson. And now, ma'am,' said Sutton, speaking more like a human being again, 'I come to my point, because when Cumby reached the last piece, the Admiral, who had been as grim as a hanging judge all this time, and all the other officers too, burst out in a roar of laughter, told my cousin to take three months' leave in England, and ordered him to dine aboard the flagship the day he returned. That is my point, do you see – Sir Francis can be savage or he can be kind, and there is no telling which.'

* * *

'There is no telling which,' said Jack Aubrey to himself as the barge carried him over the water to the flagship fairly early the next morning. His signal had not been thrown out at the Commander-in-Chief's usual unearthly hour, for the *Avon* had come in at dawn with dispatches: and with mail, including a well-filled sack for the *Surprise*. Her captain's share of the letters, or to be more exact the share that dealt with business, made it clear that it was essential that he should get a ship – preferably a frigate with a chance of prize-money – to be able to cope with the situation at home; so Sir Francis' opinion of him was now even more important than it had been before. The other letters, those from Sophie and the children, he had in his pocket, to read again while he was waiting for the Admiral.

Bonden, steering the barge, gave a significant cough, and Jack, following his eye, saw the *Edinburgh* standing in, a ship commanded by Heneage Dundas, Jack's particular friend. He glanced at Stephen, but Stephen was deep in his own thoughts, grave and withdrawn. He too had letters in his pocket for further reading. One was from his wife, Diana, who had heard an absurd story of his having a very public affair with a red-haired Italian woman: it must be absurd, she said, because Stephen could not but know that if he publicly humiliated her before people of their own world, then she would resent it very bitterly indeed. She did not set up as a moralist of any kind, she said, but she would not stomach an open affront from anyone on earth, man, woman, or freemartin. 'I shall have to deal with this directly,' said Stephen, who knew that his wife, though uncommonly good-looking, was also uncommonly passionate and determined.

Other letters were from Sir Joseph Blaine, the chief of naval intelligence, and the first, written officially, congratulated 'his dear Maturin' upon what he described as 'this brilliant coup', hoping that it would lead to the complete elimination of French agents in Malta. For a long while English moves in the Mediterranean and on its African and Asian shores had been countered by the French almost before they were made and it was clear that secret information was being sent from Malta to France. The position was so serious that the Admiralty had sent its acting Second Secretary, Mr Wray, to look into it; but the coup in question was Maturin's independent discovery of the chief French agent in Valletta and his principal colleague or accomplice, a senior official in the British administration, a Channel Islander by the name of Boulay, a man very well placed for learning facts, plans and movements of the first importance to the enemy. This discovery followed a long and complex operation carried out by Maturin with Laura Fielding's unwitting help; but it had occurred only a few hours before he was obliged to leave Valletta, and he had therefore been compelled to send his information to Mr Wray and to the Commander-in-Chief for action, Wray being in Sicily for a few days and the Admiral off Toulon. He had done so reluctantly, because the letters necessarily disclosed his status as one of Sir Joseph's colleagues, a status that he preferred to keep secret – so much so in fact that he had declined collaborating with Wray or the Admiral's counsellor and oriental secretary, Mr Pocock. Wray was a newcomer to the world of naval intelligence, coming from the Treasury, and Maturin had thought the affair too delicate for inexperienced hands; furthermore, he understood that Wray did not enjoy Sir Joseph's fullest confidence, which was not surprising, since although Wray was certainly able and intelligent he was also a fashionable, expensive man, much given to high play and not at all remarkable for his discretion. The same objection of inexperience applied to Pocock, though in other ways he made a very good head of the Admiral's local intelligence service. Yet even if both Wray and Pocock had been far more objectionable, even if they had been downright fools, Maturin would still have written: his was a very important discovery, and the first of the two men to reach Valletta had only to make use of his exact, detailed information to wipe out the French organization in half an hour, with the help of no more than a corporal's guard. Even if it had meant revealing his true identity ten times over he would certainly have written, above all to Wray, who must in all probability return to Malta well before the Admiral; for although Maturin had a very considerable experience of intelligence-work, and although he was wary, percipient, and acute enough to have survived several campaigns in which many of his colleagues had died, some under torture, he was by no means omniscient; he was capable of making mistakes and he had no suspicion of the fact that Wray was a French agent, a man who admired Buonaparte as much as Maturin detested him. Stephen saw Wray as a somewhat flashy, unsound, over-clever fellow; he did not know that he was a traitor, nor did he even suspect it.

Ever since leaving Valletta Stephen had been passionately eager to learn the result of his letters, and he would certainly have been aboard the flagship the moment she appeared, had it not been for naval etiquette and because any untimely, unusual visit on the part of a surgeon to Mr Pocock must necessarily excite comment, to some degree lessening his obscurity and with it his usefulness as an agent, to say nothing of his own personal safety.

But there were also other letters from Sir Joseph, personal letters, some parts of which would require both literal and figurative decoding – letters in which Sir Joseph spoke in veiled terms of rivalries in Whitehall and even within the department, occult influences acting on the Board, underhand dealings, his friends and followers being displaced or denied promotion; and at present Sir Joseph seemed discouraged. Yet the most recent note was dashed off in quite another tone: it spoke with keen approval of the work of a person in the United States who had sent news that a plan often put forward in the American Navy Department was now to be carried into execution, a project that for brevity's sake was called Happiness and that dealt with American activities in the Pacific. 'I shall not trouble you with the details, since you will hear them aboard the flag,' wrote Sir Joseph, 'but it appears to me that at this juncture there is a great deal to be said for viewing the coleoptera of the far side of the world, until the storm blows over; a great deal to be said for the pursuit of Happiness.'

'The vainest chase that ever was,' reflected Stephen, but with no more than a fragment of his mind, the rest of it being taken up with an intense desire to know what had happened in Malta and with wondering how to justify himself to Diana in the shortest possible time, before she should make one of those rash passionate moves so characteristic of her.

'The boat ahoy,' hailed *Caledonia*.

'*Surprise*,' replied Bonden, and the flagship instantly began preparing for the ceremony of receiving a post-captain.

Although he had spent many years at sea Dr Maturin had not gained the slightest tincture of seamanship. At one time or another he had contrived to fall between the boat that was carrying him and almost every class of ship and vessel in the Royal Navy; he had also fallen between a Maltese dghaisa and the solid stone-built quay, and between Wapping Old Stairs and a Thames wherry, to say nothing of less stable craft; and now, although the *Caledonia* had shipped a broad accommodation-ladder, a kind of elegant staircase with rails and entering-ropes covered with red baize, and although the sea was perfectly calm, he very nearly managed to plunge through the narrow gap between the lowest step and the next, and so under the flagship's side. But Bonden and Doudle at stroke oar were used to his vagaries: they seized him directly and set him cursing on the steps again with no more than a torn stocking and a slightly barked shin.

On the quarterdeck, where Jack was already talking to the captain of the *Caledonia*, he saw Dr Harrington, the physician of the fleet, who hurried over, and after the most cordial greetings and a few words about the present influenza invited him to come and look at two cases of military fever as curious as he had ever seen, occurring in twins and perfectly symmetrical.

They were still contemplating the finely-spotted patients when the message came: could Dr Maturin spare Mr Pocock a few moments, when he was disengaged?

The moment Stephen's eager eye caught sight of Mr Pocock's face he knew someone had blundered. 'Do not tell me Lesueur was not taken,' he said in a low voice, laying his hand on Pocock's sleeve.

'I am afraid he had wind of Mr Wray's approach,' said Pocock. 'He vanished without a trace. But five Italian or Maltese accomplices were taken up, and Boulay killed himself before he could be arrested: or so they say.'

'Did the Maltese and Italians yield anything upon being questioned?'

'It seems that with the best will in the world they had nothing to yield. They were fellows of no importance, messengers and second murderers working under men whose names were meaningless. Mr Wray was satisfied that they could not tell him anything before he resigned them to the firing-squad.'

'Did he give you any message for me?'

'He sent his heartiest congratulations on your success, infinitely regretting your absence, but begged you would forgive him if he did not write for the moment, he being so very much out of order, particularly as I should be able to give you an account of his proceedings. He deplored the escape of André Lesueur more than he could say, but was confident that he should soon be taken, Government having put five thousand pounds upon his head. He was also confident that with the death of Boulay all treacherous communications between Malta and France would come to an end.'

After a short silence Maturin said, 'You seemed to express some doubt about Boulay's death.'

'Yes,' said Pocock, making a pistol of his fingers

and holding it to his temple. 'He was found with his brains blown out. But Boulay was a left-handed man, left-handed in all he did; and the pistol had been put to the right-hand side of his head.'

Stephen nodded: ambiguous deaths were commonplace in the rougher levels of intelligence. 'At least I hope I may assume that Mrs Fielding's free pardon has passed the seal – that she is quite safe from any importunity of any kind?'

'Oh yes,' said Pocock. 'Mr Wray attended to that at once. He said it was the least he could do, after your extraordinary efforts. He also charged me to say that he was going home overland, and would be happy to be of any service. A courier goes off to him tonight.'

'Most obliging in Mr Wray,' said Stephen. 'And perhaps I may avail myself of his kindness. Yes. I shall entrust him with a letter that I should like my wife to receive as soon as possible.'

They both of them meditated for a while and then moved on to the next subject. Stephen said, 'You have seen Captain Aubrey's official account of the Zambra affair, of course? It would be improper in me to speak of the naval side, but since I was concerned with the political aspects, I should very much like to know how the Dey is to be handled now.'

'Ah, there I am on much safer ground,' said Pocock. 'With the French agents in Valletta I dare say I should have done no better than Mr Wray, but the Oriental world is my province, and in Mascara . . .' He drew his chair a little nearer, and contorting his hairy, ill-favoured face into an arch and even roguish look he said, 'Mr Consul Eliot and I arranged the neatest little parricide you can imagine, and I think I may promise a new and better-disposed Dey at present.'

'No doubt parricide is more readily brought about when a man has many wives, many concubines, and a numerous progeny,' observed Stephen.

'Just so. It is a usual factor in Eastern politics. Yet in the West there is still a certain prejudice against its employment, and perhaps you would be so kind as not to mention it specifically when speaking to the Admiral. "A sudden dynastic change" is the term I have employed.'

Stephen sniffed and said, 'Mr Wray stated that he was much out of order. Was this also just a form of speech, merely describing an unwillingness to write the whole thing out again, or had it a basis in fact? Was he perhaps deeply affected by Admiral Harte's death in the *Pollux*? Conceivably there was more attachment between them than appeared to the casual observer.'

'Oh, as to that,' said Pocock, 'he put on the mourning proper for a father-in-law, of course; but I do not believe he was much more affected than a poor man who suddenly inherits three or four hundred thousand pounds may be expected to be. He *was* out of order, very much out of order, but it seemed to me the effect of extreme nervous tension and exhaustion of spirits, and perhaps of the oppressive heat; between ourselves, colleague, I do not believe he has a great deal of bottom.'

'I am glad he has a great deal of money however,' said Stephen smiling, for Wray had lost a preposterous sum to him when they played piquet day after day in Malta. 'Do you suppose the Admiral will want to see me, at all? I am extremely anxious to get to the top of the Rock the moment the east wind stops.'

'Oh, I am sure he will. There is a question to do with a certain American plan that he wishes to discuss with you. Indeed, I wonder he has not called us in well before this. He is a little strange today.'

They looked at one another. Apart from the 'American plan', which was certainly that of Sir Joseph's letter, Stephen very much wanted to know the Admiral's opinion of Jack's conduct in Zambra Bay; Pocock very much wanted to know what Stephen would be at on the heights of Gibraltar at midday. Both questions were improper, but Pocock's was far less important and after a moment he said, 'Perhaps you have an appointment high on the Rock?'

'So I have too, in a manner of speaking,' said Stephen. 'For at this time of the year, unless there is a levanter blowing, prodigious vast great quantities of birds pass the Strait. Most of them are raptores, which, as I am sure you know, generally choose the shortest passage over water; so you may have thousands and thousands of honey-buzzards, kites, vultures, the smaller eagles, falcons, harriers, and hawks crossing in a single day. But they are not only raptores: other birds join them. Myriads of white storks, of course, but also, as I am credibly informed, the occasional black stork too, God bless her, a bird that I have never yet beheld, a dweller in the plashy forests of the remotest north.'

'Black storks, sir?' said Pocock with a suspicious look. 'Black swans I have heard of, but . . . Perhaps, as the time is getting on, I should give you an outline of this American plan.'

'Captain Aubrey, sir,' said Mr Yarrow, 'the Admiral will see you now.'

Jack's first impression, as he walked into the great cabin, was that the Commander-in-Chief was drunk. The little man's pale leathery face had a pink flush, his bowed back was straight, his usually cold, hooded old eyes shone with a youthful gleam. 'Aubrey, I am delighted to see you,' he said, standing up and reaching over his paper-covered desk to shake hands.

'Come, that's civil,' thought Jack, somewhat relaxing his noncommittal expression and sitting on the chair the Admiral pointed out.

'I am delighted to see you,' said Sir Francis again, 'and I congratulate you on what I reckon a thumping victory. Yes, a thumping victory, when you compare the respective losses. A victory, though no one would think so from your official letter. The trouble with you, Aubrey,' said the Admiral, looking at him kindly, 'is that you are no goddam good at blowing your own trumpet; nor, by consequence, at blowing mine. Your letter,' – nodding at the laborious pages Jack had left the day before – 'is downright apologetic instead of triumphant; it is *concerned to say* and *regrets to have to report*. Yarrow will have to recast it. He used to write speeches for Mr Addington, and he knows how to make the best of a case. It ain't a question of lying, nor of showing away or puffing yourself neither, but just of refraining from crying out stinking fish at the top of your voice. By the time he has finished with your letter it will be clear even to the ordinary land-borne public that we have won a victory, clear even to the ordinary newspaper-reading cheesemongers, and not only professional men. Will you join me in a glass of sillery?'

Jack said he would be very happy – exactly the thing for such a hot morning – and while the bottle was fetching the Admiral said, 'Never think I don't grieve for poor Harte and the *Pollux*, but in practical politics any C-in-C will always give an old worn-out ship for a new one half as powerful again. The French two-decker was the *Mars*, you know, fresh off the stocks. They managed to warp her under the guns of Zambra – *Zealous* and *Spitfire* saw her there, together with your big frigate burnt to the waterline on her reef – but they will never warp her out again – *Mars* my arse, hey? Hey? – even if her back weren't broke, which it is, because our politicoes have nobbled the Dey.' The steward, a very much smoother soul than Jack's Killick, though still a seaman with gold rings in his ears, drew the cork with a London butler's gravity and Sir Francis said, 'Aubrey, here's to your health and happiness.'

'And to yours, sir,' said Jack, savouring the fresh, flowerly, grateful wine. 'Lord, how well it does go down.'

'Don't it?' said the Admiral. 'Well, there you are, you see: on balance we are up by at least half a ship of the line and of course by your whole frigate; and the contumelious Dey is knocked on the head. Yarrow's rephrasing will make all this perfectly clear to the meanest understanding, and your letter will look extremely well when my dispatch appears in the Gazette. Letters . . . Lord above,' said the Admiral, pouring out another glass and waving his hand at the mass of correspondence, 'sometimes I wish no one had ever found out the art of writing. Tubal Cain, was it not?'

'So I have always understood, sir.'

'And yet sometimes they can be tolerably welcome. This one came this morning.' Sir Francis picked it up, hesitated, and then, saying, 'I had not the smallest expectation of it. I have not mentioned it to anyone. I should like people I respect in the service to be the first to know – it is after all a service matter,' he passed the letter over.

Jack read

Dear Sir

The great exertions, ability, and zeal, which you have displayed during your command in the Mediterranean, not only in the active operation of the fleet under your orders, but in the internal arrangements and discipline which you have established and maintained, with such effect to His Majesty's service, have been noticed by His Royal Highness with so much approbation, that he has been graciously pleased to declare His intention of honouring you by a distinguishing mark of the royal favour; I am accordingly commanded to acquaint you that His Royal Highness will confer on you the dignity of a Peer of Great Britain, as soon as it shall be known what title you would desire to bear . . .

Without finishing he sprang up, and shaking the Admiral's hand he cried, 'Give you joy with all my heart, sir, or rather my lord as I should say now – eminently well-deserved – it does honour to the whole service. I am so happy.' And indeed his face shone with such honest pleasure as he stood there beaming at the Admiral that Sir Francis looked at him with more affection than his hard old face had shown for many years. 'It is perhaps a vanity,' he said, 'but I confess it pleases me very much indeed. An honour to the service, as you so rightly say.

And you are part of it: if you read farther on, you will see he mentions our turning the French out of Marga. God knows I had no share of it – it was your doing entirely – though legally it was just within my time of command: so, you see, you have earned me at least one of the balls in my coronet, ha, ha, ha!'

They finished their bottle, talking of crowns, imperial and otherwise, strawberry leaves, for whom reserved, titles that descended in the female line, and the awkwardness of being married to a peeress in her own right. 'That reminds me,' said the Admiral, 'you could not dine aboard yesterday because you were engaged to a lady.'

'Yes, sir,' said Jack, 'to Mrs Fielding. I had given her a lift from Valletta. Her husband joined her here, coming in *Hecla*, so I asked 'em both.'

Sir Francis looked very knowing indeed, but he only said, 'Yes, I had heard she went aboard *Surprise*. I am glad it ended happy, but in general women in a ship are a very bad thing. A gunner's wife to look after your youngsters, by all means, and perhaps one or two other warrant officers', but no more. Quite apart from the moral effect, you would not believe the amount of water they waste. Fresh water for washing their smalls they will have, and they will go to any lengths to get it, corrupting sentries, ship's corporals, even officers – the whole ship's company, indeed. However, I hope you will be able to come tomorrow. I mean to indulge in a little private celebration and then I am away, back to the Toulon blockade.'

Jack said that nothing would give him greater pleasure than celebrating such news, and the Admiral continued, 'Now I must turn to a completely different subject. We have certain intelligence that the Americans are sending a frigate into the Pacific to attack our whalers: the *Norfolk*, thirty-two. She is comparatively light, as I dare say you know, and although she has a much heavier broadside than *Surprise* she carries only four long guns, all the rest being carronades; so that at anything of a distance the two could

37

be considered a match. The question is, would a man of your seniority accept such a command?'

Jack mastered the delighted smile that did all it could to spread over his face, and bidding his heart beat quieter he said, 'Well, sir, as you know I was promised the *Blackwater* on the North American station; but rather than sit idle at home while their lordships find me an equivalent, I should be happy to protect our whalers.'

'Good. Very good. I thought you would say that: I hate a man that refuses an active command in time of war. Well, now,' – picking a sheaf of papers from his desk – 'the *Norfolk* was to weigh from Boston on the twelfth of last month, but she has to convey some merchantmen to San Martin, Oropesa, San Salvador and Buenos Aires, so it is to be hoped that you will have time to cut her off before the Horn. But if not, clearly you must follow her round, and that means six months' provisions. Relations with the Spanish authorities, such as they are, are likely to be difficult, and it is very fortunate that you will have Dr Maturin. We will ask him for his views on the opportunity of putting in, but before he comes tell me if you have any particularly deserving men in the *Surprise*. I am in a promoting frame of mind, inclined to spread happiness, and although there can be no question of commissions, a few warrants or removals to a higher rate may prove possible.'

'Why, sir, that is very kind in you, most benevolent,' said Jack, horribly torn between a sense of justice to his shipmates and a very strong disinclination to weaken his crew. 'My master and gunner are both of them fit for a ship of the line; and I have two or three very promising young petty officers, perfectly qualified for a bosun's warrant in an unrated vessel.'

'Very well,' said the Admiral. 'Let my flag-lieutenant have their names this afternoon and I shall see what can be done.'

'And, sir,' said Jack, 'although there is no question

38

of commissions at present you will allow me to mention William Honey, a master's mate, who brought the news from Zambra to Mahon in the launch, and Mr Rowan, my second lieutenant, who went away for Malta in the cutter.'

'I shall not forget them,' said the Admiral. He rang the bell, and when Pocock brought Stephen in he said, 'Good morning to you, Doctor. I dare say you and Mr Pocock have been considering this American plan?'

'In part, sir. We have traced the path of the *Norfolk* down the Atlantic coast of South America, but we have not entered the Pacific. We have not yet reached Chile or Peru.'

'No,' said the Admiral. 'Nor does our intelligence reach so far. We have a reasonably detailed course as far as the Horn, and after that nothing at all. That is why it is so important to intercept her before say the height of Falkland's Islands: there is not a moment to be lost. But first I should like your opinion of the political situation in the various ports she is to call at – whether it would be advisable to put in for information or whether we might meet with obstruction or even downright hostility.'

'As you are aware, sir, the Spanish possessions are in a state of extreme confusion; but I am confident that we may put into San Martin, and Oropesa, and of course the Brazilian San Salvador. I am far less sanguine about Buenos Aires and the River Plate, however. From the very beginning the region was colonized by the offscourings of the worst parts of Andalusia, slightly relieved by a few shiploads of criminals; and of recent years the mongrel descendants of these half-Moorish ruffians have been under the tyrannical rule of a series of low demagogues, disreputable even by South American standards. There is already a great deal of ill-will towards us, because of the recent action and their humiliating defeat; and since a tyrant's position is a little less insecure if the discontent can be directed at a foreigner, who knows what imaginary crimes may not be fastened upon our people? What lies invented to mislead us, what delays contrived to hinder our progress, and what information conveyed by all possible means to our enemies? Unless we have a singularly devoted correspondent there I cannot recommend a visit to Buenos Aires.'

'I am entirely of your opinion,' cried the Admiral. 'My brother was there when we took the town in the year six, and a nastier, dirtier place he had never seen, nor nastier, dirtier people; and he was a prisoner of war there when a French officer assumed command and took it back again – they used him barbarously, barbarously. But I will not dwell upon that.' He reached for his pen and wrote energetically. 'Aubrey, here is my direct rescript for your six months' stores; and don't you let those mumping villains at the cooperage-wharf keep you standing off and on. As I said, there is not a moment to lose.'

CHAPTER TWO

It was profoundly true that not a moment was to be lost, since even the space between breakfast and dinner might see the *Norfolk* a full degree farther south if she had any luck with the north-east trades, and by so much nearer the vast expanse of the Pacific, where she might so easily never be found at all. Yet from the very beginning of this state of emergency Captain Aubrey was compelled to lose a great many of them: moments, minutes, hours and even days that fled away into the past, never to be recovered.

In the first place common decency required him to receive the ceremonial visits of Mr Gill, the frigate's master, and of Mr Borrell, her gunner, come to take their leave on being promoted into the *Burford*, 74, and to utter particularly laborious speeches, returning thanks for his kind recommendation. Then came Abel Hames and Amos Day, formerly his captains of the maintop and the foretop respectively, the first now bosun of the *Fly* gun-brig and the second of the *Eclair*, who found great difficulty in beginning to express their gratitude, but who having begun, were sadly puzzled to leave off. And when he had at last got all four over the side, heartily cheered by their shipmates, the *Berwick* came in, instantly sending the *Surprise*'s launch across, commanded by William Honey, the master's mate Jack had dispatched from off the coast of Africa to carry word of the disabled French two-decker a tolerably perilous four hundred miles to Port Mahon; and Honey was so justifiably pleased with his success that it would have been inhuman not to attend to his account of the voyage. Honey had barely finished before another boat from the *Berwick* brought the Reverend Mr Martin, her chaplain, a naturalist and a great friend of Stephen's, and

41

Captain Pullings, formerly Jack's very able first lieutenant but now promoted – a captain without a ship or any real prospect of a ship, and a captain only by courtesy at that, since his official rank (and of course his meagre half-pay) was that of a commander. They were both very cheerful and both in their best clothes, come to pay their respects to Captain Aubrey, who had to be called from the stowing of the hold, and to talk at large about earlier commissions in a variety of ships. Captain Aubrey greeted them with a singularly artificial smile, and as soon as Martin had gone off to show Stephen a paper nautilus, a *female* paper nautilus, he said to Pullings, 'Tom, forgive me if I seem inhospitable, but I have just been ordered to take in six months' stores with the utmost dispatch. Gill is removed to *Burford* and no new master has been appointed – Borell is gone too – Rowan is somewhere between this and Malta – Maitland is having a tooth drawn at the hospital – we are twenty-eight men short of complement – and unless I go and stir up those wicked dogs at the cooperage we shall be here until we ground on our own beef bones.'

'Oh, sir,' cried Pullings, to whom the significance of an urgent six months' stores was instantly apparent, 'is that indeed the case?'

'Now, sir,' said Jack's steward, walking in without any ceremony, 'I must have that there shirt.' Then seeing Pullings his acid, housewifely face broke into a smile; he put a knuckle to his forehead and said, 'My kind duty, sir, and hope I see you well?'

'Blooming, Killick, blooming,' said Pullings, shaking hands and then taking off his fine blue coat with its golden epaulettes. 'Be a good fellow and fold that carefully and find me a frock.' And to Jack, 'If you do not think it would upset Mowett, sir, I should be happy to take over the hold, or the watering party, or the gunner's stores: I am quite at leisure, you know.'

'He would rise up and call you blessed,' said Jack, 'and so should I, if you would relieve me in the hold while I run to that infernal – while I run to the port-admiral's and the cooperage. Never was such a Behemoth of vice as that master cooper. Lucifer ain't in it.'

Leaving Behemoth's lair, poorer by five guineas but with his heart eased by the promise of diligence, Jack hurried towards the Waterport gate, clasping a sheaf of papers that he consulted from time to time, commenting upon them to the short-legged midshipman who trotted at his side. Even a sixth-rate man-of-war needed an astonishing amount in the way of naval stores, while each of the warriors she carried was allowed seven pounds of biscuits a week, seven gallons of beer, four pounds of beef and two of pork, a quart of peas, a pint and a half of oatmeal, six ounces of sugar and the same of butter, twelve ounces of cheese and half a pint of vinegar, to say nothing of the limejuice, the necessarily enormous quantity of fresh water for steeping the salt meat, and the two pounds of tobacco a lunar month, for which however he had to pay at the rate of one and sevenpence a pound – an enormous bulk when multiplied by two hundred. Seamen were, furthermore, intensely conservative and most passionately attached to their rights, and although they would compromise over their beer, their very, very small beer, cheerfully and indeed eagerly accepting a pint of wine instead if they were in the Mediterranean or half a pint of rum, made into grog, in all far foreign waters, and agree that duff might be considered the equivalent of meat on stated occasions, almost any other change was sure to lead to trouble, and wise captains avoided innovation at all costs. Fortunately Jack had an efficient purser in Mr Adams, but even Mr Adams could not make the Victualling Board's local minions spread more canvas than they chose; and in any case Jack suspected that the purser, like the bosun, might be feeling a little out of humour, a little less willing to run himself into the ground, since Jack had recommended the master and the gunner for promotion, but neither Mr Adams nor Mr Hollar. The truth was that the *Surprise* had been brought to such a degree of excellence with their great guns and carronades that the ship could almost dispense with a gunner, except for minding his stores; and Jack himself could perfectly well see to the navigational side of the master's duties (in fact, he could do them rather better than Mr Gill); but at this stage a skilled and relatively honest purser was of the first importance, while an excellent bosun was essential at all times, particularly now that Jack had lost those splendid seamen, the captains of the main and foretops. In Captain Aubrey's mind there had been a conflict between loyalty to his shipmates and loyalty to his ship; the ship had won, of course, but a certain guilt haunted his conscience, still tender for these things if for little else.

Just opposite the Convent he met Jenkinson, Sir Francis' flag-lieutenant. Until this point he had only nodded or waved to his various acquaintances as he hurried along but now he stopped and after the briefest interchange of civilities he said, 'As you know, Mr Jenkinson, the C-in-C was very kind to me yesterday, so kind that I hardly liked to mention that *Surprise* was twenty-eight men short of complement. Do you think it would be possible to raise the subject today, before he sails?'

'I very much doubt it, sir,' said Jenkinson, without any hesitation. 'I very much doubt it would be opportune.' In respectful terms he said that was a matter Jack must fight out for himself with the port-admiral; and having made that plan clear he said, 'It is understood, is it not, that Dr Maturin too dines aboard the flag today? I believe there is some farther point that Mr Pocock wishes to raise, and the Admiral was afraid that his invitation was not quite clear. I had intended to come aboard you on my way back.'

'I had not understood the Doctor to be invited, I must confess,' said Jack. 'But I will make sure that he waits on Sir Francis.' He wrote in his pocket-book, tore out the sheet and gave it to the midshipman, saying, 'Calamy, run back to the ship and give this to the Doctor, will you? If he is not aboard you must find him, even if it means running up to O'Hara's tower; but I dare say the hospital is more likely.'

A hundred yards farther on Jack came face to face with his old friend Dundas of the *Edinburgh*, a friend who certainly could not be waved or nodded to.

'Why, Jack,' said Dundas, 'you look distracted. What's afoot? And why are you running about in a round hat and those vile pantaloons? If the Admiral sees you he will put you under arrest for topping it the shopkeeper.'

'Walk along with me, Hen, and I will tell you,' said Jack. 'The fact of the matter is, I *am* distracted. I was ordered to take in six months' stores yesterday and I have been hurrying to and fro among these slow sly circumspect creatures ever since, without getting any forrarder at all – I have lost my master and gunner and two petty officers – I have only one lieutenant aboard – I am twenty-eight men short. As for these clothes, they are all I have. Killick has taken everything else away, to be washed by the Gibraltar laundrywomen in fresh water, every stitch bar my square rig for dinner with the Admiral this afternoon, God help us – hours wasted, stuffing food I do not want at a time when I cannot afford five minutes and should be glad to eat a cold piece of beef and bread and butter in my hand.'

'Still,' said Dundas, 'how glad I am that you are not going home to lay the poor *Surprise* up in ordinary, or worse. May I ask where you are bound, or would that be indiscreet?'

'I do not mind telling you,' said Jack in a low tone, 'but I would not have it generally known. We are to protect whalers. And that reminds me. You always sailed with a fine ballast of books: have you anything on whaling? I am sadly ignorant about the whole subject.'

'Northern or southern?'

'Southern.'

'I had Colnett's book until I was fool enough to lend it. But I can do better than that – by God, Jack, I can do much better than that. There is a man here on the Rock called Allen, Michael Allen, that was master of the *Tiger* till he invalided from her a few months ago: a thoroughbred seaman. We were shipmates once, and we said how d'ye do on the Parade not half an hour ago. He is quite well now, and eager for a ship. And he sailed with Colnett!'

'Who was Colnett?'

'Do you not know who Colnett was, Jack, for Heaven's sake?'

'Would I ask if I knew?'

'But surely even you must know of Colnett; everybody knows of Colnett.'

'What an entertaining witty rattle you are to be sure, Hen,' said Jack in a dissatisfied tone.

'Not to know about Colnett. Lord! Only think. But of course you must remember Colnett. Just before the last war, in ninety-two I think, some merchants asked the Admiralty for a vessel to go looking for places where the southern whalers might wood, water and refit. The Admiralty let them have the *Rattler* sloop and gave Colnett long leave of absence to command her. He had been a midshipman with Cook and he took her round the Horn into the Pacific . . .'

'Forgive me, Heneage,' said Jack. 'But I must just look into the port-admiral's office. Be a good fellow and step into Richardson's' – nodding towards the open door of a cool shaded tavern – 'and wait for me over a bottle. I shall not be long, I promise you.'

He was not long. He came into the big sanded room, bowing under the lintel, his naturally florid face somewhat redder than usual and his bright blue eyes brighter still with anger. He sat down, drank a glass of pale ale, and whistled a stave. 'Do you know the words they sing to that?' he asked, and Dundas replied,

'We'll give you a bit of our mind, old hound,
Port-admiral, you be damned.'

'That's right,' said Jack.

At much the same time Stephen said to Martin, 'That

makes eight more black storks: seventeen in all, I believe.'

'Seventeen it is,' said Martin, checking the list upon his knee. 'What was that smaller bird low down on the left?'

'It was only a bar-tailed godwit,' said Stephen.

'Only a bar-tailed godwit,' repeated Martin, laughing with delight. 'Paradise must be very like this.'

'Perhaps a little less harsh and angular,' said Stephen, whose meagre hams rested on a sharp limestone edge. 'Mandeville reports that it has mossy walls. But let it not be supposed that I complain,' he added, and indeed his face, usually withdrawn and reserved, fairly shone with pleasure.

The two of them were sitting high-perched on the very chine or ridge of Gibraltar under an immense, cloudless, gentle blue sky, with the grey cliffs falling almost sheer to the Mediterranean on the left hand: on the right lay the distant bay with all its shipping, and straight ahead the dim peaks of Africa rose from a blueish haze. A soft south-west breeze cooled their cheeks, and across the strait there passed a long loose train of birds in an unhurried easy glide, sometimes single lines, sometimes much thicker troops, but always passing, the sky never empty. Some, like the black vultures and the storks, were huge; others, like the tired hobby that sat preening his red breeches on a rock not ten yards away, quite small; yet large or small they all glided on together without the least sign of animosity, sometimes wheeling in close-packed spirals to gain height but most passing quite low overhead, so low on occasion that they had seen the crimson eye of the bearded vulture, the orange of the goshawk's.

'There is another imperial eagle,' observed Martin.

'So there is too,' said Stephen. 'God bless him.'

They had long since given up counting the white storks and the various kinds of buzzard and harrier, the smaller eagles, the kites and commoner vultures, and now they concentrated upon the rarest of the rare. On the left hand, beyond the hobby, in a cleft overhanging the sea, a peregrine kept up a strong harsh hacking cry, presumably

47

expressive of desire; and on the right hand, lower down, Barbary partridges could be heard: the air was filled with the scent of lavender and lentiscus and a hundred other aromatic shrubs hot in the sun.

'There, there!' cried Stephen. 'Below the storks – to the right – that is a lappet-faced vulture, my dear sir. My lappet-faced vulture at last. You can see her pale, well-rounded thighs, almost white.'

'What a satisfaction,' said Martin, following the bird with his single, carefully shaded eye, and some minutes after it had vanished, 'There is an odd creature almost exactly over your ship.'

Stephen fixed it with his pocket spyglass and said, 'I believe it must be a crane, a solitary crane. How curious.' He also fixed Jack Aubrey on the quarterdeck of the *Surprise*, stalking to and fro like Ajax and waving his arms about. 'Why, he looks as though he were in quite a passion,' he murmured indulgently: he was used to passion in the executive officers at these times of preparation for a voyage.

But he was not used to quite this degree of passion. Captain Aubrey had just received the message, delivered by a frightened, breathless, purple-faced Calamy, that Dr Maturin sent his compliments, but 'did not choose to come'.

'Does not choose to come,' cried Captain Aubrey. 'Red Hell and bloody death.'

'He said he thought he might not dine today at all,' quavered Calamy.

'And you bring me this message, wretched boy? Do you not know that in such a case you must insist, you must explain?'

'I am very sorry, sir,' said Calamy, who at twelve was quite wise enough not to protest that he *had* insisted, he *had* explained, until he had been positively cuffed and threatened with worse if he did not go away and stop frightening the birds – his unnecessary, vehement gesticulations had already startled three Andalusian hemipodes that were just about to land – where was he brought up, to be prating so to his elders? Did he not know shame or decency at all? He now bowed his head, and his Captain asked him whether he did not know that an officer-like fellow must not be put off with answers like that from persons who, however great their learning and virtues, were essentially civilians?

But Jack was never one for prolonged moralizing, still less now, when every minute counted: he broke off, glanced fore and aft, trying to remember who was in the ship and who was not. 'Pass the word for Sergeant James,' he said, and to the sergeant, 'Pick four of your quickest-moving Marines and follow Bonden up to the top of the Rock at the double: Mr Calamy will point out the way. Bonden, go ahead and make the situation clear even to civilians, if you can: in any event I expect to see the Doctor here at two. Killick will have his number one rig ready to be put on.'

At four bells in the afternoon watch, or two by the clocks in the town, Jack was sitting in front of a small looking-glass in his sleeping cabin with a freshly-laundered cravat the size of a topgallant studdingsail spread out ready to be folded about his neck when he heard a confused thumping, bundling sound on deck, followed by Killick's shrill, indignant, shrewish voice, a cross between that of a much-tried long-soured nursemaid and of an uncommonly rough tarpaulin-hatted tobacco-chewing foremast-hand, and by some indistinct oaths.

A little before five bells he came on deck in all the glory of full dress, with the Nile medal in his button-hole, his Turkish decoration, a diamond chelengk, blazing in his gold-laced hat, and his hundred-guinea Patriotic Fund sword at his side; and there he found Stephen, looking stuffed and sullen in his rarely-worn good coat, a comparatively subfusc garment. The frigate's barge lay at the starboard mainchains, the bargemen in gleaming white trousers and frocks and broad straw hats, the Captain's coxswain standing at the tiller, with Mr Midshipman

49

Williamson and the sideboys waiting at the rail, while the bosun and his mates held their calls ready poised: it was all a shocking waste of time; but high ceremonial waste, like blazing away for King Charles' restoration and Gunpowder Plot, was no doubt necessary for the good of the service. Jack glanced about the harbour and saw boats converging upon the *Caledonia* from all the King's ships; and the port-admiral's barge had already put off from the shore. He smiled at Stephen, who gave him a bitter look, and said, 'Lead on, Macbeth.' Macbeth instantly sprang from the larboard gangway, where he had been standing by a tackle-fall, ready to get on with the ship's urgent business the moment the ceremony was over. Standing before his Captain with his huge bare red bony splay feet brought neatly together he plucked off his blue bonnet and asked, 'Wheer tu, sirr?'

'No, no, Macbeth,' said Jack, 'I did not mean you; and in any case I should have said Macduff . . .'

'Macduff, Macduff,' the cry went through the ship. 'Sawny Macduff to the quarterdeck at the double.'

'Belay there,' cried Jack. 'Scrub it. No, no. My meaning is, the officers may go over the side as soon as they please.'

Quite unmollified by this, Stephen was handed muttering down into the boat after the midshipman, and Jack followed him to the howl of silver pipes.

The Commander-in-Chief's sudden flush of benevolence had called together a surprising number of guests, and Stephen found himself tight-wedged at the bottom of the table between the *Caledonia*'s chaplain and a black-coated gentleman who had come out to act as deputy judge-advocate in some particularly delicate courts martial. Yet this party, though a little too numerous for comfort, had its advantages: the humbler people were removed from the admirals by so solid a phalanx of post-captains that they could talk away at their ease, almost as though there were no Olympians present; and presently they were making a fine convivial din.

The lawyer seemed a knowledgable man, willing to converse, and Stephen asked him how, in naval courts, a suit for tyranny and oppression might be instituted in cases of extreme disparity of rank: whether, to take an entirely hypothetical example, a froward commander-in-chief and his accomplice of post rank who persecuted an innocent subordinate might be brought before officers on the same station or whether the matter would have to be referred to the High Court of Admiralty, the Privy Council, or the Regent himself.

'Why, sir,' said the lawyer, 'if the persecution were tortious, and if it happened at sea, or even on fresh water or reasonably damp land, the Admiralty court would no doubt have cognizance.'

'Pray, sir,' said Stephen, 'just how damp would the land have to be?'

'Oh, pretty damp, pretty damp, I believe. The judge's patent gives him power to deal with matters in, upon, or by the sea, or public streams, or freshwater ports, rivers, nooks and places between the ebb and flow of the tide, and upon the shores and banks adjacent – all tolerably humid.'

At this point Stephen became aware that Dr Harrington some places higher up the table and on the other side, was smiling at him and holding up a glass. 'A glass of wine with you, Dr Maturin,' he said, with a civil bow.

Stephen returned the smile and the bow with a very good will, and drank the wine that a heavily-breathing Marine poured into his glass, his brimming glass. It was the same sillery that Jack had drunk the day before and it went down even more gratefully. 'What delightful wine,' observed Stephen to nobody in particular. 'But it is by no means innocent,' he added, slowly drinking the rest of the glass. Because of the total confusion in the frigate he had had no breakfast apart from a cup of coffee; the packet of sandwiches and the flask of cold negus that he had forgotten to take up the Rock lay in his cabin still, attended by a growing crowd of rats and cockroaches;

his usual dinner time was two hours earlier than this; the latter part of his morning had been intensely frustrating, hot, dusty and hurried; and so far he had eaten nothing but a crumb of bread: he felt the effect of the wine well before his glass was emptied – a very slight swimming in his head, the faint birth of a certain benignity, a willingness to be pleased with his company. 'Quo me rapis?' he murmured. 'Sure it destroys one's sense of free will. Jove made Hector bold and timid, timid and bold by turn, so there was no personal merit in his heroism, no shame in his running away. From a misanthrope Bacchus makes me sociable . . . Yet on the other hand I had already bowed and smiled; I had performed at least the motions of complaisancy; and how often have I not observed that the imitation begets the reality.'

His neighbour, he found, had for some time been telling him about the nice distinctions to be found in English law. '. . . it is much the same with deodands,' he continued. 'If a man leap on to a cart in motion, however slight that motion may be, and miss his footing so that he break his neck, then the cart and all it contains is a deodand, forfeit to the King. But in the case of a cart that is standing still, while the man climbs up by the wheel, and climbing falls to his death, the wheel alone is deodand. In the same way, if a moored ship is the cause of a man's death, only the hull is deodand, whereas if she is under sail the cargo too is forfeited, so long as it is within the domain of the common law: for on the high seas, my dear sir, a very different set of rules applies.'

'Deodands,' said the chaplain on Stephen's right. 'The patron of my brother's living in Kent has the grant of all the deodands in the manor of Dodham. He showed me a brick that had fallen on a mason's head, a gun that had exploded in firing off, and a very furious bull that its owner did not choose to redeem with a payment of money; and he told me of yet another fine point of law – that if a child fall off a ladder and kill itself, the ladder is not forfeit; whereas if its father do so, then it is. I mean, that the ladder becomes a deodand in the second case, but not in the first.'

'Very true,' said the lawyer. 'And Blackstone explains this by the fact that in the times of Popish superstition it was held that infants, being incapable of sin, had no need of the propitiatory Masses purchased with the deodand, or rather its redemption. Yet other authorities . . .'

Stephen's attention drifted away until the parson touched his sleeve and said, 'Dr Harrington is speaking to you, sir.'

'You will support me, colleague, I am sure,' called Harrington down the table, 'when I say that barely one in ten of our people is directly killed by the enemy, or dies from wounds received in battle. Disease or accident account for nearly all of them.'

'Certainly I will,' said Stephen. 'And perhaps it may be said that these figures suggest the relative importance of the combatant and the non-combatant officers.'

'Or perhaps it may be said,' cried a very witty, very red-faced Marine officer, 'that for every man the enemy kills, the medicoes kill nine, ha, ha, ha!'

'Come, Bowers, recollect yourself,' said the Admiral. 'Dr Harrington, Dr Maturin, a glass of wine with you.'

By this time they had moved on to a noble Hermitage (for to honour the occasion the Admiral had fairly stripped his cellar on the Rock) and as he savoured it Stephen said to himself, 'I must remember to pin Harrington for a mate.'

This he did in the rosy full-fed cheerful crowd that stood about the quarterdeck and poop with little coffee-cups in their hands during the interval between the end of dinner and the arrival of the boats, saying, 'Dear colleague, may I beg you to help me to an assistant? In general, as you know, I prefer to sail without one unless I am in a two-decker, most surgeon's mates being sad ignorant bouncing rapparees. But with the prospect of a long voyage before me, I feel I must have some strong young man skilled in drawing teeth. I have rarely been happy in my

53

tooth-drawing. In my youth it was considered far below a physician's dignity; I never learnt the knack, and recently I have had some most unfortunate experiences. I can do it, given time, of course; but often enough the tooth comes out more slowly than the patient might wish, and in little pieces. If we have a ship's barber with a turn that way I usually leave it to him, or when I can I send the case to hospital.'

'That is odd,' said Dr Harrington, 'because I have seen you carry out all the greater amputations with extraordinary speed and apparent ease.'

'Yet there it is,' said Stephen. 'Who is capable of the more is not necessarily capable of the less, as my old nurse used to say; and I should be most grateful for a young man unusually clever with his hands.'

'As for mere extraction,' said Dr Harrington, 'I know a fellow whose performance would astonish you. Look,' – opening his mouth wide, tilting it to the sun and pointing. 'Look,' he said, pointing to a gap and speaking in a strangled, inarticulate open-mouthed voice, 'second molar, right maxilla.' Then, more like himself, 'Only five days ago and yet almost no wound, as you see. He did it with his fingers alone: remarkable. But he is not a young man, and to tell you the truth, Maturin,' said Dr Harrington, bending close and shading his mouth, 'he is something of a quacksalver. How the Board ever came to pass him, I do not know. He seems to possess almost no Latin at all.'

'If he can draw teeth like that, he may do it in plain English for me,' said Stephen. 'Pray, where is he to be found?'

'At the hospital, and his name is Higgins. But I speak for nothing but his dexterity; he may be a mere empiric, or even worse.'

'Dr Maturin, if you please, sir,' said a messenger, and Stephen was led away to the secretary's cabin, where both Mr Yarrow and Mr Pocock were waiting for him. Mr Pocock said that he had received Dr Maturin's letter for the courier to carry to Mr Wray and that it had already left. Stephen thanked him, observing that in all likelihood much time would be saved, a point of real importance to him. Then there was a short silence. 'I am somewhat embarrassed to begin,' said Pocock 'since the information I am to pass on has been communicated to me in a deliberately obscure form, so that I am obliged to speak as though I were withholding many of the facts, which must seem strange and perhaps even offensive to Dr Maturin.'

'On the contrary,' said Dr Maturin. 'If, as I presume, confidential matters are concerned, I had far rather know only the details that concern me: it is then materially impossible for any blunder or inadvertence of mine to disclose the rest.'

'Very well,' said Mr Pocock. 'It appears, then, that Government has sent a gentleman to one or more of the Spanish South American colonies with a large sum of money: he is travelling under the name of Cunningham in the packet *Danaë* from the Cape, a swift-sailing brig. But the minister is now much concerned at the possibility of the *Danaë*'s being taken by the *Norfolk*, and if the *Surprise* should meet with the packet she is to warn her of the danger and, if it can be done with little loss of time, escort her into a South American port. But should this not be possible, or should the port be on the eastern, or Atlantic coast, then other measures must be taken. The gentleman has two chests of specie, and these will be left in his charge; but his cabin also contains a far larger sum in bills, obligations and so on. He is unaware of the fact, though I presume the person to whom this larger sum is consigned must have been supplied with directions for finding it. In any event, here are the directions,' – passing a slip of paper – 'and they will enable you to remove the package. And here is a note that will ensure that the gentleman understands the position. There: I have said all I was required to say.'

For some time the *Caledonia* had been filled with

55

familiar sounds, the stamp and go of some hundreds of men at the capstans, and various pipes and cries usual in unmooring ship. Now there was a pause, and Yarrow said, 'I dare say they are hauling away the cat before hooking on the fish.'

Pocock said, 'Perhaps they will stopper with a dog.'

Stephen said, 'It is my belief that they have raised a mouse, and that having seized it with a fox they will clap on a lizard.'

'Lord, what a jargon the honest creatures have invented, upon my word,' said Pocock, laughing heartily for the first time in Stephen's acquaintance with him. 'Were your terms authentic?'

'They were indeed,' said Stephen. 'And there are hounds too, somewhere about the masts.'

'So were my cat and fish,' said Yarrow. 'The master explained them to me only yesterday; and he mentioned horses, dolphins, flies, bees, a positive ark, ha, ha, ha!'

'If you please, gentlemen,' said the tall stern flag-lieutenant at the door, and all three civilians at once stopped smiling, 'the Admiral awaits your pleasure.'

The *Surprise*'s boat had long since borne her captain and his bargemen back to their labours, and the flagship's accommodation-ladder had vanished too. From the middle deck Stephen contemplated the steep and dangerous descent, the peevish sea worked up by the freshening south-westerly breeze, and the little harbour tub, manned by two amphibious strangers, bobbing like a cork down there. He hesitated, and Pocock, who understood his hesitation only too well, said, 'If you will take one step down, holding on to me, while Mr Yarrow holds my other hand, at the same time grasping this ring, I believe we may all advance together, in a kind of human chain, without too much peril.'

It was perhaps a ludicrous sight, but it served its purpose, and as the flagship, close-hauled on the starboard tack, swept nobly down towards Europa Point, packing on sail after sail, the harbour tub delivered Dr Maturin to the extremely busy *Surprise*, quite dry from head to foot, his watch still going (it often suffered when he plunged into the sea) and the curious, close-written documents he had just received unblurred by the action of salt water. He crept aboard by way of the stern ladder and found himself in the midst of a most intense activity. Jack had already thrown off his fine clothes and he was standing on the capstan calling out directions to those who were about to warp the ship two cables lengths to windward, while grave, concentrated men hurried by on either side of him, and along the gangways, and down in the waist, and all over the forecastle. 'There you are, Doctor,' he cried on seeing Stephen. 'I am sorry I had to desert you, but we must gather rosebuds while we may, you know. We are just warping up to Dirty Dick's – tallow, coals, pitch, and Stockholm tar – so if you have anything to do on shore, now is the time. No doubt you have already thought of your medicine-chest, portable soup, splints and so on?'

'I shall go to the hospital directly,' said Stephen, and this he did, as soon as the frigate touched the quay.

'Pray, Dr Edwardes,' said he to the head physician, 'do you know Mr Higgins?'

'I am acquainted with a Mr Higgins, who attends from time to time in an unofficial capacity, in case we have anything for him to do. Mr Oakes not infrequently sets him to drawing teeth, which has put our barber's nose finely out of joint, I can tell you: but it does appear that he has a real gift that way. And no doubt he can cut corns, too,' – laughing scornfully. 'If you are in need of his services – and he performed an extraction on Dr Harrington, no less – I will send for him. He is working in the wash-house at this moment.'

'I should prefer to see him in action. Do not stir, I beg: I know the way.'

Even if Stephen had not known the way, the sound of the drum would have guided him. He opened the wash-house door as the beat began to quicken and he saw Mr Higgins in his shirt-sleeves leaning over a seaman, while a benchful of other patients watched with extreme and anxious attention. The drumbeat grew faster, louder, louder still; the seaman uttered a shrill, strangled, involuntary shriek and Higgins straightened, the tooth in his hand. All the patients gave a sigh of relief, and as he turned Higgins saw Stephen standing there. 'What may I have the honour, sir?' he asked with a very respectful bow, for he had at once recognized Stephen's uniform: a surgeon's coat was by no means as gorgeous as a captain's, but to an unemployed surgeon's mate it was infinitely more interesting, since its wearer might require an assistant.

'Pray carry on, sir,' said Stephen. 'I should like to watch.'

'I beg pardon for the fair-ground noise, sir,' said Higgins with an uneasy laugh, placing a chair for Dr Maturin. He was a small wiry middle-aged man with short cropped hair and his present look of genteel complaisance sat oddly on his unwashed, unshaved face.

'Not at all, at all,' said Stephen. 'Any din that is in the patient's interest is legitimate, nay laudable. I have used gunfire before now.'

Higgins was nervous and perhaps it cramped his style, but even so his was a remarkable performance: once he was sure of his tooth he would give the drummer a nod – there was an excellent understanding between the two – and as the beat began he hung low over his patient, talking loud into his ear, pulling his hair or pinching his cheek with one hand while he manipulated the gum and tooth with the other: then at another nod the drum grew furious and at the height of the crescendo, with the patient's senses all aswim, he would exert just the necessary force, sometimes with forceps, sometimes with his bare fingers alone, in a very smooth, efficient, practised gesture.

'I am the surgeon of the *Surprise*,' began Stephen, when the patients had left, all beaming now, each with a clean handkerchief held ritually to his face.

'Oh, sir, everybody here in the medical line knows Dr Maturin,' cried Higgins, 'and Dr Maturin's valuable publications,' he added with a certain hesitation.

Stephen bowed and went on, 'And I am looking for an assistant skilled in dental surgery. Dr Harrington and my shipmate Mr Maitland speak highly of your talents, and I have seen you operating. If you wish I will ask Captain Aubrey to apply for your appointment to the ship.'

'I should be only too happy to sail under your orders, sir,' said Higgins. 'May I ask where the *Surprise* is bound?'

'That has not yet been publicly given out,' said Stephen. 'But I understand it to be the far side of the world: I have heard mention of Batavia.'

'Oh,' said Higgins, his exultation momentarily checked, for Batavia was most notoriously unhealthy, even worse than the West Indies, where whole ship's companies might die of the yellow jack. 'Yet even so I should be delighted at the prospect of repairing my fortunes in a ship commanded by such a famous prize-taker.'

It was true. In his time Jack Aubrey had taken a very great many prizes, so many indeed that he was called Lucky Jack Aubrey in the service. As a young commander in the awkward little fourteen-gun brig *Sophie* he had filled Port Mahon harbour with French and Spanish merchantmen, harrying the enemy trade in the most desperate fashion; and when a thirty-two gun xebec-frigate called the *Cacafuego* was sent out especially to put an end to his capers he captured her too and added her to the rest. Then as a frigate-captain he had taken a Spanish treasure-ship among other things, and he had had a large share in the spoils of the Mauritius, together with its recaptured Indiamen, among the richest prizes in the sea. To be sure, the Admiralty had taken the Spanish treasure away from him on the pretext that war had not been legally declared, while in his simplicity he had allowed various dishonest landsmen to cheat him out of much of the Mauritius wealth and so involve his remaining fortune that neither he nor his lawyers could tell whether he would be able to retain any of it at all; but in spite of this he still had much of the aura of Lucky Jack Aubrey as well as the nickname.

Mr Higgins was not alone in wishing to become rich, and as the news of the *Surprise*'s prospect of a long voyage spread a great many people applied to go with her; for at this stage of the war it was only frigates that could hope for those glorious encounters in which a man might earn a hundred years' pay in an afternoon. At the same time a number of parents and other relations showed a strong inclination to place their boys on the quarterdeck of one of the outstanding frigate-captains, a man with a remarkable fighting-record and one known for his care in bringing up his midshipmen – a strong desire to send them aboard the *Surprise* even if she were going to the fetid, fever-ridden swamps of Java.

When Jack had commanded the ship in the Mediterranean he had hardly been importuned at all, since it was known to be nothing more than a temporary command for one or two specific missions; but even now that the case was altered (at least to some degree) this was still not one of those long commissions in which he could settle down to the forming of young gentlemen. With reasonable luck he should intercept the *Norfolk* well before the Horn, and even if he did not he hoped to be back in a few months' time: he would therefore have refused all youngsters but for the fact that he had a son himself, young George, whose future he had ensured by making various captains promise to take him aboard when the time was ripe; and now, when these captains or their near kin asked him to do the same he could not very well refuse. Nor could he in decency dwell on the unhealthiness of Batavia, since he knew very well that he was not going there – the whole thing was a mild ruse on Stephen's part, aimed at disguising their movements from the probable foreign agents on or near the Rock and the certain neutrals who passed up and down the Strait, often calling in for stores and gossip. The result was that he now had four little boys in addition to Calamy and Williamson, four squeakers, pleasant, reasonably clean, well-mannered sons of naval families, but still a sad trial to him. 'I tell you what it is,' he said to Stephen at one of their rare meetings in the town, when they were both buying strings, rosin and sheet-music, 'I shall have to ship a schoolmaster. With Calamy and Williamson, that makes six of the little beasts, and although I can teach them navigation when things are quiet and beat them whenever they need it, it seems a poor shabby thing to send them out into the world without a notion of history or French or hic haec hoc. Seamanship is a very fine thing, but it is not the only quality, particularly by land, and I have often felt my own want of education – I have often envied those fellows who can dash off an official letter that reads handsome and rattle away in French and throw out quotations in Latin or even God help us in Greek – fellows who know who Demosthenes was, and John o' Groats. You can cut me down directly with a Latin tag. And it is no good telling an ordinary healthy boy to sit down with his Gregory's *Polite Education* or Robinson's *Abridgment of Ancient History*: without he is a phoenix like St Vincent or Collingwood he needs a schoolmaster to keep him to it.'

'I wonder whether you sea-officers may not rate literature too high,' said Stephen. 'Though to be sure I have known some sea-going boobies who can conduct their ships to the Antipodes and back with nicely-adjusted sails but who are incapable of giving a coherent account of their proceedings even by word of mouth, let alone in writing, shame on them.'

'Just so: and that is what I want to avoid. But both the schoolmasters I have seen are mere mathematicians, and drunken brutes into the bargain.'

'Have you thought of asking Mr Martin, at all? He is not very strong in the mathematics, though I believe he now understands the elements of navigation; but he speaks very fair French, his Latin and Greek are what you would expect in a parson, and he is a man of wide reading. He is unhappy in his present ship, and when I

told him that we were going to the far side of the world
– for I was no more exact than that – he said he would
give his ears to go with us. Yes: "would give both my
ears" was his expression.'

'He is a parson, of course, and the hands reckon
parsons unlucky,' said Jack, considering. 'And most sea-
going parsons are a pretty rum lot. But then they are used
to Mr Martin; they like him as a man – and so of course do
I, a most gentlemanlike companion – and they do like to
have church rigged regularly . . . I have never shipped a
parson of my own free will: but Martin is different. Yes,
Martin is quite different: he may be holier than thou, but
he never thrusts it down thy throat; and I have never seen
him drunk. If he was speaking seriously, Stephen, pray tell
him that should the transfer be possible, I should be very
happy to have his company to the far side of the world.'

'To the far side of the world,' he repeated to himself,
smiling, as he walked towards the old mole: and on the far
side of the street he saw an uncommonly handsome young
woman. Jack had always had a quick eye for a pretty face
but she had seen him even sooner and she was looking at
him with particular insistence. She was certainly not one
of the many Gibraltar whores (though she brought carnal
thoughts to mind) and when their eyes met she modestly
dropped her own, though not without a kind of discreet
inward smile. Had that first insistent look been a signal
that he would not be too fiercely repelled if he boarded
her? He could not be sure, though she was certainly no
bread-and-butter miss. At an earlier age, when he accepted
any challenge going and some that were not going at all,
he would have crossed over to find out; but now, as a
post-captain with an appointment to be kept, he remained
on his own pavement, only giving her a keen, appreciative
glance as they passed. A fine black-eyed young person, and
there was something distinctive about her walk, as though
she were a little stiff from riding. 'Perhaps I shall see her
again,' he thought, and at that moment he was hailed by
another young woman, not quite so handsome, but very

plump and jolly: she was Miss Perkins, who usually sailed with Captain Bennet in the *Berwick* when the *Berwick's* chaplain was not on board. They shook hands, and she told him 'that Harry was hoping to get his grum old parson to take a long, long leave, and then they would escort the Smyrna trade up the Med again among all those delicious islands how lovely'. But when she asked him to dine with them he was obliged to refuse: alas, it was not in his power, for he was already bespoke, and must in fact run like a hare this very minute.

Heneage Dundas was the bespeaker, and they dined very comfortably together in a small upstairs room at Reid's, looking down into Waterport Street and passing remarks about their friends and acquaintances as they went by below.

'There is that ass Baker,' said Dundas, nodding in the direction of the captain of the *Iris*. 'He came aboard me yesterday, trying to get one of my hands, a forecastleman called Blew.'

'Why did he do that?' asked Jack.

'Because he dresses his bargemen in all colours of the rainbow, and likes them to have answerable names. He has a Green, a Brown, a Black, a White, a Gray and even a Scarlet, and he fairly longed for my John Blew: offered me a brass nine-pounder he had taken from a French privateer. Somebody must have told him that Iris meant rainbow in Greek,' added Dundas, seeing that Jack still looked puzzled, if not downright stupid.

'Really?' said Jack. 'I had no idea. Yet perhaps he knew it before. He is quite a learned cove, and stayed at school till he was fifteen. What would he do if he had *Amazon*, I wonder?' – laughing heartily – 'But I do hate that way of making monkeys out of the men, you know. He is kissing his hand to someone this side of the street.'

'It is Mrs Chapel,' said Dundas, 'the master-attendant's wife.' And after a pause he cried 'Look! There is the man I was telling you about, Allen, who knows so much about whaling. But I dare say you have already had a word with him.'

'Not I,' said Jack. 'I sent round to his lodgings, but he was not in the way. The people of the house said he was gone to Cadiz for a couple of days.' As he spoke he looked intently at Allen, a tall, upright, middle-aged man with a fine strong face, wearing the plain uniform of a master in the Royal Navy, and as he took off his hat to a superior officer, a lieutenant of barely twenty, Jack saw that his hair was grey. 'I like the look of him,' he said. 'Lord, how important it is to have a well-assorted set of officers, men that understand their calling and that do not quarrel.'

'Of course,' said Dundas. 'It makes all the difference between a happy commission and a wretched one. Have you managed to do anything about your lieutenants?'

'Yes, I have,' said Jack 'and I think I have solved the problem. Tom Pullings has very handsomely suggested coming along as a volunteer, as I thought he would; and even if Rowan don't join from Malta before we sail, I can give Honey or Maitland an acting order: after all, both you and I were acting lieutenants, taking a watch, before their age.'

'What about the port-admiral and his young man?'

'I utterly refuse to have that niminy-piminy blackguard on my quarterdeck,' said Jack. 'The port-admiral may be damned.'

'I should like to see you telling him so, ha, ha, ha!' said Dundas.

Happily the need did not arise. As soon as Jack walked into his office Admiral Hughes cried, 'Oh Aubrey, I am afraid I must disappoint you of young Metcalf. His mother has found him a place in the Sea Fencibles. But sit down, sit down; you look quite fagged.' So he did: Jack Aubrey was a tall, burly man, and the labour of propelling his sixteen stone about the reverberating sun-baked Rock from dawn till dusk and beyond, trying to urge slow officials into equally brisk motion, was telling on him. 'On the other hand,' continued the Admiral, 'I have just the master you need. He sailed with Colnett – you know about Colnett, Aubrey?'

'Why, sir, I believe most officers that attend to their profession are tolerably well acquainted with Captain Colnett and his book,' said Jack.

'Sailed with Colnett,' said the Admiral, nodding, 'and is a thorough-going seaman, according to all accounts.' He rang the bell. 'Desire Mr Allen to walk in,' he said to the clerk.

It was just as well that Dundas had spoken highly of Mr Allen, for otherwise Jack would have made little of him: Allen did not do himself justice at all. From his boyhood Jack had been an open, friendly creature, expecting to like and to be liked, and although he was by no means forward or over-confident he was not at all given to shyness, and he found it difficult to conceive that the emotion could still paralyse a man of fifty or more, filling him with a repulsive reserve, so that he responded to no civil advance, never smiled, nor spoke except in reply to direct questions.

'Very well. There you are,' said the Admiral, who seemed equally disappointed. 'Mr Allen will join as soon as his order is made out. Your new gunner should have reported already. That is all, I believe: I will not detain you any longer.' He touched the bell.

'Forgive me, sir,' said Jack, rising, 'but there is still the question of hands: I am short, very far short, of my complement. And then of course there is the chaplain.'

'Hands?' exclaimed the Admiral, as though this were the first he had ever heard of the matter. 'What do you expect me to do about them? I can't bring men out of the ground, you know. I am not a goddam Cadmus.'

'Oh no, sir,' cried Jack with the utmost sincerity, 'I never thought you were.'

'Well,' said the Admiral, somewhat mollified, 'come and see me tomorrow. No. Not tomorrow. Tomorrow I am taking physic. The day after.'

Allen and his new captain walked out into the street.

'I shall see you tomorrow, then, Mr Allen?' said Jack, pausing on the pavement. 'Let it be early, if you please. I am very anxious to put to sea as soon as possible.'

'With your permission, sir,' said Allen, 'I had rather go aboard directly. If I do not attend to the stowing of the hold from the ground-tier up, I shall never know where we are.'

'Very true, Mr Allen,' cried Jack, 'and the forepeak calls for a mort of care. *Surprise* is a very fine ship – no better sailer on a bowline in the service – can give even *Druid* or *Amethyst* maintopgallantsails close-hauled – but she has to be trimmed just so to give of her best. Half a strake by the stern, and nothing pressing on her forefoot.'

'So I understand, sir,' said Allen. 'I had a word with Mr Gill in the *Burford*, and he told me he could not rest easy in his cot, thinking about that old forepeak.'

Now that they were out in the open, surrounded by quantities of people and talking about subjects of great importance to them both, such as the ship's tendency to gripe and the probable effects of doubling her, Allen's constraint wore off, and as they walked along towards the ship he said, 'Sir, may I ask what a Cadmus might be?'

'Why, as to that, Mr Allen,' said Jack, 'it might not be quite right for me to give you a definition in such a public place, with ladies about. Perhaps you had better look into Buchan's *Domestic Medicine*.'

They were received aboard by a more than usually distracted Mowett: the purser had refused to accept a large number of casks of beef that had twice made the voyage to the West Indies and back; he said they were short in weight and far, far too old for human consumption, and Pullings had gone to the Victualling Office to see what could be done; Dr Maturin had flung his slabs of portable soup into the sea, on the grounds that they were nothing but common glue, an imposture and a vile job; and the Captain's cook, having rashly and falsely accused the Captain's steward of selling Jack's wine over the side and being terrified of what Killick might do to him once they were out at sea, had deserted, getting into an outward-bound Guineaman. 'But at least, sir, the new gunner has joined, and I think you will be pleased with him. His name is Horner, late of the *Belette*, and he served under Sir Philip. He has all the right notions about gunnery: I mean, he has our notions, sir. He is in the magazine at present; shall I send for him?'

'No, no, Mowett, let us not delay him for a moment,' said the Captain of the *Surprise*, looking along the deck of his ship, which might have come out of a particularly disruptive battle, with stores, cordage, spars, rumbowline and sailcloth lying about here and there in heaps. Yet the disorder was more apparent than real, and with an efficient master already busy in the hold (for Mr Allen had disappeared almost at once) and a gunner trained by Broke already busy in the magazine it was not impossible that she might put to sea in time, above all if he could induce Admiral Hughes to give him some more hands. As he looked he saw a familiar figure come over the forward gangway, the broad and comfortable Mrs Lamb, the carpenter's wife, carrying a basket and a couple of hens, attached by their feet and intended to form part of the Lambs' private store for the voyage. But she was accompanied by another figure, familiar in a way, but neither broad nor comfortable, the young person Jack had seen in Waterport Street. She was perfectly aware of the Captain's eye upon her, and as she came aboard she dropped a little curtsy, before following Mrs Lamb down the fore hatchway, holding her basket in a particularly demure and dutiful manner.

'Who is that?' asked Jack.

'Mrs Horner, sir, the gunner's wife. That is her young hog, just abaft the new hen-coops.'

'Good God! You do not mean to say she is sailing with us?'

'Why, yes, sir. When Horner asked I gave permission right away, remembering you had said we must have someone to look after all these youngsters. But if I have done wrong . . .'

'No, no,' said Jack, shaking his head. He could not disavow his first lieutenant, and in any case Mrs Horner's presence was perfectly in accordance with the customs of the service, though her shape was not; it would be tyranny and oppression to turn her ashore now that she had installed herself, and it would mean sailing with a thoroughly discontented gunner.

Captain Aubrey and Dr Maturin, in their private capacities, never discussed the other officers, Maturin's companions in the wardroom or gunroom as the case might be; but when Stephen came into Jack's cabin late that evening for their usual supper of toasted cheese and an hour or two of music – they were both devoted though not very highly accomplished players, and indeed their friendship had begun at a concert in Minorca, during the last war – the rule did not prevent Jack from telling him that their common friend Tom Pullings was to sail with them once again as a volunteer. Jack had not proposed it, nor even thrown out any hint, although it was such a capital thing from the ship's point of view; but in fact it was a thoroughly sound move, approved by all Pullings' friends on shore. There was not the least likelihood of his being given a ship in the immediate future, and rather than sit mumchance on the beach for the next year or so, he was very sensibly going on a voyage that would give him a much stronger claim for employment when he returned, above all if the voyage was successful. 'They love zeal in Whitehall,' observed Jack, 'particularly when it don't cost them anything. I remember when Philip Broke was made post out of the horrible old *Shark* and turned on shore, he made a kind of militia of his father's tenants and drilled 'em day and night; and presently the Admiralty gave him the *Druid*, thirty-two, a wonderful sailer. Now Tom has no peasants to drill, but protecting our whalers shows just as much zeal, or even more.'

68

'You do not anticipate any inconvenience from there being two first lieutenants?'

'I should, in any other ship and with any other men; but Pullings and Mowett have sailed together since they were youngsters – they are very close friends. They arranged it between themselves.'

'I believe I have heard the first lieutenant spoken of as one who is wedded to his ship; so this will be an example of polyandry.'

'Anan, brother?'

'I mean a plurality of husbands. In Thibet, we read, one woman will marry several brothers; whereas in certain parts of India it is considered infamous if the husbands are related in any degree.'

'A precious rum go in either event,' said Jack, considering, 'and I don't know that I should much care for it myself.' As he tuned his fiddle a vision of Mrs Horner came before his mind's eye, and he added, 'I do most sincerely hope it will be the only case of polyandry we ever see in this commission.'

'I am no great advocate for it,' said Stephen, reaching for his 'cello. 'Nor even for a plurality of wives. Indeed, there are moments when I wonder whether any satisfactory relation is possible between men and . . .' He checked himself and went on, 'Did you remind the post-admiral about Mr Martin at all?'

'Yes, I did. And about our missing hands, for God's sake. I am to see him again the day after tomorrow.' He raised his bow, beat the deck three times with his foot, and at the third they dashed away into their often-played yet ever-fresh Corelli in C major.

'Well, Aubrey,' said the post-admiral, when a hot and weary Captain Jack came into his office at the appointed hour, having run all the way from the rope-walk and its singularly dogged superintendent, 'I believe I have solved your problem: and at the same time we have decided to pay you a great compliment.'

69

Jack had been deceived by many a land-shark in his time, and parted from his perilously hard-earned prize-money with pitiful ease; but in matters to do with the sea he was much more wary and now he gave the Admiral's look of smiling good will no credit whatsoever.

'As you may know,' the Admiral went on, 'there has been a certain amount of trouble in *Defender*.' Jack knew it very well indeed: the *Defender*, a badly commanded and thoroughly unhappy ship, had very nearly mutinied off Cadiz. 'And it was in contemplation to bring the troublemakers before a court-martial here: they are all in the *Venus* hulk. But it was represented that the trial must be long and time-consuming, and that the ministry was most unwilling to see still more newspaper paragraphs about disorders in the Navy; so one of the gentlemen present cried, "Send 'em to Captain Aubrey. Aubrey is the man for situations of this kind. There is nothing like a ship in first-rate order for reclaiming your scabbed sheep, as St Vincent used to say when he sent difficult hands to Collingwood." Here is a list of them.'

Jack took it with a cold, suspicious air; and after a moment he exclaimed, 'But they are nearly all landsmen, sir!'

'I dare say,' said the Admiral carelessly. '*Defender* had a recent draft from home. But any man can push on a capstan-bar and swab a deck: every ship needs some waisters.'

'And there are nothing like enough to make up *Surprise*'s complement,' said Jack.

'No. But we have several hands about to be discharged from the hospital, and you may have them too. There is nothing like sea-air for setting a man up, and long before you reach the Line they will be as brisk as bees in a bottle. Anyhow, there it is. Either take them or wait a month before another draft comes out. In my day any young captain would have seized the offer with both hands. Aye, and he would have looked grateful, too, instead of chuff and sullen.'

'Oh sir,' said Jack, 'believe me, I am fully conscious of your goodness, and am duly grateful for it. I was only wondering whether the hands about to be discharged from hospital were those my surgeon saw in the – how shall I put it? – in the rigorous confinement ward.'

'Yes,' said the Admiral, 'they are. But it don't really signify, you know. Most lunatics are only shamming Abraham to get out of work; and these are not the dangerous raving kind. They don't bite: they would not be discharged else. It stands to reason. All you have to do is put 'em in chains and flog 'em hearty in their fits, just as they do at Bedlam. Was you ever at Bedlam, Aubrey?'

'No, sir.'

'My father often used to take us. It was better than a play.' The Admiral chuckled at the recollection and then went on, 'And there is another thing you have to thank me for, Aubrey. I have managed to persuade Captain Bennet to part with this chaplain for you.'

'Thank you, sir: I am most grateful, and will send my midshipman for him at once. He is sure to be up on the top of the Rock with Dr Maturin, and we have no time to spare.'

Emerging from the office into the heat of the day he found his midshipman, the youngster who had been with him since breakfast, tagging along to carry messages if need be and half running to keep up with Jack's long stride – found him sitting on the steps with his shoes off. 'Williamson,' he said, 'the Doctor and Mr Martin will be somewhere up by Mount Misery; the sentries on the upper battery will show you where. Tell them with my compliments that by making great haste we may get to sea sooner than I had thought, so Mr Martin should stand by to come aboard with all his dunnage; and I should be glad of the Doctor's assistance with some new hands.'

'Yes, sir,' said Williamson.

'Why, what's amiss?' asked Jack, looking at his pale, dusty face.

'Nothing, sir,' said Williamson. 'The skin has rubbed

quite off both my heels, but I shall be perfectly all right if I may go in stockinged feet.'

Jack saw that the inside of his shoes was red with blood: the last miles must have been exceedingly painful. 'Well,' he said kindly, 'that shows a proper spirit. Stay here. I shall pass by Anselmo's on my way to the ship and I shall send you back an ass. You can ride an ass, Williamson?'

'Oh yes, sir. We had one at home, a dickey.'

'You may gallop if you wish. We have hurried so much already that it would be a pity to spoil the ship with a ha'porth of tar at this stage. Remember: my compliments and I should like to see the Doctor within the hour, while the chaplain should be ready to come aboard at very short notice. And don't you let them put you off with going on about their birds. You must be respectful, of course, but firm.'

'Respectful but firm it is, sir,' said Williamson.

Jack had two long, important calls to make before returning to the ship, and for the first time since the beginning of his furious drive to get to sea both were encouraging: the ordnance people, who instead of changing two of his slightly honeycombed twelve-pounders for new ones had hitherto showed a strong inclination to keep all four, were now all compliance, and even offered him a pair of handsome brass gunner's quadrants as well; while the rope-walk, having recovered from its ill-humour, showed him two new fifteen-inch cables that he might have whenever he chose to send a boat for them.

He reached the *Surprise* in a more sanguine mood, far more inclined to look cheerfully upon the prospect of admitting a score of mutineers into his ship. Pullings and Mowett accepted the situation philosophically too, for although most of the pressed hands they had known had been pretty decent, upon the whole, the quota system sometimes resembled an emptying of the inland gaols and on occasion they had had to deal with some very sinful characters indeed. 'Collingwood used to say that a mutiny was always the fault of the captain or the officers,' said Jack, 'so perhaps we shall find them as innocent as so many lambs unhung, and merely maligned. But as for the men from the hospital, I had rather the Doctor looked at them first. I do hope he will come down presently. If we can get one more thing settled, we are by so much the nearer to sailing.'

'But sir,' said Pullings, 'the Doctor is here already. They both of them came racing along the quay an hour ago, gasping and covered with dust and calling out to us not to pluck up the anchor, nor to spread the sails abroad, because they were there. They are below, now, lying in hammocks on the orlop and drinking white wine and seltzer-water. It seems they did not quite understand your message.'

'We will let them lie until we have seen the new draft. Then we will ask the Doctor to look at the hospital offering, for it seems that they are all madmen. I should be happy to have almost any pair of hands that can haul on a rope, but there are limits, even in the Navy.'

'I have heard of maniacs so devilishly cunning,' said Pullings, 'that they pretend to be sane, so they can creep into the magazine and blow up the whole ship and themselves with it.'

The draft from the hulk arrived, pale for want of sun and air, unshaved, and with red marks on their wrists and ankles from the irons; few had much in the way of bags or chests, for the *Defender*, a very badly officered ship, was also a thievish one, and most of their property had vanished as soon as they were put in the bilboes. They did not look like innocent lambs unhung. A few were striped Guernsey-frocked tarpaulin-hatted kinky-faced red-throated long-swinging-pigtailed men-of-war's men, and judging by their answers as they were entered in the ship's books some of these were right sea-lawyers too; a few were lowering, resentful sailors recently pressed out of merchant ships; but most were landsmen. They seemed to fall into two classes, the

73

one being what the Navy called bricklayer's clerks, men with a certain amount of education who said they had seen better days and whose talk impressed the simple foremast jacks, and the other made up of strong-minded independent characters, probably given to poaching and deer-stealing or their urban equivalents, who found any discipline hard to bear, let along the *Defender*'s alternate slackness and tyranny. And then of course there were a few silly, weak-headed fellows. They were not a draft anyone would have chosen, and the Surprises looked at them with pursed lips and cold disapproval; but all the officers had seen far worse.

'Nagel served with me for a while in the *Ramillies*,' said Pullings, when they had been sent forward for slops. 'He was rated quartermaster until he answered once too often. No great harm in him, but obstinate and argumentative.'

'And I saw Compton, the barber, once,' said Mowett. 'I went to a party, an entertainment, aboard *Defender* when Captain Ashton had her, and he did a turn as a ventriloquist. They had some capital dancers, I recall, as good as Sadler's Wells.'

'Now let us see the hospital men,' said Jack. 'Mr Pullings, pray see whether the Doctor has recovered his breath.'

Stephen was breathing easily enough, but from the smouldering fire in his eye it was clear that he had not quite recovered his equanimity. 'I have been practised upon,' was his only reply to Jack's kind enquiries. 'Let the discharged patients be brought forward.'

Those few Surprises who had no immediate urgent task in hand gathered for the fun, and all those who could paused in their work to see them come aboard; but the general look of pleased anticipation vanished as the first stumbled across the gangway, an ordinary-looking seaman, but weeping bitterly, his grey face turned to the sky and the tears coursing down. No one could possibly doubt his extreme unhappiness. The others were not much amusing, either. Stephen retained one whose only trouble was a limited knowledge of English and an extreme difficulty in speaking, because of a cleft palate, which made his answers very strange, a very big, diffident, gentle man from the County Clare; three head injuries from falling blocks or spars; and one genuine Abraham-man. 'The big fellow I will keep for my servant, with your leave,' he said privately to Jack. 'He is perfectly illiterate and will suit me very well. The three others might just as well be at sea as on land: I anticipate no great danger from them. Matthews is certainly feigning madness and will recover his senses when we sink the land. But the rest should never have been discharged, and must go back.'

Back they went, and as they reached the quay a message arrived from the port-admiral. 'Upon my sacred word,' said Jack, having read it, 'I am fit to go with them. All our break-neck hurry, all our stowing the hold by lantern-light, all my hellfire fagging up and down this Sodom and Gomorrah of a town, has been quite unnecessary. I need never have crammed the ship with mutineers and maniacs: I need never have taken them off his hands. The *Norfolk* has been detained a month in port – we had all the time in the world – and that wicked old hound knew it days ago.'

CHAPTER THREE

For once in her long, long naval life HMS *Surprise* had time to spare, and Jack was heartily glad of it. He would not have to drive her as he had so often driven her before, flashing out topgallants and royals as soon as she could possibly bear them and then whipping them in again a moment before they split; he would be able to husband his spars, cordage and sailcloth, a great comfort to a sailor's mind at any time but even more so when there was a possibility of the ship's having to double Cape Horn and sail westward into the great South Sea, where there was no chance of finding a spare topmast for thousands upon thousands of miles.

The possibility was slight with the *Norfolk* delayed for a full month, particularly as the *Surprise*, in Gibraltar, was much more favourably placed for reaching the south Atlantic than her quarry, and Jack thought it most probable that by making Cape St Roque and there standing off and on he would either find her on her way south or at least have news of her. It was here that the coast of Brazil tended far out to the east and Jack had raised the headland many a time on his way to the Cape of Good Hope; and many a time had he seen the trade bound for the River Plate and points south shaving St Roque close and hugging the land for the sake of the leading winds inshore: sometimes there had been as many as twenty sail of merchantmen in sight at one time, all following the same familiar tract. Yet Jack had been at sea long enough to know that the only thing about it he could rely upon was its total unreliability: he did not trust in Cape St Roque nor any other cape, but was fully prepared to carry on to Van Diemen's Land or Borneo if need be.

Still, he was glad of this respite. It would not only

76

give all hands time to breathe after their furious activity in preparing for sea, but it would also enable him to do something towards turning his new hands into the kind of seamen the ship would need on coming to grips with the *Norfolk*. When he was a prisoner in Boston he had seen her as well as several other American men-of-war, and although the *Norfolk* could scarcely be compared with frigates like the *President* or the *United States* with their twenty-four-pounders and their line-of-battle-ship scantlings she would be a tough nut to crack. She would certainly be manned by a full crew of uncommonly able seamen and she would be officered by men who had learnt their profession in the unforgiving waters of the north Atlantic, men whose colleagues had beaten the Royal Navy in their first three frigate-actions. One after another the *Guerrière*, the *Macedonian* and the *Java* had struck to the Americans.

Seeing that Captain Aubrey had been a passenger in the last of these, it was little wonder that he had a high opinion of the United States navy: to be sure, HMS *Shannon*'s victory over the USN *Chesapeake* had shown that the American sailors were not invincible, but even so the respect in which Jack held them could be measured by the zeal with which the new hands were now being put through the great-gun exercise and small-arms drill. Most of them seemed to have been taught nothing aboard the *Defender* apart from swabbing decks and polishing brass, and as soon as the *Surprise* had cleared the Strait, with Cape Trafalgar looming to starboard and Moorish Spartel to larboard, a troop of cheerful spotted dolphins playing across her bows and a topgallant breeze in the north-north-west urging her on her way, her officers took them in hand.

Now, on the third day out, their backs were bent, their hands were blistered and even raw from heaving on gun-tackles, and in some cases their fingers and toes were pinched by the recoiling pieces; but even so Mr Honey, the acting third lieutenant, had just led a party of them to one of the quarterdeck carronades, and the shriek of its slide just over his head caused Captain Aubrey to raise his voice to an uncommon pitch in summoning his steward. Or rather in trying to summon his steward: for Killick was nattering with a friend on the other side of the bulkhead, and being an obstinate, stupid man he neither would nor could attend to two things at once – he had started an anecdote about an Irish member of the afterguard called Teague Reilly and the ancedote he was going to finish. "Well, Killick," he say to me in that old-fashioned way they have of speaking in the Cove of Cork, scarcely like Christians at all, poor souls, "you being only a bleeding Proddy, you won't understand what I mean, but as soon as we touch at the Grand Canary I am going straight up to the Franciscans and I am going to make a good confession." "Why so, mate?" says I. "Because why?" says he . . .'

'Killick,' cried Jack in a voice that made the bulkhead vibrate.

Killick waved his hand impatiently towards the cabin and went on, ' "Because why?" says he, "Because the barky's shipped a Jonah for one, and a parson for two, and for three the bosun's girl put a cat in his cabin; which crowns all." '

The third summons Killick obeyed, bursting into the cabin with the air of one who had just run from the forecastle. 'What luck?' asked Jack.

'Well, sir,' said Killick, 'Joe Plaice says he would venture upon a lobscouse, and Jemmy Ducks believes he could manage a goose-pie.'

'What about pudding? Did you ask Mrs Lamb about pudding? About her frumenty?'

'Which she is belching so and throwing up you can hardly hear yourself speak,' said Killick, laughing merrily. 'And has been ever since we left Gib. Shall I ask the gunner's wife?'

'No, no,' said Jack. No one the shape of the gunner's wife could make frumenty, or spotted dog, or syllabub, and he did not wish to have anything to do with her. 'No, no. The rest of the Gibraltar cake will do. And toasted cheese. Break out the Strasburg pie and the wild-boar ham and anything else that will do for side-dishes. Tent to begin with, and then the port with the yellow seal.'

In his drive to get to sea Jack had not troubled about replacing his cook until the very last minute; and at the very last minute the wretched man had failed him. Rather than lose a favourable wind Jack had given the word to weigh cookless, relying on picking up another at Teneriffe. But there was this serious disadvantage: on the one hand he particularly wished to invite his officers early in the voyage, partly to tell them of their real destination and partly to hear what Mr Allen had to say about whaling, about rounding the Horn, and about the far waters beyond it; yet on the other there was a very old naval tradition that required a captain to give his guests a meal unlike that which they would eat in the gunroom, thus making his entertainment something of a holiday, at least in respect of food. Even in very long voyages, when private stores were no more than memories and all hands were down to ship's provisions, the captain's cook would make a great effort to prepare the salt horse, dog's-body and hard tack rather differently from the gunroom cook; and Jack Aubrey, a Tory, a man who liked old ways and old wine, one of the comparatively few officers of his seniority who still wore his hair long, clubbed at the back of his neck, and his cocked hat athwartships in the Nelson manner rather than fore and aft, was the last to fly in the face of tradition. He could not therefore borrow the services of Tibbets, the officers' cook, but was obliged to scout about for what talent the ship might contain, since Killick's genius extended no farther than toasted cheese, coffee and breakfast dishes, and Orrage, the *Surprise*'s official ship's cook, was a negligible quantity in the epicurean line. Indeed he was not a cook at all in the landsman's sense, being confined to steeping the salt meat in tubs of fresh water and then boiling it in vast coppers, while one member of each seamen's mess attended to all the fine work. In any case he had no sense of taste or smell – he had been given his warrant not because he made any claim to knowing how to cook but because he had lost an arm at Camperdown – yet he was much loved aboard, being a good-natured creature with an endless variety of ballads and songs, and uncommonly generous with his slush, the fat that rose to the surface of his coppers from the seething meat. Apart from what was needed to grease mast and yards, the slush was the cook's perquisite; yet Orrage was of so liberal a disposition that he would often let his shipmates have a mugful to fry their crumbled biscuit in, or chance-caught fish, though tallow-chandlers would give him two pounds ten a barrel in almost any port.

As the sun climbed over a light blue and sparkling sea, so the diminishing breeze hauled into the north-east, coming right aft. Ordinarily Jack would have set royals and probably skysails; now he contended himself with hauling down his driver and jib, hauling up his maincourse, scandalizing the foretopsail yard, and carrying on with spritsail, forecourse, foretopmast and lower studdingsails, maintopsail and maintopgallant with its studdingsails on either side. The frigate ran sweetly before the wind, in almost total silence – little more than the song of the water down her side and the rhythmic creak of the masts, yards and countless blocks as she shouldered the remnants of the long western swell with that living rise and turn her captain knew so well. But she also sailed through the strangest little local blizzard, sparse but persistent enough to make Maitland, who had the watch, call for sweepers again and again. It was Jemmy Ducks, plucking geese in the head: the down flew from him for the first few yards, since the *Surprise* did not in fact outstrip the wind (though she certainly gave the impression of doing so), but then it was caught in the eddies of the spritsail, whirled up, spinning again and again in the currents created by the other sails and settling all along the deck, falling as silently as snow. And all the while Jemmy Ducks muttered to himself,

'Never be ready in time. Oh, oh, all this God-damned down!'

In the silence Jack stood watching with his hands behind his back, swaying automatically to the rise and fall, watching these patterns with the keenest attention, they being a direct reflection of the true thrust of the sails, a set of variables exceedingly difficult to define mathematically. At the same time he could hear Joe Plaice fussing about in the galley. Plaice, an elderly forecastle hand who had sailed with Jack time out of mind, had begun to regret his offer of making a lobscouse almost as soon as it was accepted; he had grown horribly anxious as time wore on, and in his anxiety he was now cursing his cousin, Barret Bonden, his mate for this occasion, with a shocking vehemency and (he having become somewhat deaf) in a very loud voice.

'Easy, Joe, easy,' said Bonden, jerking him in the side and pointing forward over his shoulder with his thumb to where Mrs James, the Marine sergeant's wife, and Mrs Horner had brought their knitting. 'Ladies present.'

'Damn you and your ladies,' said Plaice, though rather less loud. 'If there's one thing I hate more than another, it's a woman. A woman aboard the hooker.'

Every half hour the ship's bell spoke; the forenoon watch wore away; the ceremony of noon approached. The sun reached its height; the officers and young gentlemen either took its altitude or went through the motions of doing so; and the hands were piped to dinner. Yet through the bellowing of mess numbers and the banging of mess kids, Plaice and Jemmy Ducks stuck doggedly to their tasks in the galley, standing there in the midst of the tide, blocking the fairway fore and aft. They were still there an hour later, angering Tibbets as he cooked and served up dinner for the gunroom – a much diminished gunroom, with only the two acting lieutenants, Howard the Marine officer, and the purser, all the other members walking hungrily about on deck in their best uniforms, they being invited to dine in the cabin.

The two seamen were still there, looking pale by now,

at four bells in the afternoon watch, when at the first stroke the officers, headed by Pullings, walked into the cabin, while in the galley Killick and the stout black boy who helped him clapped on to the tray bearing the massive lobscouse.

Captain Aubrey had a great respect for the cloth, and he seated the chaplain on his right hand, with Stephen beyond him and Pullings at the far end of the table, Mowett being on Pullings' right and then Allen, between Mowett and the Captain.

'Mr Martin,' said Jack, after the chaplain had said grace, 'it occurred to me that perhaps you might not yet have seen lobscouse. It is one of the oldest of the forecastle dishes, and eats very savoury when it is well made: I used to enjoy it prodigiously when I was young. Allow me to help you to a little.'

Alas, when Jack was young he was also poor, often penniless; and this was a rich man's lobscouse, a Lord Mayor's lobscouse. Orrage had been wonderfully generous with his slush, and the liquid fat stood half an inch deep over the whole surface, while the potatoes and pounded biscuit that ordinarily made up the bulk of the dish could scarcely be detected at all, being quite overpowered by the fat meat, fried onions and powerful spices.

'God help us,' said Jack to himself after a few mouthfuls. 'It is too rich, too rich for me. I must be getting old. I wish I had invited some midshipmen.' He looked anxiously round the table, but nearly all the men there had been brought up to a very hard service; they had endured the extremes of heat and cold, wet and dry, shipwreck, wounds, hunger and thirst, the fury of the elements and the malice of the King's enemies; they had borne all that and they could bear this – they knew what was expected of them as their Captain's guests – while Mr Martin, when he was an unbeneficed clergyman, had worked for the booksellers of London, an apprenticeship in many ways harsher still. All of them were eating away, and not only eating but looking as though they enjoyed it.

'Perhaps they really do,' thought Jack: he was even more unwilling to stint his guests than to force food down their gullets. 'Perhaps I have been eating too high, taking too little exercise – have grown squeamish.'

'A very interesting dish, sir,' said the heroic Martin. 'I believe I will trouble you for a trifle more, if I may.'

At least there was not the slightest doubt that they thoroughly appreciated their wine. This was partly because drinking it spaced out the viscous gobbets and partly because both Plaice and Bonden had salted the dish, which bred an unnatural thirst, but also because the wine was thoroughly agreeable in itself.

'So this is tent,' said Martin, holding his purple glass up to the light. 'It is not unlike our altar-wine at home, but rounder, fuller, more . . .'

It occurred to Jack that there might be something pretty good to be said about Bacchus, wine, sacrifice, and altars, but he was too much taken up with finding small objects of conversation to work it out (wit rarely flashed spontaneously upon him, which was a pity, since no man took more delight in it, even at infinitesimal doses, either in himself or others). Small things he had to find, since by convention all the sailors sat like so many ghosts, never speaking until they were spoken to, this being a formal occasion, with a comparative stranger present: fortunately, if he ran out of topics he could always fall back on drinking to them.

'Mr Allen, a glass of wine with you,' he said, smiling at the master and thinking, as he bowed, 'Perhaps the goose-pie will be better.'

But there are days when hopes are formed only to be dashed. The towering pie came in, yet even as he was explaining the principles of the dish to Martin Jack's knife felt not the firm resistance of the inner layers of pastry but a yielding as of dough; and from the incision flowed thin blood rather than gravy. 'Pies at sea,' he said, 'are made on nautical lines, of course. They are quite unlike pies by land. First you lay down a stratum of pastry, then a layer of meat, then a layer of pastry, then another layer of meat, and so on, according to the number of decks required. This is a three-decker, as you can see: spar-deck, main-deck, middle-deck, lower deck.'

'But that makes four decks, my dear sir,' said Martin.

'Oh, yes,' said Jack. 'All first-rate ships of the line, all three-deckers have four. And by counting the orlop you could make it five; or even six, with the poop. We only *call* them three-deckers, you understand. Though now I come to think of it, perhaps when we say deck we really mean the space between two of them. I am very much afraid it ain't quite done,' – hesitating over Martin's place.

'Not at all, not at all,' cried Martin. 'Goose is far better rare. I remember translating a book from the French that stated, on great authority, that duck must always be bloody; and what is true for the duck is truer still for the goose.'

'What is sauce for the duck . . .' began Jack; but he was too depressed to go on.

However, in time the Strasburg pie, the smoked tongue, the other side-dishes, a noble Minorcan cheese, dessert and a capital port overlaid the unfortunate, even vulturine memory of the geese. They drank the King, wives and sweethearts, and confusion to Buonaparte, and then Jack, pushing back his chair and easing his waistcoat, said, 'Now, gentlemen, you will forgive me if I speak of matters to do with the ship. I am happy to tell you that we are not bound for Java. Our orders are to deal with a frigate the Americans are sending to harry our whalers in the South Sea: *Norfolk*, thirty-two, all carronades apart from four long twelves. She has been delayed a month in port and I hope we may intercept her on her way, south of Cape St Roque, or if not there then at some other point off the Atlantic coast. But it is always possible that we may have to follow her into the Pacific, and since we have none of us rounded the Horn, whereas I understand that Mr Allen knows those waters well, having sailed with Captain Colnett, I should be obliged if he would let us know what to expect. And I dare say he could tell us a great deal about whaling too, a subject I for one am shamefully ignorant of, could you not, Mr Allen?'

'Well, sir,' said Allen, with scarcely a blush, his shyness having worn off with use and an unusual amount of port, 'my father and two uncles were whalers out of Whitby; I was brought up on blubber, as you might say, and I went a number of voyages with them before I took to the Navy. But that was in Greenland fishery, as we call it, off Spitzbergen or in the Davis Strait, going after the Greenland right whale and the nordcaper, with the odd white whales, walruses and sea-unicorns thrown in; I learnt a great deal more when I went with Captain Colnett to the southern fishery, which as I am sure you know, sir, is chiefly for the spermaceti whale. The spermaceti whale: and all the ships are out of London.'

'Yes,' said Jack, and seeing that Allen was straying from his course he added, 'Perhaps it would be best if you were to give us an account of your voyage with Captain Colnett: that would deal with the navigation and the whaling all in due order. But talking is thirsty work, so let us take our coffee here.'

A pause, in which the scent of coffee filled the cabin and Stephen's whole being yearned for tobacco; but it could be smoked only in the open air of the quarterdeck – some ships were so severe as to insist upon the galley – and that would mean missing Allen's discourse. Stephen was passionately interested in whales; he was also fairly eager to hear about their possible rounding of the Horn, that cape notorious above all others for danger, for endless beating into enormous westerly gales, for hope long deferred, scurvy, and ultimate discomfiture; he repressed his longing, and willed the master to begin.

'Well, sir,' said Allen, 'the Americans out of Nantucket had been taking sperm-whales off their own coast and southwards a great while, and before the last war they and some Englishmen took to going farther south by far, to the Gulf of Guinea and off Brazil and even right down to Falkland's Islands. But it was we who first went round the Horn for spermaceti. Mr Shields it was, a friend of my father's, who took the *Amelia* out in eighty-eight and came back in the year ninety with a hundred and thirty-nine tons of oil. A hundred and thirty-nine tons of sperm oil, gentlemen! With the bounty on top that was close on seven thousand pound. So of course other whalers hurried after him, fishing along the coast of Chile and Peru and northwards. But you know how jealous the Spaniards have always been of anyone sailing in those waters, and they were even worse then, if possible – you remember Nootka Sound.'

'Indeed I do,' said Jack who owed all his present happiness to that remote, dank, uncomfortable inlet on Vancouver Island, far to the north of the last Spanish settlement on the west coast of America, where some English ships, trading for furs with the Indians, had been seized by the Spaniards in 1791, a time of profound peace, thus bringing about the great rearming of the Navy known as the Spanish disturbance, which in its turn caused the first of his splendid metamorphoses, that which changed him from a mere (though perhaps deserving) master's mate to a lieutenant with His Majesty's commission and a gold-laced hat for Sundays.

'So, sir,' said Allen, 'the whalers were most unwilling to put into any port on the Pacific side, not only because the Spaniards were proud and injurious any gate, but because, being so far from home, they could never be sure whether it was war or peace, and they might not only lose their ship and their catch, but be knocked on the head too, or be kept in a Spanish prison till they died of starvation or the yellow jack. Yet when you stay out in all weathers two or three years, it stands to reason you need to refresh and refit.' All the officers nodded, and Killick said, 'That's right,' covering his remark with a cough.

'So Mr Enderby, the same as sent Shields out in *Amelia*, and some other owners applied to Government, asking for an expedition to be fitted out to discover safe harbours and sources of supply, so that the southern fishery might carry on and do better than before. Government was agreeable, but what with one thing and another it turned into what I might call a hermaphrodite voyage, half whaling and half exploring, the one to pay for the other. The Admiralty first said they would lend the *Rattler*, a good sound ship-rigged sloop of 374 tons, but then changed their minds and sold her to the owners, who turned her into a whaler with a whaling-master and a crew of twenty-five all told, as against her complement of a hundred and thirty as a man-of-war; yet the Admiralty did appoint Mr Colnett, who had gone round the world with Cook in *Resolution* and who had sailed the Pacific in merchantmen when he was on half-pay between the wars – in fact he was at Nootka Sound itself, and his ships it was that were seized! So he went commander of the expedition; and he very kindly took me along with him.'

'Just when was that, Mr Allen?' asked Jack.

'At the very beginning of the Spanish Armament, sir, in the winter of ninety-two. It fell unlucky for us, because the bounty was already out for seamen in the Navy, and we lost some of our people and could only get landsmen or boys in their place; and that delayed us till January of ninety-three, so we lost our whaler's bounty too, and our fine weather. Howsoever, we did get away at last, and we raised the Island, if my memory do not lie, eighteen days out.'

'What island?' asked Martin.

'Why, Madeira, of course,' said all the sea-officers.

'We always call Madeira the Island, in the Navy,' said Stephen with great complacency.

'Then Ferro nine days later. And we were lucky with our winds; when we lost the north-east trades a breeze slanted us right across the variables – very narrow that year – until we picked up the south-east trades in 4°North, and they rolled us down to 19°South, crossing the Line in 25°30′West. No. I tell a lie. In 24°30′West. We ran into

Rio a fortnight later and laid there a while to set up our rigging and caulk; and I remember Mr Colnett harpooned a five hundredweight turtle in the harbour. After that we sailed to look for an island called Grand, said to be in 45°South, but what longitude no one knew. We found plenty of black fish – that is what we call the small right whale, sir,' – this in an aside to Martin – 'but no island, Grand or Petty, so we bore away south and west until we struck soundings in sixty-fathom water off the west end of the Falklands. The weather was too thick for any observation for some days, so we gave them a wide berth and stood away for Staten Island.'

'Meaning to pass through the Straits Lemaire?' asked Jack.

'No, sir,' said Allen. 'Mr Colnett always said the tides and currents there worked up such lumpish seas it was not worth it. Then coming into soundings again in ninety fathoms at midnight – Mr Colnett always kept the deep-sea lead going, even with so small a crew – he thought we were too near, so we hauled on a wind and in the morning we had no bottom with a hundred and fifty fathom; so we bore up for the Horn, doubled it with more offing than Mr Colnett would have chosen – he liked to keep fairly well in with the land for the sake of the more variable winds – and the next day we saw the Diego Ramirez islands north by east three or four leagues. And what will interest you, sir,' – to Stephen – 'we saw some white crows. They were just the size and shape of those the northcountrymen call hoodies, only white. Then we had some very thick weather with the wind at west and south-west and most uncommon heavy seas; but however we fairly beat round Tierra del Fuego, and then off the coast of Chile we had fine weather and a southerly breeze. In about 40°South we began to see sperm whales, and off Mocha Island we killed eight.'

'Pray how did you do that, sir?' asked Stephen.

'Why, it is much the same as with the right whale,' said Allen.

'That is as though you should ask me how we take off a leg and I replied that it was not unlike the ablation of an arm. I for one should like a more detailed account,' said Stephen, and there was a general murmur of agreement. Allen looked quickly round. It was hard to believe that so many grown men – seamen and in their right senses too – had never seen a whale killed or at least heard how it was done, but their interested, attentive faces showed him that this was indeed the case, and he began, 'Well, sir, we always have men in the crow's nests, and when they see a whale spout they sing out, "There she blows". Everyone lays aloft as though his life depended on it – for, you know, whaling hands go not for wages but for shares – and if the next spout is right, I mean in this case if it is the sperm whale's thick low spout directed forwards, the boats are lowered down, whale-boats, of course, sharp at each end – lowered down double-quick and the men jump into them and the gear is passed after them, two hundred fathoms of whale-line in a tub, harpoons, lances, drogues, and they pull off, as fast as ever they can at first, then when they are near slow and very quiet, because if he is not a travelling whale he will usually come up again within a hundred yards of the same place if he dives and if you have not startled him.'

'How long is he likely to stay down?' asked Stephen.

'About a glass and a half – three quarters of an hour: some more, some less. Then he comes up and breathes for maybe ten minutes, and if you take care and paddle quiet you can come right close to him as he lies a-blowing. Then the boat-steerer, who has been in the bows all this time, sends the harpoon home – whale sounds at once, sometimes stoving the boat as he throws up his tail, or peaks his flukes as we say, and goes down and down, the line running out so fast it smokes against the bollard and you have to sluice it – boatsteerer and headsman change places, and when the whale comes up again at last the headsman lances him – a six-foot blade behind the flipper if he can manage it. I have known an old experienced headsman kill a whale almost at once, with him going into his flurry, as we say, when he can very easily stove you, lashing so wild. But generally it takes a long time: lance and sound, lance and sound, before he is killed. The young forty-barrel bulls are the worst, being so nimble: I do not suppose we succeed with one in three, and sometimes they tow you ten miles to windward, and even then they may carry all away. The big old eighty-barrel fish are far less trouble, and it was one of them I saw killed with the first stroke. But you are not sure of your whale till he is tried out. Shall I tell how we do that, sir?' he asked, looking at Jack.

'If you please, Mr Allen.'

'Well, we tow the whale alongside the ship and start cutting-in: we make him fast and then we either cut off the fore part, the upper part of his head that we call the case because it has the spermaceti in it, and hoist it on deck if he is a small one or veer it astern if it is not, to wait till we have done flinching, or flensing as some say. And that we do by making a cut above his fin, lifting the blubber and slipping a toggle through it, fast to a purchase from the maintop; then hands go on to the carcass with long sharp spades and cut a spiral band in the blubber about three feet wide. It is close on a foot thick on a good fish, and it comes easy away from the flesh; the purchase raises it, canting and turning the whale at the same time, do you see – indeed, we call it the cant-purchase. On deck they cut the blubber up and toss it into the try-works, which is cauldrons amidships with a fire underneath that fries the oil out: and the fritters that are left serve for fuel after the first firing. Then when all the blubber is aboard we attend to the head, opening up the case and ladling out the spermaceti, the head-matter: it is liquid at first, but it solidifies in the barrel.'

'It is a true wax, is it not?' asked Martin.

'Yes, sir, a true pure white wax when it is separated from the oil, as pretty as you could wish.'

'What can its function be?'

90

No one had any suggestions to offer and Allen went on, 'But as I was saying, you are not sure of your whale until he is tried out, barrelled and safe in the hold. Of the eight we killed off Mocha Island we only profited by three and one head, because the weather turned dirty and they broke away either towing or from the side. After Mocha we sailed along the Chile coast until about 26°South, when we bore away for St Felix and St Ambrose Islands, which lie a hundred and fifty leagues to the west. Miserable places, no more than five miles across: no water, no wood, almost nothing growing, and almost impossible to land: we lost a good man in the surf. Then back to the main and along the coast of Peru in sweet weather, lying to at night and looking for English ships by day. But we saw none, and reaching Point St Helena in 2°South with the wind westering on us we took our departure for the Galapagos Islands . . .'

Mr Allen carried the *Rattler* to the islands, looked at two of them, Chatham and Hood, without much enthusiasm, returned to the mainland with a westerly breeze, in steady drizzle, and so moved north of the equator, losing the seals and penguins that had been with them so long, and suffering cruelly from the oppressive heat. On to the well-watered, tree-covered Cocos Island, inhabited by boobies and man-of-war birds, a wonderfully welcome refreshment in spite of blinding rain and even fog – on to the shores of Guatemala, to the inhospitable island of Socorro, to Roca Partida, where the sharks were so fierce bold and ravenous that fishing was very nearly impossible – they took almost everything that was hooked, and the tackle too, and one rose to seize a man's hand over the gunwhale. On to the Gulf of California, aswim with turtles; and here Cape St Lucas was their northernmost point. They cruised for some weeks off the Tres Marias, but although they saw many whales they killed only two; then, the ship's people being sickly, they turned her head south, returning much the same way they had come, except that they spent much more time in the Galapagos, where they met with an English ship ready to perish for want of water – only seven barrels left.

Allen spoke of the noble tortoises of James's Island with something close to rhapsody – no better meat in the world – and he gave an exact, detailed, seamanlike description of the curious powerful currents, the set of the tides, the nature of the few indifferent anchorages, the sparse watering places, and the best way of cooking an iguana; and then of the measures that had to be taken to deal with the hood-ends that sprang after a heavy blow in 24°South, not far from St Ambrose and St Felix once more. He spoke of a few more whales sighted and pursued – usually with little success and once with the loss of two boats – and then, having carried the *Rattler* round the Horn again, in much better weather this time, and up to St Helena, he brought his account to an abrupt end: 'We made the Eddystone, then Portland in the course of the night, stood off and on till morning, and so ran up and anchored in Cowes Road, Isle of Wight.'

'Thank you, Mr Allen,' said Jack. 'Now I have a much clearer notion of what lies ahead. Captain Colnett's report was made known to the whalers, I imagine?'

'Oh yes, sir; and they follow his recommendations for most of the islands, particularly James's in the Galapagos, Socorro and Cocos. But nowadays when the sun has crossed the Line bringing dirty weather off the coast of Mexico, they tend to bear away westward for the Society Islands or even farther to New Zealand.'

There were a good many other questions, especially about the hood-ends, cheeks of the head and wash-boards, which quite fascinated the sailors, and then Stephen asked, 'And how did your people fare in their health, during all this long voyage?'

'Oh, sir, we had a most capital surgeon aboard, a joy to us all, Mr Leadbetter; and except for James Bowden who was killed when a boat overset in the surf he brought them all home hale and strong, though sometimes they were inclined to grow down-hearted and pine because we had so many disappointments with the whales, and those that were saddest went sick of the scurvy between the Horn and St Helena: but Mr Leadbetter recovered them with James's powder.'

After some remarks about low spirits and scurvy, mind and matter, and the influence of a general fleet-action upon constipation, the common cold and even chicken-pox, Stephen said, 'Pray, sir, can you tell us anything of the anatomy of the sperm whale?'

'Why, yes, sir,' said Allen, 'it so happens that I can tell you a little. Mr Leadbetter was a man very eager after knowledge, and since we always rummaged the whales' guts for ambergris – '

'Ambergris?' cried Pullings. 'I always thought it was found floating in the sea.'

'Or lying on the beach,' said Mowett. '*Who does not know,/That happy island where huge lemons grow,/Where shining pearl, coral, and many a pound,/On the rich shore, of ambergris is found?*'

'Our first lieutenant is a poet,' said Jack, seeing Allen's startled look. 'And if only Rowan had been able to join from Malta we should have had two of them. Rowan composes in the modern style.'

Allen said that that would have been very gratifying indeed, and continued, 'Certainly you find it on the shore, if you are lucky – there was John Robarts of the *Thurlow* East-Indiaman walking by the sea in St Jago while his ship was watering who found a lump weighing two hundred and seven pounds and went straight home, sold it in Mincing Lane, bought an estate the other side of Sevenoaks and set up his carriage directly – but it passes through the whale first.'

'In that case,' said Pullings, 'how does it come about that ambergris is never found in the high latitudes, where there are whales as thick as hasty pudding?'

'Because it is only sperms that are concerned with ambergris,' said Allen, 'and they do not go up into the northern waters. The whales you see there are a few right whales and all the rest are those wicked old finners.'

'Perhaps the sperms find the ambergris on the sea-bed and eat it,' said Jack. 'The right whales or the finners could never manage such a thing, with all that whalebone in the way.'

'Perhaps so, sir,' said Allen. 'Our surgeon rather fancied it originated in the whales themselves, but he could not really make it out. The fact that it was waxy and as he said un-animal puzzled him to the end.'

'And did you find any, when you inspected the whale's intestines?' asked Stephen.

'Only a little, I am afraid,' said Allen, 'and that only in one fish. It was rare that we could search thoroughly, since we flensed 'em all, or nearly all, at sea.'

'I have never seen ambergris,' said Mowett. 'What is it like?'

'A smooth rounded mass of no particular shape,' said Allen. 'Dark mottled or marbled grey when first you take it out, rather waxy and strong smelling, not very heavy: then after a while it grows lighter-coloured and much harder and takes to smelling sweet.'

'Eggs and ambergris was Charles II's favourite dish,' observed Martin, and Pullings said, 'I believe it is worth its weight in gold.' They reflected upon this for a while, slowly passing the brandy-decanter round, and then Allen went on. 'So since we opened the whales in any case when the weather allowed it Mr Leadbetter took the opportunity of looking into their anatomies.'

'Excellent. Very good,' said Stephen.

'And as he and I were particular friends I used to help him: I wish I could remember a tenth part of the things he explained to me, but it was all a great while ago. Teeth in the lower jaw only, I recall; the two nostrils uniting to make a single valved blow hole and therefore an asymmetrical skull; scarcely more than a trace of pelvis, no clavicles, no gall-bladder, no caecum – '

'No caecum?' cried Stephen.

'No, sir, none at all! I remember how on one calm

day with the whale floating easy by the ship we passed the whole length of the intestine through our hands, a hundred and six fathoms in all – '

'Oh no,' murmured Jack, pushing his glass from him.

' – without finding even a hint of one. No caecum: but on the other hand an enormous heart, a yard long. I remember how we put one in a net and hoisted it aboard; he measured and calculated that it pumped ten or eleven gallons of blood a stroke – the aorta was a foot across. And I remember how soon we got used to standing there among the huge warm guts, and how one day we opened one that had a calf in her and he showed me the umbilicus, placenta, and . . .'

Jack abstracted his mind from Allen's account. He had seen more blood shed in anger than most men and he was not unduly squeamish; but placid butchery he could not bear. Pullings and Mowett were of much the same frame of mind and presently Allen became aware that upon the whole the cabin did not relish his discourse and he changed the subject.

Jack came out of his reverie, hearing the word Jonah; and for a confused moment he thought they were speaking of Hollom. But then he realized that Allen had just said that in view of their anatomy it was no doubt a sperm whale that had swallowed the prophet – they were sometimes to be found in the Mediterranean.

The sailors, happy to be released from Fallopian tubes and biliary concretions, spoke of sperms they had seen within the Straits, Jonahs they had known, the horrible fate of ships in which Jonahs had sailed, and Jack's party ended in an even more civilized way, moving from the sea to the land – plays seen, balls attended, and a furlong by furlong account of a fox-chase in which Mowett and Mr Ferney's hounds would certainly have come up with their quarry if he had not plunged into a field-drain as darkness came on.

But although the cabin escaped more grisly details, the gunroom did not: here the master, unawed by the

95

Captain's presence and supported – indeed spurred on – by the surgeon and chaplain against the disapproval of his messmates, might deliver all the anatomy his powerful memory had retained; and in any case Mr Adams the purser, who was of a hypochondriacal cast, liked to hear; while anything that even remotely touched upon sexual matters fascinated Howard of the Marines.

Not all the details were grisly, however, nor even anatomical. 'I have read accounts of northern voyages, and of the pursuit of the whale,' said Martin, 'but I have never been able to form any clear notion of the economy of whaling. From that point of view, how would you compare the northern and southern fisheries?'

'When I was young,' said Allen, 'before the Greenland waters fell off, we used to reckon that five good fish would pay the voyage. On the average we might take thirteen ton of oil from each, and close on a ton of whalebone; and in those days a ton of whalebone fetched about five hundred pound. The oil was twenty pound a ton or a little better, and then there was the bounty of two pound a ton for the ship, so you would end up with perhaps four thousand five hundred. It had to be divided among some fifty people, and of course the ship had to have her share; yet even so it was a reasonable voyage. But now although the oil has risen to thirty-two pound the bone has dropped to no more than ninety, and the whales are smaller and fewer and farther off, so you need nearer twenty fish not to lose by the trip.'

'I had no idea whalebone could be so costly,' said the purser. 'What is it used for?'

'Fripperies,' said Allen. 'Milliners' and dressmakers' fripperies: and umbrellas.'

'And how does that compare with the southern fishery?' asked Martin. 'For if the only quarry is the sperm, there can be no question of whalebone in the south. The voyage must be made for the oil alone.'

'So it is,' said the master. 'And when you consider that taken one with another sperms give no more than two tons of oil, whereas a good Greenlander gives ten times as much and prime bone too, it seems a foolish venture; for although sperm whale oil fetches something like twice as much as ordinary oil and the head-matter, the spermaceti, fifty pound a ton, that does not compensate for the lack of bone. Oh damn my – that is to say, oh dear me, no.'

'Please to explain the apparent contradiction,' said Stephen.

'Why, Doctor,' said Allen, smiling on him with all the benevolence of superior knowledge – nay, superior wisdom, 'don't you see it lies in the time available? In the Arctic Ocean – in the Greenland fishery – we set out in early April to reach the edge of the ice a month later: in the middle of May the whales arrive and in the middle of June they are away, leaving nothing but those wicked finners behind them, and a few bottle-noses that are neither here nor there. If you have not filled half your barrels you may steer westward for the Greenland coast and try your luck along the drift-ice for what it's worth until August; but by then 'tis getting so cold and dark you must go home. It is much the same in Davis Strait, though you may stay a little longer in the sounds if you don't mind the risk of being frozen in till next year, your ship being crushed maybe and you eaten up by the ice-bears. Whereas the sperm lives in the temperate and tropical waters, do you see, and you may hunt him as long as you please. Nowadays most southern whalers reckon on staying out three years, killing perhaps two hundred fish and coming home with a full ship.'

'Of course, of course,' cried Stephen, clapping his hand to his forehead. 'How foolish of me.' He turned to the servant behind his chair, saying, 'Will you fetch me my cigar-case, now, Padeen?' and to the master, 'Mr Allen, do you choose to take a turn upon the deck? You have twice mentioned the finner with strong disapprobation, and Mr Martin and I would be most grateful, were you to develop your views at greater length.'

'I will be with you in five minutes,' said the master,

'as soon as I have clean-copied my noon observation and pricked the chart.'

They waited for him by the starboard hances, and after a while Stephen said, 'Were there so much as a blade of grass in view or a sheep, you might call this a pastoral scene.' He exhaled a waft of smoke that drifted forward, a coherent body, over the waist of the ship, for the breeze was still right aft, blowing with so even a breath that the countless shirts, trousers, jackets and handkerchiefs hanging on the complex system of lines rigged fore and aft all leaned southward together in an orderly manner, like soldiers on parade – no wanton flapping, no irregularity. With much the same sobriety their owners sat here and there upon the forecastle and among the maindeck guns: this was a make-and-mend afternoon, and for the new hands at least it meant turning the yards and yards of duck they had been given that morning into hot-weather clothes. It was not only the foremast jacks who were busy with their needles, either: on the larboard gangway one of the new youngsters, William Blakeney, Lord Garron's son, was learning how to darn his stockings under the eye of the lady of the gunroom, a bearded hand who had served under his father and who in the natural course of events was now acting as his sea-daddy, a capital darner who had attended to the Admiral's table-cloths in his time; while Hollom sat on the larboard ladder, showing yet another squeaker the best way of sewing on a pocket, singing quietly to himself as he did so.

'What a beautiful voice that young man has,' said Martin.

'So he has, too,' said Stephen, listening more intently: it was indeed wonderfully melodious and true, and the tired old ballad sounded fresh, new and moving. Stephen leant over and identified the singer. 'If he goes on improving like this,' he reflected, 'the men will soon stop calling him Jonah.' For the first days Hollom had eaten wolfishly, filling out with remarkable speed; he no longer looked graveyard-thin nor absurdly old for a master's mate – in fact he might have been called handsome by those who did not require a great deal of masculine determination and energy – and poverty and ill-luck no longer stared from his clothes. He had obtained an advance on his pay, enough to unpawn his sextant and to buy a fairly good coat, and since these were duck pantaloon and round jacket latitudes – no officers wearing uniform except for visits to the cabin or taking the watch – he looked as well as any of them, being exceptionally clever with his needle. He messed with Ward, Jack's conscientious, quiet, somewhat colourless clerk, a man who had been saving for years to put down the surety required before he could become a purser, his highest ambition, and with Higgins, Stephen's new assistant. He had not distinguished himself by any extraordinary display of skill or effectual drive during the furious days of fitting out, but on the other hand he had done nothing to make Jack regret taking him aboard. 'All in the lowland sea ho,' he sang, bringing the verse and the seam both to an end. 'There,' he said to the youngster, 'you finish it off by running it through half a dozen times and casting a round knot in the last turn.' He cut the thread and handed the boy the spool and scissors, saying, 'Run down to the gunner's and give these back to Mrs Horner with my best compliments and thanks.'

Stephen felt a gentle nuzzling at his hand, and looking down he saw that it was Aspasia, the gunroom goat, come to remind him of his duty. 'Very well, very well,' he said testily, taking a final draught from his cigar: he quenched the glowing end on a belaying-pin, wiped the pin over the side, and gave Aspasia the stub. She walked quietly back to the shade of the hen-coops by the wheel, chewing it, her eyes half-closed, and as she went she crossed the path of the master hurrying forward. 'I am sorry to have kept you waiting,' he said. 'I was obliged to mend my pen.' 'Not at all,' they said, and he went on, 'Well now, as for these old finners, gentlemen, you have four main kinds, and there is nothing to be said for any of 'em.'

'Why is this, Mr Allen?' asked Martin in a disapproving

tone: he did not like to hear so large a branch of creation condemned.

'Because if you plant your harpoon in a finner he is apt to knock your boat to matchwood or sound so deep and run so fast he either tows you under or takes out all your line; never was a creature so huge and fast – I have seen one run at thirty-five knots, gentlemen! A hundred foot long and God knows how many tons running at thirty-five knots, twice as fast as a galloping horse! It is unbelievable, was you not to see it with your own eyes. And if by any wild chance you do kill him or far more likely if you come upon him stranded, his whalebone is so short and coarse and mostly black the merchants will not always make an offer; nor will he yield you much above fifty barrels of indifferent oil.'

'He can scarcely be blamed for resenting the harpoon,' said Martin.

'I remember my third voyage,' Allen went on, not attending. 'We were over by the Greenland shore, late in the year, since we had not filled even half our hold. Thick weather, a northern swell making the ice creak loud, a bitter cold evening coming on, and one of our boats got fast to a finwhale. How they came to do it I cannot conceive. Edward Norris, the harpooner, was an experienced whaler and even a first-voyager can tell a finner by his spout – quite unlike a right whale's. And you can see his back fin as he rolls over and goes down again. Any gate, you see him plain when you are close enough to plant your iron. But however it happened, with fog or waves, or wind in the harpooner's eyes, there they were, fast to a finner. Up went their flag for more whale-lines and they clapped 'em on one after another: a tricky job, with the line running out so fast that it makes the bollard char and hiss as you keep pouring water on it. He carried out four full tubs and part of a fifth, close on a mile of line; and he stayed down a great while, maybe half an hour. When he came up old Bingham, the headsman, lanced him directly, and that was the end. He spouted red, threw up his flukes, and

100

set off south by west like a racehorse. They all screeched out for help – we saw the boat tearing along, throwing white water far on either side, going fast away into the murk – what they had done we could not tell – maybe a kink in the line round a man's leg and him half over the side so they dared not cut, or maybe a hitch round a sprung plank – but anyhow a moment later down they went, towed under among the ice, six men and we never found trace of them, not so much as a fur hat floating.'

'The sperm whale is not quite so swift or so formidable, I collect?' said Stephen after a pause.

'No. He could be, with that terrible great jaw. He could snap you a whale-boat in two and scarcely notice it. But he hardly ever does. Sometimes he beats you to pieces with his flukes, sounding or lashing in his death-agony; but he does not go for to do it. There is no vice in him. Why, in those early days, when no whalers had ever been in the great South Sea almost, he would lie there awash looking at you quite kind and inquisitive with his little eye. I've touched him before now, touched him with my hand.'

'Do any whales attack, unprovoked?' asked Martin.

'No. They may bump into you, and start your back-stays; but that is because they are asleep.'

'What are your feelings, when you kill so huge a creature – when you take so vast a life?'

'Why, I feel a richer man,' said Allen laughing: then after a moment, 'No, but I see what you mean; and I have sometimes thought – '

'Land ho,' called the lookout from on high. 'On deck there. High land one point on the starboard bow.'

'That will be the Peak,' observed the master.

'Where? Oh where?' cried Martin. He leapt on to the fife-rail, but insecurely, falling back with his heel and much of his weight on the first and second toes of Stephen's left foot.

'Follow the line of the bowsprit,' said the master, pointing, 'and a little to the right, between the two layers of cloud, you can see the middle of the Peak, shining white.'

'I have seen the Grand Canary!' said Martin, his one eye gleaming with brilliance enough for two. 'My dear Maturin,' – with a most solicitous look – 'how I hope I did not hurt you.'

'Not at all, not at all. There is nothing in life I like better. But allow me to tell you, that it is not the Grand Canary but Teneriffe, and that it is of no use your springing about like that. If I know anything of the service, you will not be allowed to land. You will not see the canary-bird, grand or small, upon her native heath.'

Prophets of doom are nearly always right, and Martin saw no more of the island than could be made out from the maintop as the *Surprise* stood off and on while the launch ran in, coming back through the crowded shipping with a cheerful fat brown man hung about with his own copper saucepans and warranted capable of Christmas pudding and mince pies by Captain Aubrey's very old acquaintance the present governor of the town.

'Never mind,' said Stephen. 'The great likelihood is that we shall water at some one of the Cape Verdes. How I wish it may be St Nicolas or St Lucy. There is a little small uninhabited island between them called Branco, and it has a puffin peculiar to itself, a puffin distinct from all other puffins, and one that I have never seen alive.'

Martin brightened. 'How long do you suppose it will take us to get there?' he asked.

'Oh, not above a week or so, once we pick up the trade wind. Sometimes I have known it begin to blow north of the Canaries and so waft us down with a flowing sheet past the tropic line and on almost to the equator itself: something in the nature of two thousand miles with a flowing sheet!'

'What is a flowing sheet?'

'What indeed? I seem to recall Johnson defining a sheet as the largest rope in the ship, and perhaps it is desirable that such a rope should flow. Or perhaps it is no more than one of the poetical expressions the seamen use: at all events they employ it to give the general impression of a fine free effortless progress. Their language is often highly figurative. When they reach the broad zone of calms and variable winds that lies somewhat north of the equator, between the north-east and the south-east trades, the zone that the French mariner so emphatically calls the *pot au noir*, the pitch-pot, they say that the ship is in the doldrums, as though she were low-spirited, profoundly melancholy, and she lying there with idly flapping sails in the damp oppressive heat, under a cloudy sky.'

At this point however the sky was perfectly clear, and the *Surprise*, although not yet quite her joyful self again, having too many right awkward bastards to deal with, was far from sad or despondent. In 28°15′N. she picked up the trade wind, and despite the fact that it was by no means wholehearted, all hands began to look forward to the modest delights of the Cape Verdes, those parched blackened intolerably hot and sterile islands. The ship had settled down to the steady routine of blue-water sailing: the sun, rising a little abaft the larboard beam and a little hotter every day, dried the newly-cleaned decks the moment it appeared and then beheld the ordered sequence of events – hammocks piped up, hands piped to breakfast, berth-deck cleaned and aired, the new hands piped to the great-gun exercise or reefing topsails, the others to beautifying the ship, the altitude observed, the ship's latitude and her progress determined, noon proclaimed, hands piped to dinner, the ceremony of the mixing of the grog by the master's mate – three of water, one of rum, and the due proportions of lemon-juice and sugar – the drum-beat one hour later for the gunroom meal, then the quieter afternoon, with supper and more grog at six bells, and quarters somewhat later, the ship cleared for action and all hands at their fighting stations. This rarely passed off without at least some gunfire, for although the usual drill of running the great guns in and out had great value, Jack was convinced that nothing could possibly equal the living

103

bang and leap of the genuine discharge in preparing men for battle, to say nothing of teaching them to point the muzzle in the right direction. He was a great believer in gunnery: he had laid in a personal store of powder (the official allowance being far too meagre for real training) to keep his gun-crews in practice; and since few of the ex-Defenders knew anything of the matter at all, much of this private powder went to them, so that often as the first dogwatch drew to an end the evening would be lit by fierce stabbing flames, the ship a little private storm lost on the vast face of the smooth calm lovely ocean, a little storm that emitted clouds, thunder and orange lightning.

An ocean too smooth for Captain Aubrey's liking. He would have preferred two or three almighty northern blows early in the voyage – blows of a violence just short of carrying away any important spars, of course – and this for many reasons: first, because although he had at least a month and more probably something like six weeks in hand, he would have liked even more, being persuaded that you could never have too much time in hand at sea; secondly, because of his simple-minded love of foul weather, of the roaring wind, the monstrous seas, and the ship racing through them with only a scrap of close-reefed storm-canvas; and thirdly because a thundering great blow with topmasts struck down on deck and lifelines rigged fore and aft, lasting two or three days, was almost as good as an action for pulling a heterogeneous crew together.

And they needed pulling together, he reflected: this was the last dog-watch, and as the great-gun exercise had been exceptionally good the hands had been turned up to dance and skylark. They were now playing King Arthur on the forecastle, one man wearing a mess-kid hoop by way of a crown while a set number of others flung buckets of water over him until by antic gestures, grimaces or witticisms he should make one of them smile, the smiler then being obliged to take his place. It was a very old and very popular hot-weather game, and it caused infinite mirth among those who were not penalized

104

for laughing; but as Jack, followed by Pullings, moved a few steps along the gangway, partly to watch the fun and partly to scratch a backstay in the hope of increasing the feeble breeze (a heathen gesture as old or older than the game) he noticed that almost none of the ex-Defenders were taking part, even in the laughter. In a pause between buckets King Arthur caught sight of the Captain near at hand and stood up straight, knuckling his crown, a sprightly young topman named Andrews whom Jack had known ever since he was a Marine Society boy. 'Carry on, carry on,' said Jack. 'I must get my breath first, sir,' said Andrews pleasantly. 'I've been blowing the grampus this last glass and more.'

In the momentary silence a very curious shrill and inhuman voice, not unlike that of Punch or Judy, called out, 'I'll tell you what's wrong with this here ship. The people ain't micable. And the Defenders are picked on perpetual. Extra duty, extra drill, work double tides: always picked on, day and night. Tom Pipes cuts capers over us: and the people ain't micable.'

The tradition of not informing was so strong that all except the stupidest foremast hands instantly looked down or over the gunwhale or into the twilit sky with studiously blank faces, and even the stupidest, having stared openmouthed at the speaker for a brief moment, followed suit. The speaker was perfectly obvious, Compton, once the *Defender*'s barber: his mouth hardly moved and he was looking over the bows with an abstracted expression, but the sound came directly from him: and almost at once Jack recalled that he was a ventriloquist – the extraordinary tone was no doubt part of the act. The words were meant to be anonymous, impersonal; the occasion was as unofficial as anything aboard could well be; and in spite of Pullings' obvious desire to collar the man the incident was best left alone. 'Carry on,' he said to those around King Arthur, and he watched for half a dozen buckets before walking back to the quarterdeck in the gathering darkness.

105

In the cabin that night, as they tuned their strings, Jack said, 'Did you ever hear a ventriloquist, Stephen?'

'I did too. It was in Rome. He made the statue of Jupiter Ammon speak, the creature, so that you would have sworn the words came from the god, if only the Latin had been a little better. The small dark room – the prophetic deep-voiced solemnity – it was very fine.'

'Perhaps the place has to be enclosed; perhaps the principles of the whispering gallery apply. At all events it don't answer on deck. But the fellow thought it did. It was the strangest experience: there he was, telling me things to my face as though he were invisible, while I could see him as plain as . . .'

'The ace of spades?'

'No. Not quite that. As plain as a . . . God damn it. As plain as the palm of my hand? A turnpike?'

'As Salisbury sphere? As a red herring?'

'Perhaps so. At all events the Defenders gave me to understand they were unhappy.'

The bosun's cat dropped through the open skylight: it was a lean young cat of indifferent character, somewhat whorish, and it at once began rubbing itself against their legs, purring.

'That reminds me,' said Jack, absently pulling its tail, 'Hollar is going to ask you for a really good name, a classical name that will reflect credit on the ship. He thinks Puss or Tib is low.'

'The only possible name for a bosun's cat is Scourge,' said Stephen.

Understanding dawned on Captain Aubrey quite fast, and his great fruity laugh boomed out, setting the larboard watch on the grin as far forward as the break of the forecastle. 'Oh Lord,' he said, wiping his bright blue eyes at last, 'how I wish I had said that. Get away, you silly beast,' – this to the cat, which had now crawled up his breast and was rubbing its whiskers against his face, its eyes closed in a foolish ecstasy. 'Killick, Killick there.

106

Remove the bosun's cat: take it back to his cabin. Killick, do you know its name?'

Killick detected the slight tremble in his Captain's voice, and since for once he was feeling relatively benign he said No, he did not.

'Its name is Scourge,' said Jack, bursting out again. 'Scourge is the name of the bosun's cat, oh ha, ha, ha, ha!'

'It is very well,' said Stephen, 'but the instrument itself is a vile thing in all conscience, and no laughing matter at all.'

'Martin says much the same,' said Jack. 'If you two had your way, nobody would be flogged and nobody would be killed from one year to the next, and a pretty bear-garden that would be. Oh dear me, my belly hurts. But even you cannot say that this is a flogging ship: we have not rigged the grating once since Gib. I dislike the cat as much as any man, only sometimes I have to order it.'

'Bah,' said Stephen. 'In anything but a servile constitution it would never be countenanced. Are we ever going to play our music now? It is the busy day I have tomorrow.'

Tomorrow was the day when in all probability the *Surprise*, even at her present staid pace, would cut the tropic line, a point at which Stephen liked to bleed all those under his care as a precaution against calentures and the effects of eating far too much meat and drinking far too much grog under the almost perpendicular sun: had he been the captain, all hands would have been kept to a diet of pap and water-gruel between the latitudes of 23°28′N. and 23°28′S. The bleeding was to take place on the quarterdeck, where the people would be assembled as for a muster and cross over one by one, so that none might escape by skulking about the cable-tiers or even hiding in the enormous coils themselves: for there were some, who though willing enough to shed blood in battle or even to lose their own, could not bear the notion or the sight of the deliberate incision. The afternoon was the time for it, but quite early in the morning both surgeons were busy putting a fine edge to their fleams and lancets. Higgins was still exceedingly shy of his chief, as though he were afraid that the Doctor might address him in Latin at any minute. Higgins' stock of that language and indeed of a good many English medical terms was so very slight that Stephen thought it not unlikely that he had borrowed the name and certificates of some qualified man, probably a former employer. Yet he did not regret having brought him: Higgins had already exercised his undeniable, however qualified, dental skill on two occasions when Stephen would have been unwilling to operate. The men looked upon him as something of a phoenix, and several of the *Surprise*'s steady old hypochondriacs, powerful healthy seamen who reported sick once a week and had to be comforted with pills made of chalk, pink dye and sugar, had deserted Stephen. They consulted Higgins privately, and although Stephen did not mind this at all, he was slightly disturbed by some stories that had come through to him: the live eel said to have been removed from John Hales' bowels, for example, did not sound quite orthodox, and perhaps in time the tendency would have to be checked. For the moment however he had nothing much to say to Higgins, and Higgins had nothing whatsoever to say to him: they ground on in silence.

Three decks above their heads (for absurdly enough they were working by lamplight, next to the medicine-chest, far under the waterline) Captain Aubrey was pacing up and down in the bright sunshine with Pullings at his side. Although the wind was still so faint, fainter than he had ever known the north-east trades, there was a pleasant contended look upon his face. The beautifully clean decks stretched away before him, and they were filled with mild, sensible activity as the ex-Defenders were shown how to reeve gun-tackles and house their pieces just so. From the fore-cabin came the youngsters' chorus of hic haec hoc and their mirth, mildly checked by Mr Martin, at the final his his his, his his his: after their dinner but before his own he would go through their day's workings with them, that is to say their separate statements of the ship's position at midday, determined by the height of the sun and the difference between local noon and the Greenwich noon shown by the chronometers, the whole checked by dead-reckoning. The answers were sometimes very wild: some of the boys seemed incapable of grasping the basic principles and they tried to fudge their workings by mistaken rule of thumb or plain cribbing; and Boyle at least (though from a naval family) had never learnt his multiplication table beyond five times. Yet on the whole they were a pleasant set of boys, and although Calamy and Williamson rather disliked being put to their books again after having sailed so long without a schoolmaster, and although they tended to boast and show away before the first-voyagers he did not think they were tyrannical: it seemed a cheerful midshipmen's berth, and the gunner and his wife looked after them well. Certainly Mrs Horner got up their shirts for ceremonial occasions such as dining in the cabin better than Killick: he suspected her of using fresh water.

The young gentlemen's chorus changed. They were now chanting autos autee auto, and Jack's smile broadened. 'That's what I like to hear,' he said. 'They won't be brought by the lee as we are brought by the lee when someone flashes out a Greek remark at us. They will instantly reply, "Autos, autee, auto to you, old cock: Kyrie eleison". And a classical education is good for discipline too; the hands respect it amazingly.'

Pullings did not seem wholly convinced, but he was saying that Mowett certainly thought the world of Homer when the cat, which had not yet learnt the sanctity of the quarterdeck, crossed their bows, evidently meaning to caress and be caressed. 'Mr Hollar,' called Jack, his voice carrying easily to the forecastle, where the bosun was turning in a dead-eye, 'Mr Hollar, there: be so good

109

as to take your Scourge forward and place him under cabin-arrest: or put him in a bag.'

Stephen's witticism had long since passed through the ship, growing even wittier with repetition, explanation to the dull, and elaboration, and the animal was carried along the gangway with many a cry of 'Scourge, ho!' and many a grin, for the *Surprise* was not one of those stern dismal ships where a man might not speak on deck without being spoken to by a superior.

Jack was still smiling when he observed that this was the ship's usual punishment day: was there anything serious? 'Oh no, sir,' said Pullings. 'Only a couple of squabbles, one drunk and incapable – it was his birthday, sir – and one reproachful words. Nothing that six-water grog won't cover. I had thought of leaving it out, since we are to be bled this afternoon.'

'I was about to suggest the same thing,' said Jack, and he was going on to some changes in the watch-list that would integrate the new hands more thoroughly with the old Surprises and make their life somewhat easier when he saw a sight so ugly that it checked the words in his gullet. Hollom was going forward along the larboard gangway: Nagel, an able seamen but one of the most sullen, bloody-minded and argumentative of the Defenders, was coming aft on the same narrow passage. They were abreast of one another; and Nagel walked straight on without the slightest acknowledgement other than a look of elaborate unconcern.

'Master-at-arms,' cried Jack. 'Master-at-arms. Take that man Nagel below. Clap him into bilboes on the half-deck.' He was exceedingly angry. He would do a great deal for a happy ship, but not for a moment would he put up with deliberate indiscipline: not for a moment, even if it meant running the frigate like a prison-hulk for the whole commission. He had heard St Vincent's passionate cry, uttered at a time of incipient mutiny throughout the fleet, 'I'll make them salute a midshipman's uniform on a handspike,' and he wholeheartedly agreed with the principle.

To Pullings he said, 'We shall take defaulters at six bells as usual,' and the look on his face positively shocked Howard of the Marines, who had never seen him anything but cheerful or at the worst impatient at the dockyard's delay.

While this was going on a messenger came below to ask when it would be convenient for the gunner to wait on Dr Maturin. 'At once, if he chooses,' said Stephen, wiping the oil from the last of his fleams. 'Mr Higgins, perhaps you will attend to the sick-bay.' It was the commissioned and warrant officers' privilege to consult the surgeon in privacy, and Stephen had little doubt that although the gunner was a heavy, broad-shouldered, dark, fierce-looking man, and battle-scarred, he was one of those who disliked being bled, and meant to beg off.

In a way he was right, since Horner's visit was indeed connected with the bleeding. But even before he had sat the man down Stephen realized that there was more to it than mere reluctance. For one thing, Horner's voice had nothing of the soft, gasping, self-pitying quality which seamen felt was owing to themselves, to the Doctor and to the situation when they came to see him as patients. Not at all. Horner's voice was gruff and it had a strong underlying ferocity in it. Crossing him would not answer and so far no one in the ship had ever done so. After a few general remarks and an awkward pause he said he did not wish to be bled if loss of blood would stop him doing it. He had come very near to doing it these last nights, he thought, and if losing even half a pint was to throw all aback once more, why . . . But if bleeding made no odds, why, the Doctor was welcome to take a gallon if he pleased.

Stephen had not practised so long among men who were both modest and inarticulate without coming to know what a number of meanings 'it' might assume, and a very few questions confirmed his first intuitive understanding. Horner was impotent. But what disturbed Maturin, making him fear that it was most unlikely he should be able to help his patient, was the fact that he was impotent only where his wife was concerned. Horner had already done great violence to his feelings in making this disclosure and Stephen did not like to press him on the exact nature of their relations, but he gathered that Mrs Horner was not particularly understanding; she said nothing – they never spoke about it at all – but she seemed contrarified and gave short answers. Horner was almost certain that someone had put a spell on him and he had been to two different cunning-men to have it taken off immediately after their marriage; had paid four pound ten; but they had done no good, the buggers. 'God love us,' he said, breaking off, 'they are piping hands witness punishment. I thought there was no defaulters today. I must run and put on my good coat. So must you, Doctor.'

It was in their good coats that they slipped into their places on the quarterdeck, a quarterdeck all blue and gold with formal uniforms, while abaft the mizen and along either rail the Marines stood in scarlet lines, the sun blazing on their white cross-belts and fixed bayonets. Jack had already dismissed the squabblers, the birthday drunkard and the reproachful words with the sentence 'Sixes until this time next week'; for although over a course of many years Stephen had assured him again and again that it was the amount of alcohol that counted, not the water, he (like everybody else aboard) still privately believed that grog, doubly diluted to a thin, unpalatable wash, was far less intoxicating – it stood to reason. He was now dealing with Nagel. 'What have you done? You know damned well what you have done,' said Jack with cold, concentrated and absolutely unaffected anger. 'You passed Mr Hollom on the gangway without making your obedience. You, an old man-of-war's man: it was not ignorance. Disrespect, wilful disrespect is within a hair's breadth of mutiny, and mutiny is hanging without a shadow of a doubt. It will not do in this ship, Nagel: you knew what you were about. Have his officers anything to say for him?' They had not. Hollom, the only one who could in decency have spoken up, did not see fit to do so. 'Very well,' said Jack. 'Rig the

112

grating. Ship's corporal, order the women below.' White aprons vanished down the fore hatchway and Nagel slowly took off his shirt with a sullen, lowering, dangerous air. 'Seize him up,' said Jack.

'Seized up, sir,' said the quartermaster a moment later.

'Mr Ward,' said Jack to his clerk, 'read the thirty-sixth Article of War.'

As the clerk opened the book all present took off their hats. 'Thirty-six,' he read in a high, official tone, 'All other crimes not capital, committed by any person or persons in the fleet, which are not mentioned in this act, or for which no punishment is hereby directed to be inflicted, shall be punished according to the laws and customs in such cases used at sea.'

'Two dozen,' said Jack, clapping his hat back on to his head. 'Bosun's mate, do your duty.'

Harris, the senior bosun's mate, received the cat from Hollar and did his duty: objectively, without ill-will, yet with all the shocking force usual in the Navy. The first stroke jerked an 'Oh my God' out of Nagel but after that the only sound, apart from the solemn count, was the hiss and the impact.

'I must remember to try Mullins' Patent Balm,' reflected Stephen. Near him those youngsters who had never seen a serious flogging before were looking frightened and uneasy, and over the way, amongst the hands, he saw big Padeen Colman weeping openly, tears of pity coursing down his simple kindly face. Yet upon the whole the people were unmoved; for Captain Aubrey this was a very heavy sentence indeed, but in most ships it would have been more severe, and the general opinion that two dozen was fair enough – if a cove liked to sail so near the wind as not to pay his duty to an officer, even if it was only an unlucky master's mate without a penny to his name, probably a Jonah too and certainly no seaman, why, he could not complain if he was took aback. This seemed to be Nagel's opinion too. When his wrists and ankles were cast loose he picked up his shirt and went forward to the head-pump so that his mates could wash the blood off his back before he put it on again, the look on his face, though sombre, was by no means that of a man who had just suffered an intolerable outrage, or an injustice.

'How I hate this beating,' said Martin a little later, as they stood at the taffrail together, watching the two sharks that had joined the ship some days before and that cruised steadily along in her wake or under her keel: experienced cunning old sharks that ate up all the filth that was offered but that utterly disdained all baited hooks, that provokingly kept just too deep for the exact identification of their species, just too deep for the musket-balls that were showered on them every evening at small-arms drill to have any effect, and that spoilt Captain Aubrey's early-morning swim. One he would have tolerated, but he had grown timid with advancing years and two he found excessive, particularly as a very disagreeable incident with the tiger-sharks of the Red Sea had recently changed his ideas about the whole race.

'So do I,' said Stephen. 'But you are to consider that it accords with the laws and customs of the sea, a tolerably brutal place. I believe that if we have our singing this evening you will find it as cheerful as though the grating had never been rigged.'

The grating in question had been unrigged and the deck well swabbed at least half an hour before this, for eight bells was within a few grains of sand ahead, and all across the deck just abaft the mainmast the officers and young gentlemen had the sun firmly in their quadrants and sextants, waiting for the moment when it should cross the meridian. The moment came: everyone was aware of it, but following the ancient ritual the master first told Mowett, and Mowett, stepping across to Captain Aubrey, took off his hat and reported to him that the local time appeared to be noon. 'Make it so,' said Jack, and noon it therefore became by law. Immediately after this the ship echoed to the striking of eight bells and the piping of the hands to dinner, but Stephen made his way through the uproar to the master, asked for the position, and hurried back to Martin. 'Give you joy of the day, my dear,' he said. 'We have just crossed the tropic line.'

'Have we indeed?' cried Martin, flushing with pleasure. 'Ha, ha! So we are in the tropics at last; and one of my life's ambitions has been fulfilled.' He looked eagerly about the sea and sky, as though everything were quite different now; and by one of those happy coincidences that reward naturalists perhaps more often than other men, a tropic-bird came clipping fast across the breeze and circled above the ship, a satiny-white bird with a pearly pink flush and two immensely long tail feathers' trailing far behind.

It was still there – still watched by Martin, who had refused his dinner in order not to lose a moment of its presence – sometimes taking wide sweeps round the ship, sometimes hovering overhead, and sometimes even sitting on the mainmast truck, when Stephen and Higgins began bleeding all hands. They only took eight ounces from each, but this, bowl after bowl, amounted to nine good buckets with foam of an extraordinary beauty: but they had rather more than their fair share of fools who would be fainting, because as the breeze declined and the heat increased a sickly slaughterhouse reek spread about the deck; and one of them (a young Marine) actually pitched into a brimming bucket as he fell and caused three more to lurch, so angering Dr Maturin that the next half dozen patients were drained almost white, like veal, while guards were placed over the buckets that remained.

However, it was all over in an hour and fifteen minutes, both surgeons being brisk hands with a fleam; the corpses were dragged away by their friends to be recovered with sea-water or vinegar, according to taste; and finally, seeing that fair was fair, each surgeon bled the other. Then Stephen turned to Martin, whose bird had flown by now, though not without having showed him its yellow bill and its totipalmate feet, and said, 'Now, sir, I believe I may

115

show you something that will gratify a speculative mind and perhaps determine the species.'

He asked Honey, who had the watch, for half a dozen keen anglers, and the bosun for two parcels of junk, each the size of a moderate baby. Up until this time all hands, including the Captain and his officers, had been clasping their wounded arms, looking rather grave and self-concerned, but now Jack stepped forward with much more life in his eye and said, 'Why, Doctor, what would you be at?'

'I hope the biter may be bit,' said Stephen, reaching for the mizentopsail halliards, to which the shark-hooks and their chains were attached. 'And above all I hope that the species may be determined; Carcharias is the genus, sure, but the species . . . Where is that black thief Padeen? Now, Padeen, thread the babies on the hooks – handle them as though you loved them – and let them soak up the good red blood till I have circumvented those villains behind – abaft – astern.'

He took a bucket and poured it slowly through the aftermost starboard scupper; both Mowett and Pullings uttered a dismal cry as they saw their holy paintwork defiled, but the hands who would have to clean it came flocking aft with pleased expectant looks. Nor were they disappointed: as soon as the blood-taint (though almost infinitely diluted) reached the fish they came to the surface, casting rapidly to and fro across the frigate's wake, their black fins high over the white water. Two more buckets, going astern in a pink cloud, excited them to a frenzy. They raced in, running up the ship's side, all caution gone, crossing under her keel, flashing through the wake and back again with frightening speed and agility, now half out of the water, now just under the surface, making it boil and froth.

'Drop the first baby,' said Stephen, 'and let him hook himself. Do not pluck it out of his mouth, on your souls.'

The tail man had barely time to whip a turn round

the gallows-bitts before the stout line was twanging taut, the hook well home, and the shark threshing madly under the starboard quarter while the other, in a blind fury, tore great pieces out of its belly and tail.

'Next baby,' cried Stephen, and poured in the rest of the blood. The strike of the second shark was even stronger than the first, and the two of them together heaved the *Surprise* three points off her course.

'Now what are we to do?' asked Martin, looking at their monstrous and quite shockingly dangerous catch. 'Must we let go? If we pull them in their lashing will certainly destroy the ship.'

'Sure, I cannot tell at all,' said Stephen. 'But I dare say Mr Aubrey will know.'

'Steer small,' said Jack to the helmsman, who had been watching the fun rather than his card, and to the bosun, 'Mr Hollar, a couple of running bowlines to the crossjack yardarm, and don't you wish you may get 'em aboard without ruining your shrouds.'

In the event, such was the wholehearted zeal of everyone in the ship that the enormously powerful, very heavy, very furious creatures came over the side with no damage at all, lying there on the deck looking larger than life and more savage by far, snapping their terrible jaws with a sound like a trunk-lid slamming. All the sailors Stephen had ever known had an ancient deep-seated hatred for sharks, and these were no exception. They exulted over the dying monsters and abused them; yet even so he was surprised to see a man so recently flogged as Nagel kicking the larger one, and apostrophizing it with all the wit at his command. And later, after the forecastlemen had borne off the one intact tail to decorate the frigate's stem and bring her luck and when he and Martin were busy with their dissection, Nagel came back and asked very diffidently whether he might have a piece, a small piece, of the backbone, just the scrag end, like; he had promised a morsel to his little girl. 'By all means,' said Stephen. 'And you may give her these too,' – taking three frightful triangular teeth (necessary for the identification of the species) from his pocket.

'Oh sir,' cried Nagel, at once wrapping them in a handkerchief, 'I thank you very kindly.' He thrust them into his bosom, wincing as he did so, knuckled his forehead and lumbered off forward, moving stiffly. Half way along the gangway he turned and called back, 'She'll be main delighted, your honour.'

On this day at least, Stephen was an accurate prophet. By the time of the evening singing, after a purely formal beating to quarters, the massive blood-letting and the excitement of the sharks had quite overlaid that morning's punishment. The cook obliged them with a ballad of eighty-one stanzas about Barton, the Scotch pirate, accompanied by three Jew's harps, and Mr Martin's nascent choir went creditably through part of the oratorio he hoped to perform before they returned to home waters. As a passenger in an earlier command of Captain Aubrey's, a ship of the line, he had brought the more musical section of the crew to be word-perfect and often note-perfect in the *Messiah*, and there were many of his former singers now in the *Surprise*. He had an indifferent voice himself, and he played no instrument well, but he was an excellent teacher, and the hands liked him. And when the concert proper was over many people stayed on deck for the pleasure of the evening air. Hollom was one of them: he sat on the larboard gangway with his legs dangling over the waist, and from time to time he played a few notes on Honey's Spanish guitar. He was searching for a tune and when he found it he chanted the words over twice, quite softly, then struck a chord and sang out clear and sweet, as pure a tenor as could be wished. Stephen took no notice of the words until Hollom came to the burden, *Come it late or come it soon/I shall enjoy my rose in June*, which he sang three or four times with some subtle variations and in a curious tone that might have been called an amused confidence. 'A golden voice,' thought Stephen, looking at him. He observed that although Hollom was facing the opposite

rail his eyes were in fact discreetly turned forward, and
following their direction he saw Mrs Horner fold up her
sewing and rise at the third repetition with a displeased,
rebellious expression and go below.

CHAPTER FOUR

The Indiamen were seen quite early in the morning while
Jack was in the pure green sea, with nothing below him
for a thousand fathoms and nothing on either hand but
the African shore some hundreds of miles away on the
left and the far remoter Americas on the right. He swam
and dived, swam and dived, delighting in the coolness and
the living run of water along his naked body and through
his long streaming hair; he felt extremely well, aware of
his strength and taking joy in it. And for this brief spell
while he was not in the ship he did not have to think
about the innumerable problems to do with her people,
her hull, rigging and progress, and the wisest course for
her to take, problems that perpetually waited on his mind
aboard; he loved the *Surprise* more than any ship he had
known, but even so half an hour's holiday from her had a
certain charm. 'Come on,' he called to Stephen, standing
on the cathead, looking pinched and mean. 'The water is
like champagne.'

'You always say that,' muttered Stephen.

'Go on, sir,' said Calamy. 'It's soon over. You will
like it once you are in.'

Stephen crossed himself, drew a deep breath, grasped
his nose with one hand, blocked an ear with the other,
closed his eyes and leapt, striking the sea with his buttocks.
Because of his curious lack of buoyancy he remained under
the surface for a considerable time, but he came up eventually and Jack said to him, 'Now the *Surprise* has no one
to direct her worldly or her physical or even her spiritual
affairs, ha, ha, ha!' This was true, for the *Surprise*'s boats
were all towing astern so that the heat should not open
their seams, and in the last sat Mr Martin: they were on
the edge of the Sargasso Sea, and he had already taken

120

up a fine collection of weeds, as well as three sea-horses and seven species of pelagic crab.

'Sail ho,' cried the lookout as the far haze cleared with the rising sun. 'On deck, there: a sail two points on the starboard bow . . . two sail. Three sail of ships, topgallants up.'

'Stephen,' said Jack, 'I must go back at once. You can reach the boats, can you not?' They had been swimming (if that was the word for Stephen's laborious, jerking progress, mostly just under the surface) away from the ship, and with her easy motion added to theirs something in the nature of twenty-five or even thirty yards now separated the Captain from his command, a distance not far from Stephen's limit.

'Oh,' said he, but a ripple filled his mouth. He coughed, swallowed more, submerged and began to drown. As usual Jack dived under him, seized his sparse hair and drew him up to the surface; and as usual Stephen folded his hands, closed his eyes, and let himself be towed, floating on his back. Jack abandoned him at Martin's boat, swam fast to the stern-ladder, ran straight up the side and so, pausing only for his shoes, to the masthead. After a moment he called for a glass and confirmed his first impression that they were homeward-bound Indiamen; then, hearing the shrill metallic voice of Mrs Sergeant James, he called for his breeches to be sent into the maintop.

On deck he laid a course to intercept them – it would take the *Surprise* only a trifle out of her way – and hurried below to join the smell of coffee, toast, and things frying, bacon among them. Stephen was already there, taking an unfair advantage with the sausages; and as soon as Jack sat down his other guests appeared, Mowett and the younger Boyle. From time to time young gentlemen were sent down to report the strangers' appearance and behaviour, and before the feast was over a disconsolate Calamy came to say 'that they were only Indiamen, sir; and Captain Pullings said that the nearest was the *Lushington*.'

'I am delighted to hear it,' said Jack. 'Killick, pray

tell my cook to make a special effort today: we shall have three Company's captains to dinner. And you may rouse out a case of champagne in case we meet early. Sling in half a dozen in a wet blanket from the crossjack yard, just under the windward side of the awning.'

Early they came and late they left, pink and jolly, after a dinner that ended with the Christmas pudding for which Jack's new cook was so justly famous, and measureless wine. A cheerful dinner, since two of the captains, Muffit and M'Quaid, had been embroiled with a French squadron in the Indian Ocean, together with Jack Aubrey, Pullings and Mowett in this very same ship, and they had a great deal to say, reminding one another just how the wind had veered, and how, at a given moment, M. de Linois had paid off round and put before it.

Cheerful, but as the ships slowly drew apart Jack paced up and down on his quarterdeck with a grave, considering look on his face. Muffit, an immensely experienced East India sailor, had told him that never in all his time had he known the belt of calms and variable breezes between the south-east and the north-east trades so wide. He and his companions had lost the south-easters in two degrees north and it had taken them more than five hundred miles of creeping and towing before they picked up the first true north-easter, and that no more than indifferent strong. The question that he was weighing in his mind was whether, in view of the *Surprise*'s mediocre progress, he should now bear away westwards, abandoning the Cape Verde islands and their water and relying upon the torrential rain that so often fell in storms between nine and three degrees north of the Line. The water collected in sails and awnings had a villainous taste of hemp and tar and at first it was scarcely drinkable; but the saving of several days might prove to be of the first importance, since it was by no means sure that the *Norfolk* would have had the same paltry breezes. Yet it was by no means sure that the *Surprise* would be rained on, either. The rainstorms in that belt, though sometimes almost unbelievably heavy, were limited in size: before now he had passed through the variables without once being wetted, though he had seen black masses of cloud on either horizon, or little isolated storms here and there, in three or four places at once with miles of clear water in between; and the fate of the waterless ship in the calms was horrible to contemplate. On the other hand the atmosphere of that region, though hellfire hot, was always intensely humid; you did not feel very thirsty, and much more fresh water was used for steeping the salt meat than for drinking.

His mind so ran on these things that when he and Stephen were playing that night his fingers, which should have been providing a mild deedly-deedly-deedly background to the 'cello's long statement in a slow (and perhaps rather dull) movement they both knew perfectly well, wandered off at a point of easy transition to another slow movement by the same composer, and were only pulled up by a shocking discord and by Stephen's indignant cries. Where did Jack think he was going to? What would he be at?

'I beg your pardon a thousand times,' said Jack. 'I am in the D minor piece – I have been gathering moss – but I have just made up my mind. Forgive me a moment.' He went on deck, altered the dear ship's course to south-west by south, and coming back he said with a contented look, 'There: we may die of thirst in the next few weeks if it don't rain, but at least we shall not miss the *Norfolk*. I mean,' he added, clapping his hand to the wood of his chair, 'we are somewhat less likely to miss her now. Yet on the other hand I am afraid you will have to tell poor Mr Martin that he will not see the Cape Verdes after all.'

'The poor soul will be sadly disappointed. He knows far more about beetles than I do, and it appears that the Cape Verdes rejoice in a wonderful variety of tetramerae, forbidding though they may appear to a shallow, superficial mind. I shall break it to him gently. But will I tell you something, Jack? Our hearts are not in the music tonight.

I know mine is not, and I believe I shall take a turn in the air and then go to bed.'

'You are not offended by my moss, Stephen, are you?' asked Jack.

'Never in life, soul,' said Stephen. 'I was uneasy in my mind before ever we sat down; and for once music has not answered.'

It was quite true. That afternoon Stephen had gone through the papers that had accumulated in his cabin, throwing most away and reducing the others to some kind of order; and among those he discarded was the most recent of a series of letters from a Wellwisher who regularly sent to let him know that his wife was unfaithful to him. Usually these letters only aroused a mild wonder in him, a mild desire to know who it was who took so much trouble; but now, partly because of a dream and partly because he knew that appearances were against him – that he certainly *appeared* to have been traipsing about with Laura Fielding – it reinforced an anxiety that had been with him ever since the mail first reached the *Surprise* in Gibraltar. Although by most standards their marriage would hardly have been called successful he was very deeply attached to her and the thought of her being angry with him, together with the frustration of being unable to communicate with her, overcame both the usual steadiness of his mind and his persuasion that the letter carried by Wray would convince her of his unaltered regard in spite of the fact that his explanation of Mrs Fielding's presence was necessarily incomplete and in some respects quite false. For now, in his present low state, it was borne in upon him that falsity sometimes had the same penetrating quality as truth: both were perceived intuitively, and Diana was intuition's favourite child.

He paused in the waist of the ship with the strong breeze eddying about him before he groped his way up the ladder to the quarterdeck. The night was as black as a night could be, warm velvet black with no stars at all; he could detect the ship's motion by her urgent heave and thrust, and living vibration of the wood under his hand, and the creak of the blocks, cordage and canvas overhead, but never a sail nor a rope could he see, nor even the steps in front of his nose as he crept up. He might have been entirely deprived of the sense of sight and it was only when he brought his nose above the break of the quarterdeck that his eyes returned to him, with the glow of the quartermaster at the con, a greyhaired man named Richardson, and of Walsh, the much younger timoneer. Quite close at hand he made out the hint of a darker form looming this side of the mainmast; and to this form he said, 'Good night, now, Mr Honey: would the chaplain be aboard at all?'

'It's me, sir,' said Mowett, chuckling. 'I swapped with Honey. Yes, Mr Martin is still up. He's in the launch, towing astern; and I doubt he comes in till sunrise, it being so uncommon dark and awkward. You can just make him out, if you look over the side.' Stephen looked: there was not much phosphorescence on the sea, although it was so warm, but there was enough for the troubled wake to show as it swirled about the towing boats, and in the farthest he could just distinguish the rise and fall of Martin's little net. 'Perhaps you would like to join him?' suggested Mowett. 'I will give you a hand over the taffrail, if you choose.'

'I do not choose,' said Stephen, contemplating the length of faintly luminous water and the increasing per-turbation of the train of boats – barge, gig, jolly-boat, and both the cutters, all quite far apart – that would have to be traversed before the launch was reached. 'Bad news will always keep. But listen, James Mowett, are they not tossing about in a very dreadful manner? Is there not some danger of their being drawn below the surface, engulfed in the mill-stream of the wake, and of Mr Martin's being lost?'

'Oh dear me no, sir,' said Mowett. 'No danger at all: and was it to come on to blow, to really as one might say blow, why, I should back a topsail, hale him alongside and so pass him a line. Ain't it agreeable to be moving at last? This is the first time we have done better than five knots since we laid the Rock: the barky began to speak at the beginning of the watch, and now she must be throwing a fine bow-wave, if only we could see it. *She plies her course yet, nor her winged speed/The falcon could for pace exceed.*'

'Are those your lines, Mr Mowett?'

'No, no, alas; they are Homer's. Lord, what a fellow he was! Ever since I began reading in him, I have quite lost any notion of writing myself, he being such a . . .' Mowett's voice trailed away in admiration and Stephen said, 'I had no idea you were a Grecian.'

'No more I am, sir,' replied Mowett. 'I read him in a translation, a book a young lady gave me for a keepsake in Gibraltar, by a cove named Chapman, a very splendid cove. I began because I esteemed the giver, and because I hoped to be able to knock poor Rowan on the head with some pretty good images and rhymes when he rejoined, but I went on because I could not stop. Do you know him?'

'Not I,' said Stephen. 'Though I did look into Mr Pope's version once, and Madame Dacier's. I hope your Mr Chapman is better.'

'Oh, it is magnificent – a great booming, sometimes, like a heavy sea, the *Iliad* being in fourteeners; and I am sure it is very like the Greek. I must show it to you. But then I dare say you have read him in the original.'

'I had no choice. When I was a boy it was Homer and Virgil, Homer and Virgil entirely and many a stripe and many a tear between. But I came to love him for all that, and I quite agree with you – he is the very prince of poets. The *Odyssey* is a fine tale, sure, though I never could cordially like Ulysses: he lied excessively, it seems to me; and if a man lies beyond a certain point a sad falseness enters into him and he is no longer amiable.' Stephen spoke with some feeling: his work in intelligence had called for a great deal of duplicity – perhaps too much. '. . . no longer amiable. And I should not quarrel with those who say that

Homer had no great hand in the poem. But the *Iliad*, of God love his soul, never was such a book as the *Iliad*!'

Mowett cried that the Doctor was in the right of it, and began to recite a particularly valued piece: soon losing himself, however. But Stephen scarcely heard; his mind glowed with recollection and he exclaimed, 'And the truly heroic scale, that makes us all look so mean and pallid; and the infinite art from the beginning to the noble end with Achilles and Priam talking quietly together in the night, both doomed and both known to be doomed – the noble end and its full close, for I do not count the funeral rites as anything but a necessary form, almost an appendix. The book is full of death, but oh so living.'

Four bells interrupted them, and clear round the ship came the cry of the lookouts and the sentinels: 'Lifebuoy, all's well.' 'Starboard gangway, all's well.' 'Starboard bow, all's well,' followed by all the rest. The carpenter's mate, bringing a lantern with him, reported eleven inches in the well – half an hour's pumping at dawn – and the midshipman of the watch, having fussed some little time with the lantern and the sand-glass, said, 'Seven knots one fathom, sir, if you please.' Mowett wrote this on the log-board: the lantern vanished down a hatchway, the darkness returned, even thicker than before, and Stephen said, 'There was a foolish man of Lampsacus, Metrodorus by name, that explained away the gods and the heroes as personifications of this and that, of fire and water, the sky and the sun, and so on – Agamemnon was the upper air, as I recall – and then there were a great many busy fellows who found out hidden meanings in Homer by the score: and some would have it that the *Odyssey* in particular was an enormous great bloated metaphor, the way the writer of it would have seen a superior acrosticmonger. But as far as I know not one of the inky boobies ever saw what is as clear as the sun at midday – that as well as being the great epic of the world, the *Iliad* is a continued outcry against adultery. Hundreds, nay thousands of heroical young men

127

killed, Troy town in blood and flames, Andromache's child dashed from the battlements and she led away to carry water for Greek women, the great city razed and depopulated, all, all from mere adultery. And she did not even like the worthless fellow at the end. James Mowett, there is nothing to be said for adultery.'

'No, sir,' said Mowett, smiling in the darkness, partly from recollections of his own, and partly like everybody else aboard – all the old Surprises, that is to say – he was as certain of Dr Maturin's criminal conversation with Mrs Fielding as if he had seen them kiss and clip in naked bed. 'No, sir: nothing at all. And I have sometimes thought of giving him a hint; but these things are too delicate, and I doubt it would answer. Yes, Boyle, what is it?'

'Who is this *him*?' said Maturin to himself.

'I beg your pardon, sir,' said Boyle, 'but I believe there is a hail from the launch.'

'Then lay aft and see what is afoot. Take my speaking-trumpet, and sing out loud and clear.'

Boyle sang out loud and clear, and coming back he said, 'As far as I could make out, sir, the chaplain wishes to know whether we apprehend any worsening of the tempest.'

'It is what we have been praying for this last age, after all,' said Mowett. 'But perhaps we had better bring the launch under the counter; he may be a little uneasy in his mind. Jump down and help him up the stern-ladder; there will be plenty of light from the cabin.'

'How very kind of you,' said Martin, sitting on the capstan to recover his breath after his climb. 'The boat was plunging up and down in a most alarming fashion, and I could make no observations at all this last half hour.'

'What were you observing, sir?'

'Luminous organisms, mostly minute pelagic crustaceans, copepods; but I need calmer water for it, the good calm water we have had almost all the way. How I pray it may grow quiet again before we leave the sargasso quite behind.'

'I don't know about the sargasso,' said Mowett, 'but I think you may be pretty sure of calm weather before we cross the Line.'

And indeed long, long before they crossed the Line the trade wind died in the frigate's wake and left her with her towering canvas limp, all the noble expanse she had spread to catch the lightest airs hanging there discouraged and the ship rolling horribly on the great smooth swell.

'So these are the doldrums,' said Martin, coming on deck in his best coat, the coat worn for invitations to the cabin, and looking about the hot, lowering sky and the glassy sea with great satisfaction. 'I have always wanted to see them. Yet even so, I believe I shall take off my coat until dinner-time.'

'It will make no odds,' said Stephen, whose spirit of contradiction was more lively than usual, because of a sleepless night, much of it filled with longing for his private vice, the alcoholic tincture of laudanum, a form of liquid opium that had consoled him in anxiety, unhappiness, privation, pain and insomnia for many a year but which he had given up (except medicinally) on his marriage with Diana. 'Your coat protects you from the radiant heat of the sun, and the mechanism of your body maintains it at a constant temperature: as you know, the Arab of the desert goes covered from head to foot. The apparent relief is a mere illusion, a vulgar error.'

Martin was not a man to be overborne, however; he took off his coat, folded it carefully on the hammock-cloth, and said, 'The vulgar error is wonderfully refreshing, nevertheless.'

'And as for the doldrums,' Stephen went on, 'I believe you may perhaps misuse the term. As I understand it, in nautical language the doldrums are a condition, a state; not a region. They are analogous to tantrums. A child, and God help us a grown man alas, can be in the tantrums anywhere at all. Similarly a ship may be in the doldrums wherever she is long becalmed. I may be mistaken, but Captain Aubrey will certainly know.'

Captain Aubrey knew, but since they were his guests he contrived to agree with both, though inclining somewhat in the chaplain's favour: he conceived that from seamen's slang or cant doldrums was become a general word by land, used in Mr Martin's sense of what used to be called the variables. He had a great esteem for Mr Martin; he valued him; but he did not invite him as often as he felt he should; and now by way of making amends he not only filled his glass very often and helped him to the best cuts of the leg of mutton but also strained the truth in his direction. The fact of the matter was that he felt a constraint in Martin's presence. He had known few parsons, and his respect for the cloth made him feel that a grave face and a sober discourse, preferably on topics of a moral nature, were called for in their presence; and although he did not much delight in bawdy – indeed never talked it except in bawdy company where the reverse would have seemed offensively pious – the compulsory decorum weighed upon him. Then again, although Mr Martin loved music he was an indifferent performer and after one or two sadly discordant evenings full of apology he had not been asked to play in the cabin again. Jack was therefore more than usually attentive to his guest, not only congratulating him (quite sincerely) upon his sermon that morning, not only feeding and wining him to a pitch that few men could have withstood in a temperature of a hundred and four with a humidity of eighty-five, but telling him in some detail of the sail that was to be put over the side that afternoon for the hands to swim in: those hands, that was to say, who could not take to the sea itself, for fear of drowning. This led on to observations about seamen's, particularly fishermen's, reluctance to be taught to swim; and at the far end of the table Pullings, who as a captain by courtesy was allowed to pipe up of his own accord, said, 'It is a great while since you have saved anyone, sir.'

'I suppose it is,' said Jack.

'Does the Captain often save people?' asked Martin.

'Oh dear me, yes. One or two every commission: or

more. I dare say you could man the barge with hands you have saved, could you not, sir?'

'Perhaps I could,' said Jack absently, and then, feeling that he was not doing his duty by his other guest, he said, 'I hope we shall see you over the side this afternoon, Mr Hollom. Do you swim?'

'Not a stroke, sir,' said Hollom, speaking for the first time; and he added, after a slight pause, 'But I shall join the others in splashing about in the sail; it would be a rare treat to feel cool.'

A rare treat indeed. Even at night heat seemed to emanate from the bloody moon, and during the oppressive, stifling days the sun, even from behind its frequent low cloud, made the pitch bubble in the seams of the deck and the tar melt so that it dripped from the upper rigging, while resin oozed from under the paint and drooled down the sides as the ship towed slowly south and west, all boats out ahead and the pullers relieved each glass. Sometimes a hot, capricious breeze would ruffle the oily sea and all hands would dart to brace the yards to take advantage of it; but rarely did the *Surprise* travel more than a mile or so before the breeze came foul or died away altogether, leaving her lifeless on the swell, rolling to such a degree that in spite of their strengthened and new-swifted shrouds and doubled backstays her masts were in danger of going by the board, even with the topgallants struck down on deck; and not only Mrs Lamb but also some of the *Defender*'s landsmen took to their beds again with utterly prostrating sickness.

It was a wearisome time, and it seemed to last for ever. One day's noon observation could be distinguished from the last only by the finest instruments used with the greatest skill; the heat worked right down into the lowest depths of the ship, making the bilgewater stink most vilely, so that those whose cabins lay far below, Stephen and the chaplain among them, had but little sleep. And when they came on deck in the night watches, carrying rolls of sailcloth against the soft pitch of the seams, they were cruelly chivvied from place to place as the hands, usually under their Captain's immediate command, raced to catch the last waft of air. It was a time when theories crumbled: although he was as impervious to heat as a salamander – revelled in it, indeed – Stephen shed his stuff coat, his cloth breeches, his good wool stockings, and appeared in a white banyan jacket, usually open on his meagre chest, airy nankeen pantaloons, and a broad-brimmed sennit hat, plaited for him by Bonden, whom he had taught to read many years before in these same waters: far, far kinder waters then, and a very much quicker passage, incalculably cheaper as far as expense of spirit was concerned. In the same way Jack's views on humidity did not prevent him from drinking up his whole private store of East India pale ale, nor from going over their supplies of water with the master again and again, adding up what was left in the 159 gallon leaguers of the ground tier, the 108 gallon butts, the hogsheads and half hogsheads, laid bung up and bilge free in the wings, and coming to a most discouraging sum total. Even at no more than a purser's quart a head – a far cry from the gallon of beer of home waters – the store diminished by nearly half a ton each day; and that took no account of the great quantity absolutely required for making the salt meat edible.

They did come in for the skirt of a rainstorm in 6°25'N., but it did little more than prepare their spread-out awnings and sails, cleaning them for the next hypothetical downpour. The few butts of water they collected were so brackish and tarry and full of maker's dressing from the new sailcloth that it could not be drunk in their present moderate state of need. Jack had it barrelled, however. If this went on they would give ten years' pay for a cup of a far worse brew.

He was worried: first by the lack of water, of course; but also by his lack of progress. He knew the *Norfolk*, and he knew that if she was commanded by any of the American officers he had met about the *Constitution* or as a prisoner of war in Boston she would be running south as fast as ever she could go with due regard to her masts and rigging: she might even make up her month's delay and pass Cape St Roque before him. The ship's people worried him, too. The Surprises had accepted and absorbed the Gibraltar lunatics, treating them kindly, cutting up their meat for them and bawling into their ears when they could not quite understand; but in spite of the heavy shared labour of towing ship and of the changes he had introduced into the watch-bill, most of the Defenders they could not bear. Almost all the punishment inflicted was brought about by fighting between the two sides, and Jack looked forward to the eventual crossing of the Line with real anxiety; in the traditional rough fun ill-will could take an ugly shape. He had known unpopular men maimed before this, and one actually drowned during the horse-play: that was when Jack was a master's mate in the *Formidable*. And his anxiety was increased by the fact that tempers were wearing precious thin with continual toil in the great oppressive heat, and the short commons. Of course, being sole master after God, he could forbid the ceremony; but he would be ashamed to command a ship ruled in such a manner.

Then again there was something in the air, something he could not yet define. Jack had been lucky in the matter of employment, spending most of his life afloat, and this had given him more experience of ships' companies than most officers of his seniority; and his experience had also been more extensive, since an irascible captain had disrated Mr Midshipman Aubrey at the Cape, turning him before the mast as a common hand, there to live, eat, sleep and work with the rest of the men. This had brought him intimately acquainted with seamen's ways and moods, the significance of their looks, gestures and silences; and now he was certain that something was afoot, something concealed but generally understood. It was quite certainly not a hatching mutiny and it was certainly not the heavy gambling he had known in a few ships rich in prize-money, since the Surprises now had barely a groat between them;

but there was a certain excitement and there was a certain secrecy that might have belonged to either.

He was quite right; and this something was understood throughout the ship by everybody except her Captain, her chaplain and of course her gunner. In a crowded man-of-war it was very difficult to carry out anything privately and all hands knew that Mr Hollom was having to do with Mrs Horner. He was ideally placed for such an enterprise, since he slung his hammock in the midshipmen's berth, and the gunner's realm, where Mrs Horner looked after the youngsters, was just at hand. Very few other men in the ship could be in those parts without exciting comment and now that he was reasonably well fed Hollom made full use of his opportunities.

It was generally thought that he made too full use of them; that after a discreet beginning he had grown over-confident; and that presently he would cop it, mate, cop it something cruel. Hollom was not a man to bully the hands or bring them up for punishment, so he was not at all actively disliked, but since he was not much of a seaman he was not respected either; and then in spite of his good luck for the moment, his much-envied good luck, there was always the possibility of his being a Jonah. He remained a stranger to the ship. Much the same applied to Horner, whose sullen temper and underlying ferocity made him no friends aboard, though for his part he was respected as an efficient gunner and feared as a right awkward bastard, if crossed.

So there were these two strangers to be watched, watched with the liveliest interest, in the intervals of trying to draw the ship out of the variables; and as the couple's caution grew less, so it seemed to the fascinated spectators that the explosion must be coming near. But these conjectures, though freely exchanged, never reached the cabin; and in the gunroom they were repressed when the chaplain was present.

Jack therefore remained ignorant of the specific reason for the knowing looks that he observed from his usual post by the windward hances; but even if he had known he would still have ordered the boats away when the bonitoes appeared. At dawn flying-fish had been found on deck by the score, and as the sun rose their persecutors could be seen skimming about in schools just under the surface. The boats, plying net and line with prodigious zeal, brought in several loads of fish, fish that did not have to be steeped in precious fresh water; and as Stephen remarked to Martin, the bonito, like his cousin the great tunny, was not only a warm-blooded fish but also a great promoter of Venus.

All hands, except Mrs Lamb, ate as much bonito as they could hold, and after the feast Hollom's lovely *Rose in June* could be heard coming from below, he now being off duty. The gunner came on deck to attend to one of the forecastle carronades: the song stopped abruptly. On the forecastle the gunner clapped his hand to his pocket, missed his handkerchief, and began walking back to his cabin.

The couple were saved only by the pipe of all hands as Jack decided that the patch of dark purple cloud with lightning flickering beneath it on the far north-east might possibly bring the edge of a turning squall down to them, and that it would be as well to strike the topgallantmasts, although they had been swayed up only a few hours before, to catch the last gasp of the flying-fish breeze.

It was as well that he did so, for the squall turned more sharply than he or Pullings or the master had expected; after various evolutions it came hissing across the calm sea on the larboard quarter, a line of white advancing at thirty-five miles an hour, backed by impenetrable darkness and preceded by three small pale birds racing across its front. It struck the ship with a mounting howl, laying her right over and shooting Stephen and Martin, who had incautiously let go their hold in an attempt at identifying the pale birds with their spy-glasses, into the lee-scuppers. Even before kindly hands had plucked them out the whole air was one roaring mass of rain, warm and so thick with

135

great drops and with finely-divided water-dust that they could hardly breathe as they crept up the sloping deck, and the scuppers were already spouting wide. 'I beg your pardon?' shouted Martin through the almighty, omnipresent din.

'I was only calling out "Butcher" to the Doctor,' roared Jack into his ear. 'That is what we say at sea when somebody falls down. Here, clap on to the fife-rail.'

For ten minutes the *Surprise* raced along under a close-reefed foretopsail, and as soon as the wind had moderated a little they began to spread various cloths for the rain and to rouse out barrels: but unhappily the downpour had almost spent itself in the useless flooding of the deck, and part of what was collected in the mainroyal, stretched between the stanchions of the forecastle and weighted with roundshot, was lost when Mr Hollom cast off the wrong hitch, being somewhat bemused in his intellects.

Still, in the short time it lasted they gathered water for eight days, very pure water; and the women aboard, even the almost paralytic Mrs Lamb, had filled all possible tubs and buckets – their smalls were already put to soak. And what was even better, the squall was followed by a steady breeze, perhaps the first breath of the south-east trades.

Yet these things had to be paid for, of course. The sun-baked decks leaked abominably and the *Surprise* (though bowling along so cheerfully) echoed with the sound of drips right down to the orlop and the hold itself, wetting all the storerooms, except the tin-lined bread-room, all the cabins, and all the hanging beds within these cabins; and even before the evening sun went down in its abrupt, tropical fashion, the hot imprisoned air was filled with the smell of mould: mould, blue or green or sometimes a mottled grey, growing on books, clothes, shoes, marine specimens, portable soup, and of course the great beams under which everybody slept and against which everybody except the Captain banged his head from time to time. This was not because Jack Aubrey was more dwarfish than the rest – indeed he stood rather more than six feet tall – but because his cabin had more clearance. Or rather his cabins, since he had three: the coach, to larboard, which included the lower part of the mizenmast and a thirty-two pounder carronade and in which he had his meals unless there were more than four or five guests; his sleeping-place to starboard; and then right aft the noble great cabin, stretching clean across the ship and lit by the splendid, curved, inward-sloping, seven-light stern-window, the airiest, lightest, most desirable place in the ship, Killick's kingdom, perpetually scoured, swabbed, scraped and polished, smelling of beeswax, fresh sea-water, and clean paint.

'Perhaps we might have some music tonight?' suggested Stephen, coming up from his fetid dog-hole.

'Oh Lord no,' cried Jack at once. 'So long as this charming zephyr lasts, I must sail the ship: I must stay on deck.'

'Sure it will sail whether you are on deck or not: you have capable officers, for all love, and they must sit up in any case, their watches coming in due succession.'

'That is eminently true,' said Jack. 'But in a near-run thing it is a captain's duty to be on deck, urging his ship through the water by the combined effort of his will and his belly-muscles: you may say it is buying a dog and barking at the stable door yourself – '

'The stable door after it is locked,' said Stephen, holding up his hand.

'Just so: the stable door after it is locked, yourself. But there are more things than heaven and earth, you know. Stephen, will you not sit in the cabin and play by yourself, or invite Martin, or transcribe the Scarlatti for fiddle and 'cello?'

'I will not,' said Stephen, who hated any appearance of favouritism, and he vanished into the smelly gunroom, there to play halfpenny whist with Martin, Mr Adams, and the master, a game in which concentration was rather harder than usual, since Howard the Marine was learning to play the German flute according to a method which,

137

though said to be adapted to the meanest understanding, puzzled him extremely, while Mowett was reading pieces of the *Iliad* to Honey in a low voice but with immense relish, so that Dr Maturin was not altogether sorry when the loblolly boy called him away to make his evening rounds with Mr Higgins.

On deck Captain Aubrey, eating a piece of cold or at least luke-warm pease pudding with one hand and holding on to the aftermost maintopgallant standing backstay with the other, did indeed urge his ship on with contractions of his belly-muscles and a continuous effort of his will; but he also did a great deal more than that. It was quite true that he had competent officers, and Pullings and Mowett in particular knew the dear frigate very well; yet he had known her longer by far – his initials on her foretopmast-cap had been carved there when he was an unruly mastheaded boy – and not to put too fine a point on it, he sailed her better.

He might almost have been riding a high-mettled horse whose moods and paces were as familiar to him as his own, for although he never hauled on a rope nor laid a hand on the wheel (except now and then, to feel the vibration of her rudder and the precise degree of its bite) he had a highly responsive crew, men with whom he had sailed the ship in pursuit of splendid prizes or in flight from hopelessly superior force, and through them he was in the closest touch with her. He had long since abandoned the cautious show of canvas, the snugging-down with reefed topsails of the early days of the voyage, and now the *Surprise* ran through the night with studdingsails aloft and alow as long as they would stand. As for the hands, most of them were perfectly aware that this was another occasion on which the ship was flying from a hopelessly superior force: they had observed the Captain's retention of the first barrels of noisome rainwater; through the ever-present servants they had heard all the conversations in the cabin and the gunroom on the subject; and, by plain eavesdropping, all those on the quarterdeck. And those few contrary-minded or heavy-arsed dullards who were not convinced by their shipmates' rhetoric were wholly persuaded by the succession of prime helmsmen being called to the wheel out of their turn, by the continuous presence of the skipper, watch after watch, and by his insistence that they should flash out jibs and staysails with supernatural speed.

He was still there at dawn, taking advantage of every heave of the ocean or thrust of the wind to drive the ship a little farther, a little faster. The breeze had veered southerly and at this point the *Surprise* was as close-hauled as she could be, her weather-leeches shaking; it grew much stronger with the rising sun, and now she really showed what she could do on a bowline – her lee forechains under the splendid foam of her bow-wave, a white line racing down her side in a curve so deep that her copper showed amidships, and a broad wake that fled out straight behind her, a sea-mile every five minutes. With the idlers called and both watches on deck he packed them along the weather rail to make her stiffer still, set his mainroyal and stood there, braced against the slope of the deck, soaked with flying spray, his face drawn and covered with the bright yellow bristles of unshaven beard, looking perfectly delighted.

He was still there at noon, when the breeze, somewhat more moderate but now blowing with beautiful steadiness from the east-south-east, had declared itself to be the true trade wind; and with infinite satisfaction he, the master and all the other officers found, when the sun crossed the meridian, that between this observation and the last the *Surprise* had covered 192 miles, running clean out of the zone of calms and variables.

After an early dinner he spent the afternoon in his cot, lying on his back and snoring with such a volume and persistence that men as far forward as the belfry winked at one another, grinning, and Mrs Lamb, speaking in a low voice and shaking her head, told the wife of the sergeant of Marines that she pitied poor Mrs Aubrey from the bottom of her heart. But he was up and about for

139

quarters; and since both watches had been called in the night he let the evening go with no more than the very popular and unlaborious form of small-arms exercise in which all hands, including the Marines, fired at a bottle hanging from the foreyardarm. And when at last the drum beat the retreat he astonished Pullings and Mowett by observing that perhaps tomorrow they might start painting the ship: there was not much point in scraping the decks yet, the pitch being so soft, but they would be very sorry to have any merchantman or Portuguese man-of-war see the *Surprise* in her present state of abysmal squalor.

What he said was perfectly true. Although a boat had pulled round her every morning when it was practicable, with the captain of the head and his mates swabbing all that could be swabbed, resin, tar, pitch and oily sea-borne filth had dimmed the frigate's brilliant Nelson chequer, and her gingerbread work was not at all what a loving first lieutenant's eye could have wished. But these things were generally attended to late in a voyage, when there was some likelihood that the freshness of the effect would strike all beholders dumb with admiration; and at present the *Surprise* was well over five hundred miles from the nearest point of Brazil. Furthermore painting ship almost always meant slower progress, and although of course it would have to be done before they reached soundings, Pullings would have expected Jack not to delay this side of the Line for anything but a rainstorm to fill their rows and rows of empty barrels. Yet both he and Mowett had been brought up from boyhood in a service that did not encourage the questioning of orders, and their 'Yes, sir,' came with no more than a barely measurable hesitation.

Dr Maturin had no such inhibitions. When he came into the cabin that evening he waited until Jack had finished a charming little rondo and then said, 'And are we not to make haste and cut the Line tomorrow, so?'

'No,' said Jack, smiling at him. 'If this wind holds, and it is almost certain to mind its duty as a true trade wind, I hope to cross in a little more than twenty-nine degrees of west longitude on Sunday. So tomorrow you should be quite near your old friends the St Paul's rocks.'

'Is that right? What joy: I must tell poor Martin. Tell, what was the rondo you were playing?'

'Molter.'

'Molter?'

'Yes. You know, Molter Vivace. You must have heard of Molter Vivace. Oh ha, ha, ha!' When at last he had had his laugh out, he wiped his eyes and wheezed, 'It came to me in a flash, a brilliant illumination, like when you fire off blue lights. Lord, ain't I a rattle? I shall set up for a wit yet, and make my fortune. Molter Vivace . . . I must tell Sophie. I am writing her a letter, to be put aboard some homeward-bound merchantman, if we meet one off Brazil next week, which is probable. Molter Vivace, oh dear me.'

'He that would make a pun would pick a pocket,' said Stephen, 'and that miserable quibble is not even a pun, but a vile clench. Who is this Molter?' he asked, picking up the neatly-written score.

'Johann Melchior Molter, a German of the last age,' said Jack. 'Our parson at home thinks the world of him. I copied this piece, mislaid it, and found it ten minutes ago tucked behind our Corelli in C major. Shall we attempt the Corelli now, it being such a triumphal day?'

Nobody could have called the next day triumphal. The *Surprise* had stages rigged out over her sides and all hands turned to scraping her wood and hammering the rust off her ironwork, and then laying on paint and various kinds of blacking. Early in the morning Stephen had told Martin of their approach to St Paul's rocks, which, in the right season of the year, harboured not only a large variety of terns but also two steganopodes, the brown and far more rarely the blue-faced booby; this was not the right season, but there was some hope of stragglers and as soon as their duties permitted they took chairs to various vantage points from which they might lean their telescopes to look for boobies and even

141

perhaps to view the rocks themselves, rearing lonely from the ocean.

But rarely had they settled for ten minutes before they were desired to move – to mind the paintwork, sir – for God's sake to mind the paintwork: and when they hovered near the taffrail and the elegant gilded carving they were told that they might stay a little while, so long as they touched nothing; but they were not on any account to breathe on the gold leaf until the egg-white had dried and they must certainly not lean their glasses on the rail at any time. Even the boats were better than this, although at sea-level the horizon was brought in to a mere three miles: yet presently the boats too were hauled in for scraping and painting, and when they showed a certain restiveness they were told that 'they would not like to have the barky mistaken for a Newcastle collier, by a parcel of Portuguees, nor her boats for mud-scows.'

It was Calamy who suggested that they should go into the foretop, from which (the foretopsail being clewed up) they could see almost the whole ring of the world, and that for an immense distance too: he helped them to climb up, settling them comfortably on the studdingsails that were kept there, and brought them their telescopes, a broad-brimmed straw hat apiece to preserve their brains from the now almost vertical furnace of the enormous sun, and a pocketful of those broken ends of biscuit known as midshipmen's nuts, against hunger, since dinner was likely to be late.

And it was from this lofty platform that they first saw an undoubted frigate petrel and then, following the cry of the lookout on the maintopgallantyard, the white nick on the horizon as St Paul's rocks heaved up in the south-west. 'Oh, oh,' said Martin, putting his glass to his single eye and focusing carefully, 'Can it be . . . ?' A line of heavy, purposeful birds came flying towards the ship, quite fast, not very high: a hundred yards out on the starboard beam they checked their run, poised, and plunged one after another like gannets, a headlong dive that sent

142

water jetting up. They rose, circled, dived for some few minutes more and then flew off with equal purpose to the north-east.

Martin relaxed, lowered his glass and turned a radiant face to Stephen. 'I have beheld the blue-faced booby,' he said, shaking him by the hand.

Long before this the seven-bell men had gone to their turpentine-tasting dinner, followed one glass later by the rest of the hands, with their customary bellowing. Now *Heart of Oak* was beating for the gunroom feast, and presently a messenger came up to tell them that the gentlemen were waiting.

'My best compliments to Captain Pullings,' said Stephen, 'and beg to be excused.'

Martin said much the same, and they returned to their contemplation of these barren islands, now quite near. 'Never a herb, never a blade of grass,' observed Stephen. 'Nor yet a drop of water but what falls from the sky. The birds to the left are only noddies, I am afraid: but then, on the topmost round, there is a booby, my dear sir, a brown booby. He is in a sad state of moult, poor fellow, but he is still a true brown booby. All that white is the droppings of the birds, of course, many feet thick in places; and it has so strong an ammoniac reek that it catches you by the throat. I was ashore there once when the birds were breeding: barely a foot of ground without an egg and the fowl so tame you could pick them up.'

'Do you think the Captain would stop for just half an hour?' asked Martin. 'Think what beetles might be there. Could it not be represented to him . . .'

'My poor friend,' said Stephen, 'if anything could exceed the sea-officer's brutish indifference to birds it would be his brutish indifference to beetles: and do but look at the boats in their new wet paint. I was able to go only because we were becalmed, whereas now we are running at five knots, because it was a Sunday, and because an officer very kindly rowed me over in a boat. James Nicolls was his name.' His mind went back to that deeply unhappy

143

man, who had almost certainly let himself be drowned off this very rock that was now going gently astern a short mile away: he had disagreed with his wife, had tried to make peace, and no peace came. Stephen's thoughts moved on from James Nicolls to marriage in general, that difficult state. He had heard of a race of lizards in the Caucasus that reproduced themselves parthenogenetically, with no sexual congress of any kind, no sexual complications: Lacerta saxicola was their name. Marriage, its sorrow and woe, its fragile joys, filled his mind and he was not altogether surprised when Martin, speaking in a low, confidential tone, told him that he had long been attached to the daughter of a parson, a young lady whose brother he used to botanize with when they were at the university together. She was considerably above him in the worldly consequence and her friends looked upon him with disapproval; nevertheless, in view of his now very much greater affluence, his income of £211. 8. 0 a year, he thought of asking her to be his wife. Yet there were many things that troubled him: one was that her friends might not regard even £211. 8. 0 as wealth; another was his appearance – Maturin had no doubt noticed that he had only one eye – which must necessarily tell against him; and still another was the difficulty of setting out his mind in a letter. Martin was not unaccustomed to composition, but he had been able to do no better than this: he hoped Maturin would be so good as to glance over it and give him his candid opinion.

The sun beat down upon the foretop; the paper curled in Stephen's hand; his heart sank steadily. Martin was a thoroughly amiable man, a man of wide reading, but when he came to write he mounted upon a pair of stilts, unusually lofty stilts, and staggered along at a most ungracious pace, with an occasional awkward lurch into colloquialism, giving a strikingly false impression of himself. Stephen handed the letter back and said, 'It is very elegantly put indeed, with some uncommon pretty figures; and I am sure it would touch any lady's heart;

but my dear Martin, you must allow me to say that I believe your whole approach to be mistaken. You apologize from beginning to end; from start to finish you are exceedingly humble. There is a quotation that hovers just beyond the reach of my recollection together with the name of its author, to the effect that even the most virtuous woman despises an impotent man; and surely all self-depreciation runs along the same unhappy road? I am convinced that the best way of making an offer of marriage is the shortest: a plain, perfectly legible letter reading *My dear Madam, I beg you will do me the honour of marrying me: I remain, dear Madam, with the utmost respect, your humble obedient servant*. That goes straight to the heart of the matter. On a separate half-sheet one could perhaps add a statement of one's income, for the consideration of the lady's friends, together with an expression of willingness to make any settlements they may think fit.'

'Perhaps so,' said Martin, folding his paper away. 'Perhaps so. I am very much obliged to you for the suggestion.' But it required no very great penetration to see that he was not convinced, that he still clung to his carefully balanced periods, his similes, his metaphors and his peroration. He had shown his letter to Maturin partly as a mark of confidence and esteem, being sincerely attached to him, and partly so that Maturin might praise it, possibly adding a few well-turned phrases; for like most normally constituted writers Martin had no use for any candid opinion that was not wholly favourable. 'What a wonderfully true voice Mr Hollom does possess, to be sure,' he said, cocking his ear towards the deck after a silent pause. 'A great blessing to any choir.' From this they went on to speak of the life of chaplains afloat, of naval surgeons, and of the *Surprise*. Martin: 'She is quite unlike any of the ships I have been in. There is none of that running at the men with canes and knotted ropes, no kicking, few really harsh words; and if it were not for those unfortunate Defenders and their fighting with the Surprises there would be almost no punishment days. Or at least there would be none of this distressing and I think inhuman flogging. Quite a different ship from one that I was lent to last, where the grating was rigged almost every day.'

Maturin: 'Just so: but then you are to consider that the men of the *Surprise* have served together for years. They are all man-of-war's men, with no recently-pressed landlubbers, no Lord Mayor's men among them; all tolerably expert sailors who work together and who need no running at. Nor any of the starting, reviling and threats so usual in less happy ships. But the *Surprise* cannot be taken as at all typical of the Navy, alas.'

Martin: 'No, indeed. Yet even here there is sometimes a vehemency of rebuke that I for one should find hard to bear if it were addressed to me.'

Maturin: 'You are thinking of the "Oh you wicked mutinous dogs, sons of everlasting whores." ' At a particularly busy moment Awkward Davis and his mates, eluding their young gentleman, tried to pass a light hawser aft for the painters' stages not as they were ordered but according to their own lights, and this passionate cry from the quarterdeck had greeted the parting of an entangled lower studdingsail boom. 'Harsh words, sure: but God love you, they would bear infinitely harsher from Mr Aubrey and still give no more than a tolerant smile and a droll wag of their head. He is one of the most resolute of fighting captains, and that is a quality they prize above anything. They would still value him extremely if he were severe unjust tyrannical sombre revengeful malice-bearing; and he is none of these things.'

'Certainly not: a most gentlemanlike, estimable character indeed,' said Martin, leaning over the top-rim to see the last of the rocks, now far astern, almost lost in the shimmering heat. 'Yet even so, such inflexibility . . . five thousand miles of ocean and not five minutes' stay to be contemplated. But do not think I complain – that would be wicked ingratitude after the sight of the blue-faced booby, of six blue-faced boobies. I perfectly remember your warning me that for a naturalist the naval life was one of nine hundred and ninety-nine opportunities lost and one that might perhaps be seized. Yet the Evil One will be reminding me that tomorrow we are to heave to and lie motionless Heaven knows how long for the ceremony of crossing the Line.'

A muted ceremony however, for most exceptionally it took place on a Sunday when church was rigged, and even more exceptionally it took place in a newly-painted ship, with all hands acutely aware of their best clothes on the one hand and of the wet paint, the freshly laid-on pitch tar, and the still-moist blackstrake just above the wales on the other. Furthermore Mr Martin had read a grave sermon by Dean Donne, and the choir had sung some particularly moving hymns and psalms. There were Africans, Poles, Dutchmen (a broad category), Letts, Malays, and even a mute solitary Finn on the *Surprise*'s books, but most of her people were English, and Anglican at that, and the service brought home very much to mind. In general the mood remained serious even after Sunday duff and grog, and those few volatile spirits who would be fooling were perpetually reminded to 'watch out for the paintwork, mate; mind your bleeding step,' by those who would have to make all good if anything were smeared.

The *Surprise* did back her foretopsail and lie to almost on the very Line itself; Badger-Bag did come aboard with his train, exchanging the customary greetings and witticisms with the Captain of the ship and calling for those who had not crossed the equator before to redeem themselves or be shaved. Martin and the youngsters paid their forfeit, and the others, all of them former Defenders, were brought to the tub; but there was not much zeal in the shaving – again and again Badger-Bag's style was cramped by cries of 'Mind the paintwork, Joe', and his usual obscene merriment could not really flow free on a Sunday in the presence of a parson – and presently it was over, with no harm done, only a certain feeling of flatness. And even that was remedied by a concert in the evening, the ship's first in the southern hemisphere, with all hands singing and Orrage the cook coming out very strong with *The British Tars* –

> *Come all you thoughtless young men, a warning take by me*
> *And never leave your happy homes to sail the raging sea.*

Mr Martin had not visited the Canaries, nor the Cape Verdes, nor yet St Paul's rocks, and presently it seemed that he was to be done out of the New World too. Five days later, the *Surprise* raised Cape St Roque at dawn, a dim, remote headland, and then bore away to cruise in the most frequented shipping-lanes, where the currents and the local winds brought most vessels from North America and the West Indies quite close inshore south of Recife, off the broad estuary of the São Francisco river. Quite close inshore, that is to say, from a sailor's point of view, since the land could actually be seen if one ascended to the masthead, a faint line, rather harder and a little more irregular than cloud. Here Jack meant to stand off and on, with the barge just in sight in the offing and the launch beyond it, waiting for the *Norfolk*. He had not been on his chosen station more than a few hours when the morning sun showed him the *Amiable Catherine* of London, homeward-bound from the River Plate. The *Catherine* had not the slightest wish to speak the *Surprise*, knowing very well that the frigate might press several of her best hands, but she had no choice: Jack had the weather-gage, a much faster ship, and ten times the number of men to spread her canvas. Her master came aboard with a glum face and the *Catherine's* papers: he left looking pleased and somewhat drunken, since Jack, both from natural choice and policy, always treated merchant-captains civilly. The *Catherine* had not seen or heard of the *Norfolk*, nor of any other American man-of-war in southern waters: no talk of any such thing in Montevideo, St Catherine's, Rio or Bahia. She would take great care of *Surprise*'s letters and put them straight into the post; and she wished her a very happy return.

Four more ships or barques gave the same news in the course of the day; so did a pilot-boat that came out to ask whether they wanted to go up the river to Penedo. On coming aboard the pilot startled the quarterdeck by uttering a delighted screech and kissing Mr Allen on both cheeks – the master had once spent a considerable time in the pilot's father's house in the port of Penedo, recovering from the dry gripes – but he then won the good opinion of all within earshot by assuring the Captain that no man-of-war could possibly have passed the headlands without his knowledge. The anxiety that had been growing so in Jack Aubrey's mind dissolved, leaving a delicious feeling of pure relief; although he had taken such an unconscionable time in getting there he was still ahead of the American.

'This is capital,' he said to Pullings and Mowett. 'I do not think we shall have to cruise here for so long as a week, even if *Norfolk* has had very indifferent breezes. If we stand well off, keeping the double-headed hill on our beam, she should pass inshore, which gives us the advantage of the current and the weather-gage, and then hey for Saffron Walden. Not that I think that she would decline an engagement, even if she were to windward of us.'

'The water . . .' began Pullings.

'Yes, yes, there is the water,' said Jack. 'But we have enough for nearly a week on short allowance, and in these latitudes, at this time of the year, I have rarely known a week go by without rain pouring down: we must have our casks and awnings ready at the first drop. And if it don't rain, why, we can run in – the master knows a good watering-place no great way up the river – leaving the boats to keep watch. Even if she does slip by she will not have any very great start, and we can make it up by cracking on, before she is aware.'

The long days passed, furiously hot, horribly thirsty. The heat pleased some, Stephen among them, and the

Finn, who silently took off his fur hat for the first time since Gibraltar; but Mr Adams on the other hand was all agasp and aswim, obliged to be sponged in a hammock under the weather-awnings, and Mrs Horner lost her looks entirely, going yellow and thin. It was also observed that her song-bird lost his voice: no more Gathering Flowers in May, no more Rose in June, nor no more flaming Spanish guitar on the gangway neither. But the guilty pair no longer excited any very considerable interest, partly because they seemed to have grown much more cautious, partly because their liaison had lasted so many thousands of miles that it was now almost respectable, but very much more because all hands were engaged in such strenuous gunnery practice in such heat that they had little energy left for adultery, the contemplation of adultery.

It was now that Captain Aubrey's private powder came into its own. Horner and his mates filled cartridge by the hour, and every evening at quarters the *Surprise* erupted in deadly earnest, the long savage flames and the smoke jetting from her sides in rippling broadsides running from the bow-guns aft, fired at empty beef-casks towed out five hundred yards, very often with shattering effect and with something close to the old *Surprise's* speed of one minute ten seconds between two discharges of each gun, although almost every crew contained a Defender or a Gibraltar lunatic.

In the afternoon of the fifth day the wind came off the land, bringing with it the smell of tropical river mud and green forest, but no rain, alas, only a single chrysomelid beetle on the wing, the first true South American that Martin had ever seen. He hurried below to show Stephen, but Higgins told him that the Doctor was engaged: would Mr Martin sit down and take one of the invalids' thin captain biscuits and a trifle of the sick-bay brandy? Martin had barely time to decline – a biscuit in such arid heat was a physical impossibility unless it was accompanied by something far wetter, far more voluminous than brandy – before the gunner walked out, looking black and grim.

'It may be nondescript,' said Stephen, peering at the beetle through a magnifying glass. 'I certainly have not seen it before and can scarcely even guess its genus.' He gave the creature back into Martin's hand and then said, 'Oh Mr Martin, my quotation came back to me, together with the author's name: Sénac de Meilhan. I made him speak a little more emphatically than I should have done, I am afraid. What he really said was "Even the best-conducted women – les plus sages – have an aversion for the impotent," going on "and old men are despised: so one should conceal one's wounds and hide the crippling deficiencies of life – poverty, misfortune, sickness, ill-success. People begin by being touched and moved to tenderness by their friends' distress; presently this changes to pity, which has something humiliating about it; then to a masterful giving of advice; and then to scorn." Of course the later considerations have nothing to do with the subject we were discussing, but they seem to me – Lieutenant Mowett, my dear, what can I do for you?'

'I beg your pardon for bursting in upon your beetle,' said Mowett, 'but the Captain would like to know whether the human frame can support this.' He passed a mug of the rainwater collected long ago, north of the Line.

Stephen smelt to it, poured a little into a phial and looked at it with a lens. Delight dawned upon his grave, considering face and spread wide. 'Will you look at this, now?' he said, passing it to Martin. 'Perhaps the finest conferva soup I have ever seen; and I believe I make out some African forms.'

'There are also some ill-looking polyps, and some creatures no doubt close kin to the hydroblabs,' said Martin. 'I should not drink it for a deanery.'

'Pray tell the Captain that it will not do,' said Stephen, 'and that he will be obliged to bear up, bear down, bear away for that noble stream the São Francisco and fill our casks from its limpid, health-giving billows as they flow between banks covered with a luxuriant vegetation of choice exotics, echoing to the cries of the toucan, the jaguar, various apes, a hundred species of parrots, and they flying among gorgeous orchids, while huge butterflies of unparalleled splendour float over a ground strewn with Brazil nuts and boa-constrictors.'

Martin gave an involuntary skip, but Mowett replied, 'He was afraid you would say that; and if you did I was to apply to Mr Martin and ask him in a very tactful, discreet manner whether the prayers for rain we use at home could be applied to a ship at sea. Because, you know, we are most unwilling to leave our station to fetch wet, if wet can, as you might say, be induced to come to us.'

'Prayers for rain *at sea?*' said the chaplain. 'I doubt it would be orthodox. But I will look in my books and tell you what I find tomorrow.'

'I am not sure that we shall have to wait until tomorrow,' said Jack, when this message reached him. 'Look away to leeward.' There, far down the evening wind, dark clouds were gathering on the horizon, and in spite of the brilliant sun in the west lightning could be seen flickering under them. Even here the air was electrical, and the bosun's cat sprang about the forecastle rigging in a high state of excitement, its fur standing on end.

'Perhaps it would not be tempting fate, was we to lay along the clean awnings and funnels,' said Pullings.

'Fate might bear it this once,' said Jack. 'She has hardly used us very kindly so far, I believe. And what is more, I think we might be well advised to get the topgallantmasts down on deck and rig rolling-tackles; the swell is increasing.'

Pullings did these things; and when the boats returned from their distant watch he had them brought inboard and made fast to the skid-beams rather than towing astern. All this seemed labour lost until the middle watch, when Maitland, Hollom, and the larbowlines took over from Honey.

'You are a good relief, Maitland,' said Honey, and then in a formal voice, 'Here you have her: close-reefed topsails and inner jib; course east-south-east until two bells, then wear ship and west-north-west until the end of the watch. If rain falls take appropriate measures.'

'East-south-east, then wear ship: appropriate measures,' said Maitland.

'Lord, what light-balls!' cried Hollom, the mate of the watch, pointing forward to the St Elmo's fire flickering about the jibboom and spritsail yard, brilliant in the faint moonlight.

'Don't point at them, for Heaven's sake,' said Honey. 'It brings bad luck. The awnings are in the waist, the hose is stretched along, and battle-lanterns are ready under the forecastle. If there is any justice we should have something like Noah's flood before morning, from the look of things to leeward.'

'Do you think we should tell the Doctor about the fire-balls?' asked Maitland. 'They are prodigious curious.'

'Why,' said Honey, considering, 'I did think of it; but they are only electrical, you know, and I don't know he would thank us for waking him up, just to see the electrical fluid playing the fool. If they had feathers and laid eggs, I should have sent long ago.'

Stephen therefore knew nothing of St Elmo's fire: far below, swinging in an ever-widening but always peaceful arc as the swell increased, his ears blocked with balls of wax, and his mind – hitherto much harassed by thoughts of Diana and by the oppressive unbreathable air – now soothed by a judicious dose of laudanum, he knew nothing of the torrential rain that half-drowned the ship in the graveyard watch, nor of the subsequent near-tornado that flung her so violently about amidst bellowing thunder no higher than the mastheads and an almost continuous blaze of blue and orange lightning. The laudanum he had returned to at last because after mature and wholly objective consideration he had been brought to see that as a physician he was required to sleep well enough to

153

perform his duty the next day; furthermore the poppy had not been created idly, and a rejection of the natural balms provided was contumelious pride, as heretical as the notion that because a thing was pleasant it was also sinful; and in any case this was St Abdon's day. After his long abstinence it worked beautifully: but even half a pint of laudanum (and he was nowhere near his old excesses) could not have kept out the enormous crash as lightning struck the *Surprise*, melting the shank of her best bower anchor, running along the seven foremost larboard guns and setting them off, but above all rending and shattering her iron-hooped bowsprit in the most extraordinary manner.

'The French fleet is out,' thought Stephen, three parts awake. 'I must get my instruments – go to my station – God between us and evil.' Then waking a little more as his bare feet plunged into the rainwater swilling to and fro under his hanging cot, 'Nonsense. This is the New World, and we are at war with the Americans, ridiculous as it may appear.'

However, he heard no more gunfire, and after a good deal of reflexion and some unsuccessful attempts at striking a light he made his way on deck, which was lit fore and aft with lanterns. The ship lay head to wind, and the fire-engine was playing on the smoking wreckage of the bowsprit: this last enormous blast had exhausted the storm, and although the sea was still high the sky was clearing over the land. He learnt from other nightshirted figures that this was not warfare, that nobody had been hurt, and that the situation was in hand; he retired to the almost deserted quarterdeck and sat on a carronade slide. He heard the cry of 'There she goes' as the outer forty feet of the bowsprit plunged into the sea with a rending sound and a splash, followed by a good many orders; then the officers came flooding back aft. Martin was among them, and seeing Stephen he joined him and said in a low voice, 'It appears that we have lost our bowsprit: the Captain seems deeply concerned.'

154

'Aye,' said Stephen. 'They value it much, as essential for turning into the wind; or perhaps from it.'

'Mr Allen,' said Jack, 'the breeze is fair; you know these waters. Can you take the ship up to Penedo?'

'No, sir,' said the master, 'neither with nor without a bowsprit. The shoals in the estuary are always shifting, and the river is as much pilot-water as the Hooghly: I could not in conscience venture upon it, even if we had a compass we could rely upon, which we have not, nor even if it was clear daylight. But if I may have the launch I will run in, send off the pilot, and set Lopez's yard a-working on a new spar as fast as ever they can go. With this breeze and the turn of the tide I should be there soon after dawn; and maybe the ship could stand in, cautious, and drop anchor in say twenty fathom water about two or three mile off the bar.'

'Very good, Mr Allen,' said Jack. 'Make it so.'

Since the foremast's main support had gone with the bowsprit, it took some little time to get the swift-sailing copper-bottomed launch over the side, and while this was going on Stephen said to the master, 'Mr Allen, can I be of any use to you on shore? I am moderately fluent in Portuguese.'

'Oh dear me no, Doctor, though I thank you very kindly. I am like one of the family with the Lopezes, and with the Moreiras. But I tell you what it is: if you do not mind a little wetting, and if you like to come along with me, I think I can show you something uncommon in the botanical line, if the floods have not carried it away, which ain't likely. Parson Martin is welcome too, if so inclined: no one can call me superstitious.'

The launch was a fine boat, but she was not a dry one. She skimmed through the water, shipping large packets of it at every plunge of the long swell, two hands baling and the master at the tiller, steering by the Southern Cross. Everybody was soaked and almost cold by the time they were well into the estuary, with the bar breaking the swell and the master often letting fly the sheet as he picked out the channel, straining forward to see the rises of the land in the dim grey light, the first hint of dawn. Twice the launch grounded slightly, but a seaman on either side, no more than thigh deep, soon heaved her off; and at last, seeing a tall stake with a rag on top, Allen said, 'Here we are,' and sent the boat slanting across the stream to a long low island, brought her gently to a halt in the sand of its shore, and as Macbeth leapt out with the gang-board for Stephen and Martin he said, 'I will just run up to Penedo now to arrange with the yard, and I will tell the pilot to bring you some breakfast on his way out to the ship. Shove off, Macbeth.' And when the boat was some way out on the smooth water he called back, 'Mind the alligators, gentlemen.'

They were standing on a firm white strand and already there was light enough to see that a little way up the slope there began a grove of trees: but surely too high, too massive to be trees. The light increased, and trees they were, palms of an almost unbelievable mass and height, their enormous fan-shaped leaves bursting in a vegetable explosion well over a hundred feet above their heads, and outlined sharp against the greying sky.

'Would they be Mauritia vinifera?' asked Martin in a whisper.

'Mauritia of some kind, sure; but what I cannot tell,' said Stephen.

They walked slowly, reverently into the grove: there was no undergrowth and spring tides or perhaps floods kept the ground quite clean, so that the magnificent trees rose sheer, each some ten yards from the next, a vast grey column.

Their feet made no sound as they paced on; but very soon it was darkness that they were walking into, for the dense fronds intertwined far overhead, and except at its fringes the grove was still filled with warm silent night, the pale trunks soaring up into obscurity. They turned right-handed with one accord and as they reached the outer edge again, facing the river and the strand, the sun heaved up from the eastern sea, sending an instant brilliance across the water to the other bank, no great way off. The reflected light and colour of the far bank fairly blazed upon them as they stood there in the shade of the remaining trees, a bank with a line of shining sand and then a great wall of the most intensely vivid green, an almost violent green, with palms of twenty or thirty different kinds soaring above it, all in the total silence of a dream. Martin clasped his hands as he gazed, uttering some private ejaculations; and Stephen, touching his elbow, nodded towards three trees some way up the river, three enormous cathedral-like domes that rose two hundred feet above the rest, one of them completely covered with deep red flowers.

They took a few more steps through the palms, reaching the white unshaded strand: to the left hand at the water's edge lay a twenty-foot caiman, contemplating the gentle stream, and to the right hand, full in the brilliant sun there stood a scarlet ibis.

CHAPTER FIVE

The mutilated frigate, as uncomely and as unrecognizable as a man whose nose is gone, made her way with infinite precautions through the shoals and mudbanks of the estuary with the making tide, guided by the grave pilot, who sent his men ahead to mark the turns in the channel with a pole; then she tacked painfully up the river, her head heaved round by boats at the end of each board – each short board, for by the height of Penedo the São Francisco narrowed to no more than a mile. However, they got her in at last, by torchlight, with no more than one wait in mid-channel for the ebb, and Jack found to his great satisfaction that Allen and Lopez, the owner of the shipyard, had already chosen a fine piece of timber for the new bowsprit, that the carpenters had already roughed out a splendid greenheart cap for it, and that the sheers to extract the shattered stump were to be erected first thing in the morning.

'This Lopez is a man after my own heart,' he said to Stephen. 'He understands the importance of time and the thorough leathering of a jibboom hole, and I have little doubt we shall be at sea by Sunday.'

'Only three days,' said Stephen. 'Alas for poor Martin: I told him a much longer period and he had set his heart upon seeing the boa-constrictor, the jaguar, and the owl-faced night-ape, as well as making a reasonably complete collection of the local beetles; but so much can hardly be expected in so short a time. I agree with you about Senhor Lopez, however. He is also a most amiable, hospitable man, and has invited me to stay the night and to meet a Peruvian gentleman, a great traveller, who is also a guest. This gentleman has crossed the Andes, I find, and must necessarily have seen a very great deal of the inland country.'

'I am sure he must,' said Jack. 'But I do beg of you, Stephen, not to keep Lopez long from his bed. There is not a moment to lose – think what flats we should look, was the *Norfolk* to pass by while we were sitting here – and we must start work a little before dawn: it would be the world's pity to have him stupid, sleepy and jaded. Could you not give him a hint, to the effect that you would be happy to entertain the Peruvian gentleman, if he chose to turn in?'

In the event Lopez needed no hints. He spoke Spanish only with difficulty, and seeing that both his guests were fluent, even enormously fluent, in that language and that they agreed very well, he excused himself on the grounds of early work to be done and bade them good night, leaving them on a broad veranda with a number of domesticated creatures on it, marmosets of three different kinds, an old bald toucan, a row of sleepy parrots, something hairy in the background that might have been a sloth or an ant-eater or even a doormat but that it farted from time to time, looking round censoriously on each occasion, and a strikingly elegant small blue heron that walked in and out. Two bottles of white port stood between them, two hammocks hung behind, and Lopez returned for a moment to beg them to use the mosquito-netting. 'Not that we have mosquitos in Penedo, gentlemen,' he said, 'but it must be confessed that at the change of the moon the vampires do grow a little importunate.'

They did not annoy his guests however, since the vampire really needs a sleeping prey and these two (though eyed wistfully from the rafters) never went to bed. They sat talking all night, watching the sliver of the new moon go down and the procession of great glowing stars pass across the sky: bats of a more amiable kind, two feet across, showed briefly against their light, and in the river only a few yards below could be seen the star-twinkling wake of turtles and the occasional alligator: the lion-maned marmoset in Stephen's lap snored very gently, sleeping on

159

and on in spite of the continual flow of talk. They had surveyed the infamous career of Buonaparte (no end yet in view, alas, alas), the melancholy record of Spain as an imperial power in the New World and the almost certain liberation of her colonies – 'Though when I look at the reptiles coming to the fore in such places as Buenos Aires,' said the Peruvian, 'I sometimes fear that our last state may be even worse than our first' – and now, at the tail end of the night, they returned to the geology of the Andes, and the difficulty of crossing them.

'I should never have accomplished it but for these,' said the Peruvian, nodding toward the half-finished packet of coca leaves on the table between them. 'When we were near the top of the pass the wind increased, bringing frozen pellets of snow and cutting off one's breath, already so short at that height that every step called for two or three gasping inhalations. My companions were in much the same condition, and two of our llamas had died. I thought we should have to turn back, but the headman led us to something of a shelter among the rocks, took out his pouch of coca and his box of lime and passed them round. We each chewed a ball – an acullico, we call it – and then, resuming our burdens with the greatest ease, we walked fast up the cruel slope through the driving snow, over the top and so down into kinder weather.'

'You do not surprise me,' said Stephen. 'Ever since the first acullico that you were so good as to give me I have felt my mind glow, my mental and no doubt physical powers increase. I have little doubt that I could swim the river that lies before us. I shall not do so, however. I prefer to enjoy your conversation and my present state of remarkable well-being – no fatigue, no hunger, no perplexity of mind, but a power of apprehension and synthesis that I have rarely known before. Your coca, sir, is the most virtuous simple I have ever met with. I had read about it in Garcilasso de la Vega and in Faulkner's account, but I had no idea it was a hundredth part as efficacious.'

'This of course is the best flat-leaved mountain coca,'

said the Peruvian. 'It was given me by the grower, an intimate friend, and I always travel with a substantial packet of the most recent crop. Allow me to pour a glass of wine: there is some left in the other bottle.'

'You are very good, but it would be wasted on me: ever since the pleasant tingling subsided after the first ball, my sense of taste is entirely gone.'

'What, what is that outcry?' exclaimed the Peruvian, for a screech of pipes could be heard from the *Surprise*, and a roaring of 'Out or down, out or down. Rouse and bitt. Here I come with a sharp knife and a clear conscience: out or down. Bundle up, bundle up, bundle up,' as the bosun's mates roused the sleeping lower-deck and all the frigate's open ports showed golden in the darkness.

'It is only the mariners being summoned to their duty,' said Stephen. 'They like to begin cleaning the deck before daylight; the sun must not be offended with the sight of dust. It is a very superstitious ritual, I am afraid.'

A little later the stars began to pale; there was a lightening in the east; and within a few minutes the sun thrust his rim above the far edge of the sea. The briefest dawn, and it was day, full day. Captain Aubrey stepped from his cabin and Senhor Lopez from his house. They met on the quay, Lopez accompanied by an embarrassing, unnecessary spider-monkey that had to be menaced and hissed at to make it go home, and Jack by the master for the language and the bosun for any technical questions that might arise.

By mid-morning all hands were steadily at work: that is to say, all the hands there were, for Pullings in the launch and Mowett in the barge, with their respective crews, had been left far out beyond the bar to keep watch and to gather news. But there were plenty of Surprises left; the frigate had been warped alongside the sheers and the shipwrights were busy on her head; along the wharf the great smooth chips flew as the carpenters plied their adzes on the new bowsprit, cap and jibboom; the bosun, his mates and a strong party of unusually able seamen were stripping almost all her standing rigging in order to set it up again Bristol-fashion when the new spar should be in; and an army of caulkers swarmed over her decks and sides. Few of the Defenders could be of any use at these skilled tasks, but by now they could all pull an oar, more or less, and they and the Marines were sent off to complete the ship's water at a spring a little way up the river.

'I feel exceedingly guilty, watching all these men so earnestly at work and doing nothing myself,' said Martin.

'The back of my hand to guilt,' said Stephen, lively and cheerful in spite of his wholly sleepless night. 'Let us walk out and view the country. I am told that there is a path leading behind the mangrove-swamp and through the forest to an open glade where a certain palm-tree grows. Its name I forget, but it bears a round and crimson fruit. We have so little time: it would be a pity to waste it in an idle beating of one's breast.'

Little time indeed: yet it was long enough for Martin to be bitten by an owl-faced night-ape, bitten dangerously, and to the very bone. They walked behind the mangrove-swamp, along the broad forest track with vegetation rising in a brilliant green wall on either side, a wall made of trees as its powerful basis and then of uncountable twining creepers, climbers, bushes, lianas and parasites filling all the interstices so that in the thicker parts nothing but a serpent could get through. They walked with foolish smiles upon their faces, astonished by the butterflies, the innumerable butterflies of so very many different species and by the occasional humming-bird; and once the all-pervading sound of stridulating insects had lasted ten or twenty minutes it could no longer be heard and they seemed to be walking in total silence – very few birds, and these few mute. But when they came to the glade, where the trees stood fairly wide and the ground was clear, they startled a mixed flock of parrots; and there on a well-beaten path they saw a marching column of leaf-carrying ants a foot wide and so long that it vanished in either direction.

162

Stephen contemplated the ants, distinguishing the various soldier and worker forms; and being fond of calculation he worked out the number in a square foot and the probable weight of their burden, meaning thereby to make some estimate of all the army he could see; but his arithmetic had always been slow hesitant and poor, and he was still scratching numbers with a twig on a broad leaf when he heard a startled cry from Martin, over by a hollow tree on the far side of the glade. 'Hush,' he said, frowning. 'I write three, I carry seven.' But now the cry had anguish in it too and turning he saw that Martin's hand was streaming with blood: he ran towards him, his little penknife out and ready, crying, 'Was it a serpent, at all? Was it ever a snake?'

'No,' said Martin, with the strangest mixture of delight and pain in his face. 'It was an owl-faced night-ape. He was in here' – pointing to a hole in the hollow tree – 'peering out: such a pleasant striped round-eyed inquisitive little face, that I ventured . . .'

'To the very bone,' said Stephen. 'And you will certainly lose your nail, if you live at all. Let it bleed, soul, let it bleed: I have no doubt the ape was mad, and the flow may get rid of a little of the poison, with the blessing. There, I will bind it up now, and we will hurry back to the ship. You must certainly be cauterized as soon as possible. Where is the ape?'

'I am very sorry to say he ran off directly. I should have called you earlier.'

'Let us imitate him. There is not a moment to lose. The river-bank is quicker than the mangrove-swamp. Keep your hand in your bosom; and take notice that the handkerchief is mine.'

As they ran under the powerful sun Martin said, 'It is not every man that can show a wound inflicted by an owl-faced night-ape.'

A belt of feathery bamboos to traverse and they came on to the river-bank, broad sand now, the tide being out; and there before them stood two seamen, Awkward Davis and Fat-Arse Jenks, grasping driftwood clubs and looking grim.

'Why, it's the Doctor,' cried Davis, the brighter of the two. 'We thought you was Indians – savages – cannibals.'

'Tigers,' said Jenks. 'Theshing about in them reeds, and ravening for blood.'

'What are you doing here?' asked Stephen, since both of them belonged to the launch.

'Why, ain't you heard the news, sir?' asked Davis.

'What news?'

'He ain't heard the news,' said Davis, turning to Jenks.

'You tell him, then, mate,' said Jenks.

The news, extricated from its web of irrelevant detail and the correction of minute circumstantial points, was that the *Norfolk* had passed by, steering south-south-west under all plain sail, that Captain Pullings had instantly set off in the launch for Penedo, that they had had great difficulty in finding the channel, and that this being the lowest ebb of a spring tide or close on the launch had grounded so often in this last stretch that Davis and Jenks, being unusually heavy and not being needed to row with this leading breeze, had been told to walk the rest of the way, but to mind out for the tigers. Mr Mowett in the barge, on the other hand, had carried all away, being overset on a sandbank quite early on, and would have to wait there till the ship came down.

'The launch will have got in an hour ago,' said Davis. 'Oh my eye, they will be as busy as bees by now.'

Bees indeed, and bees under an exceptionally active taskmaster. Meals, abolished for the cabin, gunroom and midshipmen's berth, were reduced to a mere snapping ten minutes for the hands; all pretty-work was abandoned; and so many extra carpenters, hired out of Jack's pocket, were set to work on the bowsprit that they barely had room to wield their tools. Then after nightfall what could be done by the light of huge fires blazing on the quay was done, and although there was still a great deal of fine-work that must wait for the sun Jack was fairly

164

confident that they should sail on tomorrow evening's tide.

'You will not mind its being Friday?' asked Stephen.

'Friday?' cried Jack, who had lost count in the fury of headlong work. 'God help us, so it is. But it don't signify, you know; we do not do it voluntarily; it is forced upon us. No, no. But leaving that aside – and pray don't mention it to anyone else, Stephen – there are two things in our favour: one is that the *Norfolk* was under no more than plain sail when she could easily have spread very much more canvas by far; so it is likely we may catch her by cracking on. The other is that this is a spring tide, and it will carry us down a great deal quicker than we came up.'

A third thing was the arrival of Mowett and the barge's crew, who, having accomplished prodigies of repair, appeared a little before dawn. With their help – and some of the cleverest riggers were among the bargemen – the work went forward at a splendid pace. The new bowsprit was home by half past ten, gammoned and frapped by eleven, and the new jibboom rigged out, with all stays and shrouds set up by the depth of low tide. Jack gave the order to splice the main brace, and turning to Pullings he said, 'The painting and titivating we must leave until we are at sea, and of course she don't look pretty; but I never thought we could have done so much in the time. Please ask the master to tell Mr Lopez that we should be happy to accept his invitation after all: he knows we shall have to leave him at the turn of the tide. Lord, I could do with my dinner: and with a glass of wine, by God!'

Glasses of wine were not lacking at that cheerful feast, nor excellent food (for the turtle counted as fish), nor yet song: indeed Jack thought the pilot came it a little too high with the shanties he had learnt aboard English and American merchantmen. But then Jack's mind was too much taken up with the flowing tide to take much delight in music, and as soon as the youngster he had posted by the chronometers came to tell him that the time was ripe he stood up, thanked Mr Lopez most heartily, and walked off, followed by Stephen and the master, disregarding the pilot's plea for a last toast to St Peter.

The tide, now at slack-water, was exceptionally high, so high that small waves lapped over the quay, since for most of the flood it had been a leeward tide, though now the wind had hauled conveniently into the south-west. Once this vast body of water began to ebb, reflected Jack, looking over to the far brimming bank, it would sweep the *Surprise* down to the sea at a splendid rate; and with even a little help from the breeze they should be well clear of the estuary before the turn, particularly as with so much water in the river they would not have to follow all the windings of the ebb-tide fairway. The uncommon height had another advantage too: Stephen stepped straight into the pilot's boat and sat there peaceably without having either fallen into the bottom or pitched over the far side or even barked his shins, while the pilot and his man rowed them out to the *Surprise*, which was already in the channel, holding on by two buoyed kedges belonging to the yard and only waiting for her commander to let go.

'So we are away,' said Martin, gazing at the brilliant sunlit wall of green to starboard as it glided by.

'If this had been a civilized voyage of inquiry we might have stayed for three weeks,' said Stephen. 'How is your hand?'

'It is very well, I thank you,' said Martin. 'And had it been fifty times more severe I should still have thought it nothing, for those few hours – such wealth . . . Maturin, if you direct your glass to that enormous tree upon the point and look a little to the right, do not you make out something very like a troop of monkeys?'

'I do. And take them to be howlers, black howlers.'

'Howlers, did you say? Yes, no doubt. I wish,' he added in a low voice, not to be overheard by the pilot, 'I wish that fellow would make less noise.'

'He is grown somewhat exuberant,' said Stephen. 'Let us move forward.'

But even when they were in the bows the pilot's merriment pursued them, together with his imitation of the jaguar's cry, a gruff Boo boo; and most disappointingly he moved the ship out into the middle of the river, so that neither bank could be seen in any detail. The tide had begun to ebb and she was running surprisingly fast under topsails and jib with a quartering wind. Fast, that is to say, until with a smooth but sudden check she came to a dead halt on a sandbank with her deck sloping from fore to aft and a huge cloud of mud and sand flowing away from her down the rapid stream. Hands had instantly started the sheets, and now as they were clewing up Jack came racing forward from his cabin calling out, 'Light along the lead, light along the lead there.' He leant far over the headrails, staring down into the water as it cleared: she had ploughed her way so far up the bank that the bottom was within a yard of her bridle-ports.

'Take a cast well out,' he said to the quartermaster, in the hope that the lead might show a narrow spit that she might be dragged off sideways. It showed nothing of the kind; and while the lead was whirling for the second cast to larboard he saw bushes and reeds under the frigate's forefoot. She was on a bank so high that it was rarely covered. Running aft to see how things were astern he saw that Pullings and Mowett were already getting the boats over the side. 'Cable out of the gunroom port,' he shouted as he passed.

The stern was unnaturally low in the water and the rudder was probably unshipped, but that did not matter for the moment. 'Just drop it under the counter,' he said, and the lead splashed down.

'By the mark twain, sir,' said the quartermaster in a shocked voice. 'And barely that.'

It was very bad indeed, but it was not quite hopeless. 'Best bower into the launch,' he called. 'Kedge and hawser into the red cutter.' He glanced over the taffrail to see whether the run of the current gave any hint of the bank's limits and he noticed that the pilot and his man were already two hundred yards away in their little skiff, pulling furiously. He said to the master, 'Start the water over the side,' and plunged below, to where the bosun and a gang of powerful tierers from both watches were passing one of the new fifteen-inch cables aft with rhythmic cries of 'Heave one, heave two, heave away, away and go.' All was well here and moving very fast, and as he ran on deck, calling aloud for the jolly-boat and a can-buoy, some part of his mind had time to thank God for good officers and a crew of thorough-paced seamen.

By the time he dropped into the jolly-boat the kedge had already been lowered into the red cutter, the best bower was hanging from the cathead, poised just over the launch, and fresh water was spouting over the side, lightening the ship at a great pace.

The jolly-boat cast to and fro like an eager dog, searching for depth and a good holding-ground, and at the first tolerable place Jack tossed the buoy over the gunwale and hailed the launch, now pulling as fast as it could with the anchor aboard and the cable trailing behind, pulling as fast as it could against the wind and the now much more powerful ebb, pulling so hard that the men's faces were crimson, while the oars bent danger-ously at the tholes. For now there was not a moment, not a single moment to lose, now less than ever, for as every seaman knew, this tide would drop thirty feet: even in the last ten minutes five inches of precious depth had ebbed from over the shoal and round the ship, and if they did not have her off this tide there would be little hope for the next, since it would not rise so high. Furthermore there was the fear of the ship's breaking her back as the water left her. 'Stretch out, stretch out,' roared Pullings in the launch, and 'Stretch out, stretch out,' roared Mowett in the cutter.

Reaching the can-buoy the launch manhandled the perilous great anchor over the side; the cutter raced on to where the jolly-boat was signalling a reasonable bottom and dropped the kedge, thus anchoring the anchor itself. Jack stood up and hailed the ship: 'Heave away. Heave away, there,' and at once the capstan on the frigate's quarterdeck began to spin.

By the time the boats were back something like the full strain was on: the capstan was still turning, but very slowly, with the men bowed to the bars and gasping. Stephen and Martin were pushing side by side, but as the boat-crews came leaping aboard, flinging themselves at the bars, Jack plucked Stephen away and took his place, saying, 'I am heavier.' Then in a huge voice, 'Heave hearty. Heave hearty. Heave and rally.' The bars were fully manned now and the capstan went round a full turn, the iron pawls going click-click-click: the strain reached something near to breaking-point and Stephen, looking aft, saw the cable as an almost straight line. It had shrunk to less than half its size.

'Sand to the nippers,' cried Jack, now hoarse with the effort of thrusting. 'Heave and rally. Heave, oh heave.'

The capstan scarcely moved. One click – a long striving pause – another reluctant click. 'Heave and rally. Heave and rally.' Then the sound of the pawls came faster, click-click-click-click; the cook cried, 'We're off' and some of those who had not found room at the bars began to cheer: but it was the anchors that were coming home. Apart from settling a little deeper into the mud the *Surprise* had not moved, and by now the tide had dropped two feet. 'Belay,' said Jack, straightening from the bar. 'Captain Pullings,' he said, having looked at the river and its banks, 'I believe the ship will cant to starboard as the tide goes out, so we must get out some shores; at the same time we must find a hard on the nearer bank for the guns, so that she may float at the top of next high water.' 'Or,' he added to himself, 'at the top of the next spring tide: oh God send us a right full height of flood tomorrow.'

'There have been times, my dearest soul,' wrote Stephen to Diana in a letter dated 'from the shore of the São

169

Francisco', 'when you were not altogether pleased with Jack Aubrey, but if you had watched him this last fortnight I believe you would allow him a certain heroic quality, a certain greatness of soul. As I said, a drunken pilot ran the ship on to a sand-bank in the middle of this river at the very height of the highest tide, and although we pulled with all our might we could not get her off; nor would she shift at the next tide which, though high, was not high enough to raise her from her oozy bed. After that there was no hope until the change of the moon, which would bring another spring tide: this was a comforting reflexion, but every day that passed set another hundred or two hundred miles between us and our quarry, a quarry upon which all Jack's happiness, his professional career and his reputation depends. Furthermore it was not at all sure that the next spring tide would reach the extraordinary height of the flood that was our undoing. Yet from that moment to this I have not heard Jack complain or cry out 'Oh d—n it all', or any of those still warmer expressions that are so often used at sea and which he is so very free with on trifling occasions. Certainly he has required everybody to work very, very hard all day long, since all the cannon have had to be taken to the shore, together with countless tons of provisions and stores, and at low water a channel had to be attempted to be dug to make it easier for the ship to be plucked off when the moment came, while the rudder also had to be rehung; but with all this I do not remember an oath, scarcely a rebuke. And the curious thing is that this coolness absolutely shocks the men; they look at him nervously, and go about their duties with wonderful diligence. It was the same with Martin and me. During the first days, when the ship had to be lightened at great speed in case she should hog or break her back, being left suspended in the middle by the neap tides, all the skilled hands were employed dealing with the guns, and Martin, the purser and I were entrusted with the jolly-boat (a vile machine) to tow heavy casks ashore; and I do assure you, we were perpetually aware of that impassive, determined and authoritative eye; we felt it upon us in all our comings and goings, and we were as meek as schoolboys.

'After the first few days however we were released, with bleeding hands and no doubt permanently injured spines, since there was no more wholly unskilled work to do; and I must confess that the last week has been singularly agreeable. This is the only tropical river I know that is not infested with mosquitoes, although it has some capital marshes close at hand, with such a wealth of wading birds – imagine, my dear, a *roseate* spoonbill if you can – and of course there is an infinitely great botanical wealth on every hand. I have rarely seen a man so happy as my friend Martin: the coleoptera alone would have been worth the voyage, in his opinion, but as well as making a collection of very curious beetles he has also seen a boa, which was one of his great ambitions. We were walking in an open part of the forest, talking about jaguars, when we were both felled to the ground by what at first I took to be a heavy branch or rather liana; yet the liana writhed with great force and I quickly perceived that it was in fact an enormous serpent that had fallen from a tree. But a serpent so horribly alarmed that it had quite lost its head; and as it strove to escape threw coils in every direction. I saw that Martin was clinging to its neck with both hands and I represented to him that this was rash, heedless, imprudent. I should have gone on to remind him of the fate of Laocoön, but a coil tightening under my chin cut me short. In gasps he replied that it was a boa – boas were notoriously good-natured – he only wished to see its vestigial hind-legs – then would let it go – he was not hurting it. By this time the poor creature had recovered its wits; it darted (if the word can be used of so vast a reptile, thick, thick, and almost endless) from his grasp with a determined lunge, raced up the tree like an inverted torrent, and we saw it no more. From its brilliant appearance and its confused state of mind I think it must very recently have changed its skin.

'But the great wealth of every day is of course

botanical, and that reminds me of the cuca or coca leaves that a Peruvian traveller gave me; when they are chewed with a little lime they sharpen the mind to a wonderful degree, they induce a sense of well-being and they abolish both hunger and fatigue. I have laid in a considerable stock, because I think it will help me to throw off a somewhat troublesome habit: you may have noticed that for insomnia and a variety of other ills I take the tincture of laudanum; and this does tend to become a little too usual. I do not think there is any question of abuse, still less of addiction, yet it creates a certain need, not unlike that for tobacco; I should be glad to be set free from it, and I am confident that these valuable leaves will prove efficacious. Their powers really do surprise me, and I shall enclose a few with my letter, so that you may try them. During this period of extremely wearing toil and anxiety I have proposed them to Jack, but he said that if they did away with sleep and hunger they were not for him – in this crisis he needed his sleep and he must have his meals – in short, he would not take physic till the ship was afloat, no, not for a king's ransom.

'She is afloat now, trim, spruce, quite unharmed, having been plucked off her bank or rather island at the height of last night's spring tide; but in doing so we lost an anchor, and recovering it took up so much time that we have been obliged to wait for the next high water, when the excellent Mr Lopez (with the blessing) will guide us down to the open sea. I was about to add the proviso "if he reaches us in time", but as my pen was poised I saw his boat come round the bend of the river. He is now aboard; and when he leaves us, having taken the ship beyond the bar, I will entrust him with this letter.'

'Will I, though?' he asked aloud, having read it over. The tone was wrong, perhaps offensively wrong. It assumed that there was no difficulty between them, and the awareness that this assumption was unwarranted gave the letter a falseness, a grating artificiality. He slowly

172

crushed the paper in his hand as he stared out over the river at the elegant little ship, swimming there in the fairway well this side of her wicked island; but then as he saw the boat pull away from her side, the boat that was to carry him aboard, with no more land perhaps until the far Pacific, he smoothed it out again and wrote 'the Dear knows when it will reach you, but early or late it brings all my love.'

The *Surprise* had sixteen days of sailing to make up; and although the *Norfolk* was probably running off her southing under no more than moderate sail, to conserve her stores, spars and canvas, she would hardly make less than five knots in the steady south-east trades, even if she double-reefed her topsails for the night: and that set her two thousand miles ahead.

The *Surprise* was therefore in a tearing hurry, and as soon as she had dropped her pilot she spread a great expanse of canvas: there was nothing unusual about this situation however; the ship and her commander had been goaded by time for nearly the whole of their career and by now hurry was almost the normal state – leisure at sea had something uneasy about it, a kind of unnatural calm. Yet in spite of the hurry Jack had no intention of pushing her to the limit of her possibilities, with everything on the very edge of carrying away, as he had often done when his chase had a ship in view or just over the horizon and when he could risk springing a topmast with a clear conscience; but he did mean to go as near to that extreme racing pace as ever he could, bearing in mind that now the far South Sea lay before him with never a ship's chandler, let alone a dockyard, on its shores; and once again he blessed the Providence that had furnished him with two officers in Pullings and Mowett who would keep her moving through the water night and day with equal determination and energy.

'Now we can get back to real sailoring again,' he said with great satisfaction as she stood out into the

South Atlantic, close-hauled on a north-east breeze that had no scent of land upon it, a purely maritime wind. 'And perhaps we can make the ship look a little less like something ready for the breaker's yard. How I do loathe being clapped right up tight against the land,' he added, glancing at Brazil, a dim band looming on the western horizon, but still far too near for a blue-water sailor, whose worst enemy was a lee shore. '*But sea-room, an the brine and cloudy billows kiss the moon, I care not,*' he observed, taking the words from Mowett's mouth; but then, reflecting that fate might regard this as a challenge, he grasped a belaying-pin and said, 'I am only speaking figuratively, of course.'

Jack was not one of the modern spit-and-polish captains whose idea of a crack ship was one that could shift topmasts five seconds quicker than the others in the harbour, in which great quantities of brass outshone the sun at all times and in all weathers, in which the young gentlemen wore tight white breeches, cocked hats and Hessian boots with gilt twist edging and a gold tassel, singularly well adapted for reefing topsails, and in which the round-shot in the racks and garlands was carefully blacked while the naturally black hoops of the mess-kids was sanded to a silvery whiteness. But he did like what little naked brass the *Surprise* possessed to gleam and her paintwork to look tolerably neat; his first lieutenant liked it even more, and curiously enough the men who had to do all the work thoroughly agreed with them. It was what they were used to, and they prized what they were used to, even if it called for starting the day with sand and holystones on the wet deck long before sunrise and even longer before breakfast, even if it called for painting exposed parts of the ship while she swooped and plunged, flanking across the Atlantic swell with four men at the wheel and most of the watch standing by to let all go with a run: not that this happened often, since in general the winds were no kinder to her than they had been in the early part of the voyage; and many a wry look did Hollom's back receive, the back of a wind-eating Jonah for all his successful cruising in the gunner's private waters.

The *Surprise* therefore proceeded southwards with all possible dispatch, spreading the smell of fresh paint to leeward; and as soon as the more vulnerable paint was dry, the sharp, exhilarating scent of powder-smoke too. It was rare that quarters passed without at least small-arms being fired, rarer still that the great guns were not run in and out – the fouler the weather the better the exercise, said Jack, since you could never be sure of coming up with an enemy on a smooth and placid sea, and it was as well to learn how to heave your five hundredweight a man against the slope of the wildly-heaving deck long before the knack was needed. There were two chief reasons for this steady preparation: the first was that Jack Aubrey thoroughly enjoyed life; he was of a cheerful sanguine disposition, his liver and lights were in capital order, and unless the world was treating him very roughly indeed, as it did from time to time, he generally woke up feeling pleased and filled with a lively expectation of enjoying the day. Since he took so much pleasure in life, therefore, he meant to go on living as long as ever he could, and it appeared to him that the best way of ensuring this in a naval action was to fire three broadsides for his enemy's two, and to fire them deadly straight. The second reason, closely allied to the first, was that his idea of a crack ship was one with a strong, highly-skilled crew that could out-manoeuvre and then outshoot the opponent, a taut but happy ship, an efficient man-of-war – in short a ship that was likely to win at any reasonable odds.

Southward then, degree after degree, southward with the warm Brazil current; and they had not passed under the tropic of Capricorn before the regular, accustomed nautical way of life, punctuated by bells, might have been going on time out of mind. The ship was now as pretty as paint could make her, her copper had been scrubbed during her involuntary dry-docking, she had her pale fine-weather suit of sails abroad, and she looked a most uncommonly elegant sight as she ran down and down wide-winged, leaving the sun behind her. The young gentlemen had been introduced to the first aorist, the ablative absolute, and the elements of spherical trigonometry; these they pursued with little enthusiasm until they were let out to learn horseshoe splicing with Bonden or some unusual knots with Faster Doodle, a man who never explained anything at all, being wholly inarticulate, but who showed it over and over again, with endless patience: he would turn in a dead-eye cutter-stay fashion ten times over, without a single word. They saw little of Mr Martin for the rest of the day, and sometimes it seemed that he was as eager as his pupils to abandon sines, tangents and secants: he was in fact arranging his very large collection of the Brazilian coleoptera, hastily gathered and only now revealing its full wealth of new species, new genera, and even new families. He and Stephen looked forward to several happy, tranquil months, classifying these creatures; although Stephen had not quite so great a passion for beetles, and although his duties (as well as his disinclination to miss any passing bird or whale) often called him away.

He had grown more and more dissatisfied with Higgins as a surgical assistant. The man was without any sort of doubt an excellent tooth-drawer, but he was deeply ignorant of physic and surgery, and not only ignorant but bold and rash. He also practised on the credulity of the foremast hands. There was something to be said for hocus-pocus, just as there was for placebos, but Higgins went far beyond what might be justified as useful to the patient; furthermore he was beginning to extract illicit fees (as well as eels, mice and earwigs) from those who were sick and from those who wished to malinger in the sick-bay for a while, taking their ease. Stephen therefore determined to look after all the patients himself, confining Higgins to their teeth; he knew that he would not entirely do away with the man's private or rather secret practice, sailors being what they were, but at least he could see that they were not poisoned, at least he could lock his more dangerous drugs away.

He saw the foremast-hands in the forenoon and then again when he made his rounds of the sick-bay, often accompanied by Jack, later in the day: the officers, on the other hand, usually made an appointment through the sickberth attendant, the loblolly-boy. Yet this was by no means invariable, particularly with his messmates in the gunroom, and Stephen was not at all surprised to hear a knock at his door some days out of Penedo – there were several commissioned or warranted stomachs still suffering from a surfeit of turtles and tropical fruit. But not at all: it was Mrs Horner, come at a moment when all hands were on deck, the *Surprise* having heaved to to speak a merchantman from the River Plate. When he suggested that he should examine her in the gunner's cabin with her husband present she declined; nor did she wish Mrs Lamb or the sergeant's wife to attend. Indeed no very prolonged or detailed examination was called for: Mrs Horner was pregnant, as she had known perfectly well since the last change of the moon. When Stephen told her so she said, 'Yes. And it was not Horner: you know about his trouble, Doctor; he told me so. It was not him, and when he finds out he will kill me. He is a terrible man. Unless I can get rid of it he will kill me.' In the long silence that followed she whispered, 'He will kill me,' to herself.

'I am very sorry for it,' said Stephen. 'I will not pretend not to know what you wish me to do: but it cannot be. I will do anything I can to help you, but not that. You must try to . . .' His invention failed; his voice died away and he was left looking at the ground, feeling all the weight of her bitter distress and of her present disappointment.

'I know him, yes,' said Mrs Horner in a dead voice. 'He will kill me.'

After some moments she regained at least an appearance of composure and stood up, smoothing her pinafore, looking pitifully young and ill. 'Before you go,' said Stephen,

'I must tell you two things: one is that any interference with the course of nature in these matters is extremely dangerous; and the other is that nature often interferes herself, since rather more than one pregnancy in ten ends in a natural miscarriage. I hope you will come to see me at least once a week; you may perhaps feel a little unwell, and the humours may have to be rectified.'

It was clear that she scarcely heard him, although she curtsied when he had finished speaking; and as she passed through the door she murmured to herself, 'He will kill me.'

'Perhaps he will, too,' thought Stephen some minutes later; he had gone on deck to shake off the painful impression of this interview and to hear what the merchantman had to say, and there only a few feet along the gangway from him stood the gunner, dark, angry, dangerous, liable to fly out for a nothing, a powerful man with long hanging arms.

Stephen was too late for anything but the parting civilities, exchanged over a quarter of a mile of heaving aquamarine sea all flecked with white as the ships filled on opposite tacks, but Pullings told him that the news was most disappointing: the *Norfolk* had not put into the River Plate, which might have allowed the hurrying *Surprise* to gain at least a few hundred miles, but had carried straight on. A Montevideo barque had spoken her in about forty degrees south, which almost certainly meant that she had increased her lead, having had fairer winds. 'Our only hope now,' he said, 'is meeting a ship that has seen her refitting at say Port Desire before tackling the Horn: otherwise we shall certainly have to follow her round. And God knows whether we shall ever find her.'

'But Mr Allen knows the haunts of the English whalers, and surely the *Norfolk*'s one function is to pursue them?'

'Yes, to be sure. But the fishery has spread far south and west these last years, and if we do not catch her along the coast in the waters the master knows, along

by Chile, Peru, the Galapagos, Mexico and California –
if she has sailed off westwards three thousand miles and
more, how are we ever to find her in all that sea? No
trade in those parts, no merchantmen to see her go by,
no port where we can hear news of her. It would call for
most uncommon luck: and luck is what we have not had
much of, this goddam voyage.'

Southward and still farther south, but never a ship did
they meet. Day after day, even week after week, the quiet
sea was empty clean round its rim, an enormous loneliness;
and all this time the winds were faint, capricious and sometimes foul: but above all faint. Three nights running Jack
had his recurrent dream of riding a horse that shrank and
dwindled until his feet touched the ground on either side
and people looked at him with strong disapproval, even
with contempt; and each time he woke up with the same
sense of sweating anxiety.

Imperceptibly the air grew colder, and the sea; and
every day the sun was at least a degree farther from the
zenith at the noon observation. By now the young gentlemen could all take its altitude with tolerable proficiency;
Jack looked at their daily workings of the ship's position
south of the Line and west of Greenwich with real satisfaction, and sometimes he would call them in to hear part
of a Latin ode (at present they were slowly mangling poor
Horace) or the declension of a noun in Greek. 'If they are
all drowned tomorrow,' he remarked to Stephen, 'their
fathers cannot say I han't done my duty by them. When
I was a squeaker nobody gave a tinker's curse whether my
daily workings were right or wrong, and as for dashing
away in Latin and Greek . . .' He also fed them almost
daily, turn and turn about, often asking the youngster of
the morning watch to breakfast with him and another or
sometimes two to dine.

During this long slow passage there was time, ample
time, for the usual invitations to resume their steady
sequence and even to grow somewhat monotonous: the
Captain dining with his officers in the gunroom, the

members of the gunroom dining in the cabin by rotation, and the midshipmen by ones and twos with both. And the farther south the ship travelled the poorer grew the fare: both cooks did their best, but private stores were running low and although Pontius Pilate, the gunroom cock, still crowed every morning when the coops were carried up on to the quarterdeck, and although his hens still laid the occasional egg, while goat Aspasia provided milk for the cabin's holy coffee, the last sheep died a little south of the fortieth parallel – it had been shorn, nay shaved, for its own good under the equator and was now unable to endure the increasing cold – and salt pork took its place on the Captain's table on a day when the chaplain was dining with him. Jack apologized for the change, since the invitation had been 'to share his mutton' but Martin said, 'Not at all, not at all; this is the best salt pork I have ever eaten – such a very subtle combination of East India spices – yet even if it had been black penitential gruel it would still have been a feast. This morning, sir, at half past eight, I saw my first penguin! A jackass penguin, as the Doctor assures me, swimming with extraordinary speed and grace hard by the ship, flying, as it were, in the element!'

The *Surprise* was in fact on the edge of the waters where the Pacific, the Atlantic and the Indian oceans run round the world in a continuous stream common to a large number of far southern animals; the sea had quite abruptly changed its colour, temperature and even character and although it was perhaps a little too early to hope for the larger albatrosses there was a strong likelihood of mallemawks, blue petrels, whale-birds and of course many more penguins. The day after this change both he and Stephen left their warm cots as soon as they heard the familiar grinding of holystones on the deck far above their heads – a sound that was felt rather than heard, coming as a vibration through the timbers and the taut cordage – and made their way to the gunroom, where the steward gave them each a bowl of hot burgoo, a kind of liquid porridge. By this time – for Martin had washed and even shaved by the light of a purser's dip – a faint grey was showing in the east, and Honey came below, bare-footed and red legged from the cold and streaming deck, to put on his shoes and stockings in the warmth. He told them that the worst of the wet would be gone, swabbed away, in five minutes, and that the night's drizzle had lifted: 'Wind at north-east and a following sea. But it is precious cold still: will you not wait until after breakfast? It will be stockfish, judging by the smell of glue.'

No, they said, they preferred to be in the open before hammocks were piped up and stuffed into those things along the sides, sadly obstructing the view. They would go upstairs in five minutes, as soon as the decks were reasonably . . .

'Oh sir, oh sir,' cried Calamy, running barefoot down. 'A huge great enormous whale – he is just alongside.'

Alongside he was, and vast he was: a sperm whale with his great blunt squared-off head abreast of the forechains, his dark body streaming aft far along the quarterdeck, perhaps seventy-five or even eighty feet of massive creature, giving such an impression of tranquil strength the ship seemed frail beside him. He lay with the upper part of his head and the whole uneven length of his back awash, and he blew: a thick white jet that spouted up and forward while a man could count three. Then after a slight pause he deliberately sunk his head for twice that time; raised it and blew again, breathed and blew, breathed and blew, all the while keeping alongside the ship with a slight rippling motion of that huge broad horizontal tail. He was a biscuit-toss away in the grey transparent water; he could be seen above it and below; and they watched him entranced, all silent along the rail.

'That is one of your old eighty-barrel bulls,' said the master at Stephen's elbow. 'Maybe ninety. The kind we call schoolmasters, though they are usually alone.'

'He does not seem at all alarmed,' whispered Stephen.

'No. I dare say he is deaf. I have known old ones

181

deaf, aye, and blind of both eyes too, though they seemed
to manage very well. Yet perhaps it is the company he
likes; they seem to do so sometimes, the lonely ones;
like dolphins. He will be going down any minute now;
he has pretty well had his spoutings out, and . . .' The
very shocking report of a musket in the silence cut him
short. Darting a glance along the rail Stephen saw the
Marine officer, still in his night-cap, with the smoking
gun in his hands and a great fool's laugh upon his face.
The whale's head plunged in a boil of water, his huge back
arching and the tail coming clear, poised there above the
surface for an instant of time before it vanished straight
downwards.

Stephen looked forward to keep his extreme anger
from showing, and on the gangway he saw a most unusual
sight for this time of day, or any other for that matter:
Mrs Lamb the carpenter's wife. She had been waiting for
the silence to end and now she hurried towards him. 'Oh
Doctor, if you please, can you come at once? Mrs Horner
is took poorly.'

Poorly indeed, doubled up in her cot, her face yellow
and sweating, her hair draggled about her cheeks and she
holding her breath for the extremity of pain. The gunner
stood there, distraught in a corner: the sergeant's wife
knelt by the bed saying, 'There, there, my dear, there,
there.' Mrs Horner had been far from Stephen's mind
that morning but the moment he walked into the cabin
he was as certain of what had happened as if she had told
him: she had procured an abortion; Mrs Lamb knew it;
the others did not, and between her fits of convulsive
agony Mrs Horner's one concern was to get them out of
the room.

'I must have light and air, two basins of hot water
and several towels,' he said in an authoritative voice.
'Mrs Lamb will help me. There is no room for more.'

Having made a rapid inspection and dealt with the
immediate problems he hurried down to the medicine-
chest. On his way, far below, he met his assistant, and

182

as there was no escape Higgins stood aside to let him pass; but Stephen took him by the elbow, led him under a grating so that some light fell on his face, and said, 'Mr Higgins, Mr Higgins, you will hang for this, if I do not save her. You are a rash wicked bungling ignorant murderous fool.' Higgins was not without bounce, confidence and resource when put to his shifts, but there was such a contained reptilian ferocity in Stephen's pale eye that now he only bowed his head, making no sort of answer.

A little later in the empty sick-bay, one of the few places in the ship where it was possible to speak without being overheard, Stephen saw the gunner, who asked him what the trouble was – what was the nature of the disease?

'It is a female disorder,' said Stephen, 'and not uncommon; but I am afraid this time it is very bad. Our great hope is the resilience of youth – how old is Mrs Horner?'

'Nineteen.'

'Yet even so you should prepare your mind: she may overcome the fever, but she may not.'

'It is not along of me?' asked the gunner in a low voice. 'It is not along of my you know what?'

'No,' said Stephen. 'It has nothing to do with you.' He looked at Horner's dark, savage face: 'Is there attachment there?' he wondered. 'Affection? Any kind of tenderness? Or only pride and concern for property?' He could not be sure; but early the next morning, when he had to tell the gunner that his wife had made no improvement at all, he had the feeling that the man's chief emotion, now that the first shock and dismay were over, was anger – anger against the world in general and anger against her too, for being ill. It did not surprise him very much: in the course of his professional career by land he had seen many and many a husband, and even some lovers, angry at a woman's sickness, impatient, full of blame: quite devoid of pity, and angry that it should be expected of them.

It was a slow dawn, with showers drifting across the

sea from the north-east; and as the light grew and the veil of rain in the south-west parted the lookout bawled, 'On deck, there. Sail on the starboard bow.'

Part of the cry reached Jack in the cabin as he was raising his first cup of coffee. He clapped it back on to the table, spilling half, and ran on deck. 'Masthead,' he called. 'Where away?'

'Can't make out nothing now, sir,' said the masthead. 'She was maybe a point on the starboard bow, hull up. Close-hauled on the larboard tack, I believe.'

'Put it on, sir,' cried Killick angrily, hurrying after him and holding out a watchcoat with a hood, a Magellan jacket. 'Put it on. Which I run it up a-purpose, ain't I? Labouring all the bleeding night, stitch, stitch, snip, snip,' – this in a discontented mutter.

'Thankee Killick,' said Jack absently, drawing the hood over his bare head. Then loud and clear, 'Hands to make sail. Topgallants and weather studdingsails.'

No more was needed. At the word the *Surprise*'s topmen raced aloft, the shrouds on either side black with men: a few cutting notes on the bosun's pipes and the sails flashed out – let fall, sheeted home, hoisted, trimmed and drawing with extraordinary rapidity. And as the *Surprise* leapt forward, her bow-wave rising fast, the lookout hailed again: the sail was there, but she had worn; she was now heading due south.

'Mr Blakeney,' said Jack to a youngster, rain-soaked but glowing pink with excitement, 'jump up to the fore-jack with a glass and tell me what you see.'

Yes, she had worn, came down the cry: Mr Blakeney could see her wake. She was going large.

Even from the quarterdeck Jack and all the rest crowding the lee-rail could see her looming far over there in the greyness, but as a pale blur, no more. 'Can you make out a crow's nest?' he asked.

'No, sir,' after a long, searching minute. 'I am sure there ain't one.'

All the officers smiled at the same moment. In these

waters any strange sail would almost certainly be a whaler or a man-of-war: but no whaler ever put to sea without a crow's nest; it was an essential and most conspicuous part of her equipment. A man-of-war, then; conceivably the *Norfolk* too had met with some accident or with very dirty weather; conceivably she had had to refit in some desolate far southern inlet; conceivably that was their quarry, just a few miles to leeward.

'On deck, there,' said the first lookout in a glum dissatisfied tone, though enormously loud, 'She's only a brig.'

The happy tension dropped at once. Of course, of course there was the packet too, the brig *Danaë*: the recollection came flooding back immediately. She too must have made extraordinarily poor progress, to be no farther on her way than this. Of course she had spun on her heel, and of course she would run as fast as ever she could until she knew who the *Surprise* might prove to be.

'Well damn her,' said Jack to Pullings. 'We shall speak her presently, no doubt. Let us hoist the short pennant with the colours as soon as they can be seen. But no sooner: there is no point in wasting valuable bunting on the desert air.' With this he returned to his coffee: and learning that Dr Maturin was engaged with a patient he moved on from his coffee to a solitary breakfast.

But there was something odd about the *Danaë*. Obviously she did not trust the *Surprise*'s colours at first sight, and it was her plain duty not to trust them; but it was strange that she should not make a satisfactory, undeniable response to the private signal either, although by now the day was reasonably clear. And it was stranger still that she kept hauling her wind a trifle, as though to get the weather-gage, while at long intervals obscure signals ran up to her mizen-peak. She was a very fast sailer indeed, as would be expected in a packet, and at present, by carrying a great press of canvas, she was drawing away from the *Surprise*.

Pullings sent to the cabin to say that he did not care

for the present appearance of things and Jack returned to the deck. He surveyed her, a piece of toast in his hand, and considered. She had made her number correctly, she was flying the right colours, and now she had broken out the signal 'Carrying dispatches' which meant that she must neither stop nor be stopped. Yet there was still that dubious private signal: it had never showed plainly, being hauled down before the entire hoist flew clear. 'Repeat it,' he said, 'And give her a windward gun.'

He put his toast carefully down on a carronade-slide and watched the *Danaë* through Mowett's telescope. Hesitation aboard her; bungling; the hoist going up and down again; the halliard jamming; and once again the essential flags vanished before the whole had been distinctly seen. He had used all these capers himself, many and many a time, to gain a few valuable minutes in a chase. In a vessel that sailed so well as the *Danaë* they were not at all convincing: they should have been combined with some wild steering, some reef-points or gaskets flying free. No, no: it would not do. She had been taken: she was in enemy hands and she meant to get away if ever she could.

Jack reflected for a moment upon the force of the breeze, the current, the bearing of the packet, and said 'Let the hands go to breakfast, and then we will turn to. If she is what I think she is, and if we catch her, you shall take her home.'

'Thank you, sir,' said Pullings, his face a great grin. From the professional point of view nothing could suit him better. There would not be the glory of a battle – the packet's armament could not possibly compete with the frigate's and would certainly not come into action – but that did not signify, since the glory always went to the credit of the captain and the first lieutenant: for a volunteer, bringing in a valuable recaptured prize would be a more evident, noteworthy testimony of his zeal, and of his good luck too, by no means a negligible quality when it came to employment.

'She will take some catching, though,' said Jack,

looking at her under his shading hand. 'You might let the Doctor know. He loves a good chase.'

'Where is the Doctor?' he asked some time later, when the *Surprise* was tearing away southwards under a perfectly astonishing show of sail with the wind on her quarter.

'Well, sir,' said Pullings. 'It seems he was up all night – the gunner's wife taken ill – and now he and the chaplain are at peace by the gunroom stove at last, spreading out their beetles. But he says that if he is given a direct order to come and enjoy himself in the cold driving rain if not sleet too as well as a tempest of wind he will of course be delighted to obey.'

Jack could easily imagine the rapid flow, the fluent run of bitter and often mutinous expressions that Pullings did not see fit to pass on. He said, 'I must ask Killick to make him a Magellan jacket too: his servant is no hand with a needle. The gunner's wife, you said? Poor woman. I dare say she had eaten something. But she could not be in better hands. You remember how he roused out Mr Day's brains on the quarterdeck of the old *Sophie*, and set them to rights directly? Forward, there: come up the forestaysail sheet half a fathom.'

The *Surprise* was now wholly given over to her chase. This was something that she, her captain and her people could do supremely well; they worked together in perfect harmony, with rarely an order needed, taking advantage of every run of the sea, every shift in the breeze, jibs and staysails continually on the move, the braces perpetually manned by keenly attentive hands. The Surprises had always dearly loved a prize; they had had more experience of taking them than most and their appetite had grown with each successive merchant ship, man-of-war or recapture, and now all the piratical side of their character was in full, intensely eager play. And though it might seem that nothing could add to the combined effect of the hunting instinct and the very strong desire of something for nothing, in this case there was also a hearty wish to do well by Captain Pullings: for Jack's promise had of course been overheard. He was very much liked aboard, and with this extra spur the men flung themselves into their work with an even greater zeal, so that although the *Danaë* was so fast and well handled that with her five miles start she might reasonably have hoped to keep ahead until the night gave her shelter, the pale sun was still well above the horizon when she was obliged to heave to and lie there with backed topsails under the frigate's lee.

'Tell the Doctor that he must come on deck and enjoy himself now whether he likes it or not,' said Jack: and when Stephen appeared, 'This is the packet we were told about. But the *Norfolk* must have taken her, since she is manned with a prize crew. This is the American officer coming across now. Have you any observations to make?'

'May we perhaps confer once you have seen him?' asked Stephen, who had no observations to make in public. 'I am happy that you should have recaptured it without any gunfire; I had no notion that the chase was going so well. Mr Martin and I had anticipated a great deal of banging and running up and down before the end.' He looked across at the *Danaë*: the smaller group of men on her forecastle slapping one another on the shoulder and calling out to the grinning Surprises were obviously prisoners who had now found a most unexpected freedom; the others, in the waist, looking desperately low and dispirited and very tired from their day-long heaving and hauling, making sail and reducing it again, were clearly her regular crew. Their captain, a youngish lieutenant, put the best face he could on it as he came up the side, saluted the quarterdeck and offered Jack his sword. 'No, sir, you must keep it,' said Jack, shaking his head. 'Upon my word, you led us an elegant dance of it.'

'I believe we might have run clear,' said the lieutenant, 'if we had not lost so much canvas south of the Horn and if we had had a heavier, more willing crew. But at least we have the satisfaction of having been taken by a famous flyer.'

'I dare say we could both do with some refreshment,' said Jack, leading him towards the cabin; and over his shoulder, 'Captain Pullings, carry on.'

Captain Pullings carried on with great effect, bringing the packet as close as she could lie so that the transfer might take place before the fading of the day and the almost certain coming of dirty weather; and for a while, before returning to their hanging stove, Stephen and Martin watched the boats going to and fro on the increasing swell, taking Surprises and Marines over and bringing back the former prisoners and the Americans, together with a long-legged midshipman and the *Danaë*'s books and papers.

'Here are her papers,' said Captain Aubrey when Stephen came for his conference. 'They do not tell us much, of course, since the English log stops when she was captured and the rest is just a bald account of her course and the weather since then: damned unpleasant weather, most of it. But the prisoners, and by that I mean the people that were captured and drafted into the *Danaë* to sail her, were more informative. Since they were taken this side of the Horn, like the packet, they do not know for a fact that the *Norfolk* is in the Pacific yet, but they do know that she took two of our homeward-bound whalers in the South Atlantic, one of them a ship that had been out more than three years and that had filled every barrel she possessed. But here is my draft of the official letter Tom Pullings will carry back with him. It will tell you the whole thing in a moment, and perhaps you would put in some style, just here and there, where you think it might fit.'

Stephen glanced at the familiar opening

Surprise at sea
(wind N by E with moderate
weather)
49°35'S., 63°11'W.

My Lord,
 I have the honour to acquaint your Lordship
that in . . .

and said, 'Listen, before I read it, tell me one thing,
will you now? Suppose there were treasure aboard that
packet, would it be safer with us or with Tom?'

'Oh, as for the treasure, I am afraid the *Norfolk* snapped
that up directly. Two iron chests full of gold, God love
us! You would hardly expect them to leave it lying about:
I am sure I should not have done so, ha, ha, ha!'

'Let it be supposed that there are documents, valuable
documents concealed in her fabric,' said Stephen patient-
ly, still in the same low tone of voice, his chair pulled up
to Jack's, 'Would they be more liable to loss with him or
with us?'

Jack cocked a considering eye at him and said, 'The
privateers are the trouble. In that craft Tom can outsail
most men-of-war except in very heavy weather, but he
will have to run the gauntlet of the privateers from the
West Indies on, both French and American. Some of them
are very fast, and he will only have a few pop-guns and
muskets and precious few men to handle them. He does
not run a very grave risk, there being such a prodigious
quantity of salt water, but even so I should say that your
hypothetical papers would be safer with us.'

'Then before it grows dark would you have the kindness
to go across into the packet with me, into the room where
the chests were found itself?'

'Very well,' said Jack. 'I wish to see her in any
case. Should we take a bag?'

'I believe not,' said Stephen, 'but an accurate yardstick
might be wise.'

His mind was uneasy. Money always had an unhealthy
effect on intelligence, often confusing the issue; and it

190

could sometimes prove a very dangerous substance to handle. He did not like the way he had been told about the hiding-place in the *Danaë*: a recollection of the letters in which Sir Joseph had told him of the murky, troubled atmosphere in London made him like it even less, and in these altered circumstances he was tempted to leave the whole thing alone. The instructions did not cover the present situation and whatever he did might turn out to be wrong. Yet if he did nothing and the packet were taken he would look an incompetent fool: or worse. But what if he found the cache empty? What if the rats had got at the papers? What if the captured Mr Cunningham was himself kin to the rats?

These thoughts ran through and through his head as he poked about under a long recess in the side of the cabin once inhabited by Mr Cunningham and his chests – the holes for the screws that had held them down were still to be seen – and it was not without a certain relief that he turned to Jack at last, saying, 'The mad brute-beasts have given me the wrong direction, so they have. There is nothing here. Perhaps it is just as well.'

'Should you like me to look at the paper?' asked Jack.

'By all means. But it is as plain as can be. "Press the third bolt-head under the larboard shelf-piece three foot nine inches from the bulkhead." '

'Stephen,' said Jack, 'I believe that is the starboard shelf-piece you are looking at.'

'Oh your soul to the devil, Jack,' cried Stephen. 'This is my left hand, is it not?' – holding it up – 'And what is on the left or unlucky or indeed sinister side is the larboard.'

'You are forgetting that we have turned about,' said Jack. 'We are now facing aft, you know. The third bolt-head, did you say?' He pressed, and instantly and with a surprisingly loud crash a metal box fell from the seam, striking the deck with one corner and bursting open. He bent to pick up scattered sheaves of bank-notes and other papers, putting his lantern down, and at the sight of the first he cried, 'God love us! What can – ' But recollecting himself he gathered the bundles together in silence and handed them to Stephen, who gave them a cursory glance, shook his head with a worried, dissatisfied air, and put them back into their box. 'The best thing I can do is to seal this at once, and give it to you to keep in a safe place. Perhaps you had better carry it back to the *Surprise* yourself: I have slipped into the water from a boat before this.'

In the great cabin once more Stephen melted the wax, pressed his curiously engraved watch-key upon it, and handed the box over together with a small piece of paper, saying, 'This slip shows the proper recipient, if any accident should happen to me.'

'It is a damned heavy responsibility,' said Jack gravely, taking it.

'There are heavier by far, my dear,' said Stephen. 'I must be away for my rounds.'

'That reminds me,' said Jack. 'I see that the gunner's wife is on your sick-list. I hope she is better by now?'

'Better? She is not,' said Stephen emphatically.

'I am sorry for it,' said Jack. 'Would a visit be in order, or one of the chickens, or a bottle of port-wine? Or perhaps all three?'

'Listen,' said Stephen, 'I do not know that she will live.'

'Oh Lord,' cried Jack, 'I had no idea – I am extremely concerned – I hope there is something you can do for her?'

'As for that,' said Stephen, 'I set nearly all my trust in the resilience of youth. She is no more than nineteen, poor child, and at nineteen one can support hell and purgatory almost, and live. Tell me, Tom Pullings will not be leaving us at once?'

'No. He keeps company until the morning. I have a great deal of paper-work to do.'

'I must write at least one letter too,' said Stephen. 'And if I possibly can I will come and help you with the captured mail,' he added, knowing Jack's extreme reluctance to read other people's correspondence, even though it might contain priceless information. 'We shall have a busy night of it.'

A busy night and a sleepless one, but in the course of it they found one letter written by an officer named Caleb Gill which gave a clear statement of the *Norfolk*'s intended movements as far as the Galapagos archipelago: from that point she was to steer westward 'to my uncle Palmer's particular Paradise, for which we have a band of colonists, who wish to be as far away from their countrymen as possible.' Uncle Palmer was obviously the captain of the *Norfolk*, and his particular Paradise might be anywhere in the South Seas; but by comparing dates and positions and what the whalers said about the *Norfolk*'s sailing qualities, Jack was reasonably confident that he should come up with her well before the Galapagos, probably at the island of Juan Fernandez, where she meant to wood and water, or in the neighbourhood of Valparaiso, where she meant to refit; and Stephen would have been quite cheerful if it had not been for two patients who weighed upon his mind, the one his old friend Joe Plaice, who had brought his head against a ring-bolt in a commonplace fall down a ladder, fracturing his skull, and the other Mrs Horner, who was not responding to his treatment in any way.

'It astonishes me that our seamen can move straight from one ship to another and sail it off with no practice,' said Martin as they stood watching the *Danaë* part company, turning in a long pure curve until her head was pointing north-north-east while the *Surprise* carried on to the west of south.

'The complexity of rigging is much the same in all, I am told,' said Stephen. 'Just as we see a clear analogy between the skeletons of vertebrates, so the mariner with his boats. In a brig I believe some ropes run forward while on a three-masted ship they run backwards, yet this is no more a source of confusion for the seaman than the ruminant's multiplicity of stomachs for the anatomist, or the howler's anomalous hyoid. Yet what I wished to say was this: I know it was your kindly intention to visit the gunner's wife, but in her present state of mental agitation and extreme physical distress I really think I should beg you not to do so until there is some improvement: I have already banished her husband. On the other hand, I should be glad of your assistance in a tolerably delicate operation as soon as there is light enough: a depressed fracture. I must trepan poor Plaice and I should like to do so today; they tell me there is dirty weather ahead, and clearly one needs a steady deck underfoot and an immobile patient. I have an improved Lavoisier's trephine, a magnificent instrument with extraordinary biting power; and if you choose, you shall turn the handle!'

The *Surprise*'s crew, like most seamen, were a hypochondriacal set of ghouls upon the whole, and they loved a surgical operation almost as much as they loved a prize. But whereas the amputation of a shipmate's arm or leg had disadvantages of which they were fully sensible, a trepanning had none: the patient had but to survive to have all his former powers restored – to be as good as new, with the glory of a silver plate and an anecdote that would last him and his friends to the grave.

It was an operation that Dr Maturin had carried out at sea before, always in the fullest possible light and therefore on deck, and many of them had seen him do so. Now they and all their mates saw him do it again: they saw Joe Plaice's scalp taken off, his skull bared, a disc of bone audibly sawn out, the handle turning solemnly; a three-shilling piece, hammered into a flattened dome by the armourer, screwed on over the hole; and the scalp replaced, neatly sewn up by the parson.

It was extremely gratifying – the Captain had been seen to go pale, and Barret Bonden too, the patient's cousin – blood running down Joe's neck regardless – brains clearly to be seen – something not to be missed for a mint of money – instructive, too – and they made the most of it. This was just as well, because it was the last gratification they had for a very long while: in some cases the last they ever had. The dirty weather, foretold by the long heavy swell from the south and west, the dropping glass and the most forbidding sky, struck them even sooner and even harder than they had expected.

Yet the *Surprise* was a well-found, weatherly ship, and she rigged preventer backstays, braces, shrouds, and of course stays throughout, as well as rolling tackles, a full suit of storm-canvas bent well in time and her topgallant masts struck down on deck. Although the gale was very heavy indeed, filled with blinding rain and sleet, and although at first it blew against the swell and cut up a wicked sea, it was not foul, and the frigate, under close-reefed topsails, raced south at a tremendous pace, half smothered in flying water, shipping green seas every other minute, so that her decks were aswim and men could never move without clinging to the life-lines stretching fore and aft.

Two days and three nights it blew, the storm-wrack as low as the mastheads, but the third day it cleared and they had a good noon observation: to his great pleasure Jack found that they were farther south than he had expected − farther south than their dead-reckoning allowed − and that they were within striking distance of Staten Island.

He and Allen had a long conference, with the charts spread out before them, charts that gave different longitudes for a good many awkward islands, reefs and headlands; and all the while they talked the decks as far aft as the taffrail were aflutter with sea-soaked clothes attempting to dry in the pale evening sun. Jack questioned the master again and again about Captain Colnett's accuracy, and again and again the master affirmed that he would take his Gospel oath on it. 'He was Captain Cook's pupil, sir, and he carried a pair of Arnold's chronometers: they lasted him all the way, always wound, never once stopping, right by observation to within ten seconds, until we were pooped south of St Helena, homeward bound.'

'A pair of Arnold's chronometers? Very well then, Mr Allen,' said Jack, satisfied at last, 'let us set course for Cape St John. And as you go forward, pray tell the Doctor that I shall be able to accompany him on his rounds this evening.'

'Well, Stephen,' he said, when the Doctor came to fetch him, 'you have a thundering long great sick-list today, I see.'

'The usual strained articulations, crushed fingers, broken bones,' said Stephen. 'I tell them, "You must have one hand for the ship, and another for yourself; and you must throw your nasty grog into the scuppers, if you are to go aloft within two hours," but they do not attend. They leap about the rigging, encouraged by the bosun, as though they were octopodes, with prehensile tails into the bargain; so of course every time there is a tempest my sick-bay fills.'

'Of course. But tell me about Mrs Horner: I thought of her often when we rolled and pitched to such an extent.'

'She was unaware of it at the time, being delirious, but in any case the hanging cot is wonderfully adapted for patients at sea. I believe I may say that she has overcome her fever – I shaved her head – and that although there is a high degree of debility the youthful resilience of which I spoke may pull her through: it may perhaps pull her through, with the blessing.'

Jack Aubrey saw very little sign of resilience when he was led without warning into the gunner's cabin, or of youth; and if it had not been for Stephen's words he would have said that her grey face, her immense dark-circled eyes, showed the marks of death. Mrs Horner had just enough strength to snatch up a scarf and wrap it round her bald head, casting a reproachful glance at Stephen as she did so, and to murmur, 'Thank you, sir,' when Jack told her that he was delighted to see her looking so much better, and that she must make haste to be quite well again for the sake of the youngsters, who missed her sadly, and of course for Mr Horner. He was about to say something about 'Juan Fernandez restoring the roses to her cheeks' when he noticed that Stephen had laid his finger to his lips, and realized that in his embarrassment he had been addressing Mrs Horner as though she were a ship some considerable distance to windward.

196

He felt much happier in the sick-bay, where he knew exactly what to say to each man and boy – the boy being one of his youngsters, John Nesbit, with a broken collarbone – and in his relief he said to Plaice, 'Well, Plaice, at least some good has come out of this: at least nobody will ever be able to say, "Poor old Plaice is down to his last shilling." '

'How do you make that out, sir?' asked Plaice, closing one eye and smiling in anticipation.

'Why, because there are three of 'em screwed to your head, ha, ha, ha!' said his Captain.

'You are not unlike Shakespeare,' observed Stephen, as they walked back to the cabin.

'So I am often told by those who read my letters and dispatches,' said Jack, 'but what makes you say so at this particular moment?'

'Because his clowns make quips of that bludgeoning, knock-me-down nature. You have only to add *marry, come up*, or *go to, with a pox on it*, and it is pure Gammon, or Bacon, or what you will.'

'That is only your jealousy,' said Jack. 'What do you say to some music tonight?'

'I should like it extremely. I shall not play well, being quite *fagged out*, as our American captive says.'

'But Stephen, we say fagged out too.'

'Do we? I was not aware. Still, at all events we do not say it with that touching colonial twang, like a cockle-woman's horn on Dublin Quay. He is close kin to that most amiable Captain Lawrence we met in Boston, I find.'

'Yes, the same that captured Mowett in the *Peacock* and was so good to him. I mean to pay the young fellow every attention in my power: I have asked him and his midshipman to dinner tomorrow. Stephen, you will not mind doing without our usual toasted cheese? There is only just enough to make a presentable dish for my guests.'

They played without cheese; they played far into the night, until Stephen's head bowed over his 'cello between two movements: he excused himself and crept off, still half asleep. Jack called for a glass of grog, drank it up, put on a comforter knitted by his wife, still full of warmth and love though somewhat mangled by Brazilian mice, and his Magellan jacket and went on deck. It was a little after seven bells in the first watch, a drizzling night; and Maitland had the deck. As soon as his eyes were used to the darkness Jack looked at the log- and traverse-boards. The *Surprise* had kept exactly to her course, but she had been travelling rather faster than he had expected. Somewhere out there in the darkness to leeward was Staten Island: he had seen engravings of its ironbound coast in Anson's Voyage and he had no wish to come up against it, no wish to be whirled about in the strong currents and furious tides that swept round the tip of South America and through the Straits Lemaire. 'Clew up the forecourse and pass along the deep-sea line,' he said.

A few minutes later there began the steady ritual of taking soundings: the splash of the heavy lead far forward, the cry of 'Watch, there, watch,' coming aft as each of the men along the side let go the last of his coils of deep-sea line, until it reached the quartermaster in the mizen-chains, who reported the depth to the midshipman of the watch and called, 'Ready along,' whereupon the lead passed forward and the sequence began again.

'Belay,' said Jack as eight bells struck and the pink, sleepy larbowlins and the master relieved the midnight deck. 'Good night to you, Mr Maitland. Mr Allen, I believe we should be off Cape St John. We have a little over a hundred fathom, gently shoaling. What do you say to that?'

'Why, sir,' said the master, 'I think we should arm the lead and go on casting until we strike say ninety fathom with white shelly ground.'

One bell: two bells. And then, 'Ninety-five fathom and white shelly sand, sir,' said the quartermaster at last, holding the lead to the lantern, and with a strong feeling of relief Jack gave orders to haul to the wind. With the

Surprise sailing away from that vile thing a lee-shore, but still heading south, he could go below and sleep in peace.

He was on deck again at first light: a clear day, with the wind freshening and blowing in strange, uneasy gusts, a troubled sea and sky, following no coherent pattern, but no land to leeward, no land at all. The master, having had the middle watch, ought to have been asleep, but he was not, and together they laid a course that should take the ship round the Horn with no great offing – just enough to allow their minds to rest easy yet at the same time to profit from the variable inshore winds, which were blowing at present from the north and north-east, as favourable as could be.

They were profiting from them still as the guests in the cabin finished the very last of Jack's cheese, watched by a disapproving Killick and his coal-black mate: disapproval on a black face, ordinarily lit by a white smile, is disapproval indeed. It had not been an easy party; the circumstances were obviously very much against convivial merriment in the first place, and then again the sanguine, readily-pleased, conversible Jack that his friends knew was a very different person from the tall, imposing, splendidly-uniformed Captain Aubrey, his face moulded by years of nearly absolute authority, who received the two much younger Americans – far more different than he had supposed. It was therefore with a general, though decently concealed, sense of release that they parted, the prisoners to return to the gunroom with Mowett and Martin, their fellow guests, and Jack to walk on the quarterdeck.

There he found that the *Surprise* was holding her course, though from the look of the sky it was unlikely that she should hold it very much longer. The master was also on deck, and from time to time he swept the horizon from the starboard bow to the beam with his telescope; there were several others with him, for word had gone round that the Horn itself might appear about this time if the sky stayed clear.

No false word either: Jack, pacing up and down
the seventeen yards of his quarterdeck, had not travelled
above three furlongs of the three miles that Stephen
insisted upon to control what he termed the Captain's
gross obesity, before the lookout gave the cry of land.
Maitland, Howard and all the valid youngsters ran up
to the maintop to see, and presently it was in sight from
the deck, not so much land as the world's grim end, a tall
blackness on the rim of the sea that continually flashed
white as the rollers broke at its foot and dashed far up
the towering rock.

More people came on deck, including the doctor
and parson. 'How very like landsmen they look, poor
fellows,' thought Jack, shaking his head kindly. He called
them over, assured them that it was indeed Cape Horn
and showed it to them through his telescope. Martin was
absolutely delighted. Staring at the far deadly precipice
with the foam surging up it to a preposterous height he
said, 'So that spray, that breaking water, is the Pacific!'

'Some call it the Great South Sea,' said Jack, 'not
allowing it to be really Pacific until the fortieth parallel;
but it is all equally wet, I believe.'

'At all events, sir,' said Martin, 'what lies beyond is the
far side of the world, another ocean, another hemisphere,
what joy!'

Stephen said, 'Why are all the people so very earnest
to double it today?'

'Because they fear the weather may change,' said
Jack. 'This is west-wind country, as you remember
very well from our trip in the *Leopard*; but if once
we can slip round the Horn, slip round Diego Ramirez,
and gain a few degrees onward, the west wind may blow
great guns if it likes – we can still bear away for the Chile
coast – we shall still have rounded the corner. But before
we get round, do you see, a south-west or even a strong
west wind would quite bar our way. We fairly dread a
south-west wind at this point.'

The sun sank behind a bank of purple cloud. The

breeze entirely died. Between the changing from one wind to another the Cape Horn current seized the ship and carried her fast eastwards; and at the beginning of the graveyard watch the south-west wind came in with a shriek.

The shriek rarely lessened in the days and weeks that followed. Sometimes it rose to a maniac pitch that threatened the masts themselves, but it never dropped below a level that in ordinary times would have been thought uncommonly severe, though now it was soon taken as a matter of course.

For the first three days Jack fought as hard as he could to preserve all that could be preserved of his precious westing, flanking across the wind right down into the sixties, where the people suffered cruelly from the ice on deck, ice on the rigging, ice on the yards, the sailcloth board-hard with frozen flying spray, and the cordage seizing in the blocks. South and still farther south in spite of the danger of ice, of the mortal collision with an iceberg in the night, south in the hope of a change; but when it came the change was for the worse: the full west wind strengthened, the enormous rollers sweeping eastwards grew more monstrous still, their white, wind-torn crests a quarter of a mile apart with a deep grey-green valley between, and the *Surprise* could do no more than lie to at the best, while for one wholly outrageous day when the entire surface of the sea – mountainous waves, valleys and all – was a flying mixture of air and fragmented water and she was obliged to scud under a goose-winged foretopsail, losing an enormous distance. Each hour of that nightmare scudding meant a day of laborious beating into the wind to regain the westing lost; and although the *Surprise* and most of her people were used to the tremendous seas of the high southern latitudes, the notorious forties and the far worse fifties, they were not used to sailing or trying to sail against them. The scale of the rollers was so vast that the frigate, opposing them, behaved more like a skiff; although she was forty yards long she could not possibly

201

span two, and hers was a violently pitching, switchback path.

This very nearly caused the end of Dr Maturin. He was about to go below – reluctantly, for there were no less than seven albatrosses about the ship – when he noticed the bosun's cat washing itself on the second step: ever since it had learnt that it was not to be starved, ill-treated, flung overboard, it had abandoned all its pretty, caressing ways; it now gave him an insolent stare and went on washing. 'That is the most pretentious cat I have ever known,' he said angrily, stepping high to tread over it. The cat gave a sideways spring and at the same moment the *Surprise* ran her bows into the advancing green wall of a roller, pointed her bowsprit at the sky and flung the already unbalanced Stephen forward. Unhappily a grating in the deck below was open and he fell a great way on to a heap of coals about to be whipped up for the hanging stoves.

Nothing was broken, but he was miserably bruised, shaken, battered, strained; and this happened at a most unfortunate time. That same evening, in a lull between two storms of sleet that came driving horizontally with the force of bird-shot, Jack gave orders to hand the fore and main topsails. The two watches were on deck and they manned the clewlines, buntlines and sheets of both together; and in both cases the clewlines and buntlines parted, almost at the same moment. Since the sheets were half-flown the sails instantly split at the seams, the maintopsail shaking so furiously that the masthead must have gone had not Mowett, the bosun, Bonden, Warley the captain of the maintop and three of his men gone aloft, laid out on the ice-coated yard and cut the sail away close to the reefs. Warley was on the lee yardarm when the footrope gave way under him and he fell, plunging far clear of the side and instantly vanishing in the terrible sea. At the same time the foretopsail beat entirely to pieces, while the maincourse blew free, billowing out with horrible strength, destroying right and left. They lowered the yard a-portlast, striving harder one would have said than it was possible for men to strive, often waist-deep in swirling water; then they lowered the foreyard too, and set about securing the boats on the booms, which were on the point of breaking loose, the *Surprise* all this time lying to under a mizen. They succeeded in the end, and then they began knotting and splicing the damaged rigging: they also carried their hurt shipmates below.

Jack came down into the sick-bay when the ship was reasonably snug. 'How is Jenkins?' he asked.

'I doubt he can live,' said Stephen. 'The whole rib-cage is . . . And Rogers will probably lose his arm. What is that?' – pointing to Jack's hand, wrapped in a handkerchief.

'It is only some nails torn out. I did not notice it at the time.'

From the sailors' point of view things improved after this: at the cost of incessant toil they could make some headway, and although the wind stayed firmly in the west there were days when it allowed them to tack rather than wear, with the heartbreaking loss of distance made good that wearing entailed in such a current and such a wind. But from the medical point of view they did not. The men's clothes were permanently wet, the men themselves were horribly cold and often low-spirited, and with great concern Stephen saw the first signs of scurvy in several of them: he had only lime-juice aboard, not the far more efficient lemon, and even the lime-juice he suspected of sophistication. He nursed his sick, he amputated Rogers' shattered arm successfully, and he dealt with the many new cases that presented themselves; but although Martin, Pratt the loblolly-boy (a gentle, unpractising paederast) and Mrs Lamb were a great help to him in the nursing – Higgins far less so – he found it heavy going. He saw little of Jack, who was almost always on deck or dead asleep; and he was surprised to find how he missed the very modest gunroom dinners – all livestock but the immortal Aspasia had perished, all private stores had been eaten or destroyed, and they were down to ship's rations, eaten quickly and in discomfort: and sometimes, when the galley fires could not be lit, they dined on biscuit and thin-sliced raw salt beef alone. Heavy going, with continual pain and a continual heavy despondency about Diana – premonitions, ill dreams, foreboding. Most fortunately he had his leaves of coca, that virtuous shrub, which kept him going by day and abolished his hunger, and his laudanum by night, which made the darkness a refuge at least.

Some of his time he spent with Mrs Horner. This had been necessary to begin with, when she had to be watched almost hour by hour, and it became habitual, partly because the gunner had a swinging, rope-woven chair, the only seat in the ship that did not hurt Stephen's wrenched, bruised limbs and creaking frame, and partly because he had taken a liking to her. There were few things he admired more in a woman than courage and she had courage in a high degree, and fortitude: no self-pity at any time, no complaint, and in the worst of her pain no more than an angry gasping wholly involuntary rattle, almost a growl.

She had early confided in him, speaking of her affection for Hollom – they were going to run away together and set up a mathematical, nautical school – she would do the cooking, housekeeping, mending, as she did for the young gentlemen here – and at first, supposing her almost whispered dreaming words to be the voice of delirium, he had allowed it, replying kindly to soothe the agitation of her mind. Later, when he sternly forbade this impropriety he found that she had long since detected his liking and that his harsh words had little effect.

As for Hollom himself, he had from the first shown intense anxiety. He could not speak of it openly, but the youngsters could, and daily one or another of them would ask Stephen how Mrs Horner did, immediately relaying his words to her lover. And although he was shy of Stephen he twice reported sick in order to ask after her and perhaps to talk about her; but this did not answer. Stephen dismissed him with half a blue pill and a black draught, told him he could not discuss his patients except to say they were well, indifferent, or dead, and discouraged any approach to confidence.

Yet as time went on, and as the *Surprise* slowly worked west and north into somewhat kinder waters, and as the resilience of youth asserted itself, which after a hesitant spring it did with remarkable speed, it became clear that Hollom had established his own lines of communication. He grew far more cheerful, and sometimes he could be heard singing in the awkward little triangular berth he shared with the Captain's clerk, Higgins and the American midshipman, or playing on Honey's guitar.

On the second day that the ship could carry courses and full topsails, the gunner, a deadly hand with a harpoon and quite pitiless, killed a seal that was looking up at him out of the sea. Stephen seized upon its liver for his scorbutic patients, and having reserved a little piece he carried it to Mrs Horner, arriving somewhat before his usual evening rounds. He found them tightly clasped together, mouth to mouth, and he said in an exceedingly angry voice, 'Leave the room, sir. Leave the room at once, I say.' And to Mrs Horner, who looked like a frightened boy with her short crop of hair standing up all round her head, and pinker than he had seen her since her high fever, 'Eat that, ma'am. Eat it up directly.' He clapped the plate down on her belly and walked out. Hollom was on the other side of the door and Stephen said to him, 'The risks you choose to run are your own concern, except in so far as they affect my patient. I will not have her health endangered. I shall report this to the Captain.'

Even as the words were uttering he was ashamed of their tone of righteous indignation and surprised by their naked jealousy; and at the same time he noticed the look of pale horror that Hollom directed beyond him. Turning he saw Jack's great bulk filling the gangway – like many big powerful portly men Jack was very light on his feet. 'What shall you report to the Captain?' he asked, smiling.

'That Mrs Horner is far better, sir,' said Stephen.

'I am heartily glad of it,' said Jack. 'I was looking for you to pay her a visit. I have good news for all the invalids. We have put our head north-north-west at last; we have the breeze on the larboard quarter and we are running eleven knots right off the reel. If I cannot promise them locusts and honey at once, at least there is every likelihood of warmth and dry beds very soon.'

And in the cabin, as Stephen slowly tuned his 'cello, thinking, 'It was common jealousy I make no doubt: disapproval too – the fellow is not worth her – a poor groatsworth of a man, vox et praeterea nihil (though a very fine vox) – but sure men in general are very rarely worth their women,' Jack said, 'I did not like to raise their hopes too much, but if this goes on, and by all accounts I have read it is very likely to go on, we should raise Juan Fernandez in a fortnight. It has been a slow, rough passage, I admit; but it is not impossible that the *Norfolk* may have had it slower and rougher still. It is not impossible,' he said, trying to convince himself, 'that we may still find her lying there, refreshing her people and taking her ease.'

CHAPTER SIX

The *Surprise* lay moored head and stern in forty fathom water on the north side of the island, in Cumberland Bay, the only sheltered road, and Jack Aubrey sat on his quarterdeck in an elbow chair with an awning over his head to keep off the sun, digesting his dinner – lobster soup, three kinds of fish, a roast shoulder of kid, sea-elephant steak grilled to a turn – and contemplating the now familiar shore of Juan Fernandez. No more than two cables' lengths away began the noble sward, a sweet smooth green with two brooks running through it upon which his tent had been pitched until that morning, a green theatre rimmed by green forest, and beyond the forest wild rocky hills rising in abrupt, fantastic shapes – black crags in general, but clothed with green wherever greenery could take hold, and not the rank lush excessive exuberance of the tropics either but the elegant green of the county Clare. On one of the nearer precipices he could see Stephen and Martin creeping up a goat-path, anxiously shepherded by Padeen, Stephen's servant and an intrepid cragsman whose enormous frame had been founded on sea-birds' eggs throughout his childhood, by Bonden, with a coil of one-inch line over his shoulder, and by Calamy, who was obviously giving advice, begging them to take care, to watch where he was putting his feet, and not to look down. They had heard of a humming-bird peculiar to the island, the cock being bright pink and the hen bright green, and since the recovery of the invalids they had spent what waking hours they could spare from the Juan Fernandez ferns and epiphytes to combing the countryside in search of a nest.

From a ravine over towards East Bay came the crackle of gunfire: that was Howard of the Marines, the American officers and a party of liberty-men who were roaming the island with fowling-pieces, shooting anything that moved. Only a small party, and one made up of those particularly skilled men who until now had scarcely had a free hour from the urgent task of refitting the ship. A small party, because for most of the frigate's people liberty had come to an end with yesterday's evening gun, and they had spent this forenoon striking camp – the hospital-tent had been an imposing affair with ample room for all the severe cases of scurvy and the other invalids – and carrying water, wood, dried fish and other stores aboard. There might still be a score of people on the island, apart from the look-out men he had established on the Sugar Loaf, which commanded a fine view of the Pacific, but they had only a short time left; they had to be back before the end of the afternoon watch, when he intended to weigh, run out of the sheltered anchorage on what little tide there was (for the wind was steady in the south-south-east) and steer as straight and fast as ever he could for the Galapagos Islands. They had not found the *Norfolk* at Juan Fernandez, which was perhaps just as well, with so many Surprises unfit for action; nor had they found any trace of her having been there, but that did not signify a great deal, since she might perfectly well have watered at Mas-a-Fuera, a hundred miles to the west, or have put into Valparaiso, where she meant to refit. They had not found the *Norfolk*; he had made a very slow passage and he had been obliged to spend a long while on the island to recover his invalids and patch up his ship; yet even so he was satisfied. The *Norfolk*'s obvious duty – always supposing that she was in the Pacific at all and not down in the high southern latitudes, still battling with the westerlies – was to proceed steadily along the coast of Chile and Peru, lying to at night and looking for British whalers by day; so if he were to crack on for the Galapagos there was a strong likelihood that he should get there first, or find her on the whaling grounds, or at the very least learn something of her destination.

He had other causes for satisfaction: although she had scarcely a bolt of sailcloth or a tenpenny nail to spare once she had put herself to rights, the ship was now taut and trim and beautifully dry; she was very well supplied with fresh water, fuel, stockfish and pickled seal, and her people were remarkably healthy. They had only buried two, and that was at sea, off Diego Ramirez; the others had responded wonderfully to fresh vegetables, fresh meat, warmth and plain creature comfort after the howling wet and incessant cold of the sixties. Furthermore they had been through so much together that they were now a united body of men, and the frightful passage had made something like sailors out of even the least promising Defenders. Insensibly they had taken on the tone of the Surprises – the old distinction, the old animosity had vanished – and they were not only far more efficient but also much pleasanter to command: the grating had not been rigged since the remote days of the south Atlantic. There was only one man who still stood out, and that was the silly little ventriloquial barber Compton, who would be prating. There was also the gunner. He was not a former Defender but he too was a newcomer and he too did not fit in. He drank heavily and he was probably going mad: Jack had seen a good many sea-officers go mad. Although the captain of a man-of-war had immense powers there was little he could do to prevent a man protected by a commission or a warrant from destroying himself so long as he committed no offence against the Articles of War, and this Horner never did; although he was a sombre, inhuman brute he was a conscientious one and he did his duty at all times: yet even so Jack could not like him. The reefers on the other hand – how well they were coming on, and what an agreeable set of young fellows they were; he had rarely known a pleasanter, more cheerful midshipmen's berth. Perhaps it was the Greek. They had behaved remarkably well coming round the Horn, although Boyle had had three ribs stove in, while frostbite had taken off two of Williamson's toes and the tips of his ears, and the scurvy, running to Calamy's scalp, had turned him as bald as an egg; and now they were having immense fun on Juan Fernandez, hunting goats with a troop of large feral dogs they had more or less tamed. He smiled, but his pleasant thoughts were interrupted by a musket-shot and the voice of Blakeney, the acting signal-midshipman. 'If you please, sir, Sugar Loaf is signalling. A sail, I believe.'

A sail it was, but the eddying breeze up there streamed the rest of the hoist directly away from the ship; and rather than wait for it to come fair Jack ran to the forecastle, filled his lungs and hailed the Sugar Loaf with enormous force: 'A whaler?' A combined yell of No came down, with gestures of negation, but the answer to his 'Where away?' could not be heard, though their outstretched arms pointed emphatically to leeward, and calling to Blakeney to follow him with a telescope Jack climbed to the fore crosstrees. He searched the hazy northern rim of the sea, but nothing could he find, apart from a school of whales blowing by the score some five miles away. 'Sir,' cried Blakeney, standing on the topgallant yard, 'the hoist has come straight. I can read most of it without the book. *Ship bearing north-north-east* something *leagues* – can't make out the numerals, sir – *steering west.*'

They were responsible men up there, Whately, a quartermaster, and two middle-aged able seamen: and to seamen *ship* meant only one thing, a three-masted square-rigged vessel. A frigate was of course a ship, and since this ship they were signalling somewhere beyond his range was not a whaler – and whalers could instantly be recognized from their crow's-nests – she might well be the *Norfolk*. Might very well be the *Norfolk*. 'Mr Blakeney,' he said, 'jump up to the Sugar Loaf with a glass. Take all the notice you can of what sail she is under and her course and bearing. Then bring the men and their belongings down: you may come as quick as you like, unless you choose to spend the rest of your days on this island. We shall never beat back to it in this breeze, once we have gone to leeward.' Then raising his voice and sending it aft, 'Mr Honey, there. All hands unmoor ship, if you please.'

Every man aboard and several ashore had been expecting the order ever since the Sugar Loaf answered the Captain's hail, and even before the bosun raised his call the deck was as busy as an upturned anthill. Purposefully busy however with capstan-bars hurrying to be shipped, pinned and swifted, topmen running to veer away the head-cable, forecastlemen vanishing below to the cable-tier, there to coil the stern-cable as the monstrous, wet, stiff and heavy rope came in; it took a great deal more than a sudden order to unmoor ship to make the *Surprise* lose her head, and busy though she seemed, or even to a landsman's eye distracted, she found plenty of time to break out the blue peter at the fore and fire a gun to draw attention to it.

The gun stopped Stephen and Martin dead, and before they could gather their wits and begin to reflect upon the reasons for the report they were turned about and hurried down the goat-path, losing half an hour's laborious climb in five minutes. Neither Bonden nor Calamy would attend to any speculation, any remarks about humming-birds, about reckless unnecessary haste, or the beetles left among the tree-ferns, for a moment; and although there was a long way to go through the sandal-wood trees and behind the sea-elephants' cove – 'the only place on the island where Venus mercenaria is to be found' cried Martin in anguish as he was heaved past it at a brisk trot – they brought their charges to the strand as the last three invalids (one broken leg that would not knit; one amputated forearm, gangrened after frostbite; and one perfectly irrelevant tertiary syphilis, acquired years ago behind a Hampshire hedge and now moving to its terminal general paralysis) were handed into the red cutter, attended by Higgins, and as the fife on the capstan-head died away, the *Surprise* being right over her stern anchor, having reached the point where the ritual words were spoken, 'Up and down, sir' and then, 'Thick and dry for weighing.' These were followed by an anxious period, for the anchor had dragged a little and there was danger of its being in foul ground. The fife struck up and the men heaved hearty, but the capstan moved slower and slower. The shooting-party arrived, all crammed into one boat, and the liberty-men flung themselves upon the bars. 'Heave and a-weigh,' called the bosun as he felt a yielding tremor from the depths, and the capstan began to turn with a fine click-click of its pawls, raising the best bower through a murky cloud of sediment. 'Heave and in sight.' But the best bower had moored the frigate by the stern, with the cable passing out of a gunroom port, and although the Surprises were pleased to see their anchor dangling there, they still had to pass it forward. This was a difficult task in itself, the best bower weighing thirty-one hundredweight, and it was harder now, since at the same time they had to warp the ship across the bay to heave up the second anchor, laid out ahead. A period of intense activity ensued, with the capstan turning steadily to the tune of *All Aboard for Cuckolds' Reach* and the bosun and his mates leaping to and fro, inboard and out, like so many passionate apes.

Some time passed before Jack had leisure to say, 'There you are, Doctor. There you are, Mr Martin. I am sorry to have torn you from your botanizing, but I am happy to see you aboard. We may have our enemy under our lee – we must sail directly, and with the wind so steady in the south anyone left behind is likely to stay there a great while. Mr Mowett, all the people are aboard, I believe?'

'No, sir,' said Mowett. 'The gunner, his wife, and Hollom are still ashore.'

'Mr Horner?' cried Jack. 'God's my life, I could have sworn he came in the launch. Give him another gun.'

They gave him three guns at long intervals while the *Surprise* moved steadily across the bay; but it was not until she was almost over her small bower, with the cable sloping steep, that he was reported at the landing-place, alone at the landing-place. 'What the devil does he mean? What the hell are they about? Gathering nosegays?' said Jack, glancing angrily over the pure sea, just ruffled now by a most welcome breeze, blowing the way of the tide. 'Send the jolly-boat for them. Yes, Mr Hollar, what is it?'

'Beg pardon, sir,' said the bosun. 'Capstan's up to his old capers again.'

'Red hell and death,' said Jack. 'Surge the messenger.' They surged the messenger, taking the strain off the cable. and Jack crawled under the bars to the iron pawl-rim. True enough: one of the pawls had already lost its tip and the other was so distorted that it might go any minute; and if it were to go when the cable was taut any heave of the sea, any lift of the ship, would be transmitted to the bars with shocking force, spinning the capstan backwards and scattering the men like ninepins, bloody ninepins.

'Shall I have the forge set up, sir?' asked Mowett.

It would have to be done sooner or later; new pawls would have to be shaped, hammered, tempered just so and fitted; but this would take hours and they would lose not only the tide but the promising little air that was stirring the pennant. 'No,' said Jack, 'We shall weigh with a voyol to the jeer-capstan.' As he spoke he saw a horrified look spread on the bosun's face. Mr Hollar had always served in modern ships and he had never weighed with a voyol: indeed it was an antiquated practice. But as a youngster Jack had sailed under some very conservative, antiquated captains; and it also happened that his very first command, the *Sophie*, an old-fashioned brig if ever there was one, had habitually used a voyol. With scarcely a pause Jack called the midshipmen. 'I will show you how we weigh with a voyol,' he said. 'Take notice. You don't often see it done, but it may save you a tide of the first consequence.' They followed him below to the mangerboard, where he observed, 'This is a voyol with a difference: carry on *Sophie*-fashion, Bonden,' – for Bonden had already brought the big single-sheaved block. 'Watch, now. He makes it fast to the cable – he reeves the jeer-fall through it – the jeer-fall is brought to its capstan, with the standing part belayed to the bitts. So you get a direct runner-purchase instead of a dead nip, do you understand?'

213

They understood; but the voyol-block, so long unused, broke under the strain. It had to be replaced by various makeshifts, and by the time the cable was truly up and down and Jack on deck again the jolly-boat was lying empty alongside, its crew already busy at their various stations. As he walked aft he saw Maitland speaking to Mowett, who came forward to meet him, took off his hat and said in an odd, formal voice, 'The gunner has come aboard, sir. He came alone. He says Hollom has deserted – will not rejoin the ship – and that Mrs Horner is staying with him. He says they mean to stay on the island. He hurt his leg in the woods and has gone below.'

The atmosphere was very strange. Jack checked his first reply and glanced about the quarterdeck. Most of the officers were there: not one had a wholly natural expression on his face. Two of the jolly-boat's crew were close by, clearing away the falls, and they looked deeply perturbed, anxious, and as it were frightened. Obviously there was something known in the ship, and obviously no one was going to tell him; even Maturin's face was closed. The decision had to be made at once and he would have to make it himself. Ordinarily any deserter had to be taken up; the example was of the first importance. But this was a special case. Searching the island with all its caves and deep recesses might take a week – a week at a time when a possible enemy was in sight! While his mind was turning to and fro he was tempted to say, 'Has the gunner made no representations about pursuing them, about recovering his wife?' when he realized that the answer was implicit in Mowett's account. The question was pointless: in any case his mind was clear and settled; he said, 'Up anchor,' adding, 'We shall deal with the question of desertion at a later time, if possible. Carry on, Mr Maitland.'

'Away aloft,' cried Maitland, and the men ran up on to the yards.

'Trice up and lay out,' and they cast off the gaskets, holding the sails under their arms.

'Let fall. Sheet home.' The sails dropped: the larboard

214

watch sheeted home the foretopsail, the starboard watch the maintopsail, and the boys and idlers the mizen. Then, slightly ahead of the order, they manned the halliards and ran the yards up; the topgallants followed, the sails were trimmed to the breeze, and as the *Surprise*, moving easily over her small bower, plucked it up with scarcely a check, they ran back to the capstan and heaved the cable in. The hands went through these motions with the unthinking ease of very long practice but in something near dead silence; there was none of the cheerful excitement of getting to sea in great haste with the possibility of action not far ahead.

Most of them had seen the gunner come aboard, his ghastly sunken face, his blood-spattered clothes; some had heard the inhuman mechanical voice in which he reported to the officer of the watch; and the crew of the jolly-boat told how he had washed his hands and head, kneeling there at the edge of the sea.

Once the ship was clear of the island's lee she set studdingsails aloft and alow and steered a course designed to intercept the stranger: Blakeney had taken her bearing with great care and he had made out that she was on the larboard tack, at least one point free under courses and topsails. The *Surprise* was now making eight knots and Jack hoped to raise her in the evening, then, taking in all but his staysails until nightfall, and lurking under the horizon as it were, to come up with her at dawn under a press of canvas.

Up at the main crosstrees he scanned the far sea with his telescope, sweeping a twenty-degree arc from the starboard leech of the foretopgallant, and below him he heard the men in the foretop, unaware of his presence, talking in low urgent voices, little more than a whisper. They were upset; more upset than could be accounted for by a master's mate bolting with a gunner's wife on a warm and pleasant island. Whales again; a perfectly enormous school of them spouting over not much more than a mile of sea; he had never seen so many together –

215

certainly more than two hundred. 'Innocent blood in the sun,' said a voice in the foretop: Vincent, a West Country lay preacher.

'Innocent blood my arse,' said another, probably old Phelps.

And beyond the whales, far beyond the whales a pale flash that was certainly not a spout: he focused his glass and steadied it – the stranger, sailing steadily along, holding her course. Hull down, of course, but quite certainly there. Turning his head and leaning down he hailed the deck: an absurdly moderate hail, as though the distant ship might hear. 'On deck, there. In topgallants.'

He made his way slowly down, gave the orders that should keep the *Surprise* out of sight but still moving on a course parallel with the stranger's, and walked into his cabin. He was very much a creature of his ship and although his life was so comparatively isolated he was keenly aware of the atmosphere aboard: in tune with it too, since his intense eager looking forward to the morning was now deadened to a surprising degree. Obviously this did not prevent him from taking every proper measure; he and the master laid a very exactly calculated course: dead-lights were shipped before dark so that not a glimmer should show aboard, and half an hour after sunset the ship swung five and a half points north, increasing her speed on the regular, unvarying breeze to seven knots, with perhaps two in reserve if she needed to spread more canvas. He said to Mowett, 'It would be inhuman to harass poor Horner this evening Let us assume that he has gone sick and ask his eldest mate to report – Wilkins, is it not? A solid man. I have no doubt about the state of the guns, but we may need some more cartridge filled, particularly if we are lucky tomorrow.'

Then as the ship sailed evenly through the moonless night with a long easy pitch and rise on the following swell and with the regular hum of her rigging transmitted to the cabin as an omnipresent comfortable sound laced through as it were with the run of the water along her side, he returned to his serial letter to Sophie. 'Although a captain is married to his ship it is with him as it is with some other husbands; there are certain things he is the last to know. There is certainly more in this than meets the eye, at least more than meets my eye. The people are shocked and I might even say grieved, and this would not have been brought about merely by what is said to have happened – a warrant officer's wife leaving him and a master's mate walking Spanish. I hate and distrust tale-bearers and I have no opinion of captains who listen to them, still less encourage them; and although I am morally certain that Mowett and Killick and Bonden, to name only three who have been shipmates with me time out of mind, know very well what is afoot I am equally certain that not one will tell me without I ask him straight out, which I shall not do. There is only one person I might decently speak to, as a friend, and that is Stephen; but whether he would tell me or not I cannot say.' He paused – a long, long pause – and then called, 'Killick. Killick, there. My compliments to the Doctor and if he should care for a little music I am at his service.' With this he took his fiddle out of its case and began tuning it, a series of pings, squeaks and groans that made a curiously satisfying pattern of their own and that began moving his mind on to another plane.

The old Scarlatti in D minor and a set of variations on a theme of Haydn's that they handed to and fro with some pleasant improvisations moved it somewhat farther; but neither was in a mood to be wholly possessed by music and when Killick came in with the wine and biscuits Jack said, 'We must turn in early: it is not impossible we may find the *Norfolk* tomorrow. Unlikely, but not impossible. But before turning in I should like to ask you something. It may be improper and I shall not take it amiss if you don't choose to reply. What do you think of this desertion?'

'Listen, my dear,' said Stephen. 'It is an awkward thing asking a ship's surgeon about any of her people, because they have nearly all of them been his patients at cne time or another, and a medical man may no more discuss his patients than a priest his penitents God forbid. I will not tell you what I think of this desertion, so, nor what I think of the people concerned in it; but if you wish I will tell you of what is commonly thought, though without giving you any warrant of its truth or falsity and without adding any views of my own or any private knowledge I may possess.'

'Pray do so, Stephen.'

'Well, now, it was generally supposed that Hollom has been Mrs Horner's lover for a considerable time, that Horner discovered it a week or so ago . . .'

'Enough to make any man run mad,' said Jack.

'. . . and that he took the opportunity of leading them to the far side of the island on the pretext of a private conversation and there battering them to death. He had a bludgeon with him, and he is shockingly strong. He is said to have carried their bodies to the cliff and thrown them over. The people grieve for Mrs Horner, so young; and she was good-natured, kind and uncomplaining too. They are sorry for Hollom to some degree, but above all they regret he ever came aboard, an unlucky man. Yet they feel that Horner was intolerably provoked; and although they do not like him they think he was within his rights.'

'I dare say they do,' said Jack. 'And if I know anything of the Navy they will not give him away. Not a scrap of evidence will they ever produce; an enquiry would be perfectly useless. Thank you, Stephen. That was what I wanted to know, and I dare say if I had been a little sharper I should not have had to ask. I shall have to take the thing at its face value, put an R against poor Hollom's name, and meet Horner's eye as best I can.'

In the event there was no difficulty about meeting Horner's eye. At the end of the middle watch the chase's lights were seen, a little, but only a very little, farther west than they should have been; and at first dawn there she lay, placidly holding her course under the low grey sky. Jack was on deck on his nightshirt, but Horner was there before him. The gunner was dressed in fresh white canvas trousers and new checked shirt; a wounded or twisted leg made his movements awkward but he stumped about his guns, inspecting equipment, sights and breeching with his usual surly competence. He came aft to the quarterdeck carronades, spreading intense wooden embarrassment all round but apparently feeling none himself: he touched his hat to the Captain, standing there with a lowered night-glass in his hand. Jack's whole heart and soul had been turned to the chase – he had been engaged in naval war for more than twenty years and he was very much of a sea-predator, perfectly single-minded when there was the near likelihood of violent action – and now in the most natural voice in the world he said, 'Good day to you, master gunner. I fear there will be no great chance of expending your stores this morning.'

The rising sun proved that he was right: it showed a line of figures leaning along the stranger's rail in easy attitudes, some with moustaches, some smoking cigars. The United States Navy, though easy-going and even at times verging upon the democratic, never went to such extremes as this; and indeed the chase turned out to be the *Estrella Polar*, a Spanish merchantman from Lima for the River Plate and Old Spain. She was perfectly willing to heave to and pass the time of day, and although she could not spare the *Surprise* anything but a few yards of sailcloth in exchange for bar iron she was generous with information: certainly the *Norfolk* had passed into the Pacific, and that after an easy passage of the Horn; she had watered at Valparaiso, scarcely needing to refit at all, which was just as well, since Valparaiso was notorious for possessing nothing, and that nothing of the very lowest quality as well as exorbitantly dear and delivered only after endless delay. She had sailed as soon as her water was completed and she had captured several British whalers. The *Estrella* had heard tell of one burning at sea off the Lobos rocks like an enormous torch in the night and had spoken to another, the *Acapulco* by name, which was being taken to the States by a prize-crew, a stout ship, but like most whalers a slug: the *Estrella* could give her fore and main topgallantsails and still sail two miles for her one: had met her under the tropic line, two hundred leagues north-north-east, a great way off. The *Estrella* would be happy to carry the *Surprise*'s letters to Europe and wished her a happy voyage; the two ships filled their backed topsails and drew apart, calling out civilities. The Spaniard's last audible words, over half a mile of sea, were 'Que no haya novedad.'

'What did he mean by that?' asked Captain Aubrey.

'May no new thing arise,' said Stephen. 'New things being of their nature bad.'

The Surprises were glad to have their letters carried back to the Old World; they were grateful for the half bolt of canvas; and they said good-bye to the *Estrella* with real good will. Yet after a night of the liveliest expectation and the triumph of seeing her lights in the middle watch, she could not be anything but an anticlimax, a bitter disappointment. There was also the intense mortification of the *Norfolk*'s having rounded the Horn so much before them and of her snapping up the British whalers they had been sent to protect. Many Surprises had friends or relations in the South Sea fishery, and they felt it keenly: Mr Allen most of all. He had always been a stern, unsmiling officer when he had the watch; not exactly a hard horse, since he never abused or wantonly harassed the men, but taut, very taut indeed; and now he became more so. He had the afternoon watch that day, when the sky lowered and began to weep thin rain; the breeze grew capricious, sometimes baffling, and he kept the hands perpetually on the run, making sail, trimming it, taking it in again, all in a harsh and angry bark.

He had had a long conference with Jack, and they had decided that in view of the *Estrella*'s information the best course was to bear in with the main, keeping as close to the homeward-bound whalers' path as possible; this was not the *Surprise*'s direct route for the Galapagos, but, insisted the master, they would lose little time – it

220

was almost as broad as it was long – because of the cold current that flowed north along the coast, carrying seals and penguins right up almost as far as the equator, the whole length of Chile and Peru. Allen's reasoning and his experience of these waters seemed conclusive to Jack, and the ship was now steering as nearly east-north-east as she could, through the cheerless drizzle.

A cheerless, uneasy ship: they had got rid of one unlucky man in *poor Hollom*, as they all called him now, but they had gained a far worse, a fellow who must necessarily bring a curse upon them all. The youngsters were pitifully affected – Mrs Horner had always been very kind to them, and apart from that they had been as sensible of her good looks as grown men – Jack abruptly shifted their quarters, making them mess with Ward, his clerk, Higgins, and the tall American midshipman: Ward did not care for their company (though they were red-eyed and as quiet as mice at present) but it was intolerable that they should stay with Horner.

The gunner celebrated his freedom by getting drunk. He compelled one of his mates to sit with him and the much less reluctant barber Compton, the one person aboard who could by any stretch of the word be called his crony. Horner was well found in stores, having three breakers of Spanish brandy left, and they drank until the graveyard watch, when to their horror the hands on deck heard his thick harsh voice singing *Come it late or come it soon/I shall enjoy my rose in June.*

Day after day the *Surprise* sailed through troubled seas, with the ship labouring heavily; and every night Horner sat drinking with the barber, whose shrill ventriloquial voice could be heard going through his set pieces again and again, followed by the deep rumbling tones of the half-drunk Horner growing confidential. It shocked the men on deck; it shocked the men below. Even when she reached the cool turquoise water of the Peru current one clear day at noon and raised the jagged line of the Cordillera of the Andes, sparkling white in the clear sky far, far on the starboard beam as she turned northward, the mood in the ship remained the same. The hands were oppressed and silent; they thought Compton mad to hobnob with the gunner and they were not surprised when one night there was the sound of fighting and he came racing up on deck, his face covered with blood and the gunner hard after him. Horner tripped and fell; they picked him up dead drunk and carried him below. Compton had no more than a cut mouth and a bloodied nose, but he was so frightened he could hardly stand, and to those who wiped him he said, 'I only told him she had been got with child.'

The next day the gunner sent to say that he wished to consult Dr Maturin, who received him in his cabin. The man was perfectly steady in his movements but there was no human contact with him; he was so pale that his tan showed ochre, a dull ochre, and Stephen had the impression that he was filled with an almost ungovernable rage.

'I have come to see you, Doctor,' he said. Stephen bowed, but made no reply. 'She was in kindle, when she took sick,' said the gunner suddenly.

'Listen, Mr Horner,' said Stephen. 'You are speaking of your wife, and I must tell you that I cannot discuss my patients with anyone.'

'She was in kindle, and you used an instrument on her.'

'I have nothing to say to you on this matter.'

Horner stood up, crouching under the beams, and said in a much rougher tone, 'She was in kindle, and you used an instrument on her.'

The door opened. Padeen stepped quickly in and took Horner from behind, circling his arms: Padeen was an even bigger man, and stronger by far. 'Put him down, now, Padeen,' said Stephen. 'Mr Horner, sit in that chair. Your mind is disturbed; you are upset, as well you may be, with so much emotion. You need physic. Drink this.' He poured half a wine-glass of his own tincture and passed it, saying, 'I will not pretend not to know what you mean; but you must understand that I have never used an instrument in that sense in all my life, nor ever shall.'

He spoke with an authentic kindness and this perhaps even more than the evident truth pierced through: the gunner drank his glass.

It was a dose that should have calmed a dozen men unused to the drug, but that afternoon Higgins came to see Stephen in a state not so much of alarm as of abject terror. 'He said I used an instrument on her – oh sir you must protect me – I am your assistant – I am your mate – you must protect me. He respects you: he don't respect me at all.' That was true enough: Higgins' patter had been repeated too often, his rapacity had become too naked, and he had been so foolish as to tyrannize over the loblolly-boy, a medical oracle of great standing with the lower deck, who revealed many of his capers, privately showing his shop-worn earwigs and the aged stag-beetle. And in any case Stephen's trepanning of Plaice had quite wiped out what little triumphs Higgins may have had with teeth.

'You had better keep out of his way until he has quietened,' said Stephen. 'You may stay in the sick-bay, reading to the invalids: I will ask Padeen to sit with you for a day or so. You must conciliate his good will, somewhat thoughtlessly impaired, by speaking to him civilly, perhaps by making him a small present.'

'Oh sir, I will give him half a guinea – a whole guinea – I will give him two guineas, honest fellow – and I shall never leave the sick-bay, except to turn in, and then never you fear, sir, I am surrounded by hammocks on all sides: and the big American midshipman is between me and the door.'

Yet on the Friday, that clouded, miserable day, when Stephen and Martin were dissecting a pelican, one of the many creatures that Howard the Marine had shot as the ship sailed along the fertile current, much frequented by penguins, dolphins and all kinds of seals, sea-lions and sea-bears, as well as unbelievably vast shoals of little fishes like anchovies and their attendant birds overhead, Martin said, 'What do they mean by a Jonah's lift?'

Before Stephen could answer Howard came below and

told them that a strange enormous thing rather like a sea-elephant had come within range: he had fired, but had hit only the young one that was with it, a veil of mist coming between him and his mark at the crucial moment. He wished they had seen the animal; it was prodigious like a human being, though bigger, and what he might call grey in colour. He wished very much they had seen it.

'I am sure you mean very kindly, Mr Howard,' said Stephen. 'But let me beg you not to shoot more creatures than we can collect or dissect, or than the men can eat, for all love.'

'Oh, you have never been a one for sporting, Doctor,' said Howard, with a laugh. 'Why, you could shoot all day long in these waters, was you fond of sporting; just now I had the prettiest right and left among a flight of cormorants. I shall go straight back to it; I have two men loading for me.'

'A Jonah's lift, did you say?' said Stephen. 'I believe it is a term they use when they speak of an unpopular or unlucky man having been pushed over the side.'

'Oh surely not,' said Martin, who was ignorant of these later developments, 'I heard it used of Mr Higgins.'

'Did you indeed?' said Stephen. 'Pray stretch the skin till I come back.'

Higgins was not in the sick-bay, nor in his berth; and as Stephen looked for him he caught significant glances exchanged by some of the men. He took the loblolly-boy aside and said, 'Listen, Jamie Pratt, when did you see him last?'

'Well, sir,' said Jamie, 'he dursen't go to the head, you know: he bottled himself up or used a pot. But last night he had a roaring old flux and went forwards, it being wholly dark. Which I ain't seen him since. I thought he was maybe with you, maybe in his berth, or maybe in the cable-tier. I heard tell he has a hidey-hole down there, being main frightened of a certain gent, as you might say.'

'Sure he will be in his place at quarters, if he has been hiding below,' said Stephen.

The drum beat, the bulkheads vanished, the frigate showed a clean sweep fore and aft, ready for battle, and all hands ran to their action-stations. Mowett made his rapid inspection, in order to be able to report to the Captain, 'All hands present and sober, sir, if you please.' He found the bosun on the forecastle, of course, the carpenter and his crew at the pumps and in the wings, and the gunner, his yeoman and his mates at their posts in the magazines; but when he came to the shady depths where Stephen, Martin and the loblolly-boy stood ready to attend the wounded, Stephen said, 'Sir, I have to report the absence of my assistant Mr Higgins.'

Quarters ended with no great-gun exercise; the drummer beat the retreat and Jack ordered a thorough searching of the lower platforms and the hold. Higgins might have been taken ill inside one of the great coils of cable on the tiers, or he might have fallen down a hatchway. The men lit their lanterns in the rapidly-gathering dusk – low cloud was already wafting through the upper rigging – and began going through the necessary motions. But their hearts were not in it: of course their hearts were not in it, since they knew as an evident fact that Higgins had been given a Jonah's lift: and no great loss, neither. And when the wailing started they all hurried up on deck, standing there in a huddle.

It was a wailing, a great long desperately sad O – o – o of immense volume, sometimes rising to a shriek, unlike any sound that had come from the sea in the experience of the oldest man aboard, and it circled the ship, coming quite close on either side: sometimes a form could be made out, but never clearly. In any case there were few who dared to look.

'What can it be?' asked Jack.

'I cannot tell,' said Stephen, 'but suppose it to be the creature whose young one was shot. Perhaps it was wounded, and perhaps it has now died.'

The voice grew louder still, almost intolerable before it broke off in a dying sob. 'Mr Mowett,' said Jack in a most uneasy tone, 'has the ship been thoroughly searched?'

'I am not quite sure, sir,' said Mowett, raising his voice above the wail, now on the larboard beam. 'I will find out directly.' There was the same answer to all his questions: yes, everything had been rummaged; and no, there was no good going down there again. They were responsible warrant and petty officers who spoke, sometimes lying to his face; and he knew and they knew that there would be no getting the men to return to remoter, darker, more lonely parts of the ship.

'God's my life,' cried Jack, the empty watch-glass catching his eye, the half-hour glass that was religiously turned even in the heat of battle, even when the ship was settling in the sea, her bottom pierced. 'God's my life. What the devil are you thinking of? Turn the glass and strike the bell.'

The Marine on duty turned the glass and reluctantly moved forward: eight hesitant bells, and the howling all around.

'Set the watch,' said Jack. 'Judas Priest, what are you all standing about for? Mr Mowett, lanterns will be allowed on the berth-deck tonight after lights out. Master-at-arms, take notice of that.'

He paused to see that the watch was indeed mustered. For a moment he thought it might not be accomplished, for although he had often seen sailors disturbed, alarmed, unsettled, he had never known them so frightened as this, nor so utterly cast down; but most of the officers were on deck, and the stolid, wholly unimaginative presence of Mr Adams, eagerly discussing the storage of bottled ale with Stephen and Martin, helped Maitland through his task. Once the last name was called Jack walked into his cabin, where he paced to and fro athwartships, his hands behind his back; and all the time the terrible great cry moved round the ship.

226

'Pass the word for the Doctor,' he said at last; and when Stephen came, 'I hear that Martin asked about a Jonah's lift: I know what is said among the people, and I have been reflecting. This cannot go on: tell me, since it is generally held that the gunner has committed monstrosities, could you certify that he is mad and must be placed under restraint?'

'I could not. Many a man has done what he is said to have done and is still reckoned sane. I could not certify a man mad on supposition no nor on the most vehement suspicion either, nor even on legal proof without examining what can be made out of his mind, to know whether he acted rationally. To know with at least that faint light of knowledge that can come from one man's fallible examination.'

'Examination?' said Jack. 'Very well.' He rang and said, 'Pass the word for the gunner.'

They sat there lost in thought as the cry went forward. The howling outside had diminished while they were speaking but now it rose to a shriek even higher than before. 'What can it be?' asked Jack again, deeply disturbed.

'Sure I cannot tell,' said Stephen, crossing himself. 'Conceivably something of the manatee kind, though the latitude is wrong entirely. God between us and evil.'

'Amen,' said Jack and the door opened – Killick appalled, could scarcely speak. 'Gunner's hanged hisself,' he brought out in a gasp.

'Have you cut him down?' cried Jack.

Stephen saw the answer in Killick's stupid look, pushed past him and ran forward, calling to Bonden and a bosun's mate as he ran.

'Lift him up till I cut the cord,' he said.

They laid him on his cot and it was there that Martin saw him, with Stephen sitting by his head. 'There is hope, is there not?' said Martin, looking at that dark, suffused, expressionless face. 'There is no question of dislocation, surely?'

227

'No drop, no dislocation,' said Stephen.

'So there is certainly hope. I have known a man hang twenty minutes and still be revived by proper measures. Why, he is still warm! Do you detect a pulse?'

'I believe I may.'

'When shall you bleed him? I do not mean to instruct you, Maturin, but should he not be let blood directly?'

'I do not think bleeding would answer in this case,' said Stephen, and after a while he went on, 'Have you ever brought a determined suicide back to life? Have you seen the despair on his face when he realizes that he has failed – that it is all to do again? It seems to me a strange thing to decide for another. Surely living or dying is a matter between a man and his Maker or Unmaker.'

'I cannot think you are right,' said Martin, and he set out the contrary view.

'Sure you speak with great authorities on your side,' said Stephen. He stood up and leant his ear to the gunner's chest, then opened his eye, gazing into it with a candle. 'But in any case he is now gone beyond my interference, God rest his soul.'

Martin shook his head and said, 'I cannot give him Christian burial, alas.' Then, after a moment, 'The wailing has stopped.'

'It stopped while you were speaking, five minutes ago,' said Stephen. 'I believe the best thing to do is to send for his mates, who will sew him up in a hammock with round-shot at his feet. I shall watch by him until the morning, when he can be slipped over first thing, without distressing the hands even further; for I must tell you, Martin, the more superstitious of them are quite capable of pining away under this kind of strain, like blacks when they have been cursed.'

But first thing in the morning or rather before it was also the time when the *Surprise* sent men to the masthead to see what the new-lit ocean might have on its surface. Rare, rare were the gifts it offered, but still the men laid aloft at a tearing pace, even in such times as these, since before now the frigate had found an opponent or a prize lying there within range of her guns. Three hundred and sixty-four mornings of the year might show nothing or only a distant fisherman but there was always the possibility of an exceptional dawn and this was one of them. The shrieking hail of 'Sail ho' cut short all the rumbling activity of holystones and bears.

'Where away?' called the master, who had the watch.

'Right in the wind's eye, sir,' said the lookout. 'Just topsails up, and a whaler, I do believe.'

A few minutes later, with the light spreading fast and the last stars dying in the west, Jack was plucked from a troubled, anxious sleep by the ship's change of course through sixty-four degrees and by young Boyle's voice loud in his ear, bringing 'Mr Allen's duty, sir, and a sail in the south-south-west, a whaler, we do believe.'

When he came on deck he found a fresh and brilliant morning, the *Surprise* close-hauled on the larboard tack, and a somewhat nervous master, who said, 'I have presumed to alter course, sir, since she may be an American or a prize of ours going home.'

'Quite right, Mr Allen,' said Jack, fixing the chase's topsails as they nicked the clear horizon. 'Quite right: there was not a moment to lose – it will be tack upon tack, as hard as ever we can pelt, to make up such a leeway.'

'Another thing, sir,' said Allen in a low voice, 'Pearce and Upjohn' – two of the Gibraltar lunatics, who had laid the hammock-shrouded gunner on the gangway – 'did not quite understand, and they launched Mr Horner over the side when the ship hauled to the wind.'

'Perhaps it was for the best,' said Jack, shaking his head. 'Perhaps it was . . . forward, there: sharp that maintop bowline. Mr Allen, I believe she will wear fore and main topgallantsails.'

With the sun a broad handsbreadth clear of the sea he was on deck again, standing there with one arm hooked round the weather mizen topmast backstay; the *Surprise* had finished her morning rituals and now all hands and her captain were settling down to the task of sailing her as fast as ever she could go without undue risk to her precious spars, sailcloth and cordage. The chase was half topsails under, thirteen or fourteen miles away, and had she been going large the frigate would probably have overhauled her by dinner-time; but they must have passed one another in the night and she was now directly to windward. The *Surprise* would therefore have to beat up against a head-sea in a stiff and freshening breeze, and she would have to make up that distance before the sun set and the moonless night hid the whaler from view. It could be done, but it called for very keen seamanship, a very close study of the ship's capabilities, and a very particular trim to carry weather-helm to a nicety.

It did not call in vain. The *Surprise* was using every possible racing manoeuvre to eat the wind out of the chase; the most expert helmsmen were at the wheel in pairs, determined not to yield an inch of leeway, perpetually watching for a smooth to edge her a little closer to the wind, while expectant hands carried out the slightest change of trim that Jack called for with the flashing perfection of long practice and the keenest zeal. For his part he felt in perfect touch with his ship: sailing on a bowline was something both he and she could do admirably well, and as he stood there, swaying to the heave of the deck, he was aware of her slightest swerve or check. He was wearing an old blue coat, for the morning was fresh although they were so near the tropic line, and the spray and even solid water that swept aft every time the *Surprise* shouldered one of the steeper seas was fresher still, turning his new-shaved face a fine bright pink. From the masthead he had seen that the whaler was British-built; he was convinced that she was an American prize, and without a word passing this conviction had communicated itself to the crew; all the old Surprises knew that if a British ship had been twenty-four hours in the enemy's possession it was not yielded up to the former owners with a polite bow and the hope of a piece of plate in acknowledgement, but became salvage, the next best thing to a prize, or in some cases even better and more direct.

When Stephen came up on to the steeply-sloping deck quite late in the day – he had been woken by the fife playing *Nancy Dawson* for the hands' noontime grog – he had an impression of all-pervading blueness: blue sky with a few high white clouds after all these days of low grey; a darker blue white-flecked sea; even blue air in the great shadowed convexities of the straining sails. 'Good afternoon to you, Doctor,' called Jack – blue coat and bright blue eyes gleaming – 'Come and take a look at our chase.'

Stephen slowly made his way aft, handed along by the jolly Marines and all the seamen who, having no immediate task in hand, were lining the weather rail so that their weight should make the ship a little stiffer, and as he went he felt the total change of mood: the people's hearts and minds were wholly set on the pursuit, intent, eager, cheerful, the past and even the events of yesterday left behind, far behind with the long-vanished wake.

'There she lays,' said Jack, nodding over the larboard beam, where the whaler could be seen standing south-east under topgallantsails with her starboard tacks aboard.

'But you are going almost directly from it,' cried Stephen. 'What kind of chase is this, at all?'

'Why, she is very much concerned with her southing, do you see,' said Jack, 'and she wears about every two hours or so: she is on the starboard tack now, as you see. Yet wearing ship takes time, and in any case I do not care to arouse her suspicions; so we do not go about – we sail as nearly south as we can, but on the other tack. I believe she is innocent as a babe unborn: takes us for a Spaniard. We put all that filth up there to encourage her to think so.' Stephen peered up, and after some searching he saw a little piece of dimity, about the size of a moderate tea-tray, fluttering at the junction of two ropes, and a few untidy reef-points. 'But next time she wears we shall be on what look like parallel courses, though in fact they will be converging, since we lie much closer as well as sailing faster; and I reckon that if all goes well – if we carry nothing away – then in four more of her boards and one or perhaps two of ours we should have the weather-gage.'

'You mean to take her, I collect?'

'That is the general idea.'

'What makes you suppose she is lawful prize?'

'She is British-built to begin with, and then although her commander sails her tolerably well he does not sail her as a man who had had her for a year or so would sail her. A weak crew, too, whereas whalers' crews are strong; they take a great while wearing. You shall watch through my glass next time they make a leg. Everything points to her being a prize, probably the ship that worthy Spaniard spoke of, the *Acapulco*.'

'When do you hope to come up with her, so?'

'Come,' said Jack, 'do not let us tempt fate. I only say that if all goes well – if we carry nothing away, and the breeze is freshening, as you see . . .'

'It is already far more like a tempest than any breeze.'

'. . . then we might, with luck, speak her before dark.'

Here the drum beat for the gunroom dinner and they parted, for Jack meant to stay on deck, eating sandwiches brought by Killick. The dinner was a hurried meal, with most of the officers, including the American lieutenant, bolting their food so that they should miss not a moment of the chase: yet there was some conversation, from which it appeared that the *Surprise* did not set royals at about three bells, when the whaler spread her topgallantsails, partly from fear of losing them, but much more so that she should not appear to be chasing – that the whaler certainly had a dirty bottom: she sagged horribly to leeward – that the people who sailed her were no phoenixes – and that nothing made Mowett happier than remembering the days they had so wisely spent at Juan Fernandez, heaving the barky down as far as possible and cleaning her copper as far as ever they could reach, painful at the time but wonderfully pleasant in the recollection.

Presently the purser, the chaplain and the surgeon were left to themselves with the greater part of a long grey pudding, made with sea-elephant suet and studded with Juan Fernandez berries, and Stephen observed, 'I have seen many examples of the seaman's volatility, but none equal to this. When you recall the last week, culminating in the events of yesterday – no longer ago than yesterday itself – when you recall the silent, anxious and I might almost say haunted faces, the absence not only of the usual laughter but even of quips and small-wit, and the collective sense of impending, ineluctable doom, and when you compare that with today's brisk gaiety, the lively eye, the hop, skip and jump, why, you are tempted to ask yourself whether these are not mere irresponsible childish fribbles . . .'

'Fribble yourself,' murmured the gunroom steward the other side of the door, where he was finishing the officers' wine with Killick.

'. . . or weathercocks. But then you reflect that these same people circumnavigate the entire terraqueous globe, sometimes in trying circumstances, which argues a certain constancy.'

'I have heard their levity put down to there being no more than a nine-inch plank between them and eternity,' said Martin.

'Nine-inch?' said the purser, laughing heartily. 'Why, if you are given to levity with nine inches under you, what must you be in a little old light-built frigate? A flaming gas-balloon, no doubt. God – dear me, there are parts of *Surprise*'s bottom where you could push a penknife through with ease. Nine-inch! Oh lord, ha, ha, ha!'

'Sir, sir,' cried Calamy, running in and standing by Stephen's chair, 'the whaler's taken in her topgallantsails – we are to go about any minute now, and we'll overhaul her by the end of the watch, as sure as eggs is eggs. Please sir' – with an affectionate look – 'may I have a slice of pudding? Chasing is desperate hungry work.'

As it happened the *Surprise* overhauled her well before the end of the watch. The whaler, the unlucky *Acapulco*, wholly deceived by the Spanish ensign that Jack hoisted when they were a couple of miles apart, backed her foretopsail and lay to while the captive American sailors stood in silent agony as the *Surprise* took up a raking position across the *Acapulco*'s bows, ran out her broadside guns in one brisk movement, replaced the false colours with the true, and called upon her to surrender.

There was not the least possibility of resistance, and her commander came across without any fuss, a disconsolate young man with spectacles. His name was Caleb Gill, and he was nephew to the *Norfolk*'s captain, who had captured so many whalers that in spite of having burnt several he was hard pressed for officers to take the others in.

The Surprises were very kind to Mr Gill, as well they might be, since he had done them no sort of harm, while his trusting nature had, with no great pains on their part, delivered them a prize, deep-laden with white-oil and spermaceti, mostly from other ships, that Mr Allen reckoned at a hundred thousand dollars.

'That is very fine, to be sure,' said Jack Aubrey, smiling at his report, 'and Heaven knows I am not one to fling a hundred thousand dollars in a gift-horse's teeth; yet in a way the carpenter and the bosun have even better news – the *Acapulco* is stuffed, *stuffed*, with spars, cordage and sailcloth, enough for a three-year cruise; she has only been out six months, and has hardly used anything at all.'

The gunroom was kind to Mr Gill, and the other Surprises were kind to his crew, which included some of the *Acapulco*'s men, who, anxious to avoid the accusation of foreign enlistment or comforting the King's enemies, told all they had learnt about the *Norfolk*'s movements, past and to come; but it was Caleb Gill who gave the information that relieved Jack's mind from a most gnawing anxiety. Gill was a reading man, nearer akin to Martin and Stephen than to most of the other sailors. His interests however had more to do with men, primitive men, and less with botany or brute-beasts than theirs; he was fascinated by the idea of the noble savage and had travelled far among the native Americans, learning all he could of their social order in peace and war, their laws, customs and history; and one afternoon, when the *Surprise* was still stripping the *Acapulco* of everything that could possibly be crammed between decks and Mr Lawrence was dining with Jack, the three of them lingered in the gunroom over a bottle of madeira. 'I was of course exceedingly mortified at being taken prisoner,' he observed, 'yet in a purely personal and private way I had been perhaps even more deeply mortified by being ordered to take command of that unfortunate *Acapulco*, since from the very beginning of the voyage my whole heart had been bent on beholding the Marquesas: your upas-tree, sir, your two-toed sloth, dodo, solitary-bird, were hardly more for you than the Marquesas were for me, particularly the island Huahiva, which my uncle has always represented as a Paradise.' 'As a Paradise, indeed?' asked Stephen, remembering a letter found in the *Danaë*'s packet, which used that very phrase. 'Yes, sir. Not perhaps quite an orthodox Presbyterian Paradise, but one so agreeable that he means to set up a colony upon it. Indeed he even has some colonists with him. I have heard differing and often muddle-headed accounts of the islanders' polity, but all agree that it pays great attention to various prohibitions or taboos and to relationship; and all agree that the people are most uncommonly amiable and good-looking, their only faults being cannibalism and unlimited fornication. But neither of these is erected into a religious system, oh no: the divine offerings are invariably swine, the cannibalism being simply a matter of taste or inclination; while the fornication has nothing ceremonial or compulsory about it.'

235

'Does your uncle mean to reform the islanders?' asked Stephen.

'Oh no, not at all,' said Gill, 'he thinks they could scarcely be improved upon. It is to be quite a utopian colony – Liberty Hall writ large – yet even so I long to see the people's way of life before it is changed in any way. And since I cannot now see it as a free man, why, I hope I shall see it as a prisoner. Captain Aubrey means to sail to the Marquesas, I take it? But perhaps my question is not quite discreet?'

'Not at all, at all,' said Stephen. 'I am not fully acquainted with his intentions, but I will ask him; and I trust that we may all three tread the shores of Huahiva before the islanders have been corrupted.'

'I hope so too. Oh yes, indeed!' cried Gill, clasping his hands with eager anticipation.

Yet when Captain Aubrey had digested his information, and when his ship had taken in all the stores she could hold, he summoned the master and said, 'Mr Allen, a little while ago you observed that Butterworth and Kyle, the *Acapulco*'s owners, had agents in Valparaiso.'

'Yes, sir; and in Pisco too, I believe. Most of the houses engaged in the South Sea fishery have agents in Chile or Peru.'

'I am very glad to hear it, because I believe they may solve one of our difficulties. I cannot afford the officers and men to take the *Acapulco* home, yet I am most unwilling to disappoint the people of their money. I therefore think of sending her into Valparaiso and delivering her up to the agents upon promise of salvage: at the same time I can liberate all our American prisoners on parole. They are decent creatures in themselves, but considered absolutely they are an infernal hell-fire nuisance, and the prospect of housing and feeding them indefinitely weighs upon me. It weighs upon Mr Adams too; and this would be killing both birds . . .' He paused, frowned, muttered 'over one stile', and went on, 'Well never mind – that would be the most seamanlike way of dealing with the situation short of making them walk the plank.'

'Very true, sir.'

'But the point is this, Mr Allen: the officer who takes her in must run the risk of being left behind. I have no intention of lying windbound in that bay; I have no intention of exchanging endless platitudes with port-admirals, generals, governors, even bishops, God forbid: but all this can be avoided by a subordinate officer on plea of urgent orders. I should therefore escort the *Acapulco* to some point within sight of land and stand off and on for a day and a night. The officer would have to take her in with no more than the prisoners and say a cutter's crew, transact the business in an expeditious manner, and instantly proceed to sea, rejoining the ship in the cutter without the slightest loss of time. From all I understand, the *Norfolk* is likely to cruise on the Galapagos whaling grounds until the end of the month, and we may catch her there by cracking on. Nevertheless I think this matter of the prize and the prisoners is worth four and twenty hours. Four and twenty hours but not a minute more: the officer would have to rejoin in that time. With your local knowledge, Mr Allen, do you think the plan feasible?'

'Yes, sir, I do. And although I not like to put myself forward you will allow me to mention that I know my way about Valparaiso, I speak the language tolerable, and I have been acquainted with Mr Metcalfe, the agent, these twenty years.'

'Very well, Mr Allen, let us make it so. Pick your men and take command of the prize at once: if we are not to reach the Galapagos the morning after the fair there is not a moment to be lost. Killick. Killick, there. My compliments to the American officers and I should like to see them directly.'

CHAPTER SEVEN

On an oppressive day and under a low and troubled sky the *Surprise* made her way along the channel between Albemarle and Narborough, the westernmost islands of the Galapagos; she was finding it uncommonly difficult, for although at present the capricious breeze was favourable she had to stem a powerful tide, setting against all reason from the north – against all reason, for as Mr Allen observed, an even stronger current beyond the Redondo Rock at the far end of the strait ran in the opposite direction at four and even five miles an hour, while the tide between Albemarle and James Island, only a little way to the east, was in full agreement with it. In her rapid, hound-like casting to and fro among the Galapagos the *Surprise* had grown used to very strong unreasonable currents and unreasonable weather – fog under the equator, for all love: penguins hooting in the fog on the very Line itself! – but this particular current showed every inclination to turn into an extremely dangerous tide-rip, and as the rock-strewn channel was one of those the master did not know Jack had taken over the deck himself.

It was the kind of navigation that he did not like at all, but this was his last chance of finding the *Norfolk* in the archipelago: she might be lying in any of the three or four sheltered bays ahead, filling up with tortoises (those from Narborough weighing between two and three hundred pounds were particularly good eating) and with what water and firewood the place could afford, and the *Surprise* might come upon her unawares. The channel therefore had to be threaded, though it was a tricky passage indeed, with a weakening, uncertain wind, a strengthening current, little room to work the ship, an iron-bound coast on either side, and – height of injustice – something very like two lee-shores, since the wind on the frigate's side urged her towards the rocks of Narborough, while the crossgrained tide and current tended to fling her upon those of Albemarle, and certainly would do so were the wind to carry out its threat of veering. The atmosphere on deck was tense, with all hands at their stations, a boat carrying a kedge and hawser out on either side, and a man in the chains continually heaving the lead and continually chanting, 'No bottom with this line: no bottom, nay, nay.'

The strait narrowed steadily and it seemed to Jack that he would almost certainly have to anchor until the height of flood, even if it meant letting the best bower go in a hundred fathoms. 'Light along the deep-sea line,' he said. For some time the shores had been less than a musket-shot apart and now they were much nearer, increasing the force of the current. All hands looked at them gravely – a wicked surf beating upon black rock on either side, and on either side a vast fissured expanse of dull black naked lava sloping up to vague mist-covered heights, the lava scattered with great heaps of volcanic clinkers, mostly black but sometimes an unhealthy red, like the waste of an enormous ironworks: here and there a crater – an inhuman landscape. Or almost all hands: the surgeon and the chaplain, either ignorant of the implications of tide-rip, unplumbed depth, uncertain breeze and want of sea-room or soaring above these things, were settled at the leeward rail, focusing their telescopes with eager, even trembling hands. They had earlier made an attempt at covering either shore, so as to miss nothing, calling their discoveries out to one another across the deck, but the officer of the watch had put a stop to this wild irregularity the moment Jack appeared, the windward side being sacred to the captain; and now they were obliged to be content with Narborough alone. Yet even so, as they confessed, there was enough to occupy a score of naturalists. They had soon discovered that the miserable sterility of the lower slopes was more apparent than real; several stunted leafless shrubs, almost

239

certainly related to the euphorbias, could be made out standing among the natural slag-heaps, and prickly pears of an uncommon height, together with tall columnar cacti, were almost common on the upper slopes; but interesting though the land was without a doubt, the sea was even more so. As the strait grew narrower so the life in it seemed to become more concentrated: the shores on either hand – and not only the little beaches of black sand and pebbles but even the seemingly inaccessible ledges – were crowded with seals, eared seals, sea-lions and sea-bears, lying on their stomachs, on their backs, on their sides, sleeping or making love or merely barking, while others played in the crashing surf or swam by the ship, stretching their necks up and staring with intense curiosity. And where the seals left any room, the higher rocks were covered with marine iguanas, black, crested, and a good yard long. Penguins and flightless cormorants shared the water, swimming with great speed just under the surface, weaving among the shoals of silvery pilchard-like fish; and in the *Surprise*'s wake a band of female sperm whales with their calves lay blowing on the surface. Over her deck flew quantities of sea-birds, which was natural enough; but what was less so was the number that assembled in the rigging, on the hammocks in their netting and on the belfrey, maddening the hands who had to clean up their copious messes – messes that quickly ate into the metal of the guns. Many a privy blow with a swab did the larger birds receive when the Doctor was not looking; but it was no use; they remained obstinately tame, settling on the gunwhales of the boats alongside and even on their very oars. Most of these birds were boobies, masked boobies, brown boobies, spotted boobies, but above all blue-faced boobies, heavy-witted birds with a slow, expressionless stare; once, in the far Atlantic, they had been the rarities of the world, but now, although the approach of their breeding-season had quickened their minds and turned the webs of their feet an even lovelier turquoise, they were nothing in comparison with the land birds – little sooty

240

finches or rails – that passed by; the land-birds being, as far as they could tell, of kinds unknown to the learned world. Yet in spite of the boobies being so common, one couple did fix Stephen's eye. They were perched on the back of a sleeping turtle, an amorous pair with glowing feet, and so great was their need and urgency (the day being unusually warm and propitious for boobies) that they were going through their ritual of courtship with extraordinary speed, and there was no doubt that the cock booby would have attained his end if the turtle had not submerged a moment too soon, leaving him strangely out of countenance.

The master paused behind them and pointing to Narborough Island said, 'There is Sodom and Gomorrah, gentlemen, I believe. But it is not so bad higher up the slope. Was the cloud to lift, you would see some green up there, bushes and trees all covered with a kind of Spanish moss.'

'Oh, we are quite confident,' said Martin, turning a happy face to him. 'This is the first time we have been near enough to see the land at all clearly – to see the iguanas plain.'

'I particularly admire the tall straight cactus,' said Stephen.

'We call 'em torch-thistles,' said the master, 'and they have a kind of juice, if you cut them down, that can be drank; but it gives you the wet gripes.'

The ship sailed on; the black, scaly shore moved slowly past; and amidst the cry of nautical orders, the patter of bare feet, the creak of yards and the general song of the wind in the rigging part of Stephen's mind wandered away. A small bird perched on his telescope, cocked its head, looked inquisitively at him, and then preened its black feathers for a while before flying off to the island, where it vanished against the lava. 'That was quite certainly a nondescript,' he said, and went on, 'I have been contemplating on the mating ceremonies of our own kind. Sometimes they are almost as brief as the boobies', as when two of a like inclination exchange kind looks and after a short parley retire from view: I am thinking of Herodotus' account of the Greek and Amazon warriors in the pause after their truce for dinner, when individuals from either army would wander among the bushes, and of some more recent examples that have fallen under my own observation. At other times however the evolutions of the ceremonial dance, with its feigned advances and feigned withdrawals, its ritual offerings and symbolic motions, are protracted beyond measure, lasting perhaps for years before the right true end is reached; if indeed it is reached at all and not spoilt entirely by the long delay. There are endless variations according to time and country and class, and the finding out of common factors running through them all is a fascinating pursuit.'

'Yes, indeed,' said Martin, 'and it is clearly of the first importance to the race: I wonder some writer has not made it his particular study. The ceremony, I mean, not the act itself, which is nasty, brutish and short.' He reflected for a moment and then smiling he went on, 'Yet a man-of-war is scarcely the place for your inquiries. That is to say . . .' His smile faded and his voice died away as he remembered Friday past, when according to the custom of the sea Horner's effects were put up for auction at the mast, and where some pitiful shawls and petticoats were seen: an auction at which no man thought it right to bid, not even Wilkins, now the frigate's acting gunner.

'Now, Doctor,' said Howard, passing him a hat with several small dead birds in it, 'ain't I a good boy? Not one is the same.' Under the weight of public opinion Howard had given up shooting, and apart from catching fish and harpooning turtles and dolphins, which made capital sausages when mixed with the ship's salt pork, his sport now consisted of killing the birds that settled about the rigging. The boobies, owls, frigate-birds, brown pelicans and hawks he strangled; the smaller ones he struck down with a switch. Stephen accepted them, because he disliked killing specimens himself, but with all the force

242

at his command he had urged the Marine to be moderate, not to take more than a few of the same kind, and prevent his men from doing them any harm.

'You are most attentive, Mr Howard,' said Stephen. 'And I am particularly obliged to you for this yellow-breasted wren, a bird I have not . . .'

'Oh, oh,' cried Martin, 'I see a giant tortoise! I see two giant tortoises. Heavens, such tortoises!'

'Where? Where?'

'By the prickly pear.'

The tall prickly pear had an almost tree-like trunk: one tortoise, craning a-tiptoe, had seized a branch and was pulling with all the force of his retractile neck and huge domed body; the other had also seized it and was pulling too, though in a different direction. Martin interpreted this as an example of slightly mistaken mutual aid; Stephen as one of self-interest; but before the point could be settled the branch or rather the series of palms broke in two and each reptile walked off with his own.

'How I yearn to set foot on at least one of these islands,' said Martin. 'Such discoveries to be made in every realm! If the reptilian order can run to such extreme magnificence, what may we not expect from the cole-optera? From the butterflies, the phanerogams? But I am tormented by the thought that the ship may sail on and on, perpetually on and on.'

Here the goat Aspasia came running to Stephen for protection. Ever since the ship had reached the coast of Albemarle, small dark-grey finches with stout beaks had been persecuting her, landing on her back and plucking out hair to line their nests. She had faced the elements, thunder, lightning, two fleet actions, four between single ships; she had faced midshipmen, ship's boys, and a large variety of dogs; but this she could not bear, and every time she heard their faint twitter come aboard she hurried to Stephen. 'Come, come,' he said, 'a great goat like you, for shame,' but he flapped at the finches and went on, speaking to Martin, 'Set your heart at rest.' Captain Aubrey has promised that once his search for the *Norfolk* is over, the ship shall lie up, or to, or in, and that we shall have leave to go ashore.'

'How you relieve my mind: I really could not have borne . . . see, see, another tortoise – a Goliath, and nearer still he walks down the slope. A ponderous tread!'

They focused their telescopes on Goliath, who paused in perfect view, so well turned to the light that they could even count his plates, comparing them with those of Testudo aubreii on the Indian Ocean, which Maturin had discovered, described and named, giving Jack his only likelihood of earthly immortality, and with the thin-shelled and lighter though still respectable tortoise of Rodriguez. Reflections upon insular tortoises, their origin – tortoises in general, whether deaf – their voices rarely heard – capable of a harsh cry however as well as the more usual hiss – all oviparous, careless of their young – crocodiles more diligent as parents – but tortoises more generally sympathetic – perfectly capable of attachment – instances of affection in tortoises.

'What is all this intemperate calling out?' asked Stephen without taking his eye from the telescope: a whole troop of tortoises had come into his field of vision, all walking steadily uphill on a distinctly beaten track.

'I believe they have seen a boat of some kind – there was some mention of a boat,' said Martin. 'Would this island yield a toad, do you suppose? There are few reptiles I prefer to toads, and a toad of such heroic dimensions . . .'

'If a tortoise, why not a toad? But now that I come to recollect, I found no batrachians of any kind on Rodriguez; and I could scarcely make an intelligent native understand what I meant by a frog, though I imitated his motions in a very lively manner, and his cry.'

'By your leave, sir, by your leave,' roared the captain of the afterguard, shouldering his way between them without the least ceremony as the pipes wailed for 'All hands about ship' and the seamen ran to their places.

'Why, Beckett, what's afoot?' asked Stephen.

But before Beckett could reply the *Surprise* began her smooth turn: the familiar cry of 'Helm's alee' was followed by 'Off tacks and sheets' and then by 'Mainsail haul'. She passed sweetly through stays in spite of the encumbrance of the cutters and at this point Stephen, looking ahead, saw a distant boat, a whale-boat, pulling towards them as fast as ever it could against the current.

The *Surprise* filled on the larboard tack, and although the tide was slackening, near its height, in a quarter of an hour she lost the distance she had taken three to gain. The boat came visibly nearer every minute, a whale-boat with six men aboard; but so great was their anxiety that even when they were within a hundred yards and the distance dwindling with each breath they still pulled furiously hard; they still hailed 'The ship ahoy' as loud as ever they could roar.

Their voices had almost entirely gone by the time they came grinning up the side, overflowing with happiness; but in a hoarse whisper, interspersed with throaty laughter, and wetted by the two buckets of fresh water they drank, standing there on the deck, their spokesman, the specktioneer, soon made their story plain. They belonged to the *Intrepid Fox* of London, James Holland master; she had been out just over two years, and although she had not been successful up until the time they came to the Galapagos it had then seemed that they might go home with a full hold, for there they found whales in plenty. They had killed three the first day and the boats were out after three more when the fog came down: they themselves were fast to a lively young forty-barrel bull that led them a great dance far to the north of the Redondo Rock, far from their mates, who could not see them nor yet bring fresh whale-lines. In the end he carried away lines and harpoon and all and left them a cruel night and day to pull against wind and current without a drop to drink, no, nor a morsel to bite. And when they got back, what did they see? Why, they saw the poor old *Fox* being fair pulled to pieces by an American frigate that was not only taking her new foretopmast out of her but also transferring what oil and spermaceti she had won – the forehold and perhaps half the main, no more – into another whaler, the *Amelia*, also from London river. Fortunately it was the evening and they were under land, coming down the coast, so they were not seen; the specktioneer had been in these waters before – he knew the island – and they were able to pull into a narrow inlet, hide the boat under driftwood and climb up to the old buccaneers' shelter. There was a little water up there, though it was briny and evaporating fast; there were tortoises and land-iguanas, and the boobies had started to lay, so they managed pretty well upon the whole, though parched. Presently they saw the *Amelia* set out, cheered by the American frigate; she was wearing American colours and she steered a little east of south. Then the next day the Americans brought a couple of hundred tortoises down to the beach, ferried them out to the ship, set fire to the *Fox*, won their anchor, cleared the channel, and stood away to the west. They hurried down to try to put the fire out, but it was no good; half a dozen barrels of whale-oil had been stove, with the oil running all over the deck, and the fire had such a hold there was no getting anywhere near. The Captain would see part of her blackened hull if he carried on up the strait: the *Fox* lay bilged on a reef to the north of Banks' Bay, just after the anchorage.

'When the American cleared the channel did she stand due west?' asked Jack.

'Well, sir,' said the specktioneer, 'maybe a point south of west. Moses Thomas and me, we went up to the shelter again and we watched her to the horizon, straight as a die, just a trifle south of west, topgallantsails on the fore and main.'

'For the Marquesas, specktioneer?'

'That's right, mate. There are half a dozen of us out there, and some Yankees too, now that the Sandwiches are not what they was, and New Zealand a disappointment, with the people eating you up if you so much as set foot on shore.'

'Good; very good. Mr Mowett, these men will be entered on the ship's books: capital hands, I am sure, to be rated able. Mr Adams will issue hammocks, beds, slops; and they will be excused duty for a couple of days, to recover. Mr Allen, we will clear the strait with the changing tide and lay a course for the Marquesas.'

'No tortoises, sir?' asked Mowett.

'No tortoises. We have been very economical with the ship's provisions and we can do without tortoise as a relish. No, no, she is eighteen days before us and there is not a moment to lose over tortoises or caviar or cream in our tea.' With this he went below, looking thoroughly pleased. A few minutes later Stephen hurried into the cabin. 'When are we to stop?' he cried. 'You promised we should stop.'

'The promise was subject to the requirements of the service: listen, Stephen, here I have my tide, my current and my wind all combined – my enemy with a fine head-start so that there is not a moment to be lost – could I conscientiously delay for the sake of an iguano or a beetle – interesting, no doubt, but of no immediate application in warfare? Candidly, now?'

'Banks was taken to Otaheite to observe the transit of Venus, which had no immediate practical application.'

'You forget that Banks paid for the *Endeavour*, and that we did not happen to be engaged in a war at the time: the *Endeavour* was not in pursuit of anything but knowledge.'

Stephen had not known this: it made him if anything angrier still, but he governed himself and said, 'As I understand it, you mean to go round the end of this long island on the left and start your voyage – take your departure – from the other side.' Jack gave a noncommittal nod. 'Well, now, were Martin and I to walk across it, we should be on the other side long before the ship. The proportions are as one to ten, so they are; and a little small boat could land us without any trouble at all,

247

and take us off. We should walk briskly, pausing only for a few important measurements and almost certainly making valuable discoveries about springs of fresh water, mineral ores, antiscorbutic vegetables and the like.'

'Stephen,' said Jack, 'if the wind and the tide had been against us, I should have said yes: they are not. I am obliged to say no.' Landing them through the surf would be difficult; getting them off again on the west side might be quite impossible; and then the 'brisk walking' of two besotted natural philosophers across a remote oceanic island filled with plants and creatures unknown to science might last until the frigate sank at her moorings or grounded on her beef bones – he had seen Maturin on shore before this with nothing more than a Madeiran woodlouse to make him lose all sense of time. But he was sorry for his friend's disappointment, so much keener than he had expected from the desperately sterile look of the islands; he was even sorrier to see a tide of anger rise in Stephen's usually impassive face, and to hear the harsh tone in which he said, 'Very well, sir; I must submit to superior force, I find. I must be content to form part of a merely belligerent expedition, hurrying past inestimable pearls, bent solely on destruction, neglecting all discovery – incapable of spending five minutes on discovery. I shall say nothing about the corruption of power or its abuse; I shall only observe that for my part I look upon a promise as binding and that until the present I must confess it had never occurred to me that you might not be of the same opinion – that you might have two words.'

'My promise was necessarily conditional,' said Jack. 'I command a King's ship, not a private yacht. You are forgetting yourself.' Then, much more kindly, and with a smile, 'But I tell you what it is, Stephen, I shall keep in as close with the shore as can be, and you shall look at the creatures with my best achromatic glass,' – reaching for a splendid five-lens Dollond, an instrument that Stephen was never allowed to use, because of his tendency to drop telescopes into the sea.

'You may take your achromatic glass and . . .' began Stephen, but he checked himself and after the slightest pause went on, 'You are very good, but I have one of my own. I shall trouble you no longer.'

He was exceedingly angry: his solution – one short side of a triangle as opposed to two of immense length – seemed to him unanswerably sound; and it made him angrier still when practically everybody aboard, and not only old friends like Bonden and Killick and the privileged Joe Plaice (who practically owned the man who had opened his skull and who lived in a state of permanent hostility with Rogers, who had only had an arm off) but Padeen, recent Defenders and the mere children of the midshipmen's berth, surrounded him with exceptional kindness and particular attention. He had always prided himself on maintaining the volto sciolto, pensieri stretti rather better than most men, and here were illiterate tarpaulins comforting him for a distress that he could have sworn was perfectly undetectable.

With a surly satisfaction he observed that in spite of the changing tide the *Surprise* did in fact make but a slow passage of her two legs, for the breeze came foul upon her twice: they slowly passed two excellent strands where a boat could have landed them and taken them off, the first in a cove beyond the reef where the blackened carcass of the whaler lay; and it was clear to him that he and Martin might have crept across the island on all fours and still have been in time. 'In half the time,' he muttered, beating the rail in an extremity of frustration.

He watched the dim, cloud-covered Galapagos vanish astern and turned in early, ending his usual prayers with one for a less rancorous mind and lying there in his cot with Boethius' *De Consolatione Philosophiae* and two measured ounces of laudanum.

Yet in spite of these he was still unusually ill-tempered at two o'clock in the morning, when Padeen roused him and very slowly and with great difficulty told him in Irish and English that Mr Blakeney had swallowed a four-pound grapeshot.

'The thing is materially impossible,' said Stephen. 'The wicked little brute-beast is lying – showing away – topping it the phoenix – making himself interesting. Such a dose I shall give him – the sorrows of Munster will be nothing to his.'

But when he found the poor brute-beast, pale, frightened, apologetic and put to sit by a lantern on the half-deck, and when he learnt that the grape in question was only one of the nine that made up the charge of the launch's four-pounder, he at once had him seized up by the heels, ran for the stomach-pump and forced a large quantity of tepid salt water tinged with rum into his body, reflecting with pleasure, as among the agonized retching he heard the clang of the ball in the basin, that he had cured his patient not only of probably mortal occlusion but of any taste for spirituous liquors for some time to come.

Even so, even with this physical and moral triumph, the next day found him still thoroughly out of humour, and when Adams observed that the Captain was to be the gunroom's guest at dinner – that the dinner was to be an uncommon fine one too, quite a Lord Mayor's feast – he said, 'Oh, indeed,' in a tone that showed no kind of pleasure. 'I have known that fellow hang about in port,' he said to himself, glancing at Jack from the lee gangway as the *Surprise* ran smoothly over the vast South Sea, pure blue now from rim to unimaginably distant rim, 'I have known him hang about most shamefully when it was a question of a wench – Nelson too and many a post-captain, many an admiral when adultery was concerned – no fine-spun scruples about the King's ship then. No, no: scruples are kept for natural philosophy alone, or any useful discovery. His soul to the Devil, false, hypocritical dog; but he is probably unaware of his falsity – pravum est cor omnium, the heart is perverse above all things and unsearchable. Who shall know it?'

Yet although Stephen was of a saturnine and revengeful temperament he had been brought up to a high notion of hospitality. The Captain was the gunroom's guest, and the ship's surgeon was not to sit there in silent dogged resentment. Putting a considerable force on himself Stephen uttered four civil remarks, and after a proper interval he said, 'A glass of wine with you, sir,' bowing low.

'I must congratulate you most heartily, Doctor, on your preservation of young Blakeney,' said Jack, returning his bow. 'How I could have told our old shipmate that we had let his son perish of grapeshot I do not know. A grapeshot in these circumstances, I mean, not a French or American one.'

'How could he possibly have come to swallow such a thing?' asked Martin.

'When I was a reefer and any of the youngsters talked too much, we used to make him hold one in his mouth,' said Jack. 'We called 'em gob-stoppers. I dare say that is how it came about.'

'May I send you a piece of bonito, sir?' called Howard from the middle of the table.

'If you please. A capital fish, bonito, capital: I could eat it for ever.'

'I caught seven this morning, sir, sitting in the mizen chains and casting along the edge of the wake. I sent one to the sick-bay, one to the midshipmen's berth, three to my Marines, and kept the best for us.'

'Capital, capital,' said Jack again; and indeed it was a capital dinner altogether: best green turtle, delicate flying squid come aboard in the night, a variety of fishes, dolphin pie, and to crown all a great dish of teal, Galapagos teal, indistinguishable in taste from Christian teal, that had been netted by Howard's sergeant, a former poacher. And Stephen noticed, not without irritation, that as he ate and drank his civility was growing less artificial, his deliberately urbane expression more nearly a spontaneous smile, and that he was in danger of enjoying himself.

251

'. . . behold the threaden sails
Borne with the invisible and creeping wind,
Draw the huge bottoms through the furrow'd sea
Breasting the lofty surge,'

said Mowett in a momentary silence as the decanters were renewed – he and Martin had been discussing poetry for some time – 'That is the kind of thing I mean.'

'Did you write that, Mowett?' asked Jack.

'No, sir,' said Mowett. 'It was – it was another cove.'

'The invisible and creeping wind,' repeated Maitland. 'They say pigs can see the wind.'

'Stay, gentlemen,' cried Howard, holding up his hand and looking round with a flushed face and a gleaming eye. 'You must forgive me, but I don't often come up with a good thing at the right moment: han't done so this commission, I believe, though I came pretty close to it once off the River Plate. So by your leave, sir,' – bowing to Jack – 'there was an old woman in the Cove of Cork that lived in a cabin with just one room, no more; she bought a pig – a *pig*, eh, that's the point, that's what makes it so apposite – and they said, "What shall you do about the smell?" Because it had to live in the same room, if you follow me: the pig had to live in the same room as the old woman. "Oh, ochone," says she, "begar, he will have to get used to it," – mistaking, do you see . . .'

But Howard's explanation was drowned in a gale of laughter, led by Killick from behind Jack's chair. Jack himself said, 'he will have to get used to it', threw himself back and had his laugh out, his face scarlet and his eyes a brighter blue than usual. 'Dear me, dear me,' he said at last, wiping them with his handkerchief, 'in this vale of tears it does a man good to laugh from time to time.'

When they were quiet the purser peered round his neighbours at the first lieutenant and asked, 'Was that piece you said just now poetry? The piece before the pig.'

'Yes, it was,' said Mowett.

'It didn't rhyme,' said Adams. 'I told it over to myself, and it didn't rhyme. If Rowan were here, he would knock your poet on the head. His poetry always rhymes. I remember a piece of his as though it were only yesterday:

Awful the grinding noise of keel and heel
With an unusual motion made the crew to reel.'

'I believe there are almost as many kinds of poetry as there are rigs,' observed the master.

'So there are too,' said Stephen. 'Do you remember that dear Ahmed Smyth, Mr Stanhope's oriental secretary, when we were going to Kampong? He told me of a curious Malay form of verse whose name escapes me, though I have retained an example:

The peepul-tree grows on the edge of the forest,
On the fishermen's strand nets lie in hopeless
   confusion;
It is true that I am sitting on your knee
But you are not therefore to suppose that you may
   take any other liberty at all.'

'Did it rhyme in Malay?' asked the purser, after a silent pause.

'It did,' said Stephen. 'The first and the third . . .'
The arrival of the pudding cut him short, a most uncommonly splendid pudding brought in with conscious pride and welcomed with applause.

'What, what is this?' cried Jack.

'We thought you would be surprised, sir,' said Mowett. 'It's a floating island, or rather a floating archipelago.'

'It is the Galapagos themselves,' said Jack. 'Here's Albemarle, here's Narborough, here's Chatham and Hood . . . I had no idea there was anyone aboard capable of such a thing: a masterpiece, upon my word and honour, fit for a flagship.'

'One of the whalers made it, sir. He was a pastrycook in Danzig before he took to sea.'

'I put in the lines of longitude and latitude,' said the

253

master. 'They are made of spun sugar; so is the equator, but double thick and dyed with port.'

'The Galapagos,' said Jack, gazing down on them. 'The whole shooting-match: there's even the Redondo Rock and Cowly's Enchanted Isle, laid down exactly. And to think we never set foot on a single one . . . sometimes ours is a very demanding profession . . .'

'*Stern daughter of the voice of God! O Duty!*' said Mowett; but Jack, musing over the archipelago, which swayed with the heave of the ship, did not hear him, and went on, 'but I tell you what, gentlemen, if we come back this way, having done what we set out to do, we shall lie in Mr Allen's cove on James Island for a few days, and everyone shall have leave to roam to his heart's content.'

'Will you not take some Galapagos, sir, before it comes adrift?' said Mowett.

'I hesitate to spoil such a work of art,' said Jack. 'But unless we are to go without our pudding' – this with a pretty knowing look as he poised his spoon above the pastry-cook's equator – 'I believe I must cut the Line.'

The Line, the Line, day after day they sailed westwards along the Line or a little south of it. They left the penguins and the seals behind almost at once, all the inshore birds and almost all the fish; they also left the gloom, the cool water and the low-hanging cloud, and they sailed over a dark blue disk, perpetually renewed, under a pale blue dome, occasionally flecked with very high white cirrus. But they did not sail at all fast. In spite of the *Surprise*'s splendid display of light fair-weather canvas – studdingsails aloft and alow, royals and even skysails and skyscrapers – she rarely logged more than a hundred miles between one observation and the next. Almost every day the breeze dozed for two or three hours after midday, or even went fast to sleep, leaving the pyramids of sail in a dismal state of sag, while vast stretches of dead calm spread over the sea, broken only by the passage of whales, sperm whales, that would sometimes pass in wide-spaced files two and even three hundred strong, heading for

Peru. And every evening at the setting of the watch the *Surprise* snugged down to topsails: there was no trusting the sudden flurries of the night, in spite of the lamblike innocence of the day.

These were waters largely unknown to the Navy – Byron, Wallis and Cook had kept much farther south or much farther north – and this slow creeping over an apparently infinite sea would have fretted Jack to the very heart if he had not learnt, through the master, that here it was always the case when the sun began to move backwards from the tropic: and it would be as bad for the *Norfolk* or possibly worse. Allen had had many a conversation with the specktioneer, a middle-aged man named Hogg, who had made the run to the Marquesas three times and the Sandwich Islands twice: and his experience, both first- and second-hand, was a great relief to all hands aboard. They sailed on as fast as they reasonably could, but not as though they had a chase in view, not wetting the sails throughout the urgent day, since they knew that the *Norfolk* would proceed at an even more moderate pace: and when she reached the Marquesas she would spend a great while cruising among the islands in search of the British whalers fishing there. There was not a moment to spare, it was true; but then not every moment had to be flogged.

Once again, and with surprising speed, the ship settled down to a perfectly regular, self-sufficing existence; very soon it became the natural way of life once more, and the Surprises looked back to the remote and bitterly cold days far south of the Horn and even to their haunted passage up the coast of Chile and Peru as to another world.

The sun rose every morning exactly in the frigate's wake; it shone on the new-cleaned decks, but soon they were hidden from view by awnings, for although this was not Gulf of Guinea hot, with the pitch bubbling from the seams and tar dripping from on high, still less the Red Sea of infamous memory, the temperature was in the eighties and shade was grateful. Everybody walked about in duck, except for invitations to the cabin; and even for them the midshipmen were excused their thick kerseymere waistcoats.

Yet they were perhaps the only people who were not quite pleased about the return to proper blue-water sailoring with everything just so, shipshape and Bristol-fashion. Greek and Latin had never indeed been laid entirely aside except for the very worst days in the fifties and sixties, but now both came back with redoubled force; and now Captain Aubrey had time to lead them through the mazes of navigation, while at night he made them learn the name, declination and right ascension of a great many stars, and find out the angular distance between these and various planets or the moon. He and Mowett also had time to set about improving their morals, which in the naval context meant leaving their comfortable hammocks very early indeed, relieving the watch well before the stroke of the bell, never putting their hands in the pockets or leaning on the rail or resting on a carronade-slide, and always attending in the tops whenever sails were reefed. 'You are called reefers,' Mowett told them one day, 'you are given a sumptuous berth, you are fed like fighting-cocks, and all that is asked of you is to attend in the tops when the sails are being reefed. But what do I find? The maintopgallantsail being supervised from the head . . .'

'Oh sir,' cried Nesbitt, stung with the injustice. 'I was caught short just that once.'

'. . . and the foretopsail apparently reefing itself while the midshipman was rioting in swinish slumber somewhere below. I really grieve for the service if it is to be officered by such creatures as you, who think of nothing but eating and sleeping, and neglecting their duty. I have never seen the like in any ship before, and never wish to see it again.'

'These youngsters think too much of their ease,' said Jack. 'They are nothing but a parcel of helots.'

'Pray have helots a particular nautical signification, like dogs, mice, fishes and so on?' asked Stephen.

'Oh no, just the ordinary sense of idle young devils,

you know – limbs of Satan. I must stir them up, and make their lives a misery.'

Whatever his attempts may have been, they were not successful; the *Surprise* had a sprightly, high-spirited midshipmen's berth, with no real oldsters to tyrannize over the rest; and so far at least its members had plenty to eat. They had long since recovered from the hardships of the far south, although nothing would bring Williamson's toes back nor the tips of his ears, Boyle's ribs had knit perfectly, while a faint down was beginning to cover not only Calamy's bald scalp but also his girlish chin. In spite of hard duty and hard lessons, and in spite of moral improvement they remained cheerful: what is more, they learnt how to swim. In the afternoon, when the ship was becalmed, most of the people plunged over the side, most into a shallow swimming-bath made of a sunken sail but some into the open sea itself, for no sharks had been seen since they left the Galapagos, at least none that followed the ship.

This was one of the delights of their westward course; another was the competitive firing of the great guns or small-arms almost every evening at quarters; but there were many more, and the most highly prized, deeply relished, during the first weeks was the conduct of the whalers, particularly of their chief, the specktioneer Hogg. He had never been in the Royal Navy. Although the war had been going on with little interruption since his boyhood he had never been pressed; as a South Sea whaler and a harpooner he had a protection, but he had never had to use it. Neither the press-gang nor the impress officer had ever troubled him, and in fact he had never set foot on board a man-of-war before the *Surprise*. His life had been spent entirely in whalers, a particularly democratic set of vessels in which the hands worked not for wages but for shares of what the ship might earn, and in which, although there was the necessary minimum of discipline, there was little sense of hierarchy among the thirty-odd people – certainly nothing resembling that of the Navy with its far greater numbers, its different worlds afore the mast and abaft it, its different essences of humanity. He was an intelligent man – he could navigate – but he had a certain simplicity; and having spent his childhood in the heathen slums of Wapping and the rest of his life among whalers he had had little contact with civilization. Meeting the officer of the watch on his first morning, for example, he called out, 'How are you coming along, mate? Prime, I hope, prime.' And when church was rigged it was difficult to make him set down in his right place. 'Well, this is a rum go,' he said in a loud voice when at last he was settled on an upturned mess-kid; and he stared very much during the hymns, clapping when they were done. When Mr Martin put on his surplice his neighbour told him in what passed for a whisper among seamen that 'Parson was now going to preach them a sermon.' 'Is he, though?' cried Hogg, leaning forward with both hands on his knees and watching the chaplain with keen interest, 'I never heard a sermon.' Then, after a few minutes, 'You've turned over two pages. Hey, there. You've turned over two pages, master.' It was true, for Martin, an indifferent preacher, generally read from some more gifted man, such as South or Barrow, and now, flustered by his new parishioners, he had indeed made a sad and obvious blunder.

'Silence, fore and aft,' cried Mowett.

'But he's turned over two pages,' said Hogg.

'Bonden,' said Jack, in a church-going aside, 'lead Hogg forward and tell him how we do it in the Navy.'

Bonden told him, but he cannot have made the principle quite plain, for the next day, when Nesbitt, the smallest of the reefers, was bawling orders to some hands in the foretop, he used a coarse expression, and Hogg suddenly turned, held him up with one hand and slapped his buttocks with the other, telling him he should be ashamed of speaking so to men old enough to be his daddy. Any court martial sitting on Hogg's crime would have been compelled to sentence him to death, for the Twenty-Second Article of War provided no less penalty. Jack caused Mowett and

258

Allen to speak to him at some length, and they brought him to some sense of the enormity of his act; but even so the rest of the ship's company did not despair of seeing the whalers tell Mr Adams just what they thought of his purser's dips, for example, or trouble the Captain for a glass of his best brandy when they felt inclined for a wet; and they often urged them so to do – 'Go on, mate,' they would say, 'don't be bashful. The skipper loves a foremast jack, and will always give him a glass if he asks civil.' It was not that they disliked their new shipmates, far from it indeed, for the whalers were not only amiable but thorough-paced seamen as well; but their innocence was a standing temptation, and in principle when the Surprises were tempted they fell.

Before church was rigged again the whalers had grown wary; although they could still be made to leap half asleep from their hammocks by the cry of 'There she blows' they would no longer go to the carpenter's mate and ask for a long stand nor to the gunner's yeoman for half a fathom of firing line; yet even so they did give a great deal of innocent pleasure when an American whaler appeared at an immense distance to windward, standing east, a vessel instantly recognizable from her double-decked crow's nest on the main. Hogg and his friends rushed aft in a body, filled with passion and a wild longing for revenge; and when Honey, who had the watch, would not instantly haul to the wind they began bawling down to Jack through the skylight, and had to be removed by the Marines.

A moment's consideration showed Jack that chasing the American would mean far too great a loss of time. He sent for the specktioneer and said, 'Hogg, we have been very patient with you and your shipmates, but if you carry on like this I shall be obliged to punish you.'

'They burnt our ship,' muttered Hogg.

Jack feigned not to hear: but seeing the man's hot tears of rage and disappointment he said, 'Never mind it, man. The *Norfolk* is perhaps not so very far away, and you shall serve them out.'

259

Even if she were already in the Marquesas she would not be so very far away by now, as these things were reckoned in the prodigious expanse of the Pacific, where something in the nature of a thousand miles seemed the natural unit. Another unit might be a poem: Stephen was reading Mowett's *Iliad* and he was keeping to one book a day, no more, to make his pleasure last; he had begun a little while after leaving the Galapagos and he was now in book twelve, and he reckoned that at the present rate of sailing he would finish just before they reached the Marquesas. He did his reading in the afternoons, for now that the days were calm and untroubled, with the necessary weeks of their western passage taken out of time as it were, a self-contained whole, he and Jack filled the evenings with the music they had been obliged to forego in more demanding waters.

Night after night they played there in the great cabin with the stern-windows open and the ship's wake flowing away and away in the darkness. Few things gave them more joy; and although they were as unlike in nationality, education, religion, appearance and habit of mind as two men could well be, they were wholly at one when it came to improvising, working out variations on a theme, handing them to and fro, conversing with violin and 'cello; though this was a language in which Jack was somewhat more articulate than his friend, wittier, more original and indeed more learned. They were alike in their musical tastes, in their reasonably high degree of amateur skill, and in their untiring relish.

But on the evening of the day in which Stephen had reconciled Achilles and Agamemnon, and when the frigate's wake was rather better than two thousand miles long, they did not play at all. This was partly because the ship was passing through an immense population of phosphorescent marine organisms, and had been passing through it ever since the dark-red sun set into the misty sea, his disc neatly divided by the bowsprit, but even more because the hands had been turned up to sing and dance on

260

the forecastle and they were making much more noise than usual. The order was purely formal, since the hands were already there, dancing and singing as they always did on fine evenings when the ship was sailing easy, and its only function was to let them know that they might keep it up, this being the whalers' particular feast-day.

'I am glad I cancelled the youngsters' lesson,' said Jack, looking up through the open skylight. 'There is scarcely a star to be seen. Jupiter is no more than a blur, and I do not suppose that even he will last another five minutes.'

'Perhaps it was on Wednesday,' replied Stephen at the stern-window, leaning far out and down.

'I said Jupiter will not last another five minutes,' said Jack in a voice calculated to drown the merriment afore: but it was badly calculated, not having taken the whalers into account, and they had just begun *Away my boys, away my boys, 'tis time for us to go* in voices that would have suited the whales themselves; Stephen answered, 'Probably Wednesday, I said,' in a rather impatient tone. 'Will you not pass me the long-handled net, now? I have asked you three times, and there is a creature I just cannot reach with this miserable . . .'

Jack found the long-handled net quite soon, but when he came to pass it there was no Stephen in the stern-window, only a strangled voice from the wake: 'A rope, a rope.'

'Clap on to the cutter,' cried Jack and he dived straight in. He did not hail the ship on coming to the surface because he knew the red cutter was towing astern: Stephen would either seize it or be towed towards it, and then they could regain the stern-window without the ship's way being checked or her surgeon being still further exposed for what in fact he was, the most hopeless lubber yet born.

No cutter: someone must have hauled the boat alongside. No Stephen either; but at that moment he saw and heard a gasping boil that rose and sank in the troubled, phosphorescent water. He dived again, swimming deeper and deeper until he saw his friend against the luminous surface. Stephen had become strangely entangled in his own net, his head and one elbow tight in its meshes, its handle down the back of his shirt. Jack got him out; but breaking the stout handle, ripping off the shirt, and at the same time holding Stephen so that his head was above water took some while, and when at last he drew breath and shouted, '*Surprise*, ahoy,' the hail coincided with the roaring chorus *There she blows, there she blows, there she blows*, taken up by the whole ship's company. He had set Stephen to float on his back, which he could do tolerably well when the sea was calm; but an unfortunate ripple, washing over his face just as he breathed in, sank him again; again he had to be brought up, and now Jack's '*Surprise* ahoy' coming at the full pitch of his powerful voice, had an edge of anxiety to it, for although the ship was not sailing fast, every minute she moved more than a hundred yards, and already her lights were dimming in the mist.

Hail after hail after hail, enough to startle the dead: but when she was no more than the blur of the planet earlier in the night he fell silent, and Stephen said, 'I am extremely concerned, Jack, that my awkwardness should have brought you into such very grave danger.'

'Bless you,' said Jack, 'it ain't so very grave as all that. Killick is bound to come into the cabin in half an hour or so, and Mowett will put the ship about directly.'

'But do you think they will ever see us, with this fog, and no moon, no moon at all?'

'They may find it a little difficult, though it is amazing how something that floats shows up on the night sea, when you are looking for it. In any case I shall hail every so often, like a minute gun, to help them. But, you know, it would be no very great harm, were we to have to wait until day. The water is as warm as milk, there is no kind of a sea apart from the swell, and if you stretch out your arms, stick out your belly and throw your head back till your ears are awash you will find you float as easy as kiss my hand.'

The minute-gun hails succeeded one another in a long, long series; Stephen floated easy; and they drifted westwards on the equatorial current, westwards and probably a little north. Jack reflected upon the relativity of motion, upon the difficulty of measuring the speed or set of a current if your ship is moving with it and you can neither anchor nor observe any fixed point of land; and he wondered how Mowett would set about searching once the alarm was raised. If the observations were conscientiously made and the log accurately heaved, read and recorded, then it would not be very hard for him to run back close-hauled or even with the wind one point free, always provided that the breeze remained steady at south-east by south and that his estimate of the current was correct: each degree of error in that would, in the course of an hour's sailing at four and a half knots, amount to . . . In the midst of his calculations he became aware that Stephen, lying there as stiff as a board, was becoming distressed. 'Stephen,' he said, pushing him, for Stephen's head was thrown back so far that he could not easily hear, 'Stephen, turn over, put your arms round my neck, and we will swim for a little.' Then as he felt Stephen's feet on the back of his legs, 'You have not kicked off your shoes. Do not you know you must kick off your shoes? What a fellow you are, Stephen.'

So they went on, sometimes swimming gently, sometimes floating in the luke-warm sea, rising and falling on the very long, regular swell. They did not talk much, though Stephen did observe that it was all very much easier, now that he was allowed to change position from time to time; even the act of floating came to him more naturally with use – 'I believe I may set up as a Triton.' And on another occasion he said, 'I am very deeply indebted to you, Jack, for supporting me in this way.'

Once Jack found that he must have slept awhile; and once they were rocked by a sudden upsurge of water quite close at hand, a looming on the swell, and they were in the enormous presence of a whale. As far as they could make out in the phosphorescence he was an old bull, rather better than eighty feet long: he lay there for perhaps ten minutes, spouting at steady intervals – they could see the white jet and faintly hear it – and then with a great inward sigh he put down his head, raised his flukes clear of the sea, and silently vanished.

Shortly after this the mist began to clear; the stars showed through, at first dimly and then brilliantly clear, and to his relief Jack saw that the dawn was closer than he had supposed. It was not that he had much hope of being rescued now. That had depended on Killick's looking into the cabin before going to bed; there was no particular reason why he should have looked in and clearly he had not done so, otherwise Mowett would have turned well before the end of the first watch. He would have cracked on with all the sail she could bear, and with all the boats strung out within hailing distance on either side he would have combed a broad stretch of sea, picking them up some time early in the middle watch: and the middle watch was already over. But if Mowett did not hear of their absence till the morning, clearly the dear *Surprise* would have sailed that much farther west, and she could not be brought back much before the evening. The probability of error from the current would be very, very much greater, and in any case he did not think they could hold out much beyond dawn – almost certainly not until the late afternoon. Although the sea had seemed so warm to begin with they were both of them shivering convulsively by now; they were waterlogged; Jack for one was overcome with an enormous hunger; and both of them were haunted by the fear of sharks. Neither had spoken for a long time, apart from the brief words when they changed position and when Jack towed Stephen on his shoulders for a while.

There was very little hope now, he admitted, yet he did long for the light. The heat of the sun might revive them wonderfully, and it was not wholly inconceivable that a coral island might appear: although the charts showed none for another three or four hundred miles, these were largely uncharted waters. Hogg had spoken of islands known to whalers and sandalwood cutters alone, their observed positions kept private. But what he really hoped for was a piece of driftwood: palm-trunks were almost indestructible and in the course of the last few days he had seen several drifting on the current, borne, perhaps, from the Guatemalan shore; and with one of those to buoy them up they could last all day and more, much more. He turned it over in his mind – the ways of dealing with a palm-trunk, and how to give it some kind of stability with an outrigger in the South Seas fashion. Almost wholly useless reflection, but even so better than the piercing, sterile, pointless regrets that had tormented him for the last few hours, regrets about leaving Sophie surrounded with law-suits, regrets for not having managed things more cleverly, bitter regret at having to leave life behind and all those he loved.

The earth turned and the ocean with it; the water in which they swam turned towards the sun. Over in the west there was the last of the night, and in the east, to windward, the first of the day; and there, clear against the lightening sky, lay a vessel, already quite near, a very large two-masted double-hulled canoe with a broad platform or deck overlapping the hulls with a thatched house upon it; and the vessel had two towering fore and aft sails, each with a curved crest reaching forwards. These however were details that Jack did not consciously observe until he had uttered a great roaring hail: it roused Stephen, who had been in something not far from a coma.

'A South Sea craft,' said Jack, pointing; and he hailed again. The vessel was very like what Captain Cook called a pahi.

'Will they take us up, do you suppose?' asked Stephen.

'Oh surely,' said Jack, and he saw a narrow outrigger canoe put off from the vessel's side, hoist a triangular sail and come racing down towards them. One young woman sat in the stern steering; another straddled the booms connecting the slender hull and the outrigger, balancing with wonderful grace. She held a spear in her hand and as the other girl let fly the sheet, bringing the canoe almost to a halt three yards from them, she was all poised to throw. But seeing what they were she paused, frowning, quite amazed; the other one laughed, a fine flash of white teeth. They were both strikingly good-looking young women, brown, long-legged, dressed in little kilts and no more. Ordinarily Jack was attentive to an elegant form, an elegant bosom, a well-rounded shape, but now he would not have cared if they had been old man baboon, so long as they took him and Stephen aboard. He lifted up his hands and uttered a supplicatory croak; Stephen did the same; but the girls, laughing, filled and ran back the way they had come, sailing with extraordinary skill and speed, unbelievably close to the wind. Yet as they swept off they smiled and they made motions signifying, perhaps, that the outrigger was too frail for any more weight, and that Jack and Stephen might swim to the two-master.

That was how Jack's willing mind interpreted them; and in fact when they reached the double canoe, which in any case was bearing down upon them, these same girls and several others helped them up on to the mat-covered deck. There appeared to be a positive crowd of young women and a good many older and stouter; but this was not time for fine observation. Jack said, 'Thank you, thank you, ma'am,' very earnestly to the cheerful helmswoman, who had given him a particularly hearty hand, and looked all his gratitude at the rest, while Stephen said, 'Ladies, I am obliged beyond measure.' Then they sat down with hanging heads, scarcely aware of their pleasure, and dripped upon the deck, shivering uncontrollably. There was a great deal of talk above them; they were certainly addressed at length by two or three of the older women, and questioned, and sometimes brown hands plucked at their hair and clothes, but little notice did they take until Jack felt the power of the sun warming him through and through as it mounted. His trembling stopped; hunger

266

and thirst came upon him with redoubled force, and turning to the women, who were still watching with close attention, he made gestures begging for food and drink. There was some discussion, and two of the middle-aged women seemed to disapprove, but some of the younger ones stepped down into the starboard hull and brought up green coconuts, a small bundle of dried fishes, and two baskets, one containing sour breadfruit pap and the other dried bananas.

How quickly humanity and pleasure in being alive flowed back with food and drink and the warmth of the sun! They looked about them, and smiled, and renewed their thanks. The stern broad-shouldered spear-girl and her jollier companion seemed to think them to some degree their property. The one opened the drinking-coconuts and passed them, the other handed the dried fishes, one by one. But not very valuable property: the spear-girl, whose name appeared to be Taio, looked at the white, hairy, waterlogged, water-wrinkled skin of Jack's leg where his trousers were rolled back, and uttered a sound of sincere and candid disgust, while the other one, Manu, took hold of a lock of his long yellow hair, now untied and hanging down his back, plucked out a few strands, turned them in her fingers and tossed them over the side, shaking her head and then carefully washing her hands.

By now the scene changed, almost as it might have done in a man-of-war, though there was no evident signal, no pipe, no bell. Part of the crew began washing most scrupulously, first hanging over the water, then diving in and swimming like dolphins: they paid no attention whatsoever to nakedness. Others took up the mats covering the platform, shook them to leeward, lashed them down again in a seamanlike manner, and heaved on the forestays, now slackening with the heat of the sun, while a third party brought up small pigs, edible dogs and fowls, in baskets, mostly from the larboard hull, and arranged them on the forward part of the deck where they sat good and quiet, as ship-borne animals so often do.

During all this activity no one had much time to stare at them, and Stephen, whose spirits had recovered wonderfully, grew less discreet in looking about. He considered first the hurrying crew, which seemed to consist of about a score of young women and nine or ten between old and young, together with an indefinite number heard but not seen in the deckhouse aft. A dozen of the young women were cheerful, unaffected creatures, good looking though often heavily tattooed, full of curiosity, talk and laughter, and reasonably friendly, though it was clear that they considered Jack and Stephen physically unattractive, if not worse. The young women and most of those of thirty or forty were more reserved if not downright inimical; Stephen suspected that they did not approve of the rescue, still less of the feeding of those saved from the sea. But whatever their opinion, all the women talked all the time, in a mellifluous language that he took to be that of Polynesia in general: all the women, that is to say, except four of the youngest who sat industriously chewing the root from which kava was made and spitting the fibrous pulp into a bowl: Stephen knew that once coconut milk had been stirred in and the mixture had stood for a while it would be ready to drink. He had read a few accounts of the islands, but since he had had no idea of visiting them this commission he had learnt nothing of their language and he retained no more than a word or two from his books, of which kava was one. He therefore sat uncomprehending in the babble and presently his mind wandered from this curious community – a sea-going convent? – to their vessel. It was obviously stocked for a long voyage, one of those very long Polynesian voyages of which he had heard, and it certainly seemed capable of undertaking one: he much admired the two smooth hulls upon which the platform and its house reposed, the windward hull acting as a counterpoise in a side-breeze, so that there was a much greater lateral stability as well as much less friction, an improvement that might well be introduced into the Navy. The idea of the Navy's considering a man-of-war with two hulls for a moment, after the terrible outcry it had raised about a slight change in the traditional stern made him smile, and his eye ran along the tall rising stems in which these particular hulls ended, their prows, as it were, or figureheads. And here some indistinct recollections of that black though ingenious Cromwellian thief Sir William Petty and his double-bottomed vessel were driven clear out of his mind, for lashed to the starboard stem was a carving some six feet high, a very lively carving of three men: the first had the second standing on his shoulders and the second the third; and these three were connected by the huge penis which rose from the loins of the first, towering past the second to a point above the third man's head and held by all three as it mounted. It was coloured red and purple and it had no doubt reached higher still, but it had been much gashed and mutilated and now there was no telling whether it was common to them all, though this seemed probable. All the figures had been castrated, and judging by the freshness and the rough texture of the splintered wood this had been done quite recently, and with a coarse instrument. 'Dear me,' he murmured, and turned his attention to the other stem. This bore a tall piece of wood, adze-flattened on its two faces with the side indented or crenellated in regular squares; it had something of the air and presence of a totem-pole and it was topped by a skull. The skull did not surprise Stephen very much – he had already noticed one rolling about among the coconut bailers and he knew they had no great significance in the South Seas – but it was with real concern that he saw and after a moment recognized the little wizened purselike objects pinned to the slab, as vermin might be to a European gamekeeper's door.

He was about to tell Jack of his discovery and his conclusions, to caution him against the least ill-humour and to advise submission, meekness, a deferential bearing and above all no hint of gallantry however innocent, when he found that he was alone. Jack had left him when the second part of the crew started their washing and the first set about arranging their hair, all this on the windward side of the platform. He walked aft along to the other side, taking great notice of the shaped planks, sewn together edge to edge and caulked with what he took to be coconut fibre mixed with something sticky, of the cordage and the sails, made of fine matting with an immensely long piece of creeper or supple-jack as a bolt-rope; and skirting the deck-house, in which several women were all talking at once in loud contentious voices, he came to the helm. It was a large paddle, but to his astonishment he found that it was not moved from side to side, rudder-fashion, but thrust down to turn from the wind and raised to luff it up. The woman who held it had a sensible, manly look as far as could be seen through the complex lines and spirals of her tattoo; she understood him quite readily, demonstrated the use of the paddle and showed him that the vessel could come tolerably close to the wind, though of course you had to reckon on a good deal of leeway – she showed the angle with her parted fingers and blew to indicate the increasing force of the wind. But she could make nothing of his other inquiries, to do with the stars, navigation by night, and the vessel's destination, even though he illustrated them with gestures.

He was trying to make himself plainer when three stout middle-aged women like bosun's mates came round the corner from the deck-house, gasped with indignation and hustled him forward at a great pace, one helping him on his way with a flying kick that would have done credit to a Spithead nightingale. All three, and some of the other women, seemed very angry; they railed and scolded for a quarter of an hour, and then Jack was given a mortar with some dried roots in it and a heavy pestle, while Stephen was put to mind a young hog. Like most of the animals on deck it was in a basket, but unlike the others it was restless, and in poor health. It had to be nursed and it would not keep still.

For some time the bosun's mates stood just behind, pinching and slapping them if the hog complained or the roots skipped out of the mortar, and sometimes for no reason at all. But presently other duties called them away and in a low voice Jack said, 'I should never have gone aft. We are clearly foremast hands, no more, and must never move from here unless we are told.'

Stephen was about to agree, and to add his recommendations about their behaviour, his hypothesis on the nature of this community and the purpose of its voyage, and some remarks on the prevalence of cannibalism in the South Seas, when Jack interrupted, saying, 'Ain't you hellfire thirsty, Stephen? I am. I believe it was those dried fish. But, you know, they don't seem to like the look of me; whereas you are almost as brown as they are.'

'This I attribute to my practice of aprication,' said Stephen, looking at his bare belly with some complacency. It was true: Stephen regularly sat in the tops with nothing on and he had none of the dank, corpselike pallor of naked Europeans. 'I have little doubt that to them you resemble a leper; or at any rate something diseased, unwholesome. The colour of your hair is disgusting. To those who are not used to it, I mean.'

'Yes,' said Jack, 'so pray be a good fellow and sing out to the girl forward there, among the coconuts.'

Stephen's first gentle call, accompanied by a timid gesture of drinking, was unsuccessful; she pursed her lips and looked coldly away, with a righteous expression. His second had more luck. Manu was passing by and she brought four nuts across and opened the shells with a shark's tooth set in a handle; and as they drank the exquisite milk she spoke to them rather severely, no doubt telling them something for their own good. At one time she put her hands together, as though in prayer, and looked emphatically aft; they could make nothing of it at all, but they both nodded gravely and said, 'Yes indeed, ma'am. Certainly. We are most obliged to you.'

Once again Stephen was about to tell Jack of his intimate conviction, derived not only from the figureheads but from

271

many little signs, forms of behaviour, caresses, quarrels and reconciliations, that they were aboard a vessel belonging to women who did not like men, who had revolted from the tyranny of men, and who were sailing away to some island, perhaps a great way off, to set up a female commonwealth; and to say that he dreaded the possibility of Jack's being gelded, knocked on the head, and eaten. But before he could do so his hog grew restless, squealed and fouled the deck; at the same time Jack was seen to be idling with his pestle, and the bosun's mates stepped in. When the mess was cleaned, and Stephen's trousers too – this they insisted upon, having an exceedingly high standard of cleanliness: they made him take them off and wring them out again and again before they were satisfied – and when all the shouting, cuffing, pinching, slapping and reproof had died down, Jack said, 'Here comes the captain, I believe; and the officers.'

She was a broad, squat woman, much darker than most, with a long trunk and short legs; she had a handsome, high-nosed, but exceedingly cross and authoritarian face; and as she made her tour of the vessel she was accompanied by two taller women, obviously stupid and obviously devoted to her. They both carried the same weapons, a three-foot palm-rib topped with a hardwood knob with mother-of-pearl eyes on either side of an obsidian beak, possibly a mark of rank, since they held them with a certain amount of pomp. She had no mark of rank – far from it: she was casually nibbling at something she held – but as she came forward the members of the crew stood with their hands clasped and their heads bowed.

'Perhaps we should adopt a respectful submissive attitude,' murmured Stephen; and as the captain came nearer he saw that what she was gnawing was a hand, a smoked or pickled hand. She looked at Jack and Stephen without any pleasure or interest and without making any reply to their bows or their 'Your most humble devoted servant, ma'am,' and 'Most honoured and happy to be aboard you, ma'am.' And having looked at them she entered

272

into a long, displeased conversation with Taio and Manu, who in spite of their clasped hands spoke up very freely in their clear young voices: Stephen suspected that they belonged to a privileged class – they were taller, lighter in colour, and their tatooing was quite different; and the captain's attitude towards Manu in particular was civiller than it was to the others.

The captain and her officers went by walking aft along the larboard side; and a little later Jack, having turned the mortar so that he could see, said, 'I believe they are rigging church.' Indeed something very like an altar appeared in the middle of the platform and six mother-of-pearl disks and an obsidian knife were laid upon it, with a variety of weapons ranged in front. Again Jack and Stephen slackened a little in their attention to work and again some sort of ship's corporal brought them back to a sense of duty with a furious roar; she then harangued them at length, with gestures, and although no single word had any meaning it was clear from her intonation that sometimes she was describing the conduct of the virtuous, sometimes that of the worthless. And behind her Taio, Manu and half a dozen of the jollier girls imitated her gestures and her expressions with such perfection that at last Jack could not contain but burst out into a strangled horse-laugh. The ship's corporal darted to the row of weapons and came at him with just such a beaked club as the officers carried, a tool designed to peck through a skull at a single blow; but in fact she only kicked him in the stomach. She had scarcely done so before the whole thing was over: everybody was shrieking and pointing over the side, where Manu had sighted a shark close on the starboard beam.

It was a medium-sized brute, twelve or thirteen feet long, though of what species Stephen could not tell; nor had he any time for deliberation, for Manu, catching up the obsidian knife from the altar, slipped into the sea between the two hulls. What happened next he could not make out, but there was a furious threshing convulsion a

273

few yards out to starboard and there were the girls and the ship's corporal laughing heartily as Manu came dripping aboard and the shark dropped astern, disembowelled but still lashing with enormous force.

Clearly no one but Jack and Stephen thought it out of the way; the others carried on with their preparations for church as though nothing of importance had happened, except that two of them helped Manu rearrange her wet hair. A bosun's mate, now dressed in a striped garment with tags, had just time to throw Jack more roots to grind and to give him a passing swipe with a rope's end and drums started to beat.

The ceremony began with a dance: two lines of women facing the captain, rhythmically advancing, retiring, waving their weapons while she chanted, and at the end of each verse they all cried *Wahu*. Their weapons were spears, the hardwood skull-splitter called pattoo-pattoo, a name that came to Stephen the moment he saw it, and clubs, some studded with human teeth, some with those of sharks; and all the women, even the kava-chewing girls, handled them most convincingly.

The dance went on and on and on, the drum-beat acquiring a hypnotic quality. 'Stephen,' whispered Jack, 'I must go to the head.'

'Very well,' said Stephen, calming his hog. 'I have seen the women do so repeatedly. They mostly go over the side.'

'But I shall have to take off my trousers,' said Jack.

'Then no doubt it would be more seemly to dip between the two floaters, holding on to the platform; for although they seem to be innocent as Eve before the apple, at least as far as nakedness is concerned, they may not view the shameful parts of a man in quite the same light.'

'I believe it was that dried fish,' said Jack. 'But perhaps I can wait. To tell you the truth, that ill-looking bitch' – lowering his voice and nodding towards the captain – 'quite daunts me. I do not know what she would be at.'

'Go on, Jack – go on while you may – it may be worse

later – go on directly – I believe they are reaching their climax.'

Rarely had Stephen given better advice. Jack had not been back to his pestle five minutes, with a look of profound relief on his face, before the dancing stopped and the ill-looking bitch delivered a long address, during which she often pointed at the men, growing steadily more passionate.

The address came to an end and the congregation got up and moved about; but this was only the beginning of the real ceremony. The fire that Jack had noticed on his way aft was brought forward – embers in a bowl that floated in another – and set down before the altar. Presently the smell of grilling flesh came forward, together with ritual cries; but glancing discreetly round Stephen observed that the captain and her officers were in fact drinking the kava prepared that morning. The flesh was only formal at this stage.

'Some say that kava is not truly intoxicating,' remarked Stephen, 'that it contains no alcohol. I wish they may be right.'

Alcohol or no, the captain, her officers and the big middle-aged women were obviously affected when at last they came forward, dancing heavily behind their leader, who held the obsidian knife in her hand. The effect would have been grotesque but for the fact that the jaw-bones they had now hung round their necks were in most cases quite fresh and that drunk or not they handled their weapons with great dexterity.

The captain's mood had been disagreeable in the first place; it was now very much worse, much more fierce and aggressive. She stood in front of the men with her knees bent, her head thrust forward, pouring out words that sounded full of blame, indeed of intense hatred. Yet she did not carry the whole crew with her; the older women were clearly on her side and they often repeated her last words when she paused for breath, but several of the younger were not. They seemed uneasy, unwilling, displeased, and Manu and the spear-girl obviously spoke for them when they broke in during the pauses or even frankly interrupted the full flow, so that on occasion at least three were talking at the same time. Manu was the chief interrupter and Stephen became even more convinced that there was a special relation between her and the captain that gave her more than usual confidence. She kept pointing away over the starboard bow towards a little patch of white unmoving cloud but every time the captain brushed her words aside with the same set of phrases and a sweep of the obsidian knife. Yet in spite of the captain's vehemence – vehemence that increased with the last few interruptions – Stephen felt that she knew she was no longer in full control, that she had gone on too long, that the climax was slipping away from her; and he was afraid she would do something exceptionally violent to re-establish the situation. Indeed she did call out some orders and the biggest of the women moved closer, some with cords, some with clubs; but once again Manu interrupted and before the captain could reply Stephen stepped forward, and pointing at Jack's loins he said, 'Bah, bah, bah. Taboo,' his third Polynesian word.

It had an instant effect. 'Taboo?' they said 'Taboo!' in every tone of affirmation, astonishment, and concern, every tone but that of scepticism. The tension fell at once: the club-bearers moved away, and Stephen sat down again with his hog, which had begun to whimper. He paid little attention to the subsequent discussion, which went on in a more normal tone, though he did notice accusations, tears and reproaches.

For a great while Jack and Stephen had thought it more prudent, more discreet, not to speak, but now Jack whispered, 'They have altered course,' and Stephen observed that the vessel was heading for the patch of white cloud.

Presently the talking died away. The captain and the officers retired to the deckhouse. Stephen's hog was taken from him and Jack's mortar; they were put to sit in the starboard hull among the drinking-coconuts, and there, towards the middle of the afternoon, they were fed with little separate baskets of raw fish, breadfruit pap and taro. But there was no cheerfulness, no merriment, no curiosity. A flatness and gloom had come over the pahi's company, so lively before; and in spite of their enormous relief it affected even Jack and Stephen as they sat there, watching the clouds and then the little island under them come closer. When Manu brought the outrigger round to take them ashore she had clearly been crying.

It was a charming little island, not ten acres in an infinity of sea, green in the middle with a grove of palm-trees, a brilliant white strand all round, and surrounding the whole a broad coral reef, two hundred yards out. Manu obviously knew the island; she put the canoe through a gap in the reef so narrow that the outrigger clipped weed from the far side. She rounded to a few yards from the shore, and as Jack stood there up to his middle, turning the canoe, she gave him two mother-of-pearl fish-hooks and a length of fine line. Then she hauled in the sheet, Jack shoved her off, and the canoe raced back for the gap with the strong breeze abeam and Manu standing up braced against it, as lovely a sight as could be imagined. They waved until she was far out at sea, but she never replied.

CHAPTER EIGHT

The sea increased during the night, so that by dawn the reef surrounding the little island was whiter still with broken water flying high, particularly on the windward side, and the solemn, measured boom of rollers filled the air. Jack was conscious of this before he opened his eyes, he was also pretty sure that the breeze had strengthened too, backing perhaps as much as a whole point, and this was confirmed when he walked quietly from their shelter under the palm-trees, leaving Stephen curled in sleep, and sat on the white strand, yawning and stretching himself.

The scene before him was one of extraordinary beauty: the sun was not yet high enough to make the coral sand blaze and glare but it did bring out the bright green of the lagoon in all its glory, the whiteness of the breakers, the ocean-blue beyond them, and the various purities of the sky, ranging by imperceptible gradations from violet in the extreme west to something wholly celestial where the sun was rising. He was aware of it, and together with the lively freshness of the day it delighted all that part of his mind which was not taken up with trying to estimate the course of the pahi while they were aboard her and their present position with regard to the *Surprise*'s probable line of return.

He had made attempts before this of course, and many of them; but at that time his wits were too harrassed to supply him with any convincing answer. He had merely assured Stephen that all was well – capital – quite in order – and had gone to sleep, far down into sleep, with waves of figures rising and falling in his head.

So many things had happened yesterday that he had not paid as much attention as he should have done to the pahi's speed or direction, but he did remember that she kept the wind between two and three points abaft the beam, apart from the last leg, and as for her speed he doubted whether it would have exceeded four knots at any time. 'An uncommon ingenious well-contrived craft,' he reflected, 'but necessarily frail, and happier on a wind than sailing large: I should not be surprised if she lay to during the night, when the sēa began to get up – I should not be surprised if she were still lying a-try at present, some few hours to leeward.'

Four miles in each hour, then, and the course, allowing for leeway and the last leg to northward, probably within half a point of west-north-west. He drew two lines in the sand, the one marking the pahi's voyage from where she took them aboard to the island, the other the *Surprise*'s westward continuation and her return close-hauled. She should now be sailing westward once again, having lain-to during the darkness at some point to the east of where they had been lost, and at present she should be somewhere near the right meridian. He dropped a perpendicular from the island to this second line and looked very grave; he checked his figures, and looked graver still. Even with all her boats spread to the utmost limit it was scarcely possible that she should see this low island so far to the north, a speck of land in such an immensity of sea, a speck shown on no chart, so that no one would expect it.

'Scarcely possible,' he said; but then with a sudden jet of hope he remembered that the pahi's sheets had been slackened off during church, almost to the point of flapping. That shortened his perpendicular: not by a great deal – perhaps a mile and a half or even two miles for every hour of dancing and harangue – but enough to loosen the cold grip round his heart a little.

The question was, how long would Mowett persist in his search, with all the boats strung out and the frigate moving slowly, perhaps steering a zigzag course to cover more of the ocean? Jack was known to be a very good swimmer, but no man could stay afloat indefinitely.

With a proper regard for the frigate's duty, for her pursuit of the *Norfolk*, how long could Mowett go on combing the apparently empty sea? Had he already abandoned it? There were Hogg's words about unmarked islands, but even so . . .

'Good morning to you, Jack,' said Stephen. 'Is it not the elegant day? How I hope you slept as well as I did: a most profound restoring plunge into comfortable darkness. Have you seen the ship yet?'

'No, not yet. Tell me, Stephen, how long do you think their ceremonies lasted yesterday? Their church, as you might say.'

'Oh, no great time at all, I am sure.'

'But surely, Stephen, the sermon went on for hours.'

'It was boredom and dread that made it seem so long.'

'Nonsense,' said Jack.

'Why, brother,' said Stephen, 'you look quite furious – you dash out your drawing in the sand. Are you vexed at not seeing the ship? It will soon appear, I am sure; your explanation last night convinced me entirely. Nothing could have been more reasonable, nor more cogently expressed.' He scratched himself for a short while. 'You have not yet swum, I find. Might it not set you up, and rectify the humours?'

'It might,' said Jack, smiling, 'but truly I have had enough of swimming for a while; I am still sodden through and through, like a soused pig's face.'

'Then in that case,' said Stephen, 'I trust you will not think it improper if I suggest that you climb up a coconut-tree for our breakfast. I have made repeated and earnest attempts, but I have never ascended higher than six feet, or perhaps seven, before falling, often with painful and perhaps dangerous abrasions; there are some parts of the mariner's art in which I am still a little deficient, whereas you are the complete sailorman.'

Complete he was, but Jack Aubrey had not climbed a coconut-tree since he was a slim nimble reefer in the West Indies; he was still tolerably nimble, but he now weighed rather more than sixteen stone, and he looked thoughtfully at the towering palms. The thickest stem was not much above eighteen inches across, yet it shot up a hundred feet; there was not one that stood straight even in a dead calm and now that a fine topsail breeze was blowing they swayed far over in a most graceful and elastic fashion. It was not the swaying that made Jack pensive – wild irregular motion was after all reasonably familiar to him – but rather the thought of what sixteen stone might do at the top end of such a lever, its motion unconstrained by shrouds, forestays or backstays, and the immense force that it would exert upon the lower part of the trunk and upon roots sunk in little more than coral sand and a trifle of vegetable debris.

He padded about the sparse grove, looking for the stoutest of them all. 'At least,' he observed, gazing up at the outburst of green high above, 'at least the spreading top will break the fall if it does come down.' And there were times during his long and arduous upward journey when it seemed that the palm must come down, must yield under the great and increasing mechanical advantage of his body heaving upon it, sometimes at an angle of forty-five degrees when the wind brought the tree far over; but no, after every plunge the palm swept up again, so fast and so far beyond the vertical that he had to cling tight, and eventually there he was among the great fronds, firmly wedged and breathing easy after his climb, he and the palm-top speeding to and fro on the now familiar trajectory, a kind of inverted swing, quite exhilarating in a way, even for one who was intensely anxious, hungry and thirsty. And as the palm came upright on its tenth backward heave, far out there to leeward he saw the pahi, lying-to. 'Stephen,' he called.

'Hallo?'

'I see the pahi, perhaps twelve miles to leeward, lying-to.'

'Is that so? Listen, Jack, are you privately eating a

nut up there, and drinking, while I perish here for mere want, the shame of it?'

The palm bowed to a gust, then rose again, slower and slower to its height, and Jack, now perched higher still among the fronds, let out a great bellowing roar, 'There she lays, there she lays, there she lays!' for clear on the horizon, farther than the double canoe and well to the south, he saw the *Surprise*'s topsails and her lower yards. She had her starboard tacks aboard and she was steering for the pahi with the wind almost on her beam. He explained this to Stephen at some length as the palm swayed to and fro. 'Is there anything you must do at this point?' asked Stephen in a moderate shout above the thunder of the sea, the sound of the wind and the high clatter of the palms themselves.

'Why no,' said Jack, in the same strong voice. 'She must be seven or eight leagues away. There is nothing I can do for quite a while, until she can see a signal.'

'Then I do beg you will cease springing about in that reckless inconsiderate way. Throw down some coconuts now, will you, and let us have our breakfast at last, for all love.'

'Stand from under, then,' said Jack, sending down a deadly rain of nuts. And setting foot on the ground some minutes later, 'No huzzay? No capers?'

'Why should I cry huzzay, or cut capers?'

'Because of the ship, of course.'

'But you always said it would be there. Why did you not choose green coconuts? These are as hard as cannon-balls; old hairy things. Cannot you tell one from another, good from bad, God and Mary preserve you? But will I open you one, to be drinking?'

'Pray do. I am fairly clemmed, with climbing and hallooing – Stephen, you have a knife!'

'Not at all: it is my pocket-lancet. I had taken it to deal with a damnable knot in my shoe-string – the valuable shoes you made me kick off – and had forgot it until last night, when it dug into my side as I lay. This I regret: had I remembered we could have made some slight acknowledgement of that dear broad-shouldered young woman's kindness. I think of her with great affection.'

Jack heartily agreed, saying all that was proper with great warmth, and adding, 'But, however, it does open an old coconut finely, and it will be most uncommon useful for boring holes, when I set about rigging up some kind of signal later on.'

This signal took him all the morning and rather more. It was a tripod made from the long ribs of palm-fronds lashed together with yarn worked from the leaves and passed through lancet-holes, the whole made fast to the topmost growth of the tallest tree and flying Captain Aubrey's shirt. It stood on its elastic base quite well, making a strange sharp conspicuous angular shape among all those billowing curves; but by the time it was finished and he had made the last of his countless journeys down that lofty stem, his heart was very low. He had in fact little or no faith in his tripod or his shirt. Throughout the morning, at intervals between spells of fine-work, he had observed that the sky was spoiling from the east, the wind strengthening and backing still more, and the great swell increasing; but much more than that he had watched the movements of the frigate and the pahi with passionate intensity: to his astonishment he had seen the pahi strike her deck-house and put before the wind goose-winged, with a square mat sail set between the masts, a rig he did not know she was capable of and one that carried her away westwards at a spanking pace. The *Surprise* had borne up to intercept her, and so both ran fast and far on converging courses a great way to the leeward of the island: they were now at such a distance that under the clouded sky he could only now and then catch the flash of the frigate's sails on the rise, while the pahi had practically vanished. He could not tell whether the frigate had spoken the pahi or not: all he knew was that both wind and sea had strengthened and that even if by some extraordinarily lucky chance the *Surprise* gained any information from the pahi, it must be fragmentary, uncertain, totally unreliable. With this wind, this head-sea and this current a square-rigged ship might beat up for the island a week on end and gain no eastward distance at all, a waste of time that could not be justified by the vague pointing of a crew of monoglot and largely hostile women, even supposing they pointed at all. Duty would require Mowett to carry on to the Marquesas.

'Never look so care-worn, brother,' said Stephen. 'Sit comfortably on the ground and listen to the noble booming of the sea, how it thunders.'

'Aye, so it does,' said Jack. 'It has certainly been blowing very hard somewhere, to raise this almighty swell. But I tell you what, Stephen, I am afraid the weather must be breaking up in these parts too; and even if it don't, perhaps we should make up our minds to staying on this island for quite a considerable time – capital fishing, I dare say, and winkles for relish, once we can get on to the reef.'

Stephen objected that the ship was just at hand; Jack replied that she had run far to the lee; Stephen said that in that case she must ply diligently to windward; and once again Jack was about to explain the increasing degree of leeway that even the most weatherly ship must make as the increasing force of the wind obliged the sails to be reefed or taken in when he reflected that his explanation would do no good. Invincible ignorance could not be enlightened; and although no doubt he might succeed in making Stephen anxious and unhappy this would not really advance them very much. He therefore listened quietly to his friend's assurance that 'Mowett would certainly find some means of overcoming these difficulties – impossible was not a word he connected with the Navy – nothing could exceed the zeal of the mariners – and should there be a little delay, it would enable him to complete his study of the island's flora and fauna – only a brief delay was required however, so pitifully meagre was the tale by land.'

'But,' said Stephen, after these comfortable words, 'I have been contemplating on coral, and my mind is staggered amazed confounded at the thought of these countless myriads of animalcula industriously sifting the lime from the sea-water for so vast a sequence of generations and in such prodigious quantities that they have formed this island, this reef, to say nothing of the countless others that do exist. And all founded upon what? Upon the skeletons of other coral-polyps, the calcareous external skeletons of other coral-polyps, in quantities that run far beyond conception, that is what. For I do assure you, Jack, that everything here, apart from these trifling adventitious vegetables' – waving towards the palms – 'is coral, living or dead, coral sand or solid coralline accumulation. There is no subjacent rock at all. How can it have begun, in this deep tempestuous sea? The force of these waves is very great: the animalculum is miserably frail. How do these islands come about? I cannot tell at all: I cannot form the beginning of a hypothesis.'

'No underlying rock, you say?'

'None whatsoever, brother. Coral, all coral, and nothing but coral.' He paused, shaking his head, and sank deep into thought while Jack looked out over the green lagoon to the leaping wall of white water on the far side of the reef, reflecting that presently he should try to find something in the way of bait and then wade out with Manu's line on the end of a palm-rib. He had gone on to think about ways of making fire when Stephen said, 'And these things being so, I become convinced that the large rounded object about the size of a moderate turtle but more lumpish there on the strand to your right, where the water is lapping it, could not be a boulder. No. I have more than half persuaded myself that it is an enormous piece of ambergris, washed up by the sea.'

'Have you not been to look at it?'

'I have not. The association of rarity, wealth and so on instantly brought that unfortunate brass box to my mind, that most unwelcome box from the *Danaë* packet which is now aboard the *Surprise*; and as the recollection came to me, so I grew perfectly convinced, as by a revelation, that rats or cockroaches or book-worms or various moulds were eating its contents, to our utter ruin – eating them with tropical avidity, a million of money. The thought fairly cut my legs from under me and I have sat here ever since.'

'It is a thousand to one we shall never have any need of the brass box, nor of the ambergris unless it can be eaten,' said Jack to himself. 'And if the weather goes on breaking up like this – if it really comes on to blow and *Surprise* is driven a great way to leeward, then it is ten thousand to one or more, much more.' But aloud, giving Stephen a hand up, he said, 'Let us go and have a look. If it is ambergris, we are made men: we have but to go to the nearest dealer and change it for its weight in gold, ha, ha, ha!'

It was not ambergris: it was a piece of crystalline limestone, mottled and in part translucent, and it fairly stupefied Maturin. 'How can such things be?' he asked, gazing out into the offing. 'There is no question of glaciers, icebergs . . . How can such things possibly come about? There is the boat. I have it,' he cried. 'This rock was brought tangled in the roots of a tree, a great tree swept away by some remote flood or tornado, cast up after the Dear knows how many thousand miles of drifting, and here decaying, leaving its incorruptible burden. Come, Jack, help me turn it – see,' he cried with a shining face as it heaved over, 'in these anfractuosities there are still traces of my roots. What a discovery!'

'What did you mean when you said boat?'

'Why, our boat, of course. The big one, the launch, come to fetch us, as you always said it would. Lord, Jack,' he said, looking up with an entirely different expression, 'how in God's name shall I ever face them, at all?'

He was still there, sitting by his rock, when the *Surprise*'s launch, following her Captain's directions from the height of his palm-tree, dashed through the perilous gap in the reef, crossed the lagoon and ran nose-up on to the shore. 'Oh, sir,' cried Honey, leaping from the bows and very nearly clasping his Captain in his arms, 'how glad I am to see you! We caught sight of the signal a couple of hours ago, but scarcely dared hope it was you. How are you, sir? And the Doctor?' – this last with a very anxious doubtful cock of his head.

'He is prime, I thank you, Honey, and so am I,' said Jack, shaking his hand; and then louder, to the crew of the boat who were staring round, on their thwarts, nodding, becking and grinning, against all decent naval order, 'Well fare ye, shipmates. You are most heartily welcome. A long pull?'

'About eight hours, sir,' said Bonden, laughing as though this were a really brilliant witticism.

'Then haul her up a couple of foot and come ashore. I dare say we shall have to push off with the turn of the tide, but you will have time to wet your whistles with a coconut or two. Mr Calamy, you will find the Doctor sitting by a rock on the other side of the island, at low-water mark: tell him – is there anything to eat or drink in the boat?'

'Which Killick put up some milk-punch and pickled seal, sir, in case you wasn't dead,' said Bonden. 'And we have our rations.'

'Tell him punch and seal, then. Tell him we are going to have a sup and a bite if he chooses to join us; but in any case he should hold himself in readiness to leave quite soon, as I fear it may come on to blow. Now, Mr Honey, pray let me know what happened.'

They had been missed a little before dawn, when a swabber of the afterguard saw the stern-windows wide open. On being told, Mowett instantly cried, 'It's the Doctor,' and put the ship about. All the officers worked out a course that should take the ship back to the point where the Captain was last known to be aboard. This course they followed for several hours, seeing driftwood four times, until they reached the position they had determined upon, which they did with an excellent observation to check it but with their hearts in their boots and their eyes fairly destroyed with having stared so long quite in vain; they

287

then lay to for the night, taking very great care to forereach a trifle to counteract the current. All the officers were on deck or in the tops, and the atmosphere was like that of an undertaker's barge with a crew of mutes. Before dawn they spread the boats out as before and at first light they began their westward sweep. Almost at once they were cheered by the sight of two more tree-trunks, battered but not water-logged, floating quite high, which renewed their hope; and shortly after this the northernmost boat, one of the cutters . . .

'The blue cutter: seven bells in the morning watch: beg pardon, your honour,' said Bonden.

. . . signalled something very likely, and they bore up; it proved to be only an empty barrel, but it was a United States Navy beef-barrel, and quite fresh.

'A beef-barrel, eh?' said Jack with intense satisfaction. 'Carry on, Mr Honey.'

Then at the changing of the watch Hogg, the whaler's specktioneer, came aft and said there was an island away to the north: asked how he knew, pointed out a patch of white cloud and a green reflection in the sky. He was supported by the other South Sea whalers, who said the islanders always navigated by such signs. Asked how far, he said it depended on the size: about twenty miles for a small one, much more for a large. There were plenty of islands not laid down on charts.

If the castaways had found a piece of driftwood, could they have reached it? What was the true set of the current? Might it have carried them so far north? Those were the questions that tormented the quarterdeck. Would it be right to leave their known course? It was decided that the distance was too great to warrant a change unless the island's existence were quite certain, but the blue cutter was ordered away north-north-east for an hour under all possible sail while the ship and the other boats carried on their sweep: this on the reasoning that if the island existed it would cause an indraught, attracting driftwood from a great way off. Time went by slowly, but at last the cutter was seen racing back; her signals were hard to make out, because now that the *Surprise* had moved farther westward she could only see the flags end-on and what was more cloud was coming up, spoiling the light. It was not until the boat was almost within hailing distance that they understood she had seen not only a low island but also a two-masted vessel far to the west-north-west of it. By this time the wind was freshening and backing east or even north of east, the sea was getting up, and greasy weather was surely on the way: Hogg and the other whalers said they had known a very heavy blow indeed in these waters after just such a swell. This was probably their last chance, they thought, so they called the boats in and altered course, 'feeling almighty queer'. They cracked on and presently the lookout on the jacks caught sight of the sail.

'That was me, sir,' cried Calamy. 'With old Boyle's spyglass, ha, ha, ha!'

Hogg went aloft and declared the sail to be a native craft, a double canoe, very like a Tuamotu pahi, though not quite the same in some particulars; and while he was considering it he also saw the island, farther off and to the east.

Mowett at once manned and provisioned the launch and told Honey to proceed to the island with all possible dispatch: for his part he was going to see whether the pahi had picked them up or whether its people could give any information – Hogg understood the language of the islands – and then to lie to until the launch should rejoin. He fixed a rendezvous in the Marquesas in case of dirty weather.

The launch was rigged as a schooner and she was a fine weatherly boat; but it had been clear from the start that beating up would never do, and they had taken to their oars, thus becoming practically invisible from the island in such a sea. After a few hours the people had grown quite tired and jaded, pulling against what was now a head-sea or close on; but then, standing up with his glass, Honey had seen Jack's shirt flying from the palm-tree and after that they had stretched out like heroes – both Davis and Padeen Colman, Stephen's servant, had broken their oars.

'Remind me to stop it out of their pay, Mr Honey,' said Jack; and when the mirth had died away (for this was perhaps his most deeply relished stroke of wit since Gibraltar), 'At least sore hands will have a rest once we are out of the lagoon. I saw the barky right to leeward, and with this breeze we should rejoin before sunset, never touching an oar. Bonden, cut along to the Doctor' – for Stephen had sent back a message by Calamy to the effect that he was not hungry – had some last investigations to make – would come presently – 'and tell him we are off and help him into the stern-sheets while the masts are stepping. It would be as well,' raising his voice – 'for nobody to wish him joy or ask him how he does. He has been taken a little poorly, what with soaking so long and drinking salt water.'

Jack need not have spoken, at least not to the seamen: in their delicacy they would never have taken the least notice of Stephen's misfortune, nor have made him feel the enormous amount of trouble he had caused; and in fact when he came sidling awkwardly down the strand they showed what might have been taken for a brutal indifference, relieved only by the singular gentleness with which he was lifted in and settled with a sailcloth apron over his knees and somebody's old blue jacket about his shoulders.

In the course of their flying voyage westwards with the launch impelled by following seas and an ever more powerful wind Stephen's spirits recovered a little, particularly when Jack gave an account of their time aboard the pahi. He could not have had a more attentive or more appreciative audience – how they laughed at his near-castration and the Doctor's terror when his pig misbehaved and the bosun's mates stood behind him – and after a while Stephen added a few details, feeling much more at his ease. Yet when the ship came in sight – when she came so close that people could be seen against the low sunset sky, running about the deck and waving their hats – he lapsed into silence again.

But the hearty unfeigned affectionate welcome and the underlying kindness so characteristic of the service, brutal though it was at times, would have dealt with a temperament far more morose than Stephen's. In any case his professional skill was called upon at once: the boarding-party sent to the pahi had been repelled with shocking ferocity. Martin and Hogg, leading the way with presents and kind words, had almost instantly been clubbed, and the seamen who dragged them back to the boat speared, beaten with heavy wooden blades, and stabbed with bamboo skewers, all in a terrible yelling screaming uproar. Five men were in the sickbay with wounds far beyond the loblolly-boy's competence, all inflicted within a few moments of the attempted boarding, while the hail of sling-stones and darts delivered as the pahi sheered off accounted for another half dozen less serious casualties.

'They did not give a damn for gunfire,' said Mowett, in the cabin. 'I don't believe they knew what it was. Every time we sent a shot near or over their heads they jumped up and down and waved their spears. I could have knocked away a spar or two, of course, but in such a sea . . . and in any case we could see you was not aboard. And as for information, they would never have given us any, I am sure.'

'You did very well, Mowett,' said Jack. 'In your place I should have been terrified they might attack the ship.'

'I have the villain,' said Stephen in the sickbay, where he was operating by the last of the daylight and seventeen purser's dips. 'I have him in my crow's-bill. A shark's tooth, as I had supposed, detached from the club and driven into the gluteus maximus to a most surprising depth. The question is, what shark?'

'May I see it?' asked Martin in a reasonably firm voice. He had already had thirty-six stitches in his scalp, while a square foot of court plaster covered his lacerated shoulders, but he was a man of some fortitude and above all a natural philosopher. 'A shark without a doubt,' he said, holding the tooth down towards the deck, for he was lying on his belly – most of the Surprises had been wounded ingloriously from behind, running away as fast as ever they could – 'But what shark I cannot tell. However, I shall keep it in my snuff-box, and look at it whenever I think about matrimony. Whenever I think about women, indeed. Dear me, I shall never pull off my hat to one again without remembering today. Do you know, Maturin, as I set foot on that floating thing, that pahi, I saluted the woman confronting me, bowing and baring my head, and she instantly took advantage of it to strike me down.'

'This is the far side of the world,' said Stephen. 'Now your calf, if you please. I am afraid we shall have to cut it bodily out. I had hoped to push it through, but the tibia is in the way.'

'Perhaps we could wait until tomorrow,' said Martin, whose fortitude had its limits.

'A barbed spearhead cannot wait,' said Stephen. 'I wish to see no proud flesh, no black mortification, no gangrene spreading upwards. Pratt, I believe Mr Martin would like to be attached; otherwise he might give an involuntary start and there I should be in an artery.' With quick practised fingers he passed a leather-covered chain round Martin's ankle and another behind his knee; Pratt made them fast to ring-bolts effectually pinning the limb and its owner. These were motions Stephen had made again and again and they were as familiar to him as his patients' unwillingness to be operated upon and all their transparent shifts.

He was very much at home in this place, with his familiar instruments, the smell of tallow, bilgewater, tow, lint, the rum and tincture of laudanum with which he deadened those whom he would be obliged to cut deep; and when he had finished bandaging the leg – Martin was silent now, having drifted away on his drug at last – he felt quite part of the ship once more.

He stood up, threw his operating coat into its usual corner, washed his hands, and walked into the cabin. Jack was writing in a book: he glanced up, said, 'There you are, Stephen,' with a smile, and wrote on, his pen scratching busily.

Stephen sat down in his particular chair and looked about the beautiful room. Everything was in its place, Jack's telescopes in their rack, his sword hanging by the barometer, the 'cello and fiddle cases lying where they always lay, and the particularly magnificent gold-mounted dressing-case cum music-stand – Diana's present to her husband – standing where it always stood, and the unlucky brass box from the *Danaë*, its seals intact, was hidden behind the foot-waling as he knew very well; but there was something amiss, and all at once he noticed that dead-lights had been fitted to the stern-windows: no one could possibly fall out of them.

'No, it is not that,' said Jack, catching his look. 'That would be locking the horse after the stable door is gone, a very foolish thing to do.'

'Still and all, there are some horses that are obliged to be controlled, I am afraid.'

'No, it was just that I think we may have a blow, and I do not choose to lose the window-glasses again.'

'Is that right? I had supposed the sea was calmer.'

'So it is, but the barometer has dropped in a very horrid manner . . . forgive me, Stephen, I must just finish this page.'

The ship rose and fell, rose and fell, a pure long following sea with never a hint of roll in it. Jack's pen squeaked on. At some distance Killick's disagreeable voice could be heard singing *Heave and ho; rumbelow*, and presently the smell of toasted cheese reached the cabin.

This was their particular delight in the evening, but there had been no cheese, toasted or otherwise, in the great cabin for some thousands of miles. Could there be such things as olfactory illusions, wondered Stephen, blinking at the lantern as it swung fore and aft, fore and aft. Conceivably. There was after all no limit at all to error. But then again, he reflected, Killick's notion of his perquisites had a right naval breadth to it: he stole as steadily and conscientiously as the bosun, but whereas the bosun, by immemorial custom, might sell his winnings without being thought the worse of so long as he was not caught or unless he criminally weakened the ship, the same did not apply to the Captain's steward, and Killick never passed anything over the side. His perquisites were for himself and his friends, and it was possible that he had preserved a piece of the almost imperishable manchego or parmesan for some private feast of his own: physical, material, objective cheese was certainly toasting no very great way off. Stephen was aware that his mouth was watering, but that at the same time his eyes were closing. 'A curious combination, truly.' He heard Jack say that it was certainly going to blow, and with that he went fast to sleep.

CHAPTER NINE

Jack Aubrey lay in his cot, savouring his resurrection; this was Sunday morning and according to ancient naval custom the day's life began half an hour earlier than usual – hammocks were piped up at six bells rather than seven – so that the ship's people could wash, shave and make themselves fine for divisions and church. Ordinarily he was up and about with the rest, but today he deliberately took his ease, indulging in perfectly relaxed sloth and in the comfort of his bed, infinitely soft and well-moulded compared with harsh, scaly palm-fronds, and infinitely warm and dry compared with the open sea. The usual swabs and holystones scouring the deck a few feet above his head had not woken him, because Mowett had allowed nothing but silent, largely symbolic sweeping abaft the mainmast. But for all Mowett's care Jack was pretty well aware of the time of the day: the intensity of the light and the smell of roasting coffee were in themselves a clock; yet still he lay, taking conscious pleasure in being alive.

At last the scent of coffee died away, giving place to the everyday smell of fresh sea, tar, warm wood and cordage, and distant bilge, and his ear caught the click-click of Killick's mate's pestle grinding the beans in the brass mortar belonging to the sick-bay; for Stephen was even more particular about his coffee than Jack, and having learnt the true Arabian way of preparing it when they were in the Red Sea (an otherwise profitless voyage) he had banished the commonplace mill. Jack's ear also caught Killick's shrill abuse as his mate let some of the beans skip out; it had just the same tone of righteous indignation as the dreadful bosun's mates aboard the pahi or Sophie's mother, Mrs Williams. He smiled again. How pleasant it was to be alive. Mrs Williams had come to stay with them; his old and horribly energetic father, General Aubrey, a member of parliament in the extreme Radical interest, seemed bent on destroying Jack's career; even apart from political considerations the Admiralty had treated him with striking injustice ever since he was a master and commander, promising him ships and then giving them elsewhere, failing to promote his subordinates, though infinitely deserving, frequently questioning some one or another of the horribly intricate accounts he was required to keep, and regularly threatening him with unemployment, with being thrown on the shore, there to live in wretched idleness on half pay. Yet how utterly trifling these things were, and the law-suits too, in comparison with being alive! Stephen, a Catholic, had already performed his action of grace; Jack's happy, thankful mind now did much the same, though in a less formal manner, revelling and delighting in what he had been given back.

Light pittering hooves could be heard overhead: Aspasia, fresh from her milking. It was even later than he had thought, he observed, and he sat up. Killick had obviously been listening outside the door of the sleeping-cabin, for it opened straight away, letting in a flood of eastern light.

'Good morning, Killick,' said Jack.

'Good morning, sir,' said Killick, holding up a towel. 'Are you going to take a dip?'

In these waters Jack usually swam before breakfast, even if it were only a plunge from the forechains and a return by the stern-ladder so as not to check the ship's way, but now he said no, he would prefer a pot of hot water. His skin and particularly the rolls of fat round his belly were still strangely waterlogged, and at present sea-bathing had no attraction for him.

'Is the Doctor about yet?' he called, stropping his razor.

'No, sir,' said Killick from the great cabin, where he was laying the breakfast-table. 'He was called up in the night, which Mr Adams had a fit of the strong fives in consequence of eating and drinking too much by way of wishing the Doctor joy of his return. But a clyster soon

296

settled his hash. Don't I wish I had given it to him myself, the b - - r,' added Killick in a low voice when he was sure that Jack could not hear, for the purser objected to Killick's way of robbing the foremast hands, the Marines, the warrant officers, the midshipmen's berth and the gunroom mess in order to keep the cabin well supplied.

With their voices diminished by the distance and the following wind Hollar and his mates could be heard calling down the hatchways, 'D'ye hear there, fore and aft? Clean shirt for muster at five bells. Duck frocks and white trousers.' 'D'ye hear there? Clean shirt and shave for muster at five bells.'

'Clean shirt, sir,' said Killick, passing it.

'Thankee, Killick,' said Jack. He pulled on his second-best white breeches, observing with regret that in spite of his soaking and his privations they were still so tight round his waist that the topmost hook had to be left undone: his long waistcoat would cover the gap, however.

'Not far from three bells, sir,' said Killick. 'Too late to ask anyone else to breakfast, which is just as well, seeing as how Aspasia was precious near with her milk this morning.'

Soft tack and therefore toast was as much a thing of the past as eggs and bacon or beefsteak and onions, but Jack's cook had turned out a highly spiced and savoury dish of Juan Fernandez stockfish, crisp on top, and Killick had produced one of the few remaining pots of Ashgrove Cottage marmalade, which went very well with ship's bread. 'How I wish Sophie were here,' he said aloud, looking at the label she had written such a great way off.

Three bells sounded. He drank the last of the coffee, stood up, looped his sword-belt over his shoulder and put on the splendid blue coat that Killick held out for him, a coat of singular elegance with its massive golden epaulettes and the ribbon of the Nile medal in a buttonhole, but one made of a stout broadcloth more calculated for the English Channel in winter than the equator. 'But, however,' he reflected, as his temperature rose, 'I do not have to do it up. It is worse for the others,' and in the gaiety of his heart he added, 'Il faut souffrir pour être beau' as he clapped on his cocked hat.

'Good morning, Oakes,' he said to the Marine sentry at his door, and 'Good morning, gentlemen,' as he stepped on to the quarterdeck. In the general chorus of 'Good morning, sir,' hats flew off, and immediately afterwards a dozen waistcoats partly vanished under close-buttoned coats.

Automatically Jack looked up at the sails, the rigging and the sky; all was just as he could wish – a whole topsail breeze in which she could carry the fore topgallantsail if she were pressed. But the sea was not all he could wish by any means. The heavy blow that made him ship deadlights yesterday evening had not come about, but the following swell had not subsided – indeed, the pitching made it difficult for the hands to arrange their bags, brought up so that the 'tween decks could be cleaned, in the usual pyramid on the booms, and it was traversed by a curious diagonal cross-swell that cut up the surface in an uneasy, fretful way: an ugly sea, and one that he was not used to, in spite of all his experience. The forthcoming ceremony however was one that he knew by heart; it was performed in all well-regulated men-of-war once a week except in a very heavy weather and he must have seen it at least a thousand times.

The subdued conversation on the lee side of the quarter-deck died away. The quartermaster at the con cleared his throat, and as the last grain of sand fell into the lower part of the half-hour glass he cried, 'Turn the glass and strike the bell.' The Marine on duty moved forward, very careful of his step with such a pitch and with the whole ship's company watching him, and struck five bells.

'Mr Boyle,' said Maitland, the officer of the watch, to the young gentleman acting as mate of the watch, 'beat to divisions.'

Boyle turned to the Marine drummer, who stood there

298

with his sticks poised, said 'Beat to divisions,' and the drum instantly roared out the generale.

The seamen, who had been standing about in amorphous groups, taking great care of their best, beautifully washed, ironed and often embroidered clothes, now hurried to form lines according to their various divisions – forecastlemen, topmen, gunners and afterguard only, for the *Surprise* had no waisters – toeing well-known seams on either side of the quarterdeck, on the gangways and the forecastle. The Marines were already drawn up far aft, near the taffrail. The midshipmen inspected the hands in their division, tried to make them stand up straight and soldierly and stop talking and then reported to the lieutenants and the master; the lieutenants and the master inspected them again, tried to make them stop staring about and hitching up their trousers, and reported that the men were 'present, properly dressed and clean' to Mowett, who stepped across the deck to Captain Aubrey, took off his hat and said, 'All the officers have reported, sir.'

'Then we will go round the ship, Mr Mowett, if you please,' said Jack, and first he turned aft, to where the Marines were standing as straight as ramrods in their scarlet coats: their cross-belts were brilliant with pipeclay, their muskets and side-arms shone again, their hair was powdered to a turn, their leather stocks were as tight as stocks could well be and allow a little circulation of the blood; and although awnings had been rigged, the eastern sun, not yet at its height, beat on their backs with shocking force. They might not be beautiful, but they were certainly suffering. Accompanied by Howard, his sword drawn, and by Mowett, he passed along the rows of faces, many of them nameless to him even now and all of them impersonal, gazing out beyond him, wholly without expression.

'Very creditable, Mr Howard,' said Jack. 'I believe you may dismiss your men now. They may put on their duck jackets and wait quietly under the forecastle until church.' Then, still with Mowett and with each of the divisional officers in turn, he went round the rest of the ship.

This was quite a different ceremony. Here he knew every man, many of them – indeed most of them – intimately well, knew their virtues, vices, particular skills, particular failings. And here there was no remote impassive gaze, no eyes trained to avoid the charge of familiarity or dumb insolence. Far from it: they were very pleased to see him and they smiled and nodded as he came by – Davis even laughed aloud. Furthermore it was perfectly obvious to all concerned that a rescued captain, just returned to his ship by a combination of extraordinary luck and extraordinary exertions, could not decently find fault with his ship's company. As an inspection his tour was therefore a matter of pure though amiable form; and it very nearly turned into a farce when the bosun's cat joined them and marched steadily in front of the Captain, its tail in the air.

Far below, under the grateful freshness of a windsail, Stephen was sitting with his patient Martin. They were not exactly bickering, but in both the spirit of contradiction was distinctly present and active: present in the chaplain because of his wounds and in Stephen because of a more than usually wretched night on top of two really trying days. 'That may be so,' said he, 'yet in the public mind the service is often associated with drunkenness, sodomy and brutal punishment.'

'I was at a great English public school,' said Martin, 'and the vices to which you refer were by no means uncommon there; they are I believe fairly usual whenever a large number of men are gathered together. But what is unusual in the service, and what I have not encountered elsewhere, is the essential good-nature. I do not speak of the seamen's courage and altruism, which need no comments of mine, though I shall never forget those noble fellows who dragged me back into the boat from the pahi . . .'

Stephen, cross-grained though he was that morning, really could not disagree. He waited until Martin had finished and then said, 'You did not happen to notice a tall slim broad-shouldered young woman with a spear, very like an undraped Athene?'

'No,' said Martin, 'I saw nothing but a swarthy crew of ill-looking female savages, full of malignant fury, a disgrace to their sex.'

'I dare say they had been ill-used, the creatures,' said Stephen.

'Perhaps they had,' said Martin. 'But to carry resentment to the point of the emasculation you described seems to me inhuman, and profoundly wicked.'

'Oh, as far as unsexing is concerned, who are we to throw stones? With us any girl that cannot find a husband is unsexed. If she is very high or very low she may go her own way, with the risks entailed therein, but otherwise she must either have no sex or be disgraced. She burns, and she is ridiculed for burning. To say nothing of male tyranny – a wife or a daughter being a mere chattel in most codes of law or custom – and brute force – to say nothing of that, hundreds of thousands of girls are in effect unsexed every generation: and barren women are as much despised as eunuchs. I do assure you, Martin, that if I were a woman I should march out with a flaming torch and a sword; I should emasculate right and left. As for the women of the pahi, I am astonished at their moderation.'

'You would have been still more astonished at the force of their blows.'

'It is the black shame of the world that they should be deprived of the joys of love – Tiresias said they were ten times as great as those enjoyed by men, or was it thirty? – leaving aside the far more dubious pleasures of motherhood and keeping house.'

'Tiresias represents no more than the warm imaginings of Homer: decent women take no pleasure in the act, but only seek to – '

301

'Nonsense.'

'I quite agree with you in your dislike of interruptions, Maturin,' said Martin.

'I beg your pardon.' Stephen cocked his ear to the mouth of the wind-sail and said, 'What is all that huzzaying on deck?'

'No doubt they have taken the pahi, and now you will be able to carry your charitable theories into practice,' said Martin, but without any real ill-humour.

They both listened attentively, and while they were listening feet came running aft. Padeen opened the door and stood there making inarticulate sounds, pointing a thumb over his shoulder. 'Himself, is it?' asked Stephen. Padeen smiled and nodded and passed Stephen his coat. Stephen put it on, buttoned it, and stood up as the Captain and the first lieutenant came in.

'Good morning, Doctor,' said Jack. 'How are your patients?'

'Good morning, sir,' said Stephen. 'Some are a little contradictory and fractious, but a comfortable slime-draught at noon will deal with that. The others do tolerably well, and are looking forward to their Sunday duff.'

'I am heartily glad to hear it. And I believe you will be glad to hear that we have picked up another of the *Norfolk*'s barrels. A pork-barrel this time, fresh and floating high, marked Boston in December of last year.'

'Does that mean we are close to her?'

'There is no telling within a week or so, but it does mean that we are probably in the same ocean.'

After some more remarks about barrels, their drifting and signs of wear, Martin said, 'I believe, sir, that you mean to read one of Dean Donne's sermons this morning. I have told Killick just where to find it.'

'Yes, sir, I thank you, and he did find it. But now that I have looked it over I feel that it would come better from a learned man, from a real parson. I shall confine myself to the Articles of War, which I do

302

understand and which in any case are obliged to be read once a month.'

This he did: in the pause that followed the singing of the *Old Hundredth*, Ward, who on these occasions acted as parish clerk as well as captain's clerk, stepped forward, took the slim folio of the Articles from beneath the Bible and passed it to Jack, who began in a strong, minatory voice (though not without a certain relish), 'For the regulating and better government of his Majesty's navies, ships of war, and forces by sea, whereon, under the good providence of God, the wealth, safety, and strength of this kingdom chiefly depend, be it enacted by the King's most excellent Majesty, by and with the advice and consent of the lords spiritual and temporal, and commons, in this present parliament assembled . . .'

His words came down the wind-sail in snatches as the breeze strengthened on the top of the swell and diminished when the *Surprise* sank into the trough, and fragments of the Articles mingled with Stephen's and Martin's conversation, which now moved off, by way of the phalarope, to the less dangerous ground of birds.

'Did you ever see a phalarope, at all?' asked Stephen.

'Never a live one, alas; only in the pages of a book, and that a most indifferent cut.'

'Will I describe him to you?'

'If you please.'

'All flag officers, and all persons in or belonging to his Majesty's ships or vessels of war, being guilty of profane oaths, cursings, execrations, drunkenness, uncleanness, or other scandalous actions in derogation of God's honour, and corruption of good manners . . .'

'But the hen bird is much larger and much brighter; and she is a creature that does not believe that a hen's duty is merely to tend her nest, brood her eggs, and nourish her chicks. I once had the happiness of watching a pair from a fisherman's cabin on the far far tip of the County Mayo; there was a group of them in the neighbourhood, but it was this particular pair I watched, so close to the cabin they were.'

'If any ship or vessel shall be taken as prize, none of the officers, mariners, or other persons on board her, shall be stripped of their clothes, or in any sort pillaged, beaten, or evil-intreated . . .'

'The evening she had laid the last of her clutch – '

'Forgive me,' said Martin, laying his hand upon Stephen's knee, 'but how many?'

'Four: snipe-shaped and much the same colours. That same evening, then, she was away and the poor cock had to look after them himself. I was afraid some harm had come to her, but not at all, there she was – and I knew her well from her face and the odd white streak on the side of her bosom – swimming about on the sea and the little lough this side of it and playing with the other hens and the unattached cocks. And all the while the poor fellow brooded the eggs there not fifteen yards from me under a turf-stack, covering them as well as he could from the rain and never eating but five minutes or so in the day. It was worse when they hatched, because clearly they had to be fed single-handed, the four of them bawling and screeching all the day long; and he was not very handy at cleaning up after them either. He grew anxious and thin and partially bald, and there she was on the lough, chasing the other phalaropes and being chased by them, crying pleep, pleep, pleep and never doing a beak's turn by way of labour or toil. There was a fowl that knew how to live a life of her own, I believe.'

'But surely, Maturin, as a married man you cannot approve the phalarope hen?'

'Why, as to that,' said Stephen, with a sudden vivid image of Diana dancing a quadrille, 'perhaps she may carry things a little far; but it does go some way towards redressing a balance that is so shamefully down on the one side alone.'

'Any person in the fleet who shall unlawfully burn or set fire to any magazine or store of powder, or ship, boat, ketch, hoy, or vessel, tackle or furniture thereunto belonging, not then appertaining to an enemy, pirate, or rebel . . . shall suffer death.'

These words came down the ventilator with unusual force, and after a rather solemn pause Martin asked, 'Just how does one define a hoy, Maturin?'

'As this is a Sunday, I will tell you candidly that I do not know,' said Stephen. 'But I have heard it used by way of reproach, as "You infernal two-masted Dutch hoy" or "The place was all ahoo, like the deck of the Gravesend hoy." '

Only a very little later Jack used these same words, *as this is a Sunday*, when he refused a request submitted by the hands through the captains of the tops to the bosun, by him to the first lieutenant, and by Mowett to the Captain. The idea was that as the Doctor was very curious to see a prize-fight, his return to the ship might be celebrated by a series of contests on the forecastle that evening, the more so as the Marines and even the whalers had long been prating of their extraordinary skill and courage in the ring. 'No,' said Jack, 'as this is a Sunday, I am afraid I cannot countenance prize-fighting. I am sure Mr Martin would agree that Sunday is no day for semi-slaughter, for real fighting, bare-knuckle fighting. But if they choose to ask Sails to run up properly padded gloves, and if they like to set to, sparring and boxing like Christians, with nothing on the murdering lay, no wrestling, no cross-buttock falls or gouging or strangling, no head in chancery or catching hold of pigtails, why, I cannot see that the Archbishop of Canterbury himself could object.' Then turning to Stephen, 'I never knew you were interested in prize-fighting.'

'You never asked,' said Stephen. 'I have seen many a squalid scuffle, of course, many a Donnybrook Fair, but as I was telling Bonden the other day although it is so much a part of modern life, I have nev-er seen the peculiarly English prize-fighting. I was very near to it once. I met a particularly amiable young man in a stage-coach, a pugilist named Henry Pearce – '

'The Game Chicken?' cried Jack and Mowett together.

'I dare say: they told me he was a famous man. And he invited me to see him fight some other hero – Thomas Cribb, was it? – but at the last moment I was disappointed of my treat.'

'So you met the Game Chicken,' said Mowett, looking at Stephen with a new respect. 'I saw him fight the Wapping Slasher on Epsom Downs until they were both of them groggy and very nearly blind with blood, and after an hour and seventeen minutes and forty-one rounds Pearce was the only one who could come up to the scratch, although he had had five knockdown blows and the Slasher had fallen on him twice, squelch with all his weight, the way some bruisers do when there is a big purse.'

'How you have missed seeing one in all this time I cannot tell,' said Jack, who had often travelled fifty miles to see Mendoza or Belcher or Dutch Sam, who had frequented Gentleman Jackson's establishment, and who had himself lost two teeth in friendly encounters. 'But at least that can be repaired this evening. We have some capital bruisers aboard: Bonden won the belt at Pompey, with eight ships of the line and three frigates competing; Davis is a smiter that will stand like a Trojan until his legs are cut from under him, and one of the whalers is said to be very dangerous. Mowett, the hide we use for covering the laniards would be better than sailcloth, if we have any that is supple enough.'

'I will go and see, sir.'

'Lord, Stephen,' said Jack when they were alone, 'how pleasant it is to be aboard again, don't you find?'

'Certainly,' said Stephen.

'Only this morning I was thinking how right they were to say it was better to be a dead horse than a live lion.' He gazed out of the scuttle, obviously going over the words in his mind. 'No. I mean better to flog a dead horse than a live lion.'

'I quite agree.'

'Yet even that's not quite right, neither. I know there is a dead horse in it somewhere; but I am afraid I'm brought by the lee this time, though I rather pride myself on proverbs, bringing them in aptly, you know, and to the point.'

'Never distress yourself, brother; there is no mistake, I am sure. It is a valuable saying, and one that admonishes us never to underestimate our enemy, for whereas flogging a dead horse is child's play, doing the same to a lion is potentially dangerous, even though one may take a long spoon.'

In this case the enemy was the swell, and in their eagerness for the entertainment all those concerned had underestimated it and continued to do so in spite of the evidence of their senses up to and indeed beyond the last possible moment: even when it had increased to such an extent that the ship was pitching headrails under and a man could scarcely keep his feet without holding on there were those who swore it was all a mere flurry – it would die away well before sunset – they should certainly have their fight, and any ugly Dutch-built bugger that spoke to the contrary was a croaker, a goddam crow, a fool and no seaman.

'I am afraid you will be disappointed of your treat again,' said Jack. 'But if this sea dies down, and if the work of the ship allows, you shall have it tomorrow.'

The swell, in so far as it was a vast, regular up and down, certainly diminished, yet Stephen, lying there awake in the morning, felt a strange uneasy motion that was neither a strong pitching nor a heavy roll but a quick sudden kind of lurching with no decided direction, unlike anything he had known before. This lurching caused the ship's timbers to work and it had obviously been going on for some considerable time, since there was a good deal of water washing to and fro in his cabin, and his shoes were afloat.

'Padeen,' he called several times; and after a listening pause, 'Where is that black thief, his soul to the Devil?'

'God and Mary be with you, gentleman,' said Padeen, opening the door and letting more water in.

'God and Mary be with you,' said Stephen, 'and Patrick.'

Padeen pointed upwards through the decks and after some gasps he said in English, 'The Devil's abroad.'

'I dare say he is,' said Stephen. 'Listen, Padeen, just reach me those dry shoes from the little net on the wall, will you now?'

His cabin was not far from the ship's centre of gravity and as he made his way up the ladders the motion increased, so that twice he was nearly flung off, once sideways and once backwards. The only person in the gun room was Howard's Marine servant, who said, with a frightened look, 'All the gentlemen are on deck, your honour.'

So they were, even the purser and even Honey, who had had the graveyard watch and who should have been fast asleep; but in spite of the gathering there was little talk and apart from good mornings Stephen himself said not a word. The horizon all round was of a blackish purple and over the whole sky there rolled great masses of cloud of a deep copper colour, moving in every direction with a strange unnatural speed; lightning flashed almost continually in every part and the air was filled with the tremble of enormous thunder, far astern but travelling nearer. There was a steep, irregular sea, bursting with a tremendous surf as though under the impulsion of a very hard gale: in fact the breeze was no more than moderate. Yet in spite of its moderation it was strikingly cold and it whistled through the rigging with a singularly keen and shrilling note.

The topgallantmasts had already been struck down on deck and all hands were now busy securing the boats on the booms with double gripes, sending up preventer stays, shrouds, braces and backstays, clapping double-breechings on to the guns, covering the forehatch and scuttles with tarpaulins and battening them down. Aspasia came and nuzzled his hand, pressing against his leg like an anxious dog: a sudden jerk nearly had him over, but he saved himself by grasping her horns.

'Hold on, Doctor,' called Jack from the windward rail. 'The barky is skittish today.'

'Pray what does all this signify?' asked Stephen.

'Something of a blow,' said Jack. 'Forecastle, there: Mr Boyle, guy it to the cathead. I will tell you at breakfast. Have you seen the bird?'

'I have not. No bird these many days. What kind of a bird?'

'A sort of albatross, I believe, or perhaps a prodigious great mew. He has been following the ship since – there he is, crossing the wake – he comes up the side.'

Stephen caught a glimpse of wings, huge wings, and he ran forward along the gangway to get a clear view from the bows. The fall from the gangway into the waist of the ship was not much above six feet, but Stephen was flung off with unusual force, and he hit his head on the iron breech of a gun.

They carried him aft and laid him on Jack's cot, dead apart from a just perceptible breathing and a very faint pulse. It was here that Martin found him, having crawled up from the depths.

'How good of you to come, Mr Martin,' cried Jack. 'But surely you should not be about, with your leg . . . I only sent to ask whether you thought he should be let blood, since you understand physic. We cannot bring him round.'

'I cannot advise letting blood,' said Martin, having felt Stephen's unresisting, impassive head. 'Nor brandy,' – glancing at the two bottles, one from the cabin, one from the gunroom. 'I do know something of physic, and am persuaded this is a cerebral commotion – not a full coma, since there is no stertor – which must be treated by rest, quiet, darkness. I will consult the Doctor's books, if

I may, but I do not think they will contradict me in this; nor when I say that he would be far better downstairs, where the sideways motion is so much less.'

'You are quite right, I am sure,' said Jack, and to Killick, 'Pass the word for Bonden. Bonden, can you and Colman and say Davis carry the Doctor below without jerking him, or should you be happier with a tackle?'

'A tackle too, sir, if you please. I would not slip with him, no not for a world of gold.'

'Make it so then, Bonden,' said Jack; and while the tackles were being set up, 'What do you think, Mr Martin? Is he bad? Is he in danger?'

'My opinion is not worth a great deal, but this is obviously much more than an ordinary stunning fall. I have read of comatose states of such a kind lasting for days, sometimes growing deeper and ending in death, sometimes giving way and dispersing like natural sleep. When there is no bone broken I believe internal haemorrhage is often the deciding factor.'

'All ready, sir,' said Bonden. The strongest men in the ship were with him, and between them, wedged against stanchions and bulkheads, they lowered Stephen inch by inch, as though his skin were made of eggshell, until he was back in his own cot, with Padeen by to curb its swinging. The cabin was small and somewhat airless, but it was dark, it was quiet, it was in the least agitated part of the ship, and here the hours passed over him in black silence.

On deck all hell broke loose as they were striking the maintopmast half an hour later; the preventer top-rope reeved through the fid-hole parted at the very moment a deluge of warm rain beat down on the ship, so thick they could scarcely breathe, much less see. From that time on until full darkness and beyond it was an incessant battle with mad blasts of wind from every direction, thunder and lightning right overhead, unbelievably steep seas that made no sense at all, bursting with such force that they

310

threatened to engulf the ship – bursting as though they were over a reef, although there was no bottom to be found with any line the ship possessed. All this and such freaks as a waterspout that collapsed on their astonished heads, bringing the maindeck level with the surface for several minutes; and without a pause thunder bellowed about them, while St Elmo's fire flickered and blazed on the bowsprit and catheads. It was a time or rather – since ordinary time was gone by the board – a series of instant shifts and expedients, of surviving from one stunning thunderclap and invasion of water to the next and between them making fast such things as the jollyboat, the binnacle itself and the booms that had carried away. And all the while the pumps turned like fury, flinging out tons of water that the sea or the sky flung right back again. Yet even so it was the hands at the pumps who were the least harassed; although they had to work until they could hardly stand, often up to their middles in water, often half-choked with flying spray or still more rain, immeasurable quantities of rain, at least they knew exactly what to do. For the others it was a perpetually renewed state of emergency in which anything might happen – unheard of, shockingly danger-ous accidents such as the seventy-foot palm-trunk that a freakish sea flung bodily aboard so that its far end wedged in the mainshrouds while the rest lashed murderously to and fro, sweeping the gangways and the forecastle just as an equally freakish squall took what little storm-canvas the ship dared show full aback, checking her as though she had run on to a reef and laying her so far over that many thought she was gone at last. Indeed, if a windward gun had broken loose at this point of utmost strain it would certainly have plunged right through her side.

It was not until sunset that the weather began to have a direction and some sort of a meaning. The whirling turn-ing formless blasts passed north and westwards and they were succeeded by the pent-up south-east wind, which, though full of flaws and slanting squalls, blew with enor-mous force, eventually bringing up a swell which rivalled that they had known in the fifties, so very far south.

It was a hard blow, a very, very hard blow, with a dangerous following sea; but it was what they were used to in their calling, and compared with the maniac day it was positive relief. The hands were piped by half-watch and half-watch to their very late supper; Jack ordered the splicing of the mainbrace and made his way below. He went first to the sick-bay, where he knew there would be some injured men, and there he found Martin splinting Hogg's broken arm in a most workmanlike fashion: Pratt was standing by with bandages and lint and it was clear that Martin had taken over. 'This is very good of you, Mr Martin,' he cried. 'I hope you are not in too much pain yourself. There is blood on your bandage.'

'Not at all,' said the parson, 'I took Maturin's potion, the tincture – pray hold this end for a moment – and feel very little. I have just come from him: I found no change. Mrs Lamb is with him at present.'

'I will look at your other patients and then, if it would do no harm, I will go and see him.' Considering the extraordinary severity of the day there were surprisingly few casualties, and apart from the broken arm none very serious: he felt encouraged as he went down the ladder and quite hopeful as he opened the cabin door. But there under the swinging lantern Stephen looked like a dead man: his temples were sunk, his nostrils pinched, his lips were colourless: he was lying on his back and his grey closed utterly motionless face had an inhuman lack of expression. 'I thought he was gone not five minutes ago,' said Mrs Lamb. 'Perhaps with the turning of the tide . . .'

There was no change at two bells in the middle watch, when Jack came down to sit with him for a while before turning in. There was no change when Martin hobbled up to take a first breath of morning air on the ravaged quarterdeck, desolation fore and aft, and stood for a while watching the ship tearing along under no more than close-reefed topsail and jib over a dark

312

indigo sea laced with white streams of foam and broken water, tearing along with fag-ends of rope flying, broken spars at every turn, and the rigging giving out a general note two full tones lower than usual, tearing along just ahead of great following seas that rose to the height of the mizentop.

'What shall you do now?' he asked at breakfast in the gunroom, after he had answered all their questions about Stephen.

'Do?' said Mowett, 'Why, what any ship must do in such a blow – scud and pray we are not pooped and that we may not run into anything by night. Scud, knotting and splicing as we go.'

There was no change when Martin came to a makeshift dinner in the cabin. Jack said, 'I am not to teach you any-thing about medicine, Mr Martin, but it occurred to me that as the injury was much the same as Plaice's, perhaps the same operation might answer.'

'I too have been thinking of that,' said Martin, 'and now I have had time to read in some of his books on the subject. Although I find no depressed fracture in this case, which is the usual reason for trepanning, I fear that there may be a clot of extravasated blood under the point of impact which is having the same effect.'

'Should you not try the operation, then? Would it not relieve the brain?'

'I should not dare to do so.'

'You turned the handle when Plaice was done.'

'Yes, but I had an expert by me. No, no, there are many other considerations – I have a great deal more to read – much of it is dark to me. In any case no amateur could possibly operate with the ship in such a state of violent motion.'

Jack was obliged to admit the truth of this; but his face grew stern and he tapped his biscuit on the table for a few moments before forcing a smile and saying, 'I promised to tell you about the weather when we had time to draw breath: it seems that we were on the southern side and near

313

the tail of a typhoon that has travelled off north-westerly. That would account for the whirlwinds and the seas from every quarter, do not you agree, Mowett?'

'Yes, sir,' said Mowett. 'And we are certainly in quite different waters now. Have you noticed the quantities of long thin pale sharks around the ship? One of them took the bullock's hide we had towing under the mainchains to soften it. When I went below to ask Hogg how he did he said he had often seen them, approaching the Marquesas; he also said he did not think the weather had blown itself out yet, no, not by a chalk as long as your arm.'

Dinner ended on that note. As Martin took his leave he said he would pass the afternoon reading, very attentively watching the patient's symptoms, and perhaps practising with the trephine on some of the seal's skulls he and Maturin possessed.

Late that night he said he was becoming more and more nearly convinced that the operation was called for, above all since Stephen's breathing had now become slightly stertorous; and he showed passages in Pott and La Faye supporting his view. But what, he asked, was the use of his growing conviction with the ship plunging about like this? In so delicate an operation the slightest lurch, the slightest want of balance and exact control might mean the patient's death. Would it be possible to heave the ship to?

'That would make no difference to the absolute motion,' said Jack. 'Indeed, it would make the heave and roll come quicker. No, the only hope is that this sea should go down, which, bar a miracle, it cannot do in less than three or four days, or that we should lie to under the lee of some reef or island. But there is no reef or island laid down on the chart until we reach the Marquesas. Of course there is the alternative that you should – how shall I put it? – that you should steel yourself to the act. After all, naval surgeons cannot wait for calm weather; and if I remember right, Plaice was operated on in a close-reefed topsail breeze.'

'Very true, though the sea was fairly calm. Yet we

must distinguish between timidity and temerity; and in any case, even if I were quite certain it was right, in view of my inexperience and remaining doubts, I certainly could not operate without the full light of day.'

But even when the full light of day came it did not bring full conviction: Martin was still torn with uncertainty.

'I cannot bear the sight of Maturin just fading away like this for want of care – for want of a bold stroke,' said Jack: the pulse under his attentive fingers was now so faint that it was not above once in five minutes that he could be sure of it.

'I cannot bear the thought of Maturin being killed by my want of skill or by some wretched jerk of the deck under me,' said Martin, whose improvised Lavoisier trephine had made some shocking plunges right through the practice skulls. 'Fools rush in where angels fear to tread.'

The *Surprise* raced westwards over the same dark-blue enormously heaving sea, under a brilliant sky filled with high white clouds, re-rigging, re-reeving, fishing the sprung mizenmast. Her mainshrouds on the weather side, shattered by the palm-trunk, had already been replaced, set up and rattled down, and her Captain had his usual walk restored. The quarterdeck was just fifty feet long and by stepping short at a particular ring-bolt, now worn thin and silver-bright, he could make fifty of his turns fore and aft amount to a measured mile by land. Up and down he went amid the busy noise of the ship and the steady, omnipresent great voice of the wind and the very powerful sea; with his bowed head and his stern expression he seemed so absorbed that the other people on the quarterdeck spoke very quietly and kept well over to leeward, but he was in fact perfectly aware of what was going forward and at the first cry of 'Land ho' from the maintop he sprang into the shrouds. It was a furious hard climb with the huge wind tearing him sideways and his shirt-tail out, billowing round his ears, and he was glad the lookout had been sent no higher. 'Where away, Sims?' he asked, coming into the top through the lubber-hole.

'Three points on the starboard bow, sir,' said Sims, pointing; and there indeed, as the ship rose on the swell, was land, quite high land with a hint of green, an island some eleven or twelve leagues away.

'Well done, Sims,' said Jack, and he slipped down through the hole again. Even before he reached the deck he began roaring for the bosun, who was busy on the forecastle. 'Leave that for the moment, Mr Hollar,' he said, 'and get me light hawsers to the mastheads.'

'Aye aye sir,' said Hollar, smiling. This was an old trick of the Captain's, horrible in appearance but wonderfully effective. The hairy, brutish hawsers and cablets allowed him to carry sail that would otherwise tear the masts out of the ship, and this had won the frigate many a charming prize before now, or had allowed her to run clear away from much superior force.

'Mr Mowett,' he said, 'four good men to the wheel, and let them be relieved every glass. We are going to crack on. Mr Allen, please to con the ship: course north-west by west a half west.'

Then, half an hour later, catching sight of Hogg supported by his mates on the gangway he stepped forward and said, 'Well, specktioneer, do you make it out?'

'Yes, mate, I do,' said Hogg. 'If you look under them clouds not moving, under their floor, like, don't you see a bright round, and dark in the middle?'

'I believe I do. Yes, certainly I do.'

'The bright is surf and coral sand, and the dark is trees: there ain't much lagoon.'

'How do you know that?'

'Why, because lagoon shows green, in course. Quite a high island, from the amount of cloud. I wonder you never saw it, Bill,' – this to his supporter. ''Tis as plain as plain.'

'All stretched along and a-tanto, sir,' said the bosun.

'Very good, Mr Hollar,' said Jack, and raising his voice, 'All hands to make sail.'

The new course brought the great wind almost on to the frigate's quarter, and methodically he began spreading her canvas. They had long since swayed up the topmasts, though not of course the topgallants, and he gave her a little high storm-jib first, then the main staysail, then instead of the close-reefed maintopsail the maintopmast staysail. Each time he paused for the *Surprise* to take up the full force of the new thrust: this she did with immense spirit, with the buoyant living grace which so moved his heart – never was such a ship – and when she was moving perhaps as fast as she had ever moved, with her lee cathead well under the foam of her bow-wave, he laid one hand on the hances, feeling the deep note of her hull as he might have felt the vibrations of his fiddle, and the other on a backstay, gauging the exact degree of strain.

They were used to the Captain; they had nearly all of them seen him cracking on like smoke and oakum and they were pretty nearly sure he had not finished. But no man had expected his call for the forecourse itself and it was with grave, anxious faces that they jumped to their task. It took fifty-seven men to haul the foresheet aft, to tally and belay; and as the strain increased so the *Surprise* heeled another strake, another and yet another, until she showed a broad streak of copper on her windward side, while the howl in the rigging rose shriller and shriller, almost to the breaking-note. And there she steadied, racing through the sea and flinging a bow-wave so high to leeward that the sun sent back a double rainbow. Discreet cheering started forward and spread aft: everybody on the quarterdeck was grinning.

'Watch your dog-vane,' said Jack to the helmsman. 'If you once let her be brought by the lee, you will never see Portsmouth Point again. Mr Howard, pray let your men line the weather gangway.'

Four bells. Boyle walked cautiously down the sloping

317

deck with the log and reel under his arm, followed by a quartermaster with the little sand-glass.

'Double the stray-line,' called Jack, who wanted an accurate measurement, with the log-ship well clear of the wake before the knots were counted.

'Double the stray-line it is, sir,' replied Boyle in as deep a voice as his puny frame could manage. When the red tuft had been shifted fifteen fathoms he took up his station by the rail, asked, 'Is your glass clear?' and on being told, 'Glass clear, sir,' heaved the log well out, holding the reel high in his left hand. 'Turn,' he cried as the end of the stray-line went by. The sand streamed down, the reel whirred, the knots fleeted by, intently watched by all hands who had an eye to spare. The quartermaster opened his mouth to cry 'Nip', but before the last grains had run through Boyle uttered a screech and the reel shot from his hand.

'I am very sorry, sir,' he said to Mowett after a moment's confusion. 'I let the reel go.'

Mowett stepped across to Jack and said, 'Boyle is very sorry, sir, but he let the reel go. The line ran clean out and I suppose the pin was stiff: it took him unawares.'

'Never mind,' said Jack, who in spite of his intense underlying anxiety was deeply moved by this splendid measurement of flying speed. 'Let him try with a fourteen-second glass at six bells.'

By six bells the upper part of the island was clear to those on the deck, a hilly little island, with clouds just above it; and from the maintop could be seen the tremendous surf beating against its shore. No lagoon on this windward side, but there seemed to be reefs running out some way on the north-east and south-west with lighter-coloured water beyond them.

The wind had diminished by now and the *Surprise* logged no astonishing number of knots, but there was that ineffaceable memory, dear to all the people, of a whole 150 fathoms being run straight off the reel before the glass was out; and in any case she was still bringing the land a mile closer every four or five minutes.

'Mr Martin,' said Jack in the sick-bay, 'we have raised an island, as I dare say you know, and in an hour's time we should be under its lee: or it may be possible to land. In either case I beg you will hold yourself in readiness to operate.'

'Let us go and look at him,' said Martin. Padeen Colman was sitting there, his beads in his hand: he shook his head without a word, meaning 'No change'.

'It is an awful decision,' said Martin as they stood swaying with the motion of the ship, looking down at that stern mask. 'Above all because the symptoms do not quite agree with any of the books.' Once again and this time at greater length he explained what he understood to be the nature of the case.

He was still doing so when Mowett came and said softly, 'I beg your pardon, sir, but there is a signal flying from the island.'

The island had come very much closer during Jack's time below and the signal was quite clear in his glass: a torn blue and white flag on a high-standing rock. Jack climbed into the foretop with his first lieutenant and from there the shore line was as plain as could be: cliffs with rollers bursting high on them on this eastern side and then a reef tending away southward and west. He called down the orders that put the ship before the wind under a close-reefed main topsail and forecourse: she skirted the end of the reef and hauled up round it, coming to the verge of the island's lee. Here the reef enclosed a considerable lagoon, and on its landward shore, intensely white under this brilliant sky, he saw a number of men, probably white men, from the trousers and occasional shirt: some were running to and fro but more were making emphatic gestures northwards.

The *Surprise*, with little more than steerage-way on her now, moved cautiously along the outside of the reef: quite close, but still in such deep water that the man in the chains perpetually cried, 'No bottom with this line; no bottom, nay, nay.'

319

Although there was still a powerful swell, the wind was very, very much less here, and its near silence gave their slow gliding the feeling of a dream. The reef slipped by, sometimes with little palm-grown islands on it, coconut-palms, often laid flat or broken off short, and beyond the reef the calm lagoon; beyond that the shining strand, backed first by palms and then by a rising general greenery whose wind-ravaged state could be seen only in a glass; and on the strand the white men ran and capered and pointed. They were not much more than a mile away, but the shifting airs under the island's lee did not carry their voices, which were reduced to an occasional faint 'Ahoy, the ship ahoy,' or a confused babbling.

'I believe that is a gap, sir,' said Mowett, pointing along the broad reef: and just beyond an island with three uprooted palms and three still standing, there was indeed a channel through into the lagoon.

'Flat in forward, there,' cried Jack, staring intently; and as the *Surprise* edged nearer to the gap, he heard a concerted howl from the strand, no doubt a warning, for a sunken ship lay clean across the fairway. An unnecessary warning however; in this clear water and with the ebbing tide she was clear from her stem, which was wedged just below the surface in the coral of the little island, to her stern far down in the rocks of the other side. Her bowsprit and masts had gone by the board, her back was broken, her midship gunports had been stove in, and there was a gaping hole from her starboard mainchains to her quarter-gallery, a hole through which passed long pale-grey sharks, blurred by the ripple and the swell; but she was perfectly recognizable as the *Norfolk*, and Jack at once called out, 'Hoist the short pennant and the colours.'

This seemed to cause some consternation on shore. Most of the men ran off northwards; a few still stood staring; the capering stopped and there were no more gestures. Jack returned to the quarterdeck and the ship sailed gently on, following the reef. The shore turned inward, opening a little cove in which there stood a cluster of tents and shelters where a stream ran out of the woods over the sand. Here there were more people, more distant now that the lagoon was wider and quite inaudible; but now, evidently by command, they all pointed their right arms northwards to the place where the stream flowed through a long winding channel in the reef, quarter of a mile broad at this point.

There were no breakers here, on this most sheltered part of the coast, but even so the swell still rose high on the glistening coral and receded with an enormous sigh. 'I will be damned if I venture the ship in there, on an ebbing tide, without sounding,' said Jack, looking at the light-green channel, and he ordered a boat away.

It could just be done, said Honey, returning, but it would be nip and tuck until the flood; and the coral rocks on either side and on the bottom were razor-sharp. There was no great current now, near slack-water; but the tide must scour through at a great rate, to keep the bottom so clean, unless indeed that was the effect of the heavy blow. If the ship were to go through, perhaps he had better buoy one or two of the worst places.

'No,' said Jack. 'It don't signify. We are in forty fathom water with a good clean ground; we could anchor if we chose. Mr Mowett, while I stand off and on take my barge and a proper guard of Marines, proceed to the shore – flag of truce and ensign of course – present my compliments to the captain of the *Norfolk* and desire him to repair aboard without delay and surrender himself prisoner.'

The barge had not been painted since they were off the River Plate; the bargemen had not had time to renew their broad-brimmed sennit hats; the uniforms of the lieutenant, the midshipman and the Marines were not as fresh as they had been before undergoing antarctic cold and equatorial heat; but even so the Surprises were quite proud of their turn-out, so very far from home and after such an uncommon savage blow. They watched the barge thread the channel and cross the broad, smooth lagoon,

and during the long pull many of the watch below passed
a small private telescope from hand to hand, looking for
women on the shore: in spite of their shocking experience
with the pahi they still looked for women, looked very
eagerly indeed. Those who had been in the South Sea
before had attentive, silent listeners: 'As free and kind she
was as kiss my hand,' said Hogg, speaking of the first he
had known, in the island of Oahua. 'And so were the rest.
Some of the men had to be tied, and carried aboard slung
on a pole: they would have jumped ship else, though they
had forty and fifty pound due to them in shares.'

'There ain't no women,' said Plaice to a young main-
topman after a long and searching stare. 'Nor no men
neither. It is a desert island, apart from those Boston
beans walking up and down. But that there, sheltering
the biggest tent by the stream, that's a breadfruit-tree, I
dare say.'

'You can —— your breadfruit-tree,' said the young topman bitterly.

'That's no way to talk to a man old enough to be your
dad, Ned Harris,' said the captain of the forecastle.

'Saucy young bugger,' said two others.

'I only meant it by way of a joke,' said Harris, reddening.
'I was talking lighthearted.'

'You want your arse tanned,' observed the yeoman
of the signals.

'There's a precious lot of sharks about,' said Harris,
by way of changing the subject. 'Uncommon long thin
grey ones.'

'Never you mind if they are grey or pink with orange
stripes,' said the captain of the forecastle. 'You just keep
a civil tongue in your head, Ned Harris, that's all.'

'They're putting off with the American captain, sir,'
said Killick, in the cabin.

'Undo this damned hook for me, will you, Killick?'
said Jack, who was getting into his uniform. 'I must be
growing fat.'

He looked into his dining-cabin, where a cold collation

had been spread to welcome the captain of the *Norfolk*, ate one of the little salt biscuits and then buckled on his sword. He did not wish to appear too eager, strutting about on his quarterdeck throughout his prisoner's approach – it was a damned unpleasant thing having to surrender in any case, as he knew from experience, without having people crow over you – but on the other hand he did not wish to appear casual, as though the surrender of a post-captain were of no great importance.

He waited until it seemed to him that the moment was as nearly right as possible, put on his cocked hat, and went on deck. A quick look showed him that Honey had everything in hand: midshipmen quite respectable, sideboys washed and holding their white gloves ready – rather hairy, big-boned sideboys now – Marines at hand, and the ship, which had been toing and froing, now standing gently in, just stemming the tide, to receive the barge.

He began his usual pacing; but at the third turn a glance at the short figure sitting there between Calamy and Mowett in the stern-sheets made him look again, look much harder. It was too late to start staring with a spyglass, but from his time as a prisoner of war in Boston he was very well acquainted with American naval uniforms, and there was something amiss.

When the barge was a little nearer he said to the Marine sentry, 'Trollope, hail that boat.'

The Marine was on the point of saying, 'But it's our own barge, sir,' when a glazed, disciplined look came over his eyes: he shut his mouth, drew a deep breath and called, 'The boat ahoy.'

'No, no,' came Bonden's answer, very loud and clear, meaning that no commissioned officer was coming to the *Surprise*.

'Carry on, Mr Honey,' said Jack, withdrawing to the taffrail: the sideboys stuffed their gloves into their pockets, the midshipmen abandoned their reverential looks, and Howard dismissed his men. The barge hooked on and

Mowett bounded up the side. His face was quite aghast as he came hurrying aft to Jack. 'I am very sorry, sir,' he cried, 'but the war is over.'

He was immediately followed by a cheerful short thick round-headed man in a plain uniform coat who brushed past Honey and approached Jack with a beaming smile, his hand held out. 'My dear Captain Aubrey, give you joy of the peace,' he said. 'I am delighted to see you again, and how is your arm? Very well, I see, and much the same length as the other, according to my prediction. You do not remember me, sir, though without boasting I may say you owe me your right arm. Mr Evans was actually filing the teeth of his saw, but I said No, let us give it another day – Butcher, formerly assistant surgeon in *Constitution* and now surgeon of *Norfolk*.'

'Of course I remember you, Mr Butcher,' said Jack, his mind filled with the recollection of that painful voyage to Boston as a wounded prisoner after the American *Constitution* had taken the British *Java*. 'But where is Captain Palmer? Did he survive the wreck of the *Norfolk*?'

'Oh yes, yes. He was battered, but not drowned. We did not lose a very great many people compared with what it might have been. All our clothes went, however, and I am the only man with a respectable coat. That is why I was sent – Captain Palmer could not bear the idea of going aboard a British man-of-war in a torn shirt and no hat – he desires his best compliments, of course – had the pleasure of meeting you in Boston with Captain Lawrence – and hope you and your officers will dine with him on what the island affords tomorrow at three o'clock.'

'You spoke of a peace, Mr Butcher?'

'Oh yes, and he will tell you about that in more detail than I can. We first had the news from a British whaler – how blank we looked when we had to let her go, a splendid prize – and then from a ship out of Nantucket. But tell me, sir, what is this I hear about Dr Maturin, that you wish to open his head?'

324

'He had an ugly fall, and our chaplain, who understands physic, thinks it might save him.'

'If it is a question of trepanning, I am your man. It is an operation I have performed scores, nay hundreds of times without losing a patient. That is to say except in a very few cases of vicious cachexy, where it was only done to please the relations. I trepanned Mrs Butcher for a persistent migraine, and she has never complained since. I have the greatest faith in the operation; it has brought many men back from the edge of the grave, and not only for depressed fractures, either. May I see the patient?'

'A very fine instrument indeed,' said Butcher to Martin, turning Stephen's trephine over and over in his hands. 'With many improvements unknown to me. French, I believe? I remember our friend' – nodding towards Maturin – 'saying he had studied in France. A trifle of snuff, sir?'

'Thank you, but I do not take it.'

'It is my only indulgence,' said Butcher. 'A very fine instrument; but I do not wonder you hesitated to use it. I should hesitate myself, even in a swell as moderate as this, let alone the sea you describe. Let us get him ashore at once: this pressure must not be allowed to continue another night, or I will not answer for the consequences.'

'Can he safely be moved?'

'Of course he can. Wrapped in blankets, made fast to a padded six by two plank with cingulum bandages – a crosspiece for his feet, of course – and raised and lowered vertically by tackles, he will come to no harm, no harm at all. And if Captain Aubrey could send his carpenter to knock up a hut a little more solid than our canvas, why, the patient will be as well off as in any naval hospital.'

'Mr Mowett,' said Jack, 'I am going ashore with the Doctor. It will be too dark by the height of flood for you to try the channel, so you will anchor the ship, gackling your cables a good twenty fathom. In all probability I shall rejoin when things are well in hand, but if I do not, you will come in tomorrow evening. Do not forget to gackle your cables, Mowett.'

Stephen, more corpse-like still with his face shrouded from the sun, was lowered into the boat – the launch this time, as being more roomy than the barge – and it pushed off, loaded deep with the carpenter, his crew, a working-party, a good deal of material, and some stores that Jack thought might be welcome to castaways.

Captain Palmer had hobbled down to greet him at the landing-place, a little hard on the left-hand side of the stream, away from the tents. He had done what he could to improve his appearance, but he was an unusually hairy man by nature, and a grizzled beard, together with his ragged clothes and bare feet, gave him the look of a vagrant: he had also been miserably bruised and scraped at the time of the wreck and he was covered with makeshift plasters and bandages where the coral rock had rasped him to the bone. The hair and the plasters made the expression on his face difficult to interpret, but his words were both polite and obliging. 'I hope, sir,' he said, 'that you will come and drink what we have to offer while everything is being fixed; for I conclude the gentleman on the plank under the awning is your surgeon, come ashore to be opened by Mr Butcher.'

'Just so: Mr Butcher was so very kind as to offer his services. But if you will forgive me, sir, I must see to some kind of a shelter first, while there is still light. Do not stir, I beg,' he said as Palmer made a move to accompany him. 'On our way in I noticed a glade that will probably answer very well.'

'I shall look forward to your visit, as soon as you have settled on your place and given your orders,' said Palmer with a courtly bow.

This bow was almost the only acknowledgement between the two sides. The small group of men behind Palmer, presumably his remaining officers, uttered no word, while the surviving Norfolks, some eighty or ninety of them, stood at some distance on the right-hand side

326

of the stream; the Surprises stood on the left, and they stared heavily at one another across the water like two unacquainted, potentially hostile bands of cattle. Jack was surprised. In this absurd, unnecessary war there had been little real ill-feeling except on the part of the civilians, and he had expected much more spontaneous pleasure, much more calling out between the hands. He had little time for these reflections, however; the well-drained, open, light, airy place he wanted for his shelter was by no means as easy to find as he had imagined. The hurricane had littered the ground with branches, some of them huge; there were great trees uprooted and others dangerously unsteady; and it was not until late twilight, after driving hard work, that the roof was on and the patient laid out on the solid, sweet-smelling table, newly cut from fresh sandal-wood.

'I hope the want of light will not trouble you, Mr Butcher,' said Jack.

'Not at all,' said Butcher. 'I am so used to operating between decks that I really prefer a lantern. Mr Martin, sir, if you will place one there, by the beam, while I set the other here, I believe we shall have the benefit of the converging rays. Captain Aubrey, was you to sit on the barrel by the door, you would have an excellent view. You will not have long to wait: as soon as I have put the last edge on this scalpel I shall make the first incision.'

'No,' said Jack. 'I shall go to see Captain Palmer, and then I must get back to the ship. Please to let me know the moment the operation is over. Colman here will wait outside to bring me word.'

'Certainly,' said Butcher. 'But as for your going back to the ship tonight, never think of it, sir. The flood-tide comes in through that channel like a mill-race; a boat could not possibly row against it, and the wind is foul.'

'Come along, Blakeney,' said Jack to his midshipman: he closed the door and walked quickly away: his stomach was strong enough for most purposes, but not for seeing Stephen's scalp turned down over his face, inside out, and a trephine deliberately cutting into his living bone.

At the bottom of the glade they could see the Surprises eating their supper in the lee of the launch, a noble fire burning before them. 'Cut along and have a bite,' said Jack. 'Tell them that everything is in train; and when they have finished their supper let Bonden bring the stores I put up for the Americans.'

He walked slowly on, listened to the sea on the distant reef and sometimes glanced up at the moon, just past the full. He liked neither the sound of the one nor the look of the other. Nor did he like the atmosphere on the island.

He crossed the stream, still deep in reflection. 'Halt,' cried a sentry. 'Who goes there?'

'Friend,' replied Jack.

'Pass friend,' said the sentry.

'There you are, sir,' said Palmer, ushering him into his tent, lit with a rescued top-light turned very low. 'You look anxious: I hope all is well?'

'I hope so,' said Jack. 'They are operating now. They will send me word as soon as it is over.'

'I am sure all will be well. I have never known Butcher miss his stroke; he is as clever as any surgeon in the service.'

'I am very happy to hear you say so,' said Jack. 'It should not take long, I believe.' His ear was already cocked for approaching footsteps.

'Do you understand tides, Mr Martin?' asked Butcher, slowly shaving hairs off his forearm with the scalpel.

'Not I,' said Martin.

'A fascinating study,' said Butcher. 'Here they are particularly curious, being neither semi-diurnal nor quite diurnal. There is an immense reef to the west of this island and I believe it is that which pens up the current and causes the anomaly: but whether it is that or a whole raft of other factors, a spring tide, like tonight's, comes in with great force, torrential force, and the flow lasts nine

328

hours or more. It will not be high water till morning, and your captain is as one might say marooned for the night, ha, ha! Will you take snuff, sir?'

'Thank you, sir,' said Martin. 'I never do.'

'Mine was a waterproof box, glory be,' said Butcher, turning Stephen's head and considering it with pursed lips. 'I always fortify myself before operating. Some gentlemen smoke a cigar. I prefer snuff.' He opened his box and took so vast a pinch that a good deal fell down his shirt-front and more on his patient; he flapped it off both with his handkerchief and Stephen gave a tiny sneeze. Then painfully he drew a deeper breath, sneezed like a Christian, muttered something about spoonbills and brought his hand up to cover his eyes, saying, 'Jesus, Mary, and Joseph,' in his usual harsh, grating voice, though very low.

'Pin him,' cried Butcher, 'or he will be sitting up.' And through the door to Padeen, 'Hey there, go fetch a rope.'

'Maturin,' said Martin, bending over him, 'you have come to yourself! How happy I am. I have prayed for this. You had a great fall, but are now recovered.'

'Put out that goddam light,' said Stephen.

'Come, sir, lie back and set your mind at ease,' said Butcher. 'We must relieve the pressure on your brain – just a little discomfort, a little restraint – it will soon be over . . .' But he spoke without much hope, and when Stephen did sit up, desiring Padeen not to stand there in the door like a great dumb ox but to fetch him a draught of good fresh water for the love of God, he put down his scalpel, saying quietly, 'Now I shall never have a chance of using the new French trephine.'

After a silent pause, Captain Palmer said, 'Well, sir, and how did your ship come through this blow?'

'Pretty well, I thank you, upon the whole, apart from some lost spars and a sprung mizen; but most of the storm had already passed over, somewhat to the north, I believe. We only caught the southern skirt, or the tail.'

'We were in the heart of it, or rather the forefront, since we had no warning; and it hit us at night. A sad time we had of it, as you may imagine, particularly as we were shorthanded, having sent so many men away – ' Palmer hardly liked to say 'in prizes' so he repeated 'having sent so many men away', merely changing the stress. It was evident from his account that the typhoon had struck the *Norfolk* much earlier than the *Surprise*: it had also set her far north of her reckoning, so that on the Thursday morning, when they were driving before an enormous sea with no more than a scrap of sail on the stump of the foremast, to their surprise and horror they saw Old Sodbury's Island fine on the starboard bow.

'This island, sir?' Palmer nodded. 'So you knew it, then?'

'I knew *of* it, sir. The whalers sometimes come here – indeed, it is named for Reuben Sodbury of Nantucket – but they usually avoid it because of the very long and dangerous shoals a few miles to the west – shoals that were right under our lee. So rather than run plumb on to them, with no hope at all, we bore up for Old Sodbury. Two of my men, whalers from New Bedford, had been there before and they knew the pass.' He shook his head, and then went on, 'Still, we did at least strike at the very tail of the ebb, so most of us could scramble from the bows to the little island and so along the reef to the shore. But we saved nothing – no boats, no stores, no clothes, almost no tools, no tobacco . . .'

'Have you not been able to dive for anything?'

'No, sir. No. The place is alive with sharks, the grey kind, Old Sodbury's sharks. My second and a midshipman tried, at low water: they didn't leave us enough to bury, though they were not big fish.'

They heard the sentry's 'Halt. Who goes there?' followed by a strangled gasp, then the sound of blows, and Bonden's strong, 'Now then, mate, who are you a shoving of? Don't you know he's dumb?'

'Why didn't he say so, then?' said the sentry in a faint voice. 'Let me up.'

Padeen burst in and touched his forehead with a bleeding knuckle; he brought out no clear word, but his message was plain on his shining face, and in any case Bonden was there to interpret: 'He means the Doctor was not opened at all, sir – recovered by himself, sprang up like a fairy, damned everyone all round, called for water, called for coconut-milk, and is now asleep, no visitors allowed. Which I brought the stores, sir. And sir, it may be turning dirty outside.'

'Thank you, both of you: you could not have brought better news. I shall be with you presently, Bonden. Now here, sir,' – opening the chest – 'are some little things we brought along: no caviar or champagne, I am afraid, but this is smoked seal, and this salt pork and dolphin sausage . . .'

'Rum, port wine and tobacco!' cried Palmer. 'Bless you, Captain Aubrey! I sometimes thought I should never see them again. Allow me to freshen your coconut-milk with some of this excellent rum. And then if I may I will call in my officers, the few I still have, and introduce them.'

Jack smiled while Palmer was uncorking the bottle; it was not what he was about to say that made him so cheerful but rather the thought of Stephen sitting up and cursing. The rum was poured, the mixture stirred. Composing his face Jack said, 'There is something one might almost say sacred about wine or grog or even perhaps beer that water or coconut-milk does not possess; so before I drink with you, it is but right that I should say you must consider yourself a prisoner of war. Of course I shall not proceed to extremes. I shall not insist upon your coming back to the ship with me tonight, for example, or anything of that kind. No manacles, no irons or bilboes' – this with a smile, although in fact the *Constitution* had handcuffed the captured seamen from

331

the *Java*. 'Yet I thought I should make the position clear.'

'But, my dear sir, the war is over,' cried Palmer.

'So I hear,' said Jack after a slight pause, in a less cordial voice. 'But I have no official knowledge of it, and your sources may be mistaken. And as you know, hostilities continue until they are countermanded by one's superior officers.'

Once again Palmer spoke of the British whaler, the *Vega* of London, that had lain to for him and had told him of the peace – had shown him a newspaper bought in Acapulco, fresh from New York with an account of the treaty; and he spoke of the Nantucket ship, whose officers and men all talked about it as a matter of course. He spoke in great detail, and most earnestly.

'Obviously,' he said, 'I cannot argue with twenty-eight great guns; but I hope I can reason with the officer who commands them, unless he is only concerned with blood-shed and destruction.'

'Certainly,' said Jack. 'But you must know that even the most humane of officers is required to do his duty, and that his duty may sometimes be very disagreeable to his feelings.'

'He is also required to use discretion,' said Palmer. 'Everyone has heard of those miserable killings in the remote parts of the world long after peace has been signed, deaths that every decent man must regret. Ships sunk or burnt too, or taken only to be given back after endless delay and loss. Aubrey, do you not see that if you use your superior strength to carry us back to Europe, just at a time when this wretched, unhappy war has been patched up, your action will be as bitterly resented in the States as the *Leopard*'s when she fired into the *Chesapeake*?'

This was a shrewd blow. At one time Jack had commanded that unlucky ship, a two-decker carrying fifty guns, and he knew very well that one of his predecessors, Salusbury Humphreys, had been ordered to recover some deserters from the Royal Navy from the American *Chesapeake*, a thirty-six gun frigate; the American commander was unwilling to have his ship searched, and the *Leopard* fired three broadsides into her, killing or wounding twenty-one of her people. She succeeded in recovering some of the deserters, but the incident very nearly caused a war and did in fact close all United States ports to British men-of-war. It also meant the shore for most of the officers concerned, including the Admiral.

'Conceivably Captain Humphreys was just within his legal right, firing upon the *Chesapeake*,' said Palmer. 'I do not know: I am no lawyer. And conceivably you would be within the strict letter of yours if you were to carry us to Europe as prisoners. But I cannot think that such a cheap victory over unarmed, shipwrecked men would be much to the honour of your service or would give you much satisfaction. No, sir, what I hope you will do is use your wide powers of discretion and carry us to Huahiva in the Marquesas, not a hundred leagues away, where I have friends and can shift for myself and my men; or if you do not like that, then I hope you will at least leave us here and let our friends know where they can find us. For I presume you will now go home by the Cape, passing close by the Marquesas. We can hold out here for a month or two, although food is short because of the hurricane. Think it over, sir; sleep on it, I beg. And in the meantime let us drink a health to Dr Maturin.' At these words a most enormous lightning-flash lit up his anxious face.

'With all my heart,' said Jack, draining his coconut-shell and standing up. 'I must get back to the ship.'

Long and vehement thunder drowned the beginning of Palmer's reply but Jack did catch the words '. . . should have told you before . . . nine- or ten-hour flood, impossible to pull against in the channel. Pray accept of this bed,' – pointing to a heap of leaves covered with sailcloth.

'Thank you, but I shall go and ask for news of Maturin,' said Jack.

On leaving the trees he looked out beyond the white

line of the reef for the *Surprise*'s riding-light, and when his eyes grew used to the darkness he made it out, low in the west, like a setting star. 'I am sure Mowett will have gackled his cables,' he said.

The launch had been hauled well above the high-water mark and turned bottom-up on broken palm-trunks so that it formed a low but commodious house; its copper could be seen gleaming in the moon, and from beneath the gunnel the acrid smoke of a dozen pipes drifted to leeward. Bonden was walking up and down at some distance, waiting for him. 'Dirty weather, sir,' he said.

'Yes,' said Jack, and they both stared up at the moon, peering now and then through racing, whirling cloud, though down here there was no more than a shifting, uneasy breeze. 'It looks very like the mixture as before. You have heard about the nine-hour tide, I collect.'

'Yes, sir. A very nasty piece of work caught me up when I was coming back from the tent. An Englishman: he told me. Also said he was a Hermione, and there was several more in the *Norfolk*, a score or so apart from other deserters. Said he would point them out if you would hold him safe and guarantee he would get the reward. They were main terrified at the sight of *Surprise* – thought she was a Russian ship at first, and cheered, then grew main terrified when they saw what she really was.'

'I am sure they did. What did you say to this Hermione?'

'Told him I'd tell you, sir.'

The heavens lit from rim to rim, showing a vast solid blackness rushing across the sky from the south-east. Both ran for shelter, but before Jack could reach his the wall of rain caught him and soaked him through. With ludicrous precaution he silently opened and closed the door and stood dripping there in the hut, while the hissing roar of falling water and the crash of thunder filled the outside world; with equal absurdity Martin, reading a book by a shaded lantern, put his fingers to his lips and pointed at Stephen, lying there curled on

334

his side sleeping peacefully, naturally, and occasionally smiling.

All night he slept, though a rough night it was, as rough as Jack had known, and noisier. For when the wind really began, which it did with a sudden shriek at one in the morning, it had not only the masts and rigging of a ship to howl through but all the island's remaining trees and bushes; while the tremendous surf, coming more from the south than it had before, produced a ground-bass of equal enormity, more to be felt with one's whole being than really heard through the screaming wind and the headlong crash of trees.

'What was that?' asked Martin, when the hut reverberated with hammer-blows during a particularly violent blast.

'Coconuts,' said Jack. 'Thank God Lamb made such a good job of the roof: they are mortal in a breeze like this.'

Stephen slept through the coconuts, slept through the first bleary light of dawn, but he opened an eye during the lull that came with the sunrise, said, 'Good morning to you, now, Jack,' and closed it again.

With the same precautions as before Jack crept out of the door into the streaming wind-wrecked landscape. He hurried ankle-deep down to the shore, where he observed that the launch had not moved, and there, standing on the broad bole of a fallen tree and bracing himself against a still unbroken palm, he searched the white, torn ocean with his pocket glass. To and fro he swept the horizon, watching until every trough in the swell became a rise; near and far, north and south; but there was never a ship on the sea.

CHAPTER TEN

'Two thoughts occur to me,' said Jack Aubrey without taking his eye from the hole in the wall that commanded the western approaches to the island, the rainswept waters in which the *Surprise* might eventually appear. 'The one is that by and large, taking one thing with another, I have never known any commission with so much weather in it.'

'Not even in the horrible old *Leopard*?' asked Stephen. 'I seem to recall such gusts, such immeasurable billows . . .' He also remembered a remote landlocked antarctic bay where they had lain refitting for weeks and weeks among albatrosses, whale-birds, giant petrels, blue-eyed shags and a variety of penguins, all of them hand-tame.

'The *Leopard* was pretty severe,' said Jack, 'and so it was when I was a mid in the *Namur* and we were escorting the Archangel trade. I had just washed my hair in fresh water that my tie-mate and I had melted from ice, and we had each plaited the other's pigtail – we used to wear them long like the seamen in those days, you know, not clubbed except in action – when all hands were called to shorten sail. It was blowing hard from the north-north-east with ice-crystals driving thick and hard: I laid aloft to help close-reef the maintopsail, and a devil of a time we had with it, the bunt perpetually blowing out to leeward, one of the lines having parted – I was on the windward yardarm. However we did manage it in the end and we were about to lay in when my hat flew off and I heard a great crack just behind my ear: it was my pigtail, flung up against the lift. It was frozen stiff and it had snapped off short in the middle; upon my word, Stephen, it had absolutely snapped off short like a dry stick. They picked it up on deck and I kept it for a girl I was fond of at that time, at the Keppel's Knob in

Pompey, thinking she would like it; but, however, she did not.' A pause. 'It was wet through, do you see, and so it froze.'

'I believe I understand,' said Stephen. 'But, my dear, are you not wandering from your subject a little?'

'What I mean is, that although other bouts may have been more extreme while they lasted, for sheer weather, for sheer quantity and I might almost say *mass* of weather, this commission bears the bell away. The other thing that occurred to me,' he said, turning round, 'is that it is extremely awkward talking to a man with hair all over his face; you cannot tell what he is thinking, what he really means, whether he is false or not. Sometimes people wear blue spectacles, and it is much the same.'

'You refer to Captain Palmer, I make no doubt.'

'Just so. This last spell, crammed in here with Martin and Colman, and with you so indifferent, I have not liked to speak about him.' By this last spell he meant the three days of excessively violent storm that had kept them in the hut with scarcely an hour's intermission; the wind had now diminished to a fresh gale and although the rain had started again it no longer had the choking, blinding quality of the earlier deluge and people were already creeping about the island picking up battered breadfruit, particularly the sort with large chestnut-like seeds, and coconuts, many of them broken in spite of their thick husks. 'Just so. I really could not tell what to make of him. My first notion was that what Butcher had said and what Palmer said was true – that the war was over. It did not occur to me that an officer would tell a direct lie.'

'Oh come, Jack, for all love! You are an officer and I have known you lie times without number, like Ulysses. I have seen you hang out flags stating that you were a Dutchman, a French merchant, a Spanish man-of-war – that you were a friend, an ally – anything to deceive. Why, the earthly paradise would soon be with us, if government, monarchical or republican, had but to give a man a commission to preserve him from lying – from

337

pride, envy, sloth, gule, avarice, ire and incontinence.'

Jack's face, which had darkened at the word lie, cleared at that of incontinence. 'Oh,' cried he, 'those are just ruses de guerre, and perfectly legitimate: they are not direct lies like saying it is peace when you know damned well it is war. That would be like approaching an enemy under false colours, which is perfectly proper, and then firing before hauling them down and hoisting your own at the last moment, which is profoundly dishonourable, the act of a mere pirate, and one for which any man can be hanged. Perhaps it is a distinction too nice for a civilian, but I do assure you it is perfectly clear to sailors. Anyhow, I did not think Palmer would lie and my first idea was to carry them all to the Marquesas and set them free, the officers on parole not to serve again until exchanged if there had been a mistake – if the treaty had not been ratified, or something of that kind. Yet although the capture as I saw it was no more than a formality, I wished to make the point right away; I did not like to go on doing the civil thing, dining to and fro and drinking together, and then saying, "By the by, I must trouble you for your sword." So at this first meeting I told him he was a prisoner of war. I said it not exactly with levity – apart from anything else he is a much older man, a greybeard – but with a certain obvious exaggeration: I said he should not be compelled to go back with me to the ship that very night, and that his people should not be handcuffed. To my astonishment he took this seriously, and that made me begin to think perhaps there was something amiss; I remembered that when I first came ashore I had thought it strange the Norfolks were not more pleased to see us, the war being over and we being as it were their rescuers: and I felt the whole thing was somehow out of tune, badly out of tune.'

'Tell me, Jack, just how would you have expected him to reply to your statement that he was a prisoner?'

'As I made it, I should have expected any sea-officer to have replied by damning my eyes, in a civil way of course, or by clasping his hands and begging me not to confine them all in the hold nor to flog them more than twice a day. That is to say, if he really believed it was peace.'

'Perhaps the cetacean facetiousness I have so often noticed in the Royal Navy may not have crossed the Atlantic. And then again, if there is deceit, may it not originate in the English whaler? The *Vega*, after all, had every inducement to elude capture.'

'The *Vega* may have tried it too, of course. However by this time I felt so doubtful that I did not speak to Palmer about parole or the Marquesas or anything of that kind; because if in fact the war was still carrying on I should certainly have to pen them all up. It would be gross neglect of duty not to do so. It was not just his solemnity that made me so doubtful, but a hundred little nameless things, indeed the whole atmosphere; though his full motive escaped me. And then on my way back to the hut I learnt that Palmer had some Hermiones on board, quite apart from several ordinary deserters. Surely I must have told you about the *Hermione*?' he said, seeing Stephen's blank expression.

'I believe not, brother.'

'Well, perhaps I have not. It was the ugliest thing in my time, apart from the glorious end. Very briefly it was this: a man who should never have been made post – who should never have been an officer at all – was given the *Hermione*, a thirty-two-gun frigate, and he turned her into a hell afloat. In the West Indies her crew mutinied and killed him, which some people might say was fair enough; but they also murdered the three lieutenants and the Marine officer quite horribly, the purser, the surgeon, the clerk, the bosun and a reefer, hunting him right through the ship; then they carried her into La Guayra and gave her up to the Spaniards, with whom we were then at war. A hideous business from beginning to end. But some time later the Spaniards sailed her to Puerto Cabello, and there Ned Hamilton, who had the dear *Surprise* at that time, and a damned good crew as well, took the boats

339

in at night and cut her out, although she was moored head and stern between two very powerful batteries and although the Spaniards were rowing guard. His surgeon, I remember, commanded a gig, a splendid man named M'Mullen. The Surprises killed a great many Spaniards, but most of the mutineers escaped; and when Spain joined us against the French a good many of them removed to the States. Some shipped in merchantmen, which was foolish, because merchantmen are often searched and whenever one was found he was taken out and hanged without a hope: their exact descriptions, tattoo-marks and everything, had been circulated to all the stations and there was a thumping price on their heads.'

'And there are some of these unfortunate men among the *Norfolk*'s crew?'

'Yes. One of them has offered to point out the rest if he is allowed to turn King's evidence and have the reward.'

'Informers – Lord, the world is full of them, so it is.'

'Well, now, this puts quite a different face upon it. Palmer has a score or so of Hermiones as well as other deserters aboard: the other deserters are liable to be hanged if they are taken, though they may be let off with five hundred lashes if they are foreigners, but for the Hermiones it is certain death; and although they are no doubt a pretty worthless set it is Palmer's clear duty to protect them: they are his men. Even as nominal prisoners of war they would have to be mustered and inspected and entered on the ship's books, and they would almost certainly be recognized and laid in irons, there to rot till they hang; but if they were merely rescued as castaways in time of peace they could be shuffled aboard with the rest. That seems to me his reasoning.'

'Perhaps these men are the band referred to in the ingenuous Mr Gill's letter that we captured in the packet. I quote from memory, "My Uncle Palmer's Paradise, for which we have some colonists, men who wish to live as far from their countrymen as ever can be." '

340

'May I come in?' asked Martin at the door: he had on a tarpaulin jacket, and in one streaming hand he held a barrel-hoop, also covered with tarpaulin, that served as a primitive umbrella, while with the other he kept the upper part of his shirt together, his bosom being stuffed with coconuts and breadfruit. 'Pray take these nuts before they fall,' he said; and as Jack turned from the hole, 'You have not seen the ship yet, sir, I suppose?'

'Oh no,' said Jack. 'She could not possibly be here today: I am only arranging my tube so as to sweep as much of the north-western horizon as possible when the time comes.'

'Would it be possible to form an estimate of how long she will take to come back?' asked Stephen.

'There are so many factors,' said Jack, 'but if they were able to make just a little northing towards the end of the first day, when the extreme force of the storm had dropped, and then to have brought the wind say two points on the quarter, so as to diminish the leeway as much as possible until they could shape a course for the island after the third day, why, then I think we might start looking for them in a week. Mr Martin, may I ask you for the jacket? I am going to see the men.'

'I met Mr Butcher during my walk or rather scramble,' said Martin as Captain Aubrey's steps went splashing away down the rain-soaked glade. 'He too possesses shoes and he too had made his way up the stream almost to its source. He inquired for you most earnestly, said that he was delighted with my account and that he would attend at a moment's notice if there were any renewed pressure or discomfort. But he also spoke of the ship in a way that made me very uneasy indeed. It appears that there is a chain of reefs and submerged islands a little to the west, a chain of great length, extending perhaps a hundred miles, and that it is almost impossible that the *Surprise* should not have been driven on some part of it.'

'Mr Butcher may be an excellent surgeon, but he is not a sailor.'

341

'Perhaps not, but he reported this as the considered opinion of the *Norfolk*'s officers.'

'I should not prefer their opinion to Captain Aubrey's. He knows of these reefs – he mentioned them when we were discussing the curious tide – and yet he spoke quite confidently of the ship's return.'

'Oh, I was not aware he knew of them. That is a great comfort to my mind, a very great comfort. I am quite easy again. Let me tell you about my walk. I did succeed in reaching the higher denuded ground; it was there, where the stream can be crossed as it flows over an uncomfortable bed of shattered obsidian and trachyte, that I met Mr Butcher, who agrees that the island is obviously volcanic; and it was there that I saw what I took to be a flightless rail, though perhaps it was only wet.'

Wet: the whole island was soaking wet, saturated with water; where the trees, great ferns and undergrowth stood on very steep slopes there had been landslides, leaving the dark rock bare, and the stream that came out at the landing-place was now a broad river, pouring thick mud and débris into the lagoon.

Jack's path took him along its left bank, strewn with tree-trunks and tangled, wrecked vegetation, and on the far side he saw Captain Palmer: Jack took off his hat and called out, 'Good day to you, sir,' and Palmer bowed and said something about 'the wind backing – more rain, maybe.'

These acknowledgements, repeated sometimes twice a day, were all the communication they had for the ensuing week. It was a dismal week upon the whole, with a good deal of rain, which kept the stream full; a week in which their hopes of fishing were disappointed. The vegetable food within easy reach had already been gathered; most of the broken coconuts and bruised breadfruits were rapidly going bad in the damp heat, and the Surprises had taken great pains to unlay cordage and spin fishing-lines as quickly as they could. But the lagoon was in a state of unexampled filth and most of its inhabitants had deserted it, though some, indeed, had been cast up dead in stinking swathes on the highwater-mark. The lean grey sharks were still there, however, and they made wading and casting surprisingly dangerous, they having a way of coming in to very shallow water; but in any case casting produced nothing but floating logs. Even when they righted the launch – a very heavy task – and rowed out things were not much better: most of the fish they caught were snatched hook and all by the sharks, and those they managed to preserve were ill-looking bloated purple creatures with livid spines that Edwards, one of the whalers and an old South Sea hand, said were poisonous – the spines were poisonous, the fish unwholesome. Fishing from the reef at low tide was a little more rewarding, but this too had its drawbacks: there were broad patches of stinging coral and many sea-urchins with wicked spines that broke off short when trodden upon, piercing bare feet deep and turning bad; two men were attacked and bitten by moray eels as they groped for clams, and a harmless-looking fish not unlike the rock-cod of Juan Fernandez brought all those who ate him out in a scarlet rash, accompanied by black vomit and the temporary loss of sight; while lame seamen were ten a penny, for although they were used to running about on deck barefoot, the smooth wood did not give their soles any great toughness – they usually put on shoes to go aloft, for example – and thorns, volcanic glass and coral rock soon wounded them.

In spite of the rain, the tangled and sometimes almost impenetrable vegetation, and the spiny creeper that made walking barefoot so unpleasant, men did move about the island, however, impelled by hunger or in one case by fear. On Thursday Bonden said to Jack, 'That fellow Haines, sir, the Hermione as wanted to peach on his mates, he's afraid they know and are going to scrag him: says, may he come over to our side?'

Jack checked his first violent reply, reflected, and said, 'There is nothing to prevent him making himself a shelter in the woods somewhere behind us, shifting for himself and hiding until the ship comes in.'

For those who had shoes walking was less painful, of course, and Martin and Butcher met quite often; Butcher was a friendly, rather loquacious man and during these meetings the chaplain learnt that the Norfolks had hoped for the visit of a Russian man-of-war, known to be on a cruise of exploration in the central Pacific, or for that of one or another of the half dozen New Bedford or Nantucket whalers fishing in these waters or passing through them. Yet since these hopes, though lively, were necessarily indefinite, they had also intended to make a boat from the wood of the wreck, a boat in which an officer and two or three of the best seamen would sail to Huahiva for help: once the trade-wind had returned to its usual steadiness the journey, even with the long dog-leg to avoid the dreaded western reefs, would be only about four hundred miles, nothing in comparison with Captain Bligh's four thousand in this same ocean. But they had very little in the way of tools – only a small box that some freakish wave had flung on the reef – and the wreck had scarcely begun to break up; so far it had yielded no more than the hatches from which they had made their almost useless fishing-raft.

Towards the end of the week the rain diminished; crossing the upper part of the stream became easier and more men from either side came into contact with one another. This led to the first trouble. Like all the other whalers Edwards had most bitterly resented the burning of the *Intrepid Fox* and when he met an American he called him a whoreson longshoreman and no seaman, a poxed nigger's bastard, and gave him a blow with the stick he was carrying; the American made no reply but instantly kicked him in the private parts. They were separated in time by the carpenter and one of his mates and the American withdrew, followed by cries of 'Yankee poodle' and 'Keep your side of the bloody stream,' for the Surprises felt it to be a self-evident truth that all the territory this side was theirs. It must have seemed a natural limit, since the same day, a little lower down, Blakeney was chased back across the water by a tall American midshipman with a red beard, who told him that if he were found poaching on their preserves again he should be cut up for bait.

But these incidents excited no great attention, all minds being turned to Sunday, the earliest day upon which the Captain had said the ship might be seen: most of the week's weather, though wet overhead and underfoot, had been favourable for her return, with the wind moderating and hanging a little south of south-east, and the great all-shaking crash of the swell on the outer reef dropping to a steady, half-heard thunder.

Sunday, and Jack's razor made the round of the officers, while the two surgical instruments trimmed the foremast hands, trimmed and scraped them painfully, none being an expert shaver – that was the ship's barber's job – but the pain was endured gladly, there being a pagan notion abroad that the more they suffered the more certainly they should see the ship. Church was rigged in the lee of the launch, with an awning spread and a reading-desk run up from stretchers and a thwart, lashed rather than nailed. Jack sent a note to Captain Palmer saying that if he, his officers and men chose to attend, they would be welcome; but Palmer declined on the grounds that few of his people belonged to the Anglican communion and none was in a state to appear at a public ceremony. His reply was civil and well-turned, however: it was necessarily verbal, since the Norfolks were as destitute of paper and pen as they were of everything else, and it was delivered by Mr Butcher; he remained for the service, which in spite of the lack of books was carried through creditably to the end. The Surprises ashore included five of the ship's truest and most determined singers, and the others followed them through the familiar hymns and psalms in a fine convincing volume of sound that carried out over the lagoon and far beyond the reef. Mr Martin did not venture upon a sermon of his own but turned once again to Dean Donne, quoting directly where he could rely on his memory and paraphrasing where he could not. All those present, apart from the score or so of Americans who sat here and there on the farther bank, had heard the matter before, a very real advantage for so intensely conservative a congregation. They approved of it; they admired it, and they listened with something of that same earnestness with which their eyes searched the horizon, straining for the slightest fleck of topsails against the pure blue sky.

It was odd, among so many seafaring men, accustomed to the uncertainty of the ocean and the unpredictability of anything to do with a voyage, that such importance should have been attributed to this first day of Jack's forecast, as though it possessed some magical quality; yet such was the case on both sides of the stream, and when the frigate was not seen that Sunday the Surprises, at least, were strangely cast down.

She was not seen on Monday, nor Tuesday, nor Wednesday, although the weather was so good; and as the week wore on Jack noticed that Palmer's bow grew daily less profound until by Friday it was little more than a casual nod. A great deal can be conveyed by a salute and no great perspicacity was called for to see that the Norfolks were perfectly aware that they outnumbered the Surprises by four to one, that every day increased their confidence and spirits, and that it would be difficult to oblige Palmer to deal with his people's share of the increasing hostility, with the isolated fights and scuffles that threatened to develop into general violence.

Jack blamed himself extremely. He should have stayed in his ship: his presence on shore had done nothing more towards furthering Stephen's operation than that of any of the other officers. He had behaved like an anxious old woman. Or if he had felt absolutely obliged to go ashore to deal with Palmer he should in the very first place have attended to the tide, for in spite of their partial obliteration by the hurricane an intelligent seaman's eye could have detected the signs of its unusual period and great force in the channel; and in the second place he should certainly have brought a party of Marines; even perhaps

346

the launch's carronade. As it was, all the weapons the Surprises possessed were his sword, Blakeney's dirk and pocket-pistol, and the boat-hook; the seamen all had their knives, of course, but then so did most of the Norfolks.

'I fear you are grieving for the *Surprise*, brother,' said Stephen as they sat alone outside the hut, looking down to the evening sea. 'I trust you do not despair of our friends?'

'Despair? Oh Lord, no,' cried Jack. 'She is a sound, well-found, weatherly ship, and Mowett has a crew of thorough-paced seamen. Even though he may not have known of that damned reef, I am sure that when her cables parted his first instinct would have been to keep her from going away to leeward as much as ever he could; and from what I remember of the changing direction of the wind and from all I can learn of the position of the shoal, he must have weathered its northern end. No, what I am afraid for is that wretched fished mizen. Mr Lamb is of the same opinion. How he regrets not having clapped on a double woulding while there was yet time!'

'Would the loss of the mizen be very grave, at all?'

'Not for going before the wind, since with the breeze right aft it wears no sails; but for beating up, for turning to windward – in short for getting back to this island – it is absolutely essential. If the fished mizen went, then clearly the *Surprise* would have to bear away. She would necessarily go away to the westward, and Mowett would steer for Huahiva.'

'He could then return, however, having found a new mast?'

'Yes. But it would take some finding, and with Lamb and his mates all here it would take some assembling, fitting and stepping; but above all he would be compelled to beat up against the trade-wind and the current day after day. He could not be here for a month.'

'Oh, oh,' said Stephen, with a significant look.

'Just so. The situation here is not going to remain steady for a month, nor anything like so long.' There were voices behind the hut, and although Captain Aubrey had the highest opinion of the launch's crew as shipmates and seamen, he knew they were very much given to eavesdropping – the theoretically watertight compartments of a man-of-war were pierced through and through by this universal practice and most schemes were known to the men who were to carry them out long before the order was given, while most people's domestic affairs were also the subject of informed discussion. Certainly this had its uses and it gave the ship something of a family quality; but in the present case Jack did not wish to have his views widely known, for the contacts between the two sides were not solely hostile by any means, and the more peacable men from either ship, meeting in the higher woods, the vague no-man's land beyond the rising of the stream, would often fall into conversation, particularly if they happened to be neutrals. It was a Finn, for example, who told the *Surprise*'s Pole, Jackruski, that there was a strong party led by two sea-lawyers, who maintained that the *Norfolk*'s officers, having lost both their ship and their commissions, had at the same time lost their authority, and that this made discipline hard to maintain, particularly as the *Norfolk*'s bosun and her hard-horse first lieutenant, dreaded by all, had both been drowned.

These particular voices in fact belonged to Martin and Butcher, who were walking down the path together. Butcher had come to call on Dr Maturin and to convey a message to Captain Aubrey from Captain Palmer. Captain Palmer presented his best compliments, and begged to remind Captain Aubrey of the agreement that the stream should mark the boundary between their territories, with the exception of the fore-shore on the Surprises' side of the water, which the Norfolks might traverse without let or hindrance to reach the beginning of the eastern reef: Captain Palmer was however concerned to report that a small group of his men had been turned back that morning, jeered at and pelted with seaweed; and he trusted that Captain Aubrey would at once take the proper measures. 'Pray tell Captain Palmer, with my compliments,' said Jack, 'that if this was not mere horseplay the culprits shall be dealt with, and if he wishes he may attend or send an officer to witness punishment: in any event you will present my expressions of regret and assurance that it will not occur again.'

'Now, Stephen,' he said when they were alone, 'let me give you an arm up towards the top of the island. There is a flat place over the black cliff that gives a splendid visto. You have not been there yet.'

'By all means,' said Stephen. 'And on the way we may possibly catch a glimpse of Martin's flightless rail. But perhaps you will have to bring me down on your back; my legs are still miserably weak.'

The flightless rail crept silently into a bush at the sound of Captain Aubrey's heavy-footed gasping approach, but the bare volcanic platform they eventually reached did provide them with a stretch of some thirty miles of white-flecked ocean westwards and on either side, with two separate schools of whales, one to the north, the other to the south, and with a plunging view of the entire leeward side of the island with the stream running dark and troubled into the still turbid lagoon, the white line of the reefs, and foreshortened people walking about on the sand.

Mr Lamb and two of his mates were putting the finishing touches to a little house they had begun making for themselves the very day after that ominous Sunday when the ship did not appear.

To them, from among the trees, entered the young carpenter of the *Norfolk*, who called out an affable greeting: 'What cheer, mates.'

'What cheer,' they replied in noncommittal voices, putting down their tools and looking at him with a studious lack of expression.

'It might come on to blow tonight, but we have had a fine clear day so far, and must not complain.' The Surprises did not choose to commit themselves on that either,

and after a pause the Norfolk went on, 'You wouldn't lend
a man a saw-sett, I suppose? Mine went down with the
barky.'

'No, mate, I wouldn't,' said Mr Lamb. 'Because why?
Because firsto I never lend tools anyhow, and secondo
because that would be comforting the King's enemies,
which is death at the yardarm and may God have mercy
on your soul, amen.'

'But the war's over,' cried the Norfolk.

'You tell that to the Marines, cully,' said Mr Lamb,
laying his right forefinger along the side of his nose. 'I
wasn't born yesterday.'

'I met your mate in the woods Thursday,' said the
Norfolk, pointing at Henry Choles, carpenter's crew,
'under a breadfruit tree.'

'Under a breadfruit tree it was,' said Choles, nodding
solemnly. 'Which it had lost three branches as thick as
the mainmast. I passed the remark at the time.'

'And we wished one another joy of the peace. So
he believes it's peace. Of course it's peace.'

'Henry Choles is a tolerable good craftsman, and he
is as honest as the day is long,' said Mr Lamb, gazing
at him objectively. 'But the trouble with him is, he was
born on the Surrey side, and not so very long ago neither.
No, young chap,' – this to the Norfolk, quite kindly – 'I
was out of my time before you stopped shitting yellow,
and I never seen any set of men behave like your mates
in time of peace. I reckon it is all a pack of lies to get
sent home free, gratis and for nothing, and to do us out
of our head-money.'

'Stephen,' said Jack, passing his little pocket-glass, 'if
you look steadily just this side of the horizon, where I
am pointing, I believe you will see a steadier line of white
water trending away to the right. I take it to be the shoals
they spoke of. A damned awkward thing to find under your
lee by night. From here you would have to steer almost due
north for half a day on a breeze like this.' The 'breeze like
this' was the warm steady trade, eddying about them on

this sheltered platform but singing steadily over the high ridge behind, a fine topgallantsail wind. 'However, what I really meant to say was this: I intend to lengthen the launch to take her to Huahiva. It must be done fairly soon, or we shall have no launch left to lengthen; ill-feeling is growing stronger and when the island is stripped bare of food it will obviously grow stronger still. I do not think Palmer has a strong hold over his men, and the Hermiones have an even greater motive for knocking us on the head than the others, above all now that Haines has deserted them and they know they are detected. And every day the *Surprise* does not appear makes them bolder.'

'Why must you lengthen the launch?'

'To get everybody in. She was loaded to the gunnels when we brought you ashore. She must be lengthened if she is to face the open sea.'

'A long task would it be, at all?'

'Inside a week, I believe.'

'I will not ask, have you thought they may take it away from us when it is done, or even before? I know they wish to be away to Huahiva themselves, to bring a whaler back for their friends, God forbid.'

'It had occurred to me. I do not think their spirits are high enough to make the attempt before we start work; and then I think that if we are brisk enough we can find means to dissuade 'em when it is done. No, my chief concern is victualling, victualling for what may be quite a long voyage, since I have no instruments. As for water, we have barrels enough for a fortnight at short measure and I hope we can still find a few hundred sound drinking-coconuts; but the question is food. Now that fishing has failed us – and I had banked on drying them as we did at Juan Fernandez – I should like to know whether there is anything you can suggest. The pith of the tree-ferns? Roots? Bark? Pounded leaves?'

'Sure we did pass a little dwarvish sorts of yam on the way up, an undoubted Dioscorea – I called out to you, but you were far ahead, snorting, and did not attend – yet

351

they do not really thrive here, any more than the land-crab, alas, and I should place my chief reliance upon the shark. He may not be very palatable; his appearance cannot recommend him anywhere; but his flesh, like that of most selachians, is reasonably wholesome and nourishing. He is easily taken; and I recommend that his upper flanks should be cut in long thin strips, dried and smoked.'

'But Stephen,' said Jack, glancing towards the wreck of the *Norfolk*, 'think what they must have been feeding on.'

'Never let us be missish, my dear: all earthly plants to some degree partake of the countless dead since Adam's time, and all the fishes of the sea share at first or second or hundredth hand in all the drowned. In any case,' he added, seeing Jack's look of distaste, 'sharks are very like robins, you know; they defend their territory with equal jealousy, and if we take ours over by the far channel no one will be able to reproach us with anthropophagy, even at one remove.'

'Well,' said Jack, 'I am too fat anyway. Please to show me your yams.'

The yams sprawled down a scree descending from the island's highest point: the path to the platform skirted the lower edge of the fall and here Stephen showed the climbing stems and typical leaf and a single misshapen tuber that he found by turning a few stones. 'They are not happy here, poor stunted things; it is not a scree they want at all but deep damp earth. Yet if you were to climb there is a fair possibility that you might find the parents of these dwarfs, a fine prosperous stock with great stout roots growing in a long-filled crater at the top of this scree, a territory from which these miseries have overflowed. I shall wait for you here, being but feeble. If you should chance upon any beetles on your way up, put them gently in your handkerchief, if you please.'

Stephen sat; and presently, with a beating heart and that very particular lively fresh happiness that had not changed since his boyhood, he saw the flightless rail walk out on to a bare patch of ground, stretch one useless though decorative wing, scratch itself, yawn, and eventually pass on, allowing him to breathe again.

Jack climbed, travelling along the edge of the scree and sampling yams every now and then; they began if anything even more dwarvish and misshapen, not unlike the potatoes he grew himself at home; but stimulated by the hope of Stephen's crater and the recollection of the monstrous tubers he had seen in former times, insipid great things that would feed a boat's crew for a day, he climbed on. The top was much farther than he had thought, and a recent deluge, blocking the crater's outlet, had turned it into a lake, with the no doubt enormous yams rotting under ten feet of putrid water. But the greater height gave him an even greater expanse of ocean and as he sat there recovering his breath he gazed at the far western reef, or chain of sunken islands. The horizon lay far beyond it now and he had a much clearer view of its length and breadth: a most formidable shoal indeed, with never a gap or channel that he could make out. And obliging his mind to be as cold, objective and analytical as it could be, he gauged the *Surprise*'s chances of having weathered it, in the exact circumstances of that wicked night. Not as much as one in three was the answer, and his eyes filled with tears.

A series of atolls far to the north was the most dangerous place, he reflected; and while he stared at it, taking in the whole naked-eye field of vision, it seemed to him that he saw something dark beyond and he reached for his glass. Dark it was: a ship it was. He lay flat, resting his telescope on a rock and covering his head with his coat against all outside light. He had known at once that she was not the *Surprise* but it took him ten minutes, a quarter of an hour, of very careful focusing and staring to be certain that she was an American whaler, steering south.

She was on the western side of that immensely long shoal: if she meant to call at this island she would have to work clean round it and then beat up; but unless the wind increased she could easily do so in a week. He fixed the bearings in his mind and ran down the scree. 'Forgive me, Stephen,' he said, 'I must hurry down to the camp: there is not a moment to be lost. Follow me at your own pace.'

'Mr Lamb,' he said in an even voice, having recovered his wind, 'a word with you.' They walked along the highwater-mark. 'I wish you to lengthen the launch by eight feet so that she may take us to Huahiva, there probably to rejoin the ship. Can you do that with the tools and materials at your disposition?'

'Oh Lord, yes, sir. We could cut some lovely natural aprons and timber-heads not fifty yards from the shore.'

'I meant at once, with the wood you have. There is not a moment to lose.'

'Why, sir, I reckon I could; but it would mean pulling down the Doctor's place straight away.'

'He shall have a tent. But before we lengthen the boat we must be armed: what can you turn into hangers or boarding-pikes without jeopardizing your work?'

The carpenter reflected. 'For hangars or cutlasses I can't do much, seeing as how I must keep my saws; but for boarding-pikes, Lord love you, sir,' – laughing very cheerfully – 'I could arm the hosts of Midian, if so desired. I tossed a whole keg of ten-inch spikes into the boat, and Henry Choles, thinking I had forgot, tossed in another. And your ten-inch spike, with its head flattened and given a curl on the bick of the anvil, its body shaped just so, and the whole tempered at cherry-pink in loo-warm seawater, gives a very serviceable pike. Not Tower of London work, they may say; but when they have six inches of converted spike in their weams, there's little odds whether it's London work or local.'

'Have you your forge and anvil here?'

'No, sir, but I can soon fudge up a pair of bellows, and there are all these old black stones for our anvil.

Sam Johnson, the armourer's mate that rows bow oar is just the man; he served his time to a cutler, and is uncommon neat.'

'Capital, capital. Then let that be put in hand at once, together with the shaping of the staves. Twenty will answer very well: I have my sword, Mr Blakeney has his dirk and a pistol – in any case he could scarcely manage a pike – and I do not suppose Mr Martin would think it right. We shall also need three shark-hooks, fast to as much of the bridlechain as we can spare: indeed, they had better precede the pikes, and they will give colour to the lighting of the forge. But, Mr Lamb, let the whole thing be done as privately as possible, among the trees. The launch will go a-fishing as soon as the hooks are ready and some sort of a light frame will be required for drying and smoking about thirty stone of shark in strips. At the same time it would be as well to make sure our casks are water-tight. And I cannot impress upon you too strongly, Mr Lamb, that there is not a moment to lose: all hands will work double tides.'

All hands were much shocked at this. During their weeks ashore on Old Sodbury, with little more than the formal skeleton of ship's routine maintained and with a great deal of wandering about by themselves in the woods or on the reef in search of food or fishing with a line from the rocks, they had lost the habit of brisk motion and instant unquestioning obedience; they were also still fractious from the absence of tobacco and grog, and it was with indignation and a sense of outrage that they heard their Captain 'roaring like a bull in a bush' as Plaice put it, insisting that everything should be done at the double if not triple and even wielding a rope's end – a weapon very few had ever seen him use except on his midshipmen in the privacy of the cabin – with horrible force and accuracy.

'It is like being in a prison-ship,' said George Abel, bow-oar in Johnson's absence, 'only worse. "Jump to it, you idle lubber. Quick's the word and sharp's the action, damn your eyes." What has come over him, topping it the slave-driver?'

'Perhaps this will pacimollify him,' said Plaice, spitting towards the moderate-sized shark towing behind, pursued by its kin.

'Rowed off all!' cried Bonden, and the launch ran crunching up the strand. Abel instantly leapt out and seized not the painter but the stout line hitched round the shark's tail, with which he and half a dozen others hauled the creature from the sea, its followers rushing in so close for a last bite that they were only just awash.

Abel and his mates cut the shark's head off with the carpenter's axe and looked up for approval – a fish just the size required, and hardly bitten at all. This was no time for idle gaping, they were told; this was not Bartholomew Fair; they might join Mr Blakeney's party and run, *run*, not waddle, to the north-east point of the island, where there were still coconuts to be found. Any man that did not bring back twenty would curse the day he was born.

They left at the double, passing the forge among the trees, where the bellows wheezed and the sweating armourer hammered, naked but for an apron; and they met files of worried-looking men running down from the ruins of the hut with loads of timber, while others, equally anxious, brought in faggots of pike-staves as straight and knot-free as they could find.

So they spent the day, never sitting down, never merely walking; but that was not enough. They were divided into watches as though they were on board, and each watch spent part of the night turning the long strips of shark's flesh on the framework by the fire and teasing coconut-fibre into oakum for caulking the lengthened boat; and it was striking to see how much their sleeping minds returned to shipboard time and its four-hour rhythm – each watch relieved the other almost as regularly as though the bell had been struck throughout the night. It was as well that there was a watch on deck as it were, for at two in the morning a curious wind got up and for three or four hours it blew hard from the north-west, working up a heavy short sea against the swell and endangering the fire, the unsavoury, glue-smelling food, and the new pitched tents.

It was a sea that drove straight into the lagoon through the two channels; it came on the flood-tide, hissing far up the beach, and there was not a sailor who did not know that it must work upon the wrecked frigate. The Norfolks themselves were not very early risers in general but a little after sunrise, when the Surprises were at their breakfast, a small part of them crossed the stream and hurried along the tide-line, on their way to the beginning of the reef. Although it was understood on both sides that they had a right of way they did not care to go by in the presence of many of the Surprises and their officers and most pretended not to notice them, though two of the more friendly, the more conversable, uttered a discreet howl and gave a jerk of the thumb.

Although in fact the wreck had not yet opened to any significant extent and although the red-bearded midshipman reported this to Captain Palmer, more men went by in the course of the morning; but it was not until half past eleven that they came back, twenty-five or thirty of them, dragging the *Norfolk*'s larboard headrails and some of her forecastle planking. By this time most of the Surprises were scattered about the island, engaged on various urgent tasks, and the carpenters were almost alone, busily sawing the launch in two: though Mr Lamb himself had retired privately into the bushes. The only other man on the beach was Haines, a cooper by trade, who had won a kind of half-acceptance by making himself useful to Mr Martin, and who was now attending to the very troublesome barrels. He ran away as soon as he saw the Norfolks, pursued by shouts of 'Judas'; but there were no former Hermiones among the band and they did not pursue him for any distance – a few made as if to catch him, but only for the fun. Another group came up

357

to the carpenters and asked them what they were doing
– commended their tools, their workmanship – said they
too would presently be building their own boat, now the
wreck was breaking up – and talked on at some length in
spite of surly answers or none at all. Then suddenly their
leader cried 'Look! Look!' pointing inland. The carpenters
turned their heads. The Norfolks seized a compass-saw, a
sheet of the launch's copper, a handful of spikes, a pair of
pincers, a small auger and a rasp and ran away laughing.
It was a laughing matter for a hundred yards or so: one
man tripped and lost his rasp, and another threw down
his awkward sheet of copper to run faster; but by the time
Choles overtook the man with the compass-saw he was
already among his fellow Norfolks. Choles tried to snatch
the saw, but they flung him down: Choles' friends came to
his help, one hitting out with a carpenter's maul, breaking
an arm directly, and Mr Lamb came running from the
wood with a dozen Surprises. At this the Norfolks all
drew together, wielding pieces of wood, and withdrew
steadily across the water into their own territory, leaving
most of their timber on the bank. The Surprises had two
carpenter's axes and an adze and they would have gone on
to recover the tools if they had not been stopped this side
of the water by an enormous roar of 'Belay, there' from
Captain Aubrey, some way up the hill.

They hurried back to him, the carpenters all talking
together, calling for an instant raid with the pikemen to
recover the tools.

'Mr Lamb,' he asked, 'how necessary are the lost tools
for the immediate work in hand?' But he was obliged to
shake the carpenter by the shoulder before Lamb's face,
pale with fury, showed much sense, and shake him again
before he made a coherent reply to the effect that the
compass-saw would be needed tomorrow.

'Well then,' said Jack, 'get on with your work until
dinner-time. I shall attend to the matter in the afternoon.'

He ate his own dinner – a discouraging piece of shark,
grilled, and coconut for pudding – in company with

Stephen and Martin. They talked in a general way about flightless birds and the colonization of remote oceanic islands, and he followed fairly well; but by far the greater part of his mind was taken up with his forthcoming interview with Palmer.

This morning's incident had to be dealt with, of that there was no doubt. Anything more of this kind would lead to open bloody battle, and although with his pikemen and axes he could probably sustain it, continual open violence would delay the launching of the boat intolerably and even perhaps make it impossible. There was not only the lengthening but the re-rigging, the caulking, the victualling and a thousand other things. A final attack, an attempt at taking the launch once it was ready – that was another matter, and if it could not be avoided by the various stratagems he had in mind he was reasonable confident that it could be dealt with by main force, particularly if the pikes could be kept in reserve, for the full daunting effect of surprise. What he must aim at was comparative tranquillity for three days, and then, before she was obviously ready, they could run her down to the beach before moonrise on Thursday night, pull out into the lagoon, lie there at a grapnel, step the masts, complete the re-rigging and the half-deck, out of reach from the shore, and sail on the evening tide. The question was, how much command did Palmer have over his men? He had lost almost all his officers either by drowning or by being sent away in prizes – no doubt many of his best seamen too – and he was very much alone, unseconded. How much were the former Hermiones an integral part of the *Norfolk*'s crew? Could they draw many of the others with them? How much was Palmer influenced by his remaining officers, the surgeon and the shadowy master or lieutenant who kept so very much out of sight? These were questions whose answers he should have to read on Palmer's hairy enigmatic face that afternoon.

When dinner was finished he took a few turns on the level sward in front of the tent and then called his coxswain. 'Bonden,' he said, 'I am going to see the captain of the *Norfolk*. Give my hat and coat a shake over the side, will you?'

'Yes, sir,' said Bonden, who was perfectly prepared for the visit. 'Which I have put a shaving edge on your sword, taken Mr Blakeney's pistol, drawn and dried the charges, and knapped the flints.'

'Just the thing for a cutting-out expedition, Bonden,' said Jack, 'but this is a genteel morning call.'

'Morning call my arse,' muttered Bonden, shaking the Captain's coat vehemently, some way to leeward. 'How I wish we had the carronade.' He slipped the pistol into his pocket – there was already a long thin dangerous blade of the kind called a gully inside his belt and a jacknife on a laniard round his neck – passed the hat and followed his Captain.

It was indeed the air of a social call that Jack gave his visit, and Palmer, a man of breeding, responded with trivialities of much the same kind; but while the small-talk was running its smooth insipid course Jack observed that the man he was speaking to had changed very much since their last interview: Palmer was obviously ill; he looked much older; he had shrunk; he was under great tension and Jack had the impression that he had been quarrelling furiously within the last few hours.

'Now, sir,' said Jack at last, 'it seems that some of our men got into a foolish scrape this morning. I do not believe that any real harm was meant, but it was the kind of horse-play that might have turned very ugly.'

'It did turn very ugly. John Adams' arm was broke: Mr Butcher is setting it now.'

'I am sorry for that; but what I meant by ugly was half a dozen men stretched out dead for a miserable compass-saw – for a foolish young seaman's prank. I did manage to call my carpenters off – they had axes, you know – but it was not easy and I should not like to have to do it again. Perhaps you may have noticed that men ashore, if the ship is not just at hand, are never so easy to control.'

360

'I have noticed nothing of the kind,' said Palmer sharply, darting a suspicious look from under his bushy eyebrows.

'Well I have,' said Jack. 'And it appears to me, Captain Palmer, that there is such a state of hostility between our men that it is like sitting in a powder-magazine with a naked light. The least thing may cause an explosion. So I must beg you will give very strict orders that this dangerous sort of caper should never be repeated: and incidentally I must have my compass-saw again. I do not suppose there was ever any intention of really stealing it.'

The tent wall bulged slightly in and it was fairly clear that Palmer was in contact, either by whispering or nudging, with someone outside. 'You shall have your compass-saw,' he said. 'But I must tell you, Captain Aubrey, that I was on the point of sending for you . . .'

'Sending for me?' said Jack, laughing. 'Oh no, no, no. Nonsense. Post-captains do not send for one another, my dear sir. And even if they did so far forget themselves, I must remind you that you are at least *de jure* my prisoner.'

'Of desiring you to come, then, so that I might officially acquaint you that this island is American territory, by right of first discovery, and direct you to remove to the far side of the northern reef, where your men will not hinder the recovery of the *Norfolk*'s timbers and stores.'

'I cannot accept your contention about sovereignty for a moment,' said Jack. 'In any event it is a political question quite outside my competence. But as to your notion of putting a greater distance between our men, I entirely agree. You have noticed, I am sure, that we are lengthening our boat. When the work is finished I shall take my people so far that there will be very little likelihood of trouble. But for that I must have my tools again.'

'You shall have them,' said Palmer, and he uttered a hail that began well but died in a most pitiful quaver. 'You shall have them,' he muttered again, passing his hand over his eyes. They came in a piece of sailcloth, the spikes, pincers and compass-saw, brought by the red-haired midshipman, and while Jack was making some civil remarks about his satisfaction Palmer broke out in a strong voice, 'Finally, Captain Aubrey, since you maintain that a state of war still subsists, you must be prepared to take the logical consequences of your words.'

'I do not understand you, sir,' said Jack: but Palmer, obviously unwell, replied only with a choking excuse and hurried out of the tent. Jack stood there for a moment in the opening and then, asking the midshipman to send word if Mr Butcher would like to consult Dr Maturin, handed the tools to Bonden and took his leave.

The path from the tent to the stream was bordered with close-packed tree-ferns, and in their deep shade stood men, a dozen or so on either side and more to be guessed behind the trunks; they were silent as Jack approached but when he passed their voices could be heard, low and urgent, arguing – English voices. 'Scrag the bugger now,' cried one and a stone hit Jack's shoulder. Almost immediately the strong metallic Boston shouting of the midshipman echoed through the trees and Jack walked on, crossing the stream in the usual place.

'Mr Lamb,' he said, coming up to the dismantled launch, 'here are your tools. Ply them like a hero and I believe we may still be afloat the day I had reckoned on. You may have every man-jack you want to hold a plank or shape a treenail.'

That evening and the next day the launch began to take shape again, and on the Wednesday it was fairly covered with men fitting, joining, faying, rasping and hammering under their Captain's immediate eye, for by now the victualling, such as it was, had been completed: net after net of coconuts stood ready to be loaded; the strong-smelling parched shark lay there in flat sailcloth bales; and only the water-casks stood apart, still leaking badly. The boat was screened from public view by casually draped sails and Jack thought it unlikely that the Norfolks knew just what stage they had reached. He had told Martin that although the launch would probably be ready late on

362

Friday he would not put to sea until the next day, because of the foremast jacks' superstition; and this Martin had handed on in perfect good faith to Butcher. And quite apart from that Jack felt reasonable confident that there would be no attempt at seizing the boat until dawn on Friday at the earliest, if indeed there was an attempt at all; and by then she would already have been floating out on the lagoon for some hours. But by way of precaution he had the pikes stowed close at hand, and he took a casual shot or two with the pistol, to show that ammunition was there in plenty.

The entire period since his remote sighting of the American whaler had been one of the most intense driving activity, but this Wednesday outdid all the rest. Although for the purpose of deceit the launch's masts were not to be stepped, a great deal of rigging could be prepared in advance; so on this afternoon there was not a skilled hand but was hard at work – carpenters, riggers, sailmakers, caulkers, ropemakers, stripped to the waist and labouring under the shade of the palm fronds with such concentration that they rarely spoke.

In this connection neither the chaplain nor the surgeon could be looked upon as skilled hands, and they had been sent with net bags to gather yams. They had most conscientiously filled their bags, but they had spent even more of their time persecuting the rail, creeping after it through bushes until it made a dash across the open part of the scree, running as fast as a partridge and leaping down a ten-foot drop with a despairing cry. Now, before going down to call on Mr Butcher and inquire for Captain Palmer, they were resting on the high platform, lying on their backs with their heads on the yams, gazing up at the cloud that hung over the island, perpetually torn away to leeward and perpetually renewed from the south-east.

'Gmelin says that the Siberian rail sleeps buried in the snow,' observed Martin.

'Where did you find that?'

'In Darwin. Speaking of the early spring flowering of Muschus corallinus he says

Down the white hills dissolving torrents pour,
Green springs the turf, and purple blows the flower;
His torpid wing the Rail exulting tries,
Mounts the soft gale, and wantons in the skies –

and this he justifies in a note, citing John George Gmelin as his authority.'

'Sure, I honour the Gmelins; but there is something about rails that excites credulity. In my part of Ireland it is said that the land-rail, the corncrake, changes into a water-rail at the approach of autumn and then turns back again in spring. I trust Dr Darwin did not really believe in this hibernation: he is a respectable man.'

'Did you ever look into his *Zoonomia*?'

'I did not. But I do recall some lines of his *Origin of Society* that a lewd cousin of mine used often to recite:

"Behold!" he cries "Earth! Ocean! Air above,
And hail the Deities of Sexual Love!
All forms of life shall this fond pair delight,
And sex to sex the willing world unite."

Do you suppose, Martin, that that is what they are doing, down there on the strand? Hailing the deities, I mean. Seafaring men are wonderfully devoted to them, according to my experience.'

'Certainly they are making a most prodigious outcry.'

'Joyful, they sound.'

'Demented.'

'I shall look over the edge,' said Stephen, getting up. 'Oh my God,' he cried, for there on his left hand, not two miles from the shore, was an American whaler. She had rounded the southern headland and she was in full view of the shore, which was crowded with Norfolks, roaring and cheering, quite beside themselves. The red-headed midshipman and another youth had already raced out along the reef with incredible speed to warn her of the

dangerous passage with the wreck across it. Some were
running aimlessly up and down, bellowing and waving,
but a score of men, a tight, eager pack, were after Haines
in his red checked shirt; he dodged among the barrels,
among the heaps of firewood, among the stores; he was
headed off from the shelter of the trees, headed off from
the launch, and hunted fast along the sea. They brought
him down at the edge of the stream, disembowelled him
and threw him into the water. Yet far the greater number swarmed round the boat, which the Surprises were
desperately trying to push down to the hard sand and
the sea. Some snatched away the slides, others flung
her precious stores about or staved the water-casks with
great stones in a mad destruction, and others, perfectly
without fear of the pikes or anything else, tripped up the
men who were shoving or threw whatever came to hand
on the highwater-mark – seaweed, driftwood, lumps of
coral – or even pushed in the other direction. Some had
been put out of action – Jack's sword-arm was red to the
elbow – but it had no effect; and presently the launch
was hopelessly deep in dry sand. Once this was so, once
escape was impossible, the attackers drew off, to line the
sea and cheer their long-awaited whaler. All the Surprises
were now inside the boat, which bristled with pikes, an
impregnable stronghold for the time being. But for how
long a time?

Stephen's heart was big to bursting with the violence
of his grief, yet even as he looked distractedly from side
to side his mind told him that there was something amiss,
the more so as the cheering had now almost entirely died
away. The whaler had a huge spread of canvas aboard, far
too great a press of sail for her possibly to enter the lagoon:
she was tearing along with a great bow-wave and she sped
past the mouth of the farther channel. A cable's length
beyond the opening her main and fore topgallantmasts
carried clean away, as though brought down by a shot,
and she instantly hauled to the wind, striking her colours
as she did so. Her pursuer came racing into sight round

the southern cape, studdingsails aloft and alow on either side – a dead silence from the motionless Norfolks below – fired a full, prodigal broadside to leeward, lowered down a boat and began to reduce sail, cheering like a ship clean out of her mind with delight.

'She is the *Surprise*,' said Stephen, and he whispered, 'The joyful *Surprise*, God and Mary be with her.'